BELOW

MiLE

ZERO

Cre8tve 1

Published By Cre8tve1 Corporation, 2405 Staples Ave., Key West FL 33040

Visit our Web site at www.Cre8tve1.com

ISBN 0-9789237-0-7

Printed in the United States of America

Acknowledgements

This book is dedicated with love and gratitude to June Cridland
Babineau, partner, wife, lover, spiritual guide, and friend;
to Sola, who believed and gave me the courage to believe;
to Samuel (Sy) Krinsky, the father I would have wished for, whose
encouragement kept me going;
and to the community of Key West, where dreams are the stuff of life.

Author's Note

Other than a greater degree of comfort and familiarity with advancing technologies, people have not evolved; there are no new emotions; love, hate, fear and desire continue to shape our destiny.

Foreword

A letter to the Publisher:

My name isn't on any tax rolls and I'm not in the phone book. I've been pretty thorough about ensuring my privacy, and that will probably get me screwed.

With my history I can't go to anyone for help because most of the police I've met are corrupt, and those who aren't have no reason to believe or help me.

I am a survivor. I got through Vietnam and the drug wars in America in the 70's, more or less intact. There were casualties in both wars; I lost my family in the last one, but I got out with a little piece of paradise I could call my own. I've been living comfortably in Key West since the 80's and figured on being here until I'm old and gray. But all that has changed....

Let me explain: This guy I met washed up here about five years ago. He was flat broke and on the run from some pretty bad people in New Orleans. An old partner of mine helped him dry out and get back on his feet. Eventually he became a friend of mine...and I don't make friends easy, experience has taught me it's a good way to get dead.

Looking at what's been happening over the past couple of weeks, and what's probably going to happen next, most likely I will be dead or in prison for the rest of my life by the time you get around to reading this.

I've been talking to this writer I know. I figure the only way I have of getting the record straight is to have him set it up like a work of fiction. I know this has been done before, so that the truth can come out.

He'll have to change the names and the details enough, so that no one else can be hurt, but with enough truth in it to get people asking questions about why the DEA is importing cocaine from Cuba and killing people in America.

This writer doesn't know I'm writing to you. I don't want anything out of this, I've got enough to live well, if I can survive this mess, but I'd like him to catch a break, so I'd appreciate it if you could not mention my contacting you. I'd like him to think he got a book deal on his own.

Tony Amundsen

BELOW MILE ZERO

(A novel of Key West)

Brooke Babineau

**People who like this sort of thing
will find this the sort of thing they like.**

- Abraham Lincoln

In this world a man must be either
anvil or hammer.

- Henry Wadsworth Longfellow

Let the blow fall soon or late,
Let what will be o'er me;
Give the face of earth around
And the road before me.
Wealth I seek not, hope nor love,
Nor a friend to know me;
All I seek, the heaven above
And the road below me.

- Robert Louis Stevenson

CHAPTER 1

March (?) 1992:

I remember—I use the term loosely—driving non-stop, fueled mostly by Scotch and cocaine. The need that carried me across three states, an inexplicably compelling need, was to see the Art Deco district of Miami Beach. For what purpose, as I crossed the Florida State line, I no longer recalled, though it had seemed supremely important when I'd set out. Given my nearly hallucinatory state, I was amazed to find myself still in one piece and nearing my goal. That is, until the Alligator Alley Parkway threw me headlong into a confusion of interchanges, turnpikes and cloverleaves. Using the rather limited deductive powers at my command, reasoning; since Miami was on the southeastern tip of the mainland and I was traveling east then, naturally, I had to turn right and go to the end of the road. The next major signage announced Homestead and Key Largo. The former I'd never heard of, the latter was the title of a pretty good 'Bogie-Bacall' movie. Mentally I shrugged and said, "Why not?" After all, it really didn't matter where I was going, only that I was going.

Mourning the loss of a business, a friend, and the only woman I'd ever loved, my one-man wake, most of it on auto-pilot, had begun two days earlier, on the first day of Mardi Gras, when I discovered that my good friend and office manager, Bobby, had put my company up his nose.

We'd managed acts; primarily club bands and dancers. I'd been content to live on the road, babysitting players and romancing club owners while Bobby ran the office, doing the bookings and cooking the books. Every night since Nicole's death was spent in pursuit of oblivion, so I was more numb than surprised when L'Angousette's bill collector found me.

The air at Le Clubbe Jazz Hott was thick and steamy as a cauldron of jambalaya, the band was cooking, and I was immersed in the humid press of flesh. The promise of sex throbbed to the primal beat of Cajun rhythms. Smashed, as usual, I was immune to the flashy crowd of hedonists lush with feral women on the prowl. As I made my way toward the stage door, the crowd parted and something large loomed in front of me. Nearly seven feet tall and almost as big around, Gordo would have made a good wall. Two things convinced me to follow him; the first, my reluctance to make a scene in the crowded nightclub that was a place of business; the second, Gordo's nerve-killing grip. His hand clenched my upper arm as easily as a normal human might grasp the handle of a baseball bat—the word normal had probably never been associated with this guy or with his owner, Pierre Auguste L'Angousette.

Langouste, a French corruption of his name, or the Lobster, as he was called on the street—though, never to his face—was someone you didn't screw around with and live to brag about it, at least not in one piece. I'd had history with him. None of it had been good. If Bobby'd let Langouste get his hooks so deeply into the business that his leg breaker had been sent around to collect directly from me, then there probably wasn't much left.

Pinned against the sweaty walls of the men's room, wondering if I'd leave with two functioning knees, the message was short and to the point: Twenty-four hours to make good on my partner's debts.

A message was being sent but it wasn't about money, it was a different kind of debt. Gordo's obligatory "or else" gave me a cold, hollow feeling in the pit of my stomach exactly the size and shape of his fist, so I did what any sane person would have done under similar circumstances. The evening was a liquor-sodden blur of leering faces and rundown places, which reinforced the futility of trying to prevent my already tenuous world from further crumbling to pieces.

Sometime after four I stumbled back to the suite of rooms in the Vieux Carré, which served as the agency's office and provided a convenient, though seldom-used pied-à-terre when I wasn't on the road. Sleep was out of the question. I sat on the balcony listening to the rain, thinking, remembering:

Twenty-three when I got married, I was a kid, really And much, much too young. We'd gotten along beautifully during the one-year engagement, mostly because I was blissfully unaware there was an agenda in place.

I was in love, mostly with the idea of being in love. Francesca— "...pronounced: Fran-sess-ka, not –chess-ka..." —was in love, too. She loved the idea of being the first of her high-school clique to get a husband. Being first, for her, was very important. However, once the deed was done and it dawned on her—rocket scientist that she was— that I was quite happy designing, building, and riding custom motorcycles and not in using my Fine Arts degree to climb any sort of ladder, either social or—according to her—evolutionary, she left. In so doing, Francesca was about to score again; with the deliciously daring status accrued to being a divorcée.

During the hearing, the lawyers had had a ball getting her to talk about the abuse she'd never experienced. The judge had gotten his jollies watching her show where her imaginary bruises had been.

It wasn't all bad; I finally won her approval for the "filthy, dirty, little motorcycle business" I'd built up from nothing when she saw the amount of the settlement that landed in her lap. To pay my way out of that den of thieves, I'd had to sell everything: shop, tools, the inventory of parts and bikes, and the house I'd inherited when my parents died in a head-on with a drunk driver. Thankfully, they missed the fireworks.

According to the people who make up aphorisms: misery loves company. The only thing I wanted, after the feeding frenzy, was to run as far as possible from everyone and everything. With running came the wildness. I didn't realize it then but I was running from myself, and in the process I began to find myself.

> **The past was steep and rugged,**
> **The wolves they howled and whined;**
> **But he ran like a whirlwind up the pass,**
> **And he left the wolves behind.**
>
> **- Thomas Babington Macaulay, Baron Macaulay**

After too many odd jobs and going down to the end of every road just to see what lay there, burning out the pain along with several million brain cells, my odyssey landed me in New Orleans. I had a mint '52 Harley Davidson panhead I'd kept off the books, a rouged-out leather jacket, and a pair of greasy jeans. My ponytail reached my belt, and I had a thick copper-red beard. There were a few crumpled bills in my pocket and I was loving-the-hell out of 'The Big Easy'.

Given my predilection for sticking my nose where it didn't belong and an affinity for the unusual and truly bizarre, it wasn't long before I discovered that a coal-eyed Cajun princess had permanently perched herself on the back of my bike and in my heart. A 'dancer' by profession, Nicole was the most beautiful woman I'd ever seen. Not stilt-legged, cool and untouchable like a fashion model, but beautiful in the manner of real flesh and blood women, she did things to me that still get me hard when I think about her, which, regrettably, is most every night.

The first thing "Nikki" taught me was not to drag my knuckles when I walked. Once I'd grasped that concept she then eased me into learning about entertainers and entertainment as a business. I mourned selling the bike, seeing my escape route vanish, but the seed money it provided had been necessary to give the business a fair start. Over the next five years we built one of the best independent operations in the state. We weren't big but we had the prettiest women and the hottest bands. Everyone knew, loved, and respected Nicole.

"The personal touch, Cher," Nicole insisted, "is more important than anything else." She believed that we had to be there for our clients and customers alike. It was solely because of her, her caring and her great, good heart that our business relationships became like family. It was people first, and the money really did take care of itself.

March 1, 1992:

Tap City! Other than the slender roll in my pocket and the classic '64 Continental convertible around the corner, I was at ground zero. The smiling vulture behind the service counter in the bank had cheerfully snipped my credit cards into little pieces while I stood there wondering how I'd been so blind. A hot needle of agony stitched a thread of knots above my left eye. I needed anesthetic. I needed a drink

In the office, sipping Johnny Walker Black Label from the bottle, staring at the posters on the walls, I was seeing that one tiny room—all we could afford—lit by her enthusiasm. Her eyes bright with a vision of what the future could bring, so real that she'd convinced me it could be ours. Anything had seemed possible...then.

> **The dupe of friendship, and the fool of love;**
> **have I not reason to hate and to despise myself?**
> **Indeed I do; and chiefly for not having hated and**
> **despised the world enough.**
>
> **- William Hazlitt**

A key rattling in the lock, brought me back to the present. I lowered the bottle to the desk with my left hand. The fingers of my right found the .380 resting in my lap.

"Howdy, partner."

Bobby spun around his suitcase banged the wastebasket, sending a scatter of balled-up papers across the floor.

"What's wrong, Cher? Not even a happy-birthday, where-you-at?" My cheery voice belied my true feelings.

"You, you supposed to be on your way to B-B-Baton Rouge with F-Fat City. You know how Elmo g-g-gets when he has to travel with the band and you're n-not there to hold his hand."

His slight stammer was more pronounced than usual, the weak grin curling his lips was little more than a reflex action.

"Save the crap, Bobby." I said softly.

Playing for time, he turned to close the door.

"I don't—"

Noticing the carpet in the corner pulled back and the open floor safe, the denial died in his mouth. The sound of the door clicking shut behind him seemed magnified in the tiny office.

"There's a—" he tried to jump track.

"No, there isn't...not anymore." When I took the baggie from my inside pocket—there was almost an ounce of white powder—and dropped it on the desk, Bobby's Creole-dark skin paled to gray. He reached for it but his hand froze in mid-air when he saw the pistol in my hand. Slowly, he slumped down on his side of the partners' desk.

"Oh! Yeah-h-h! And Gordo, you remember Langouste's bill collector...?" I asked warmly, as if reminding him of an old friend. "He and I, we had ourselves a little tête-à-tête at the club last night. You know, telling me about my good friend and partner; letting me know what's been going down with your 'white line fever' while I've been on the road? Most enlightening, if you know what I mean?"

Bobby swallowed nervously, easing a suddenly too-tight collar. His finger left a dark smear on the sky-blue silk.

"Then this morning, I saw the nice man at the bank." I fingered the baggie on the desktop. "Too bad I got here before you could get away with that, hey?"

Light tickled the sweat blossoms dotting his receding hairline. He was scared, and with good reason. Part of me—the not-so-nice part—had been looking forward to this all morning. Bobby's mouth began to jerk out of neutral, beginning what would surely prove an award-winning plea for help. Seeing his resemblance to a rodent, a pop-eyed rat with a greasy twirled moustache, I wondered why I'd never noticed that before.

"For the moment," I began, cutting him off.

"B-b-but—"

The sound of my hand smacking the desk was loud, sharp as a gunshot. He jerked back as if struck by a bullet. I absorbed the sting and used the pain to focus my anger.

"Listen to me..." The words were spoken quietly, which may have scared him more than if I'd ranted and raved.

"For the moment, this—" I indicated office and contents, "—is still mine, so I can hire or fire anybody I want." I saw resignation and defiance stiffen his posture, while relief lightened his eyes. Stretching it out, I continued with mock sincerity. "I really regret having to do this, after all we've been through, but..." I slid the contract across the desk. "I'm firing me."

He looked at me in disbelief; waiting for the second shoe to drop without realizing that it already had.

"Of course, there isn't much left." I added in the conciliatory tones of a game show host. "But, hey! I guess you know that."

The pistol in my hand made a lie out of my cheery consolation. The paper trembled as he picked it up and read. I was acutely aware of the hard weight in my hand. I could feel the slight resistance of the trigger against my finger. It would take only the merest flinch, to send a bullet into his heart but that would be too quick, too kind. This was better, much better.

"Sign it." The words were spoken softly, the tone deadly.

Scarcely able to hold the pen, Bobby scrawled his name on the line opposite mine.

Stuffing my copy, along with the bag of white powder and pistol into my jacket pocket, I headed for the door but he couldn't leave it alone. I had planned to avoid any physical contact, mostly because I wasn't sure I would be able to stop. Hearing him whining about being the victim and how it wasn't his fault, I felt reason receding into the background as the wild man in me came out. An animal growl rumbled in the back of my throat. Familiar hands grabbed the front of his trademark giraffe-skin vest and twice, in quick succession, they crashed him against a wall before lifting him clear of the floor to slam him bodily across the desk.

Punk!

The sound of his breath, as the wind was knocked out of him, blew into my face. The rank metallic stench of panic aroused a sudden and urgent need inside me, like a sex-starved alley cat catching a scent of heat-musk, I wanted his naked throat in my hands, to feel the life squeeze out of his wretched body through my fingers.

Our faces were millimeters apart. His eyes were stretched wide in terror.

I heard Nikki's voice in my head, "Life's one big joke, baby...just gotta remember to laugh at it."

I did. Once. It was a sharp, harsh sound like something breaking. With it, the room came back into focus. Breathing heavily, as if starved for oxygen, I willed my fists open.

Pausing at the door, my hand on the knob, I turned for one last look. I congratulated Bobby on his promotion and wished him luck, knowing that none of it would be good.

A strangled cry flew out of the open transom behind me. A nasty grin—the like of which I hope never to see on anyone else—twisted my face and tightened the skin around my eyes.

Only a few scattered fragments of my last Mardi Gras remain. The rest of the downward pirouette, into the insanity that marked my thirty-fifth birthday, remains mercifully lost in some dark corner of toxic blackout.

*   *   *

Numb from the neck—both down and up—I may not have consciously understood that I was in Key West. What I do remember is wandering through quaint pastel neighborhoods, being waved to by strangers as they wobbled down lumpy roads on fat-tired bicycles, singing aloud from the sheer joy of being alive in a tropical paradise. The mood was infectious. I must have performed a familiar ritual because passersby cheered when I pressed my lips to the worn center of the Mile Zero. The sign on the corner of Whitehead and Fleming Streets marked the 'End' of Route 1. Across Whitehead was the 'Begin' sign.

Needing to discover what Nirvana must surely lay hidden there I crossed Fleming. What followed was a succession of crowded watering holes where I was so well liked that I quickly grew an entourage of kindred spirits, which multiplied as my spendthrift tour progressed ever deeper below Mile Zero.

> **Licker talks mighty loud**
> **w'en it git loose fum de jug.**
>
> **- Joel Chandler Harris**

It was with the high-flying clarity borne on whiskey wings that I knew I had found my destiny. After only a few hours in Key West I had more true friends than the ten years left behind me in Louisiana. What I couldn't find, the next morning, was my wallet, car, or any of those warm-hearted 'bubbas' who had taken me into their hearts. All that was left was a smelly pile of crumpled rags on the floor of the city drunk tank, with me inside them. Having collected enough musicians from assorted jails and lock-ups, I couldn't help recognize my new surroundings for what they were. Though, try as I might, I could not remember how I came to be there. When I sat up, my missing custom-tailored silk suit and hand-made Italian shoes assumed a secondary importance to stopping my head from exploding.

The arresting officer later explained to the judge that the owner of the Cadillac Eldorado didn't know me, didn't want to know me, and though he hadn't seen anything funny in my using the back seat of his car as a crash pad, he wasn't interested in pressing charges. The judge had a more liberal sense of humor, except when it came to swallowing my "tall tales" of being a man of some importance. Without wallet or ID to back up my story, I chose to not further try his patience and closed my mouth.

One of the pieces of paper stuffed into my hand was a voucher for a free meal. The mere thought of food was violently repellant; I was perspiring pure alcohol, my mouth tasted like something left on the road for dead, and the hydraulic vise grinding my brain rendered any attempt at human speech or thought virtually impossible. My bene-factor, a fast-talking, church lady, had steadfastly waited for me, the last "unfortunate" from the morning's docket. In addition to the meal ticket, she had a program for me that included counseling, job assist-ance, and "...a golden opportunity to take responsibility for (my) life by accepting Jesus into my heart as my one true Savior."

Despite her obvious sincerity, I couldn't help notice the involunt-ary wrinkling of her nose at my proximity. In the growing heat of the day, I didn't want to be standing that close to me.

I jammed the giveaways into an unfamiliar pocket, mumbling a promise to go and see about the job right away. —I would have promised anything to escape the churning noises my insides were making not to mention the shrill scrape of her voice across the vast and tender galaxy of my hangover.— Pursuing me down the court-house steps, as I went in search of a drink to steady my nerves, she called out that there'd be a cot for me at the Men's Shelter. The well-disguised looks of envy I received from a hunting pack of lawyers confirmed that I really had it made. Lucky me!

Her papers and my promises went into a trash basket on the corner.

I got maybe a foot inside the cool oasis of the Green Parrot saloon before the bartender hollered, grabbed a baseball bat and chased me back out into the street. I was just as quickly shooed away from the next bar I looked like I might try to enter. Unlike the other night, this was a completely new reality. All alone on a crowded street everyone saw me, but none would look at me save to ensure avoiding contact.

Surrounded by sleek stiletto heels and patent leather pumps, a grimy, disheveled creature with a patchy beard and wild hair stared back at me from the store window. Inside, the clerk looked like he was reaching for a gun.

For of fortunes sharp adversitee
The worst kinde of infortune is this,
A man to have ben in prosperitee,
And it remembren, when it passed is.

- Geoffrey Chaucer

Beset by images of men on street corners with spray bottles and squeegees, will-work-for-food signs and cardboard boxes for homes, men with loss in their eyes, men I had ignored, I wept openly while pawing through the trash basket desperate to find those precious slips of paper.

Every step of the four miles from the candy-colored antiquity of Key West, over the Cow Key Channel Bridge to Stock Island, was a purgatory.

Once, I'd heard a joke about how falling from a tall building didn't hurt...it was the sudden deceleration at the bottom. I wasn't laughing. My fall had not been from a very great height but it had been unbelievably quick and the impact had been shattering. The worst part was in knowing that it was my fault. I could have saved Bobby from his fate and me from mine, if I had had the guts to take control of the business after Nicole's death. Instead, I had gone into hiding. I was good at hiding. Road trips, nightclubs, concerts; with enough drugs and liquor to keep reality at bay, it was easy to hide.

I would've killed for a shooter of Wild Turkey...anything to numb the pain.

When in disgrace with fortune and men's eyes
I all alone beweep my outcast state,
And trouble deaf heaven with my bootless cries,
And look upon myself and curse my fate...

- William Shakespeare

Half out of my head from heat and hangover, dying of thirst and near exhaustion, I hobbled down a desolate dead-end road on Stock Island, beyond a decaying dog racing track, past Alex' auto wreckers. Mangroves, stinking, mosquito-laden, crowded in on the right. On my left, three junkyard brawlers snarled at me through barbed wire. There was more value in the rusted and gutted wrecks behind the fence than the one inside tattered rags I was wearing.

An insistent honking woke me from my mutterings. Reeling down the middle of the road. I turned around, stuck out my thumb and got my first sight of Charlie. —Cabs of Japanese pickup trucks were never designed for something that big, few things are.

Stopping beside me with the engine running, he stated, "There's nothing down that road." I heard the implied "for you" in the tone of his voice.

Scrabbling for the do-gooder's chit in my pocket, I held it out to him in a shaking hand, explaining that I had business out there, that I had a job at a salvage company located at the end of this very road.

Refusing to touch it, he looked at the stained and wrinkled scrap of paper. I saw his eyebrows arch in disbelief. There was a skeptical half-smile stretched across his round face and a challenge in the steely-blue eyes surrounded by webs of sun-scorched lines.

"I need a whole man, not a half-drunk." He grunted a sour chuckle.

The crushing despair, seeing my last chance vanish before my eyes caused something to snap. There was a crackling, sizzling pop somewhere inside my head. My vision blurred to red. The next thing I knew I was trying to drag a man twice my size through the tiny window of his truck. I must have passed out because I next found myself lying flat on my back with him towering over me—he would have towered if I'd been standing, but from that angle he looked twelve feet tall.

"You either got guts or brain damage. I'm not sure which," he said in a thoughtful Virginian drawl then laughed; this time it was with genuine humor. "Bubba, if you want work bad enough to tackle me then work you'll git." Gesturing over his shoulder with his thumb. "In the back. 'Til we can get you smelling a damn-sight better that's where you ride"

Unsure what I was in for—but knowing that riding was infinitely preferable to walking—I scrambled aboard fitting myself into a small corner amid a rusty jumble of cables, tools and odd machine parts.

It was from that vantage that my new life appeared as we rounded the last curve in the road.

Inside a tall chain-link fence topped with rolled razor wire, five fuel tanks, each as big as a house, framed the gateway, Faded logos on their rusty white exteriors admitted that they had, in better days, owed allegiance to Gulf Oil.

Ringed with water on three sides, the spit of land was almost a quarter mile long and nearly three hundred yards at its widest. Heat waves shimmied above a bare coral expanse graded flat and baked hard by the sun.

The east and southern shorelines were natural, fringed with mangroves and congested with debris at the water's edge. Just offshore, a large black barge had been grounded. Tilted at an angle, it was loaded with rusty steel construction members and large pieces of heavy equipment, the nature of which I could only guess.

A row of decrepit fishing boats, propped up on shores, dominated the center of the property. Near the closest of the four derelicts, stood a faded blue Trav-l-lift with several missing wheels and the engine compartment a gaping hole. Abandoned and forgotten, this was clearly the end of the line for those decaying hulks, which further drove home the nature of my own status.

I saw a dust devil spring into life, stir the pale-yellow ashes of someone's dreams of prosperity, and die. It was over ninety degrees but a shiver ran down the middle of my back and gave my shoulders a violent rattle.

We stopped by a large single-story building. Of the layers of painted over names and signs, each a testament to the progression of businesses that had tried to make a go of it, in letters over six feet tall, one word was still partially decipherable: CO M S RY.

Beyond, perhaps half a mile across at its widest lay a deep-water inlet. Beginning in the shadow of a large ice plant at its mouth, the opposite shore was a profusion of boats of all sizes and descriptions filling the docks four-deep, unloading at fish packing plants and taking on supplies from row upon row of warehouses. Everywhere, people were working, money was being spent and made, everything was motion and momentum.

At the narrow end of the watery cul-de-sac, clustered about finger piers, fuel docks, bait shops and marinas, a forest of sailing masts swayed, rigging rapping and tinkling brightly in the wakes of cabin cruisers and speedboats. Brilliant hulls, sparkling brightwork, and pristine pennants radiated a multi-hued psychedelia of wealth and grace.

On this side of the inlet a rectangular cove of cracked concrete had been cut into the coral, reinforced here and there with rusty sheets of pleated steel and hung with rotting tires. Moored to the near side, in front of the CO M S RY building sat a sad rust-bucket. —While living on the Mississippi I'd seen plenty, though usually from a comfortably insulated, air-conditioned distance.— Having begun life as a steel barge, nearly a hundred feet long, it was maybe a third of that wide. Squatting on the starboard bow, like the skeletal remains of some prehistoric insect, was a scabrous crane minus its track-driven chassis. A dredging bucket lay open on its side by the base. Further aft, a blocky structure with watertight doors and portholes, was capped by a wheelhouse its roof nearly twenty feet above the deck was a jumble of antennae and spotlights.

A sinking sensation pulled inside of me, like riding an elevator in a tall building, plunging downward, ever downward.

Between the floating disaster and the defunct tank farm sat a huge mound of trash that dwarfed both in sheer mass and ugliness. Ragged pieces of boat cabins, sections of hulls, miles of rusty chain, cable, machinery, parts, pieces, and seaweed covered fish traps, supported the half-rotted carcass of a sea-plane, complete with a pair of impact-crushed pontoons and half a wing.

The elevator gathered speed as it passed the sub-basement level.

Everything looked almost as bad and confused as I felt. Since I didn't have many options, anything, even this was better than the nothing I had.

I jumped down from the pickup. Tremors rattled my bones as my knees absorbed the impact. When my internal elevator ride lurched to a stop, a little voice called: 'Everyone out for Rock Bottom.'

*   *   *

Each day, I soon learned, began at first light and ended well after sunset with me so totally whipped I could hardly see straight let alone walk. I quickly fell into a love-hate relationship with the job; I loved hating it. But I was determined to show this guy that I was worth something. Thinking back, I guess I was trying to prove it to myself.

The majority of our work seemed to revolve around adding to and whittling away at the huge pile of junk on the dock, which I'd dubbed Mt. Trashmore. We scavenged every kind of wreckage on and under the water then cut down and chopped up everything into usable and saleable parts. Marine and aviation rigging was broken down and sorted into basic components, saving all of the little bits; nuts, bolts, and fasteners in plastic pails. Every bit, no matter how small, exotic, damaged, or obsolete, had value. I sometimes wondered how far down the list of salvaged items my name would appear?

My probation lasted for two weeks; most of that time was spent trying to keep up with a guy who didn't seem to know the meaning of the word 'tired'. One of Charlie's favorite tricks, when we had finished working on a particular section of Trashmore, was to heft the two oxy-acetylene tanks, in one smooth motion, up onto his shoulders as if they were nothing before moving to the next site. I was the pathetic wretch struggling not to fall behind as I tried to keep the torch and its long loops of double hose from dragging across the ground.

Slowly, days stretched into weeks, gathered momentum and spun into months. Hard work and good food filled out the work clothes Charlie'd found for me—what I'd arrived in he'd deemed only fit for burning. A sensible person—not me—would've stood upwind. I clearly remember the foul taste, burning eyes, racking coughs, and the sound of Charlie's booming laughter, as the remnants of my past went up in flames.

Adapting to the workload, I began missing my vices but quickly learned that alcohol and tobacco had no place in the scheme of things. Charlie'd made a promise, which I learned was to him a sacred bond, that I "...would shape up and fly right come Hell or high water." True to his word he kept me on a pretty tight rein and increased the daily chores proportionately, so that they continued to demand every last bit of strength I could muster. Before long the cravings were gone.

At six months I tipped the scales at a hundred and eighty; in New Orleans I had averaged one-thirty. The brown hair I'd tied back in a long ponytail, was now sun-bleached to copper and gold, and cut hot-weather short. I also noticed that my eyes, previously a smoke and booze tinted red, had deep amber and green irises surrounded by clear sparkling whites, and instead of the pasty green-gray night-crawler pallor the sun had baked my skin to a rich golden bronze. Each day still finished with me dog-tired but I was now keeping pace and

Charlie noticed. Despite our size difference—my slender five-eight to his massive six-foot four—the almost twenty-year age difference between us had become a determining factor. More often than not, sweat running from his thick black hair that was generously salted with life, when Charlie called it a day I was still going strong.

I knew that my place on the salvage list had moved up when he included me in the planning phases of our jobs and began teaching me the intricacies of marine salvage. I thrived on each new challenge, and as my experience grew, we began implementing, with increasing frequency, many of my ideas.

New Orleans slipped further into the past.

Over the next two years our mutual respect grew and developed into a friendship the quality of which I'd never before known. There were no ulterior motives only a quiet and genuine liking for each other, strengthened by shared risk and hard work. There wasn't a job we wouldn't tackle from installing piers to raising sunken fishing boats. Once, we salvaged a crashed helicopter far out in the heart of the Gulf of Mexico...but that's another story.

* * *

July 1, 1994:

I was going through the latest batch of mail, sorting bills into 'gotta pay', 'they can wait', and 'gimme a break'. Standing out from shopping flyers and political pamphlets destined for the circular file folder, was an invitation for bids to deliver Customs-seized drug boats from Key West to the impound docks near Jacksonville for auction.

As long as there is a market for contraband there will always be people willing to take the risk. The one thing Key West is and has always been famous for is smuggling. Consequently, four Federal forces: Customs, DEA, Coast Guard, and the Navy all actively hunt the waters surrounding the Florida Keys.

Charlie'd rated our chances of winning the contract at somewhere between slim and none, but I had argued long and hard, so (probably just to shut me up) he sent in the forms. We'd been experiencing a dry spell and had been praying for some activity. According to Baseball philosopher 'Satchel' Paige: "Careful what you ask for, 'cause you might get it."

Well, we asked and we got:

Upon our return from our first one-boat delivery, we found three newly confiscated vessels awaiting transport and reports of three more en route. It had taken us two days to ready the first for the voyage, followed by three days at maximum throttle to reach the impound docks, a half day to secure a rental van and transfer our gear aboard before the nine-hour drive back to the Keys. If we were going to keep up with the rapidly building felony fleet and not default on our contract, we had to find a better way of doing our job. I cannot tell how many times I've regretted coming up with the "great idea" that Charlie agreed to try.

Watermen tend to be a strange lot, a breed unto themselves, addicted to the drug of being afloat. Like junkies without a fix, many seem unable to function for extended periods of time on dry land and need a rolling deck beneath their feet in order to feel the world is right. In the Keys there's seldom a shortage of men looking for work; some between seasonal fishing runs; others land-locked owing to their vessels being cash-poor or laid up for repairs. Shore-bound for any of an infinite number of reasons, in order to survive, many are willing to take risks outside the law. We hired ten sailors who preferred staying hungry to breaking the law then divided them into five two-man crews. Each boat was fitted with a primary radio and a handheld back up, along with provisions, tools, and emergency gear to cover any contingency. For our tug we chose the largest of the now-seven vessels, a decommissioned Coast Guard cutter (caught off Loggerhead Key loaded to the gunnels with fifty-pound bales of Colombia's finest hemp), to which we cabled our half-mile long string of boats. We then herded our motley convoy out into the Gulf Stream and headed due north.

Where lies the land to which the ship would go?
Far, far ahead, is all her seamen know.
And where the land she travels from? Away,
Far, far behind, is all that they can say.

- Arthur Hugh Clough

Chugging through that first night, the rhythmic beat of the heavy diesels thrummed, resonating through the steel hull. Above me the sky was bright with constellations just beyond my fingertips. Orion's belt glinted sharply in the inky blackness, pointing the way as it had done since man first went to sea. There was comfort in that constancy, because on the water the touchstones of one's existence often assume a different perspective. Things left behind can change radically during one's absence; wives can take lovers; possessions can vanish forever; the past can jump out suddenly, viciously appearing without warning; or worries may fade into obscurity. New Orleans, for me, may as well have been on the other side of the planet and my time there of no more substance than the fragments of a bad dream.

Money doesn't talk...it shouts. Good-paying jobs in the Florida Keys were rare. Lawful good paying jobs, rarer still. Word of our success spread so quickly that hardly a day went by without calls looking for openings on our burgeoning crew list. The continuous carousel over the next six months generated a river of cash. The bank was happy. Charlie's accountant was happy. Scarcely able to stop long enough to draw breath, a sea of red ink evaporated before our eyes.

I suppose it was inevitable that a black cloud would appear, if only to complement the silver lining we'd engineered. Perversely, it came on a clear day, pounding on the bay door of the CO M S RY building then throwing open the Judas-gate with a resounding crash. I watched through the parted flash curtains of the welding cubicle, as Charlie listened to our black cloud, a paunchy ginger-haired gorilla in a Deputy Marshal's uniform whose diatribe was punctuated by sharp and pointy gestures. As the extended index finger rat-tat-tapped the breast of his coveralls, I thought Charlie might, after considering him a new and particularly loathsome variety of bug, step on him. Many's the time I've wished he had.

The spit of land the salvage yard was on—some twenty-five acres —had been confiscated from the estate of the former owner; something to do with taxes, I supposed. Because Charlie leased the section with the cove and warehouse from the government, we were, therefore, operating at the sufferance of the bureaucracy. When the drones in Tallahassee figured out that, due to the sensitive nature of the cargoes of the impounded vessels, it might be prudent to control the area where they were unloaded, they installed Deputy Marshal Ronald Schott to oversee the dock and harbor area. With an official presence, to keep an eye on the vessels, pending their disposition, the auctions could now come to the boats. Which meant our transportation contract was unnecessary.

A true martinet, Schott lost no time in imposing a host of rules and regulations to be strictly adhered to by anyone setting foot in his domain, as I quickly found out one morning when he refused to let me through the gate. I was only admitted when Charlie, who'd been in town picking up parts, showed up and verified that I did, in fact, work there. That one of our salvaged fishing boats had almost sunk at the dock, due to the delay and a faulty bilge pump, was of less consequence to our conscientious Deputy Marshal than the misspelling (his) of my name on the access list. Doubtless, there was a good reason for everything he did, but no one—me especially—much cared for the way he went about it.

As it has long been my belief that somewhere in the world there is, in addition to one's true love, someone who is in direct opposition to every thing we do or are, day-to-day events soon indicated that my special someone might indeed be Ronald Schott. Although I was ever willing to bury the hatchet, anatomically speaking, my choice of burial sites would have done little to ameliorate the situation beyond granting me temporary relief plus a prolonged stay in a correctional facility.

Unfortunately, quite a bit of the antipathy Deputy Marshal Schott felt towards me fell on Charlie. I suspected that it must have been costing him dearly, but he would never have said a word had I not confronted him.

Hardheaded to a fault, Charlie's loyalty was fierce to behold. I was deeply touched by his sincerity when he argued with me, suggesting we look for another site for the salvage operations, but I understood that the universe had decided it was time for me to go.

I'd learned a lot about myself during our association, and had grown to like the guy I saw in the mirror. Rather than see my friend continue to get his assets stuck in a crack because of my presence, I decided to see what the future might hold in store for me back on the beach. A few nights later, over herbal tea and pizza, Charlie and I toasted the dissolution of our partnership. At his insistence, I accepted a full share of the boat delivery profits and a near-new maxi van, one we'd bought to transport crews and equipment from Jacksonville. My bankroll, however generous, was far from adequate to support a lifestyle as a playboy, especially in a money sponge like Key West where it's often been said that the only sure way to leave the island with a small fortune is to arrive with a large one.

Among other things 'the Rock', as the island is affectionately called by its inhabitants, is a party town; there's always a dozen or so get-togethers in full swing. Many are promotional launches for the latest daubings of a newly discovered artiste, some foster great opportunities "potentially worth a ton of money with room to maybe squeeze in one or two more lucky investors." Seasonal events are usually based on survival, primarily of hurricane and tourist inundations. Most happen out of equal parts boredom and the 'just for the pure hell of it' attitude that distinguishes long-time denizens. Outside of transient 'snowbirds' and tourists, it really is a very small town; the kind of place where everyone seems to know everyone else, or pretends they do. Again and again I saw the same faces saying the same things, lit with the same faint hopes that somehow tonight might be different, while knowing—perhaps, fearing—it never would. That really wasn't what I needed. Party scenes were no longer my metier, and though I appreciated the good intentions of one particular hostess who appointed herself my personal matchmaker, I really wasn't ready for another relationship. I wondered then, even as I do now, if ever I will be?

After two months playing on the water during the day and drifting through the evenings like a ghost, from one party to the next, all I managed to accomplish was to teach myself the rudiments of wind surfing and how to smile a lot while saying nothing. I knew I needed a challenge, something productive, someplace to channel my energies.

*   *   *

Monk:

The heat index was striving for a triple-digit day. Inside the narrow lanes and alleys of Old Town, melting asphalt swallowed motorcycle kickstands while air conditioners growled from windows, dripping and filling the air with a musty stench. A mile off Smathers Beach, on Key West's eastern shore, I was covered in cool salt spray, working a 15- to 25-knot wind. After three hours of windsurfing near the limits of my skill level I was starting to feel the strain, so when the wind started to gust up, I decided to call it a day and leave the fast stuff to the half-dozen or so die-hards and hot-doggers. I was maybe half a mile offshore and working the long leg of an easy run back to the beach when suddenly, from the direction of the Casa Marina Hotel (where the rich folks vacation) a Hobie-Cat blew past the point off White Street Pier. It was running before the wind, dangerously heeling over onto one pontoon. I watched in horror as each course correction caused the Cat to slew further sideways to the heavy wind until a gust caught the tiny vessel between hull and water and lifted it clear of the surface. The Cat's lightness, speed, and high center of gravity conspired to send it tumbling through the air. Halfway through its second rotation, the tip of the mast whipped around smartly and whacked the water, snapping the hollow aluminum shaft in half with a sharp crack. Wobbling, horribly, the Hobie performed one last aerial three-sixty before slamming down hard, lost inside a spectacular burst of spray.

Shearing across the face of the wind toward the capsized vessel, I looked for survivors. A couple of empty orange life vests floated near one of the pontoons. Abandoning my board on the fly, I smacked into the water in a shallow dive that carried me well under the spread of pink and white Dacron. Snagged in a tangle of lines and trapped under the sail I found the unconscious pilot, floating face down. I dragged him clear and supported the back of his neck to keep his face out of the water. Blood ran freely from a deep gouge above his hairline. He wasn't breathing. Treading water, administering mouth-to-mouth, I was keenly aware of the blood in the water and its potential attraction to the shark and barracuda that haunted the nearby reefs. Also, my board and the capsized catamaran were both drifting rather briskly before the wind. I couldn't leave off trying to resuscitate the stricken man to go and fetch either of them.

I saw a movement to my left and turned. Instead of dreaded gray fins slicing through the water, a couple of young wind-surfers were coming over for a closer look. After several very long minutes the two teens had caught and righted the battered vessel then helped me load the injured man aboard. Working at getting him breathing on his own,

I sent one of the teens ahead to call for help then directed his partner in rigging a makeshift gaff then had him short-reef the sail to the remaining piece of mast. Though broken from the accident, the catamaran still represented the surest way to get the injured man to help.

While Trey, of the pierced nose and acid-green wet suit, steered a line toward the beach, I concentrated on blowing air into the unconscious man's lungs and pumping his chest. As I tried to force life into him, the repetitive movements focused my mind on death and the suddenness with which it can come.

"Dude...?" Trey asked. "Is he...like, gone?"

Just then the man bucked once, coughed, and began retching up gouts of Atlantic Ocean.

"Maybe not." I laughed aloud without really knowing why.

"Coo-o-l!" Trey and I beamed at each other. A warm shiver ran up my spine and brought tears to my eyes. Trey blinked rapidly several times before turning his attention back to keeping us on course.

Despite his injuries and having narrowly survived a harrowing experience, the man, upon learning from Trey that I was the guilty party, launched an embarrassing and non-stop praise of my efforts. My refusal to accept reward for happening to be in the wrong place at the right time served only to make him all the more determined. Not only was his face a mask of blood, but he slurred his words and seemed disoriented. Also, the pupils of his eyes, I noticed, were unequal in size and wandering disconcertingly in the classic pattern of severe concussion. I had seen enough of death, and his agitation began to worry me, so, in order to calm him, I agreed to accept his repeated offers of dining with him to discuss his appreciation for my "noble deed."

A siren became audible in the distance and rapidly grew louder as we neared land. A fair-sized crowd had already gathered on the beach. Arnie, Trey's surfer friend, led the way for two paramedics carrying a cervical board and emergency kits. He flashed us a thumbs-up as they came forward, and, with the assistance of a half dozen volunteers, helped beach the Hobie Cat. Our injured man insisted he was going to walk to the ambulance until he tried to get up and almost collapsed. Under weak protest, he allowed himself to be strapped to the board then lowered from the catamaran. The crowd parted, closed ranks and turned to follow the paramedics and their burden to the ambulance.

The two surfers and I stayed behind. Quietly, we untied our boards from the stern of the ruined Hobie.

"No big deal..." they responded when I thanked them for their help, but it was and we each knew it. We shook hands then made good our escape.

No good deed goes unpunished,

- Clare Boothe Luce

Several days later, I was in the parking lot across from the beach setting up my board, when one of the people from Boats 'n Boards rentals came over and handed me a business card from my rescuee. Printed on the back was a request for me to contact him at my earliest convenience. I tossed the card onto the dashboard, along with receipts and other useless scraps of paper, locked up then headed for the water. A few hours later, when the winds shifted then tapered off, I decided I'd had enough. By the time I had my board beached, broken down, and stowed I had accumulated no less than seven identical cards— another half dozen or so were tucked under the windshield wipers on the van.

Now and then, I have been known to take a hint.

Later that night I was treated to an evening at Antonia's, the premiere Italian restaurant on Duval Street where, over a sumptuous feast of Osso Buco accompanied by the single glass of red wine I allowed myself, in honor of the occasion, I listened to the impeccably attired attorney—sporting two black eyes and a bandage covering half his forehead—as he reaffirmed his intent to see me suitably rewarded for having saved his life.

"I simply will not take no for an answer. Now, tell me: what do you want?"

"A good meal," I answered, raising my glass in toast and taking a microscopic sip of an exceptionally good San Geovese.

"Dear boy...! You saved my life. And, I estimate my existence to be worth considerably more than a little lamb and a giggle of grape," he said, offhandedly referring to what must surely have been a healthy three-figure tab.

"Now that that's said, how can I thank you? Do you want anyone sued?"

"Not that I can think of," I said, laughing.

As our meal progressed and we discussed some of the things I had done prior to my inadvertent role as lifeguard, I confessed that I was, indeed, at loose ends.

"A job? Do you need one?"

I couldn't see myself working in a law office, and said as much.

"I," Monk said, his spoonful of Spumoni poised in midair, "have an idea. What do you know about buildings?"

"We're inside one," I offered fatuously. The look I received was in direct contrast to the sweetness of the rum-flavored ice cream, and precluded any further pursuit of facetiousness; this was business.

"You mean construction?"

"Precisely," he mumbled around another spoonful. "I have—or rather—I look after a number of clients who own various properties and buildings throughout the Keys. And, I am in need of a project superintendent, someone to oversee—"

"Whoa, cool your jets, Mr. Rothschild, I know nothing about—"

"One of the first things you have to learn, dear boy, *is*..." he said, gesturing imperiously with his spoon "...if I'm going to make your fortune for you, when I'm creating, you will kindly do me the courtesy of not interrupting, and..." he added warmly, "...my *friends* call me Monk.

"Now, as I was saying, I need someone I can trust. As you've already proven yourself on that count, the rest is academic."

He waved his spoon denying any refusal.

"Tut-tut, don't look so concerned, you will be amply compensated for ensuring that my clients and I aren't cheated. I've made up my mind. I won't hear another word on the subject, except *yes*."

Weighing my options, bizarre as it might seem, I really had no reason not to take him up on his offer; since nothing else had come my way, so if an obviously wealthy and influential pillar of the community wanted to make life easier for me who was I to say no?

"Why not? I'll try anything once." Echoes of Charlie's ritual response rang in my ears as I took Monk's already outstretched and waiting hand. Monk positively glowed.

"And twice, if it feels good...said the actress to the bishop," he added, laughing aloud at what I was soon to learn was one of a seemingly endless series of variations on his favorite joke.

Within the next three days I found myself embroiled in my first assignment: renovating the project superintendent's (my) residence, a spacious cottage incongruously located in the Bahama Village—read: po' folk—section of Old Town directly adjacent to the high wall surrounding the Truman Annex enclave (read: rich folk). Understanding, if I was going to oversee the work of construction people, I'd better be able to talk their language and know what I was talking about. Also, because I would have to live with whatever mistakes I made, there was an incentive to get the job done right...the first time.

In order to preserve its architectural heritage (one of the attractions that draws tourists and tourist dollars to the island) the City of Key West imposes a host of rules and regulations whenever any of the buildings in Old Town are renovated. Introducing a different color scheme or replacing window shutters with anything other than the original style required the written approval of the OIHS. The Old Island Historical Society wields considerable power and can, if it so chooses, stop a job in an instant. The resulting paperwork, fines, and penalties, not to mention time wasted in variance hearings before the red tag is lifted can easily double or treble the cost of any project, unless of course, one is well-connected or wealthy enough to get the Bubba-system greasing the rails for you.

The lessons I'd learned from Charlie, about doing business with fairness, integrity, and hard work paid off. I played fair and square making sure that every item on the job lists was done according to code. There were plenty of headaches in the course of my education, but once the contractors and tradesmen saw that I really was trying to do it right they responded in kind. With their help, I learned the ins and outs of antique joinery; a legacy of the old-time ships' carpenters whose work can be found in many of the elder structures on the Rock.

At the end of the first year, when I received an unexpected bonus check for ten thousand dollars, I figured Monk and his clients must have been satisfied with my efforts, too.

*   *   *

**He was born with a gift of laughter
and a sense that the world was mad.**

- Scaramouche, Rafael Sabatini

CHAPTER 2

July, 1, 1996:

Glassed-in elevators, balconies, a bridge spanning a deep gorge, even standing on a ladder could turn my knees to jelly and my insides to water. As far back as I can remember, I have been afraid of heights. Yet, twenty-five minutes after arriving at the small airstrip in Homestead, Florida I was a fully qualified Ground School graduate, had the certificate to prove it, and was about to face my fears.

Mentally reviewing the jump commands, as the smiling instructor cinched me into a harness so tightly I could barely stand, I was led out of the equipment room and across the tarmac to where a small plane sat with its engine idling. Once white, it was now liberally stained and streaked with grease. There was a very large hole in its side where a door should have been.

I began to suspect my being there may have had less to do with tidal influence or the alignment of the planets, than the onset of the middle-age crazies. To commemorate having, successfully, survived thirty-nine years (nine more than I had once believed possible) my birthday present to me this year was the gift of free fall.

Inside the austere aluminum cabin, a late-fifties husband-and-wife team in matching black and turquoise jumpsuits nodded to me as I entered then continued chatting with two, on-leave German soldiers on a sky diving vacation across America.

Except for the rising blare of the un-muffled engine, which quickly rendered conversation below a shout virtually impossible, all was serenely surreal. The earth spiraled below into a green, brown and tan crazy quilt drawn together with highway stitching. At five thousand feet, after much nodding, waving and thumbs-up gestures all around, the husband-and-wife couple were gone. Shortly after the two soldiers followed. Soon it would be my turn. At that moment, I was pleased I had forked over the extra twenty-five bucks for the "Deluxe Pro-Package" that gave me an additional mile of altitude.

The pilot signaled as the altimeter rolled past ten thousand feet. Harnessed to the front of my guide, Bob—a retired Army Airborne paratrooper who'd seen it all—we knee-walked forward in tandem to the hole in side of the plane. The rim of the hole, I noticed, was lined with a split garden hose. In sequence, as we placed our feet on the narrow strut that jutted away from the fuselage, I saw tiny threads flapping along the trailing edge. The surface had been made nonslip by gluing cut-up sections of old sanding belts along its length. What other improvisations, I wondered, had been employed to safeguard my well being?

Standing in the full rush of air speed that tried to bully us from our perch, it suddenly became clear that this was not an academic exercise. At Bob's command, with only a few misgivings about the sanity of this escapade, I pried my fingers loose from the wing support and brought my hands into the official "pushing away position" in front of my shoulders. Then, bending my knees, lifting my feet clear of the strut, I transformed myself into baggage buckled to the front of Bob's harness.

Suddenly, my stomach became light as the plane faded to a distant buzz somewhere above. Yahoo-ing my exuberance at the top of my lungs then hearing Bob's groan, I gathered that others had expressed themselves similarly. Obviously, he was no longer impressed.

My perception shifted; awed by the immensity of the world and how small my place in it, while plummeting like a rock towards the planet. For a fantastically intense forty-two seconds, I drank undiluted of the raw, razor-edged drug called adrenaline, the flavor of which addicts find impossible to explain to the uninitiated—like describing brown to a blind man.

Thrilling...? Yes. Satisfying...? No. It was close to what I had been seeking but it wasn't exactly right; it was all over far too quickly.

Something had gotten under my skin from the experience. Perhaps it had been there all along, hidden deep down inside, and was starting to work its way out, because the following year, instead of after-shave or underwear for my birthday, I used my annual bonus to sign up for a "MTN" pilot's course at the Lookout Mountain Flight Park outside Chattanooga, Tennessee.

Shrouded in ground fog and morning shadows, class was conducted in a grassy field in the river valley far below the ridgeline. Chilled by mist, soaked to the knees by dew, I walked open the zipper on a twenty-foot-long nylon bag for the first time, exposing a mystery of poles, rods, cables, and Dacron. Two other "virgins" and I looked about in obvious helplessness and in wonder, as a flock of giant aluminum insects slowly began to take shape and stretch their acid-hued wings. Three instructors, finishing their coffees by the long and narrow storage shed, chose up who would focus on the "newbies" that morning. I noticed all three had implausibly muscular legs showing below their short pants. That should have been a clue.

On any given day, there were one to three dozen damp, shivering, would-be pilots working through the intricacies of Assembly 101 under the watchful eyes of a team of blue-jerseyed trainers. Once the gliders were assembled, advanced trainees hauled—or, for a nominal fee—had them "caddied" up the steep track to the top of a hundred-foot cut-bank just to the left of the set-up area. Meanwhile, we "fledges" towed our wings, bumping along on their large balloon-like plastic wheels, to the sixty-foot high, and softly rounded, knoll over a quarter of a mile away. There, we staggered up and stumbled down the red clay with 70-odd pounds of hang glider strapped to our backs, as we learned about lift, control, and glide angles; not everyone's idea of fun but it had been a while since anyone had accused me of aspiring to normalcy.

One unexpected lesson was in humility. A rancher from New Zealand, a frail looking sixty-year-old barely half my size, who started on the same day as me, had, after ten days, already gone on to launch from the mountain and was now doing the things that were the substance of my dreams.

After six weeks of plowing furrows down the slopes of the bunny hill, and having two beginners' classes pass me by and graduate to "the big dog", dreaming seemed as close as I would ever get to achieving the holy state of "air time." Possibly, I could have picked up a few extra dollars tilling soil with my dragging feet for some of the local farmers, but as the end of my vacation loomed closer I began to seriously think about whether or not I was wasting my time. One day my instructor filled a backpack with rocks, attached it to the apex and launched the glider; it flew perfectly level and surpassed the average distances flown off the bunny slope. The lesson was clear; I had been trying too hard. I wasn't sure if I knew how, but the next morning, after having decided to take it easy, and coast out the last two weeks with a minimum of effort, all the pieces magically came together.

In no time at all, it seemed, I stood harnessed, helmeted, staring into the green abyss beneath an azure sky. The landing zone was a tiny spot several miles away. It appeared too small to land in and far too close to the heavy ring of tall trees surrounding it. Daunted, I watched as one pilot after another made the approach, bled off speed as they floated downfield and flared perfectly to nail dead center on the mowed target circle. Cheers and whoops of appreciation chorused from the small crowd of spectators perched along the ridge on either side of the launch ramp. Then it was my turn.

My hands were slippery on the tape-wrapped foam covering the down tubes, as I carried the glider to the top of the concrete incline. Watched over by three instructors, I hooked-in and performed my "hang-check," a handy little ritual that ensures pilot and glider do not become separated after launch. Once completed, I stood and seated the "apex pinch" of the tubular aluminum control frame down onto my shoulders. Anticipating, reacting to the tiny shifts of air, I slowly balanced the weight of the glider. A fluid fulcrum to the weight of leverage, I tried to "feel" the distant wingtips. Poised, ready for that moment of calm air, I became aware of a subtle dissociation from my surroundings. Although my heart was crashing, banging against my ribs like a caged animal trying to escape, it was as if I was calmly, objectively watching through someone else's eyes. Could I make the "Leap of Faith" I heard a spectator question? Trying not to listen as she nattered on jovially about the lunacy of, "...taking a running jump off a perfectly good mountain."

The soft gusts rolling up out of the valley softened then died. Ribbony telltales on the end of the ramp hung limp.

It was time.

In a sandlot-dry and somewhat shaky voice I called, "Clear!" Then, as a testament to how effective the training had been or how exceptionally stupid I can be when I really put my mind to it, without any hesitation I ran toward the precipice.

The instant my weight shifted to my right foot, now well beyond the ramp, with nothing but a thirteen-hundred-foot drop down the face of the ridge below, a synaptic twitch in my brain demanded: "What have you done!?"

Sheering away from the face of the ridge, a large bump of warm air, like the breath of an invisible giant, moved around me, buoying up my glider. Intuitively, I eased the bar out and to my right, wheeling around into the column of warmth, seeking out its strength, feeling its shape and size. Peripherally, I sensed a presence to my right. A red-tailed hawk had stationed itself off the tip of my wing, mirroring my angle of approach to the air mass. We were in tune, in the thermal, moving with it, anticipating the nuances of its shape, its texture, as it rolled along the heart of the wide valley, carrying us higher, ever higher. The perspective broadened as we rose above the top of the ridge. The world began to take on a convex shape as we rose, gliding in formation carving wide, lazy spirals, staying in the heart of the lift. The hawk turned its head. Our eyes met. An electric shiver ran up and down my spine, radiating outward and rippling across my flesh. The chains that bind us humans to the Earth had fractured, broken, and fallen away. Freedom! Like two waves breaking around a point and flowing together, joy and peace flooded my senses, rushing pell-mell through the dry wash of my heart. When I was a child, this, was what I had imagined being an angel must feel like. In that moment I knew, had I not promised a friend I would return to Key West, nothing would have prevented me from staying in the mountains, indefinitely.

Three glorious flight-filled days later, preparing for my departure, keeping my word didn't feel like the rich and rewarding thing it was supposed to be. Bound by a set of ethics I had adopted as my own, mixed feelings or not, I headed south with a new-to me-glider bagged, tagged, and stored, awaiting my return.

Once I fulfilled my obligation to Monk I vowed to return, to pursue this new love. Unknown to me, events set into motion years before in New Orleans would prove me wrong.

*   *   *

CHAPTER 3

August 18, 1997:

Except for the monolithic roadside sculptures of kudzu-covered trees, the scenery grew progressively more monotonous by the hour as the rocky ridges of northern Georgia surrendered to undulating farm hills, which melted down into the dead, flat purgatory of inland Florida. The only respite came when US-1 finally escaped I-95 and the mainland, and fled like a fugitive from an insane asylum down over the fragile chain of coral Keys...a very slow fugitive.

Transports and dump trucks, Winnebagos and pickups pulling boats and trailers confounded the crawl of family-crammed vans and SUVs into impatient stutter-stopped knots, sometimes stretching for miles, punctuated by death defying passing sprees. Tempers and dashboard gauges rose higher and higher along the narrow 45MPH two-laned, double-solid highway.

A half-rotted Pinto with a wobbly rear wheel loitered along in front of me in the stop-and-start crawl. A hand-lettered sign filling the back window proclaimed to one and all:

Nub Buford's
Baptist Church

--

The church with a vision
and a mission

At odds with the divine message was the Pinto's rusty bumper, loaded down with NRA stickers and a wired-on BAD-ONE vanity plate. I pondered for almost an hour on the natures of the "vision" and the "mission" that conspired to create this rolling oxymoron, before I found a restaurant with a shaded parking lot. This time, I vowed my arrival in Key West would be both gentle and conscious, considerably different from my first visit to this amazing little part of the world.

> **I have been here before,**
> **But when or how I cannot tell:**
> **I know the grass beyond the door,**
> **The sweet keen smell,**
> **The sighing sound, the lights around the shore.**
>
> **- Dante Gabriel Rossetti**

Outside the restaurant heat shimmered the air making the sluggish southbound procession appear as a passing mirage. At the far end of the parking lot, my black Maxi-van sat deep in the lush shade of a sprawling Banyan tree. This year's birthday adventure, hang gliding in the mountains, had surpassed being just another vacation. It felt like I was on the verge of discovering a place I'd been searching for without knowing it existed, and the idea of spending another moment stuck in traffic was too absurd to consider.

With the four cargo doors open to the gentle breeze, I fed a little Miles Davis into the stereo, took an iced tea from the cooler, laid back, and siesta-ed while sunlight strobed, rippling off the transparent aqua waters of the Gulf of Mexico like diamonds on pale silk. A patrol of four pelicans skimmed by in close formation, inches above the surface. Nearby, from a thick stand of bougainvillea, a black and orange 'junkie bird' sang out his lament: "Oh-oh, I lost my needle" a counterpoint to the cool jazz sounds of *So What!*

This was the same tropical beauty that had greeted me on my first trip toward Mile Zero. Only then, it had been wasted on me. Disturbing fragments of that long-ago, tumble-down time crowded in as slumber carried me away.

**It is a melancholy of mine own, compounded of
many simples, extracted from many objects, and
indeed the sundry contemplation of my travels,
which, by often rumination, wraps me in a most
humorous sadness.**

-    **As You Like It, William Shakespeare**

I opened my eyes. The sun had set fire to the horizon and turned
the Gulf waters into molten copper. The traffic had thinned and flowed
easily. My snooze, despite the memories, had helped rejuvenate my
holiday mood.

Perceptions, I considered, while letting the engine warm up, have
a way of changing when viewed through the soft filter of time. The
intervening years had rounded off some of the sharp edges, though not
as many as I would've liked. That first sober day on the Rock back
then had been one of my worst; a baptism in fire, if you will and,
conversely, my saving grace.

Mile marker 23 flared out of the darkness in my headlights, raced
past and disappeared behind me. I'd made it as far as the Saddle Bunch
Keys. There were enough cars on the road ahead for a loose chain of
rubies to show the shape of the road beyond my headlights. In the
distance, the pale glow of Key West bounced off the night sky.

Like most people, I can do a pretty good job of covering over the
less than stellar moments in my life, and those first days on Key West
certainly qualified. Also, I knew that if I hadn't fallen as hard as I did
then, the bounce back from rock bottom might never have gotten me
my second chance at a real life.

It was almost ten by the time I'd navigated the van through the
narrow side streets of Bahama Village. Stretching, groaning, popping
the strain of two days on the road out of my back, I promised myself
that the next time the trip would be one -way. It felt good, thinking
about escaping the Rock; knowing there was only one thing I had to
do before I could return to hang gliding above the mountains of
Georgia.

*   *   *

And be these juggling fiends no more believ'd,
That palter with us in a double sense;
That keep the word of promise in our ear,
And break it to our hope.

- Macbeth, William Shakespeare

CHAPTER 4

August 20, 1997:

If I hadn't given my word to Monk I would have stayed at Lookout Mountain for good, but Charlie had taught me that a promise was a bond of honor, and Monk *was* a friend. Montgomery ("Monk" to his friends) Rothschild Esq. was primarily a property locator, deal facilitator, investment counselor, and given the right situation, an occasional investor. The pumped-up land prices in the Keys provided him with enough referral fees and commissions to support his penchant for expensive boyfriends, frivolous toys, and the occasional flutter in Florida's big money game; real estate.

The problem was Monk should never have been a lawyer. It's not that he wasn't sufficiently depraved or amoral to suit the demands of his profession, he was just in the wrong line. Monk's real talent was music. He could make a guitar cry like a Gypsy with a broken heart. As his fingers danced across the strings, one could almost hear the creak of painted wagons and violins sighing in the moonlight. Monk was good—in fact, very good—and with guidance and training, he might've been great. However, The General, Monk's mother and the guiding/driving force in his life had wanted him to be a lawyer. It was as simple as that. Consequently, the music business's loss was an equally disastrous blow to the Florida Bar Association.

* * *

My patience is now at an end.

- Adolf Hitler

CHAPTER 5

WESTBOUND, SOMEWHERE OVER THE GULF OF MEXICO...

Thursday, October 23, 1997, 23:25 EST:

Colonel Betancourt was not guilt-free, though painful, he admitted to himself, he had allowed complacency to subvert his value system, but no longer, he vowed. "This cannot continue."

It was the constant nature of the compromises forced upon him, upon his honor as a soldier and a man, requiring him to take part in these so-called "missions" that he found impossible to endure any longer.

"I will *not* permit this again" he addressed the mirror in the pilots restroom before bending to splash water on his face. "It will end tonight, and I will do what I must." Relieved, now that he had decided no longer to sit idle, his course of action had become clear.

His life had been molded in the crucible of honor that he had inherited from his father and the grandfather he'd been named for but had never met. A captain for the Dons in their fight against the Rough Rider invaders from America, the first Jorge Santiago Betancourt had been a man of exemplary courage and honor, as had all the men of his family who lived and died in service to their homeland.

To the Betancourt men—according to the stories the Colonel had heard since childhood—duty to country came before family or self. Though he had lacked the courage, initially, to stand firm against the corruption that now plagued his homeland his death tonight would uphold his family tradition, appease his conscience, and right a terrible wrong.

*   *   *

As I was going up the stair
I met a man who wasn't there.
He wasn't there again today.
I wish, I wish he'd stay away.

- Hughes Mearns

CHAPTER 6

October 10, 1997:

During the two hundred-plus years of its existence, the two-story office building had seen any number of alterations to its appearance, as had most of the 'downtown' section of Old Town. Most of the changes had been wrought for obvious reasons though many may have seemed odd or strangely eccentric. The latest, inspired by greed; thanks to Monk's mother, the General, meddling in his business a new T-shirt shop—one of almost ninety on the thirteen blocks of Duval Street—had gobbled up nearly ninety percent of the ground floor. All that remained of the once elegantly designed lobby entrance to Monk's upstairs offices was a narrow, high-ceilinged doorway.

On Friday morning, exactly five weeks and two days after my return from soaring above Lookout Mountain, I started up the steep staircase letting my hand glide over the satiny perfection of the oiled and polished oak handrail, automatically feeling for irregularities I knew I wouldn't find. Every post and spindle gleamed in the light from the three wrought-iron and frosted glass wall sconces, set one-each between an ascending row of bulls-eye windows whose stained-glass panels blazed like fire opals in the morning sun. A river of plush burgundy cascaded down over the restored and matched Dade County Pine stair treads, drawing one's eyes up to the ornate tin-plate ceiling pattern hovering above the gaslight era, second-floor waiting parlor.

The design for the lower entrance and stair chamber had been mine. Though I had orchestrated the physical renovation of the suite of vacant offices into the new home for Monk's law practice, the theme on the top floor was solely the General's. Perhaps best described as early-neo-classical-rediscovered, it was a trendy blend of wood grain with just enough fake worm holes and artificially induced rot spots to warm the hearts of—as the General referred to them—"the Great Unwashed." The renovation was for the benefit of tourists looking to buy bite-sized pieces of paradise through a well-established member of the community; the contrived seediness was meant to convey an air of antiquity to a practice that was scarcely six years old.

Despite a long hard campaign against his mother's choice of a particularly bilious color for the walls, I was outvoted not only by Monk, who was predictable when it came to the General but also by his staff, all of whom I'd heard in private denunciation of "*THAT PINK!*"

To my eye, the effect was hideous but the old battle-axe loved it. And, as she allowed that I had done a "better-than-average job" (from her a rave review) my invoice would be paid. I resolved to bite my tongue, swallow the blood, and accept the check with good grace.

Historically correct, according to the OIHS, the offices, once finished, did resemble the gaudy boudoir of the notorious 19th-century prostitute who had once held court there. In that respect, I supposed, there was a certain undeniable symmetry between the professions of past and present occupants.

"...even a broken clock can be right twice a day." The approaching sound of the General's metallic bray drifted downstairs. I froze in mid-step, listening, as Monk's fruitless attempt to defend whatever 'faulty timepiece' the General was currently maligning became so much verbal road kill.

"It's up to you..." she lied "...you know I trust your judgement..." she lied again "...and I only want the best for you, but..."

The rest of her campaign to manipulate Monk into seeing things her way was mercifully cut off, as the door to the general business office of the law practice in the front part of the building above Duval Street swung shut. I decided to quietly slip upstairs and into Monk's office in the back of the building to wait for his retreat from the lash of her tongue. Besides, that would give me an opportunity to say hi to—

"...and another thing..."

I stopped again.

"...this *deal*..." (the word dripped with venom) "...has to be kept running until we can get a return on your, your gamble. I don't see how you could have gotten involved in such a, a stupid, infantile thing."

She was in full harangue as they headed back to Monk's office. By the sound of it, she was harrying him every step of the way. Images came to mind of snarling hyenas snapping at the heels of a faltering gazelle, as it fled in terror.

"It was a high-yield investment opportunity, you said, you—*we*—needed..."

The door swung shut, cutting short the balance of his plea/excuse/argument. My heart went out to Monk but this was family business and, thank goodness, I was an outsider. Since a good piece of work, sorting out what to leave behind and what to take with me to Georgia, still lay ahead of me I decided to come back after the weekend.

*   *   *

CHAPTER 7

October 13, 1997:

The second Monday in October ushered in the first relief from the tropical swelter, when a large mass of polar air moving down from Canada breathed its cooling influence, soothing tempers and temperatures alike. Its arrival, coincidentally or not, corresponded with the General's return to stirring the cauldrons of mischief and malice in her West Palm Beach coven where, thankfully, she spent most of the year.

Thoughts of autumn in the mountains, of what to take and what to leave behind, started to filter in as I spent the morning completing the last item on my punch-out lists for the renovation. An indulgence really, I was checking for unfilled nail holes. Since the work in Monk's offices was essentially complete, it was a time of savoring the rewards of a job well done. Sometimes, simple pleasures are the best.

I was up a ladder—metaphorically speaking a creek would have been more appropriate for what was about to happen—smoothing a tiny dab of wood filler into the corner join of crown moldings above Monk's desk when he hung up the telephone. The call had disturbed him; all the signs were there, if one knew what to look for. Like a gambler's tell, a quirky mannerism that signals when an opponent is bluffing or holding an unbeatable hand, Monk's tendency to pant when he got excited was a weakness that he worked hard to correct. Often, a little too hard.

"I may have a little something for you," he said, breathing a little too carefully while projecting an outwardly calm demeanor. Monk relied on his boyish grin to get his way; when I looked at him, he had the wattage turned way up.

I shivered without really knowing why.

Monk dearly loved shiny toys. Like a magician mesmerizing his audience, diverting attention away from the hand holding the Ace of Spades, he arranged and rearranged the regiment of dust-collectors and gewgaws that covered almost a third of his shiny desktop. Knowing that such tricks really did work—I had seen many strange and inexplicably bizarre things happen in this office over the years—I wondered how anyone with even half a brain could succumb to such an obvious ploy?

The miniature crystal Shar-Pei, I noticed, *did* catch the light rather nicely.

"This island is growing...more and more people are coming here every year...last week there were eight cruise ships in port, with an average of two-thousand people per boat...."

Most lawyers love the sound of their own voice, especially when it concerns money. Monk was no exception. Carefully separating the superfluous sales-pitch verbiage from the remaining ten-percent, which may or may not have represented all of the facts, I learned Monk had been brought into a land development deal by another local lawyer. His partner, Morton Kiley had apparently suffered a fatal heart attack in his Jacuzzi sometime last Friday night, and was only discovered early this morning by his cleaning lady, after having spent the entire weekend in soak.

"Puffed up," Monk wrinkled his nose in delicate reference to the dearly departed, as he held up a tiny but cunningly carved ivory netsuke rat, "like a dumpling in a stew pot."

Kiley, it seemed, had been overseeing the construction of a block of upscale beachfront condos. Now that he was dead their contractual agreement dumped that responsibility and, providentially, all of the profits squarely into Monk's lap. I could tell that Monk was truly torn up over the sudden loss of a trusted business partner and valued colleague; briefly, I considered offering him a handkerchief to wipe away the drool gathering at the corners of his mouth.

Monk handed me a copy of Kiley's latest progress report showing the project was almost eighty-five percent complete, on schedule, and coming along nicely.

"I don't imagine it should take someone with your organizational talents and expertise more than ten—let's say twelve—weeks, absolute maximum and.." Monk's grin gained another thousand candlepower. "...you must know that there's no one else I'd rather have in with me on something like this."

In my three years with Monk there had been a couple of instances when I'd helped extricate him from the machinations of land sharks, the kind who wore Armani suits and casually drop seven- and eight-figure numbers. Unscrupulous developers can make unsound buildings look even more attractive an investment than solid ones, unless you know what to look for or have someone who does hold your hand. Holding Monk's hand could become habit forming. The work was simple and, when it suited his purposes, Monk could be generous but something more compelling than money or job security was calling me back to the mountains.

Reminding him that my strong suit was renovation, *historical* renovation, I confessed I wasn't sure I could handle the needs of a modern concrete prefab-slab structure or even certain I wanted to try.

Rationalization may be one of the most irresistible forces in nature. Having said that, it was after another fifteen minutes of soft manipulation when I began thinking: What could be the harm? The extra money *would*, after all, allow me a greater range of options in my new home in the mountains....

I'd almost let myself be talked into accepting the deal, when the telephone interrupted Monk in mid-suction. Did I really *want* to do this? I asked myself while Monk took the call. The message was too short to allow an answer.

Monk replaced the receiver then stood slowly, almost regretfully; implying it was necessary to postpone our conference. Inwardly, I was grateful for the time it would give me to decide what I was going to do. Pleading a need for privacy, Monk came around the desk. As I stood he placed a hand on my shoulder then used it to steer me to the door, explaining that an important client had just arrived for an urgent consultation. When he opened the door to show me out a gray-suited, gray-haired man entered. With neither greeting nor acknowledgement of our presence, he went directly to Monk's desk where he opened a

black attaché case and began to set up shop. Monk pressed one of
three fat rolls of drawings standing beside the door into my still
outstretched hand, saying that we would continue our discussion later.
Agreeing to look them over, I left without ever giving the gray man a
second thought.

*   *   *

High Season:

A bewildering blare of Rock, Salsa, and Hip-Hop pouring out of
shops and bars, competed with the full-volume pump and bump of a
parade of car stereos and the amplified, overlapping scripted narratives
of three Conch Tour buses, creating a wall of pure noise. Between the
gantlet of one- and two-story brick and wood-frame buildings, Duval
Street, the core of Key West commerce, was a dazzling carnival of
sound, motion and color.

Seated in the only Tropical zone in the contiguous United States,
Key West is both blessed and cursed with the perfect winter climate.
While most of America was dusting off storm windows and replacing
worn weather stripping, Duval Street's sidewalks were swollen with
hustlers, hawkers, large-bellied waddlers, and sunburned dawdlers.
The latter, two of the more common species of migratory snowbird
that swamp the island each year during Season, are easily distinguishable by their bright and incongruously colored plumage often
festooned with camcorders and camera accessories. With the actual
details of their vacations preserved for proper viewing from the
comfort of Lay-Z-Boys and couches, these strange birds concentrate
their attention on the consumption of every comestible in their paths.
(The average life-span of a conch fritter is about point-three seconds; a
frozen Key Lime Margarita, slightly more.) A sweaty crush of blank-
eyed gawkers (a related sub-species) crowded the sidewalk in front of
the mammoth bar on the corner.

I understood wanting to visit the infamous Hemingway hangout,
but doubted if it would matter to the patrons that they were worship-
ping in the wrong church. (The original Sloppy Joe's was a dark and
seedy little dive now called Captain Tony's, half a block away down a

side street.) Ten in the morning and it was standing room only. Indeed, Season had started in earnest.

Duval Street, already an obstacle course, would soon be jammed to a standstill during Fantasy Fest weekend, only two weeks off. Each year it seemed to get worse; this promised to outdo the previous ones. That should have been enough to reinforce my decision to leave. However, thanks to my being one of a small cult of local eccentrics who preferred to adapt to the heat and humidity rather than succumb to the addiction of air-conditioning, the tropics were firmly set in my bones. Winter in the mountains of northern Georgia, without a little time to acclimate, could be a harsh and painful reality. I hadn't experienced snow in over sixteen years. A move in the springtime *would* mean a more natural and graceful period of adjustment. Another three or four months on the Rock, the thin-blooded devil on my right shoulder advocated, might be the very thing.

I wanted someone, more objective than Monk, to bounce the idea against. Charlie, my truest sounding board and reality check, was still out of town. Having undertaken a salvage job near Andros Island, at the western tip of the Bahamas three weeks before my homecoming, he wasn't due back for another week or so. The cryptic message he'd left on my answering machine mentioned a big shakeup at the docks, "...an auspicious event of epic proportions..." he promised to fill me in when he got back. All things considered, a grunt-and-sweat session at the Iron Works seemed a viable alternative. Sometimes, after throwing around the aggregate weight of a small car, things had a way of falling into perspective.

*   *   *

Tony:

Incongruously located in a strip mall, between *Audio-Blast*, a car stereo store and *Milady's* dress shop, *Iron Works* was not just another gym. Vacationers, accustomed to upscale health spas and looking for a light workout followed by a sauna or an avocado facial before cocktails, usually did a quick about-face. Like some hellish factory of pain and punishment, the atmosphere, punctuated by screams, growls, and great metallic clankings, was so dense with the stink of sweat and exertion that it stained the walls and fogged the mirrors that failed to make the squared tunnel behind a commercial storefront look bigger than it was. Audio-blasters next door couldn't have cared less—they wouldn't have heard a thermonuclear detonation over the thundering nonstop rock and roll—but what must the dress shop's clientele have thought about the noises coming from the other side of their wall, or of the gym's denizens who more closely resembled berserkers, gladiators, and evolutionary throwbacks than modern man? I suspected, by the occasionally lingering gazes, that it might actually have been a draw for some of their clientele.

Tony Amundsen, owner and manager of Iron Works, a rumored one-time smuggler, could have been cast as the lead, had someone wanted to film a remake of 'Captain Blood'. Not only did he bear a startling resemblance to Errol Flynn but there was a piratical movie star-like quality about him; his charisma was almost electric. Behind the counter in front, Tony was mixing something pink in a blender for a trio of the cheerleader/beach bunny types he attracted to the club in a never-ending procession. He returned my nod, shrugged then smiled as if to say: "It's a dirty job, but...."

I laughed easily—he often had that effect on me. His trademark carefree air and easy grin did little to distract one's noticing a physique that was a living testament to 400-pound bench presses, or detract from the gravity of the discrete tattoo adorning the inside of his left forearm. Even without understanding that the small arrowhead field with an upright sword crossed by three diagonal lightning bolts was the insignia of the Special Forces, most people sensed he was someone who should be treated deferentially. One of those rare, larger-than-life individuals who seem a breed apart from the rest of us, Tony had survived the war in Vietnam in the 60's and, it was rumored, the Drug Wars in America in the 70's with his sense of humor and lighthearted good nature intact. Never had I seen him lose his cool, even while quelling an occasional bodybuilder's "roids rage" or when dealing with the thousand-and-one irritants that can plague a small business owner on the Rock.

*   *   *

CHAPTER 8

Reflecting on arguments in favor of extending my stay on the Rock, while Tony goaded me into pushing more weight for more reps than I'd thought myself capable, helped me decide to go for it...providing the job looked like it was something I could handle. I wanted to see Monk's project site for myself, so I finished my workout with a pair of one-mile bicycle sprints along Flagler Boulevard, up the middle of the island, finishing with a cool-down ride along the western sea wall.

Traffic noises faded behind as I left North Roosevelt Boulevard and headed towards Monk's bonanza, at the tip of the narrow, crooked finger of land that separates the charter boat docks of Garrison Bight from Fleming Bay. Many of the secondary roads on the Rock are pot-holed and twisted, little more than asphalt-covered game-trails, the lane leading out to the job site was no exception. Rounding the last turn, partially obscured behind a magnificent stand of giant rubber trees, a tall and blocky shape slowly came into view. I quit pedaling and coasted to the side of the road, stopping beside an ancient dark blue pickup truck boasting more rust than body.

If I squinted just right, the original structure, a two-story Victorian house, well proportioned and nicely suited to the generous dimensions of the grounds, which overlooked the spread of Fleming Bay, could be seen. Several slabs and the remaining two corners of the arc, showed where a Chatahoochee stone driveway had once been. Judging by a scatter of twigs and excavated stumps nearby, its graceful sweep had once embraced several large shade trees, complemented by lush stands of tropical palms, frangipani and bougainvillea.

Strains of: "*...and, they paved paradise and put up a parking lot....*" played somewhere inside a neighbor's house.

The refrain kept repeating in my head.

The vertical block of concrete, which grew out of the smaller structure, dwarfed house, property and neighborhood alike. My first impression, on seeing the construction site, was that it looked bad. Once I recovered from my initial shock and became more objective, it looked even worse.

Hanging from the empty door and window holes, like the web of some malignant spider, black, orange, and gray power cords cascaded down the walls, interlacing piles of construction debris, before linking to the T-pole set against the chain-link security fence along the east side of the property line. The courtyard formed in the angle of the building join was an obstacle course, possibly inspired by Stephen King. Garnished, almost festively, with pink and yellow ribbons of insulation, spilled boxes of nails, jagged and rusty re-bar cutoffs, razor-sharp angles and curls from the galvanized roofing, the whole conspired with steel strapping bands and enough PVC pipe to trip, trap, and pierce the unwary or unlucky.

'Be a miracle, I thought, if someone wasn't injured or killed. Perhaps, someone had been? Why was no one at work? I checked my watch—after one-thirty—the sound of silence was deafening. But an accident wouldn't have completely shut down a job-in-progress? Maybe a code-violation? I scanned the permit box for red tags. Seeing none, I let my breath out. I would make the call to the City offices, regardless.

Obviously, Monk had never set foot on the premises; he didn't lie that well; he seemed really to believe the status report he'd shown me. Besides, what would have been the point? The physical evidence would reveal the truth soon enough.

This was to have been a project in its final stages of construction, yet the shell wasn't fully dried-in. Black holes gaped where doors should have been hung. Only a third of the south and eastern faces had windows, and the majority of those were visibly out of plumb. Even the roof, the most important component after the walls went up, was only three-quarters finished. (Rain can ruin a building if left uncovered for very long; in a hot and humid environment like the Keys, warp and deterioration start fast.) Thankfully, someone, a sub-contractor, I guessed, who prided himself on quality workmanship—looking at the surrounding chaos, it was apparent that he had been in the minority —and didn't want to do the same job twice, had had the good sense to use heavy-gauge tarps to cover the unfinished areas. By the way it had been triple-battened, the temporary cover had, evidently, been meant to last for an indefinite period of time. That, in and of itself, told me something.

I locked my bike to a tilting steel gatepost. The gate and chain-link fence lay nearby in sections.

The sheer amount of waste, as I explored the site, made me shake my head in wonder. Under scaffolding, awaiting a non-existent siding crew sat split-open stacks and warping flats of cedar shakes next to broken cases of nails. Nearby, sheets and rolls of wire mesh turned brown from exposure lay forgotten. From the layers of dust and dirt plus the scatter of empty beer cans, it was obvious that there hadn't been any real work going on here for some time. Several interior rooms were filled with stacks of unpainted doors; most were water-stained and warped beyond salvage. What *was* going on?

Following the darkest tracks in the dust led me to the main foyer, where a crude utility stairway was framed into what was meant to have been an elevator shaft.

Where was the elevator?

On the second floor, I discovered half of the common landing had been walled off with thick plywood sheeting, probably, the foreman's office and lockup. The plywood door firmly secured by a stout padlock would have to keep for another time, if there was going to be another time, which I had strongly begun to doubt.

At odds with the drab gray of unfinished concrete, a splash of cool azure blue visible at the far end of the corridor caught my attention. I entered what was, judging by its location, meant to be a living room, drawn to one of the empty holes awaiting installation of picture windows that might never arrive. To my right, the Atlantic stretched wide beneath clear skies. A swarm of shrimp boats, nets like butterfly wings hanging from lowered outriggers, as they followed the ship channel south, were dwarfed by the pristine white bulk of an approaching cruise ship. A small plane angled down over the towed rainbow of a parasail then flew behind the cordon of coconut palms surrounding the airport. Directly ahead, a-dozen-or-so houseboats lay peacefully at anchor in Fleming Bay, maybe two or three hundred yards from shore. Beyond them a small fleet of sailing yachts lay at anchor. Altogether a stunning vista—sunrise would be a spectacular event—that would inspire real estate mavens to rave endlessly about the "million-dollar-view." Only five minutes from shopping yet comfortably aloof from the insanity of a tourist town, anonymity with accessibility, a pricey commodity anywhere, especially here on the Rock.

Key West is not a big island—less than 10 square miles—and like many things, moorage is always at a premium, particularly, free moorage. I grinned as I counted fourteen boats jammed tight as pigs at feeding time, along both sides of a new dock apparently built for the use of the condo residents. A dirty white cabin cruiser berthed across the end of the dock had the look of a live-aboard. Something else to check; I made a note.

I then made the mistake of looking down. The grounds and the private beach below were buried under a mountain of construction trash from the north side of the 'tumor', which is how I'd begun to think of the three-story structure. Shaking my head at the amount of sheer waste, I picked up the dust trail again. The deeper I ventured into the belly of the beast, the sorrier I began to feel for the poor slob who would try to turn it around. Reaching the top floor, my ruminations were interrupted by the sound of voices and a familiar pungent aroma. Both seemed to be coming from inside a corner bedroom just ahead.

Centered in the rough opening, meant to hold a pair of French doors, close to the edge of a wide balcony back-lit by a commanding view of the bay, sat a red cooler with a white top. On either side of the cooler were two large, untidy lumps. I recognized the one on the left, clutching a perspiring Coors can while noisily sucking on a fat joint. The lump's name was Duffy. I remembered him only too well— though I doubted him capable of recalling his own name, on even a good day.

"'S a closed job-site 'n we ain't hiring." He slurred, having turned in response to the elbowed signal of Lump #2. Squinting his red-rimmed eyes at me—probably in an effort to look assertive—he added, "I'm the boss here, so get the fuck outta here. See?"

By appearances, Duffy was succeeding in doing on land what he had nearly accomplished in the Gulf Stream. —After almost sinking one of our convoyed vessels to Jacksonville through unadulterated stupidity and drunkenness, Charlie'd threatened to keelhaul him. I couldn't recollect why I'd talked him out of it.

Duffy made as if to rise, but he was so far gone that he almost lost his balance and had to grab hold of the steel corner column in order to save himself from falling off the open balcony. With neither the time nor the inclination to match wits with an unarmed opponent, deciding not to make any further decisions until I had spoken to Monk, I left. Raucous laughter and catcalls echoed hollowly in the naked apartment, following my retreat through the empty concrete shell and down the utility staircase. I was tempted, but knew I would prove nothing by indulging in a rough-and-tumble with a pair of drunken dirtbags.

After a refreshing shower I stood, a towel wrapped around my waist, enjoying the cool indulgence of an open refrigerator while meditating on the comparative merits of Lo-Cal yogurt versus a plain salad, when the phone rang. It was Monk saying he needed to speak to me in person and right away. I heard the uneasiness in his voice.

My stomach growled.

When I mentioned I hadn't eaten, to his credit—as I hoped he would—he suggested we meet at El Loro Verde in fifteen minutes. Since my favorite Mexican restaurant was only a ten-minute walk from my front door, and there was no point in getting overly fanatical about this diet stuff, I shut the fridge door and accepted the invitation I had shamelessly promoted.

*   *   *

**Does it not also appear strange to this assembly that
a lawyer should have his hands in his own pockets?**

- Mark Twain:

CHAPTER 9

After waiting half an hour for Monk to show up, I
poured my third cup of coffee, draining the carafe. Arturo, the owner,
was already bringing me more of the rich Mocha-Java the restaurant
served as a house blend. Figuring Monk had been waylaid and I'd be
dining alone, I thanked him and accepted his suggestion of the lunch
special. As he turned to go, I saw a cab pull to the curb outside. A
moment later a car door slammed shut then Monk appeared in the
doorway. I saw him weaving a little as he waited for his eyes to adjust
from the blinding sunlight. His usually fastidious appearance was
noticeably disheveled. I was a little concerned at the changes only a
few hours had wrought.

"What do you call a lawyer at the beach, buried to his neck in
sand...?"

He blinked slowly.

"Not enough sand."

Monk dropped into the booth opposite me then gave me a bleak
look. A hard liquor-stink rolled off him. I guessed, from his lack of
response to our long-standing joke swap, that after hearing about the
true state of the project since we'd spoken, he'd consoled himself to
the point of intoxication and wasn't in the mood to be jolly-ed out of
his funk.

I guessed wrong.

Cutting off Arturo's smiling, menu-in-hand approach with a quick
headshake, I poured Monk a black coffee, listening as he related a
conversation he'd had earlier. A senior DEA officer, he said, had paid

him a visit, informing him that the condo site was suspected of being used to land drug shipments smuggled into the country, and was under surveillance. The late Morton Kiley, it seems, had—as astute business-men sometimes do—attempted to diversify. Unfortunately, his choice of investment strategies ran contrary to prevailing laws. The DEA-man indicated that Monk could curry favor with the powers that-be by allowing everything to continue uninterrupted for the present, while they gathered evidence.

Clearly unhappy about this development Monk became even more distressed when I told him about the condition of his 'windfall'. Some of his other investments, he confided, had become bogged down, what with aggressive time-share sales forces grabbing potential customers, and the lion's share of the real estate revenues, right off the street. Add to that the expensive remodeling of his offices, and he was hurting.

I didn't want to touch that one, especially in his present condition; I was still waiting for the final check to be cut and was counting on it to fund my transition to northern Georgia.

It took a couple of seconds for Monk to realize that the insistent *peep-peep-peep* was coming from his pager. When he excused himself to check his messages, Arturo appeared with a steaming fresh carafe. A willing accomplice in keeping Monk's cup filled, he winked as he made the twenty offered in thanks disappear into thin air.

Obviously not pleased with whatever he'd heard, Monk returned and slumped, head-in-hands, staring down but probably not seeing the bright Guatemalan tablecloth. I waited a few moments, freshened his cup then pushed it under his nose. Taking a deep draft, he looked up at me with a heavy-lidded gaze, then plunged back into a repetition of the sad state of his affairs. While he rambled on, I thought about the thick roll of plans in my office at home, the total chaos at the project site, not to mention having Drug Enforcement agents and smugglers thrown into the mix.

Innocent bystanders sometimes had a way of becoming "fatally injured" as reported in the Solares Hill's weekly police blotter.

Beginning to get a little weepy, Monk blurted out: "There's no one else I can trust. Every cent I could lay my hands on is sunk into this, this hole in the ground."

Monk seemed oblivious of his surroundings or the potential embarrassment of making what was tantamount to a public confession of private business. Thankful the place was almost empty. I signed to

Arturo, who had stayed discreetly out of earshot, to call a cab for Monk. Sensing that coffee and the tiny basket of rolls would be it for lunch, my stomach growled its complaint.

"Please, you've got to help me. I...I...."

The desperate stamp of fear in Monk's eyes suddenly transported me back to a gray and rainy morning in the tiny Vieux Carré office. His eyes were Bobby's eyes—

"You must..." Monk changed gears, reversed, then said, "...if you help me out on this one, I'll, I'll...."

The rank panic stench on Bobby's breath—

Monk grabbed both of my hands. He swallowed—probably, his pride—then, in a rush, offered me a percentage of the project sales.

In an instant, I was returned to the sunny Tropics. Despite my misgivings, I couldn't say no. Monk, after all, was my friend, and. here was an opportunity to really profit from my abilities, to invest in myself. Besides, I was a much different person from the one I'd been in New Orleans. Wasn't I?

While we waited for Monk's cab, I solemnly promised—for the umpteenth time—to be in his office "first thing" with a plan to take control of the project and turn it into a winner.

So much for the early-to-bed scenario: the rest of the day and far into the night, I traveled a long and arduous journey through the floor plans and elevations of a fifty-thousand square-foot block of numbers, angles and spaces; learning what lay hidden in its secret places; remembering what still needed to be done or done over; improvising on how and where could I cut corners, be more efficient; incorporating what had already been done, and what embellishments—undone as yet—could be done without.

At nine the following morning, while Monk stood at his wet bar dumping the contents of several gelatin capsules into a beaker of orange juice, I told one very fragile and excruciatingly hung-over attorney that the project was salvageable, possibly. Apart from the waste and unsightly appearance, the building was structurally sound. The project could work, providing we had the right crew and a little luck.

After three years, I had accumulated a pretty healthy Rolodex of construction talent. Both foremen I wanted were available. Each had worked with me before and had a good understanding of how to organize, improvise, and make things flow like a well-oiled machine, so I wasn't overly concerned with that aspect.

Monk poured several ounces of clear liquid from an unmarked bottle into the blender then added equal measures of green Spirulina powder and red Tabasco sauce, as he reminded me of the DEA's insistence that, for the present, the project continue as established. Cutting off any further conversation on the subject, he threw the switch on the blender.

The tiny motor shrieked. Monk cringed in pain as the contents of the blender made a high-pitched gargling noise and turned into a vile-looking gray-green sludge.

I had to admit, it did make sense: the crew, or what I'd seen of it, might very well be involved in something illegal. With someone like Duffy in the mix that was almost a given.

Monk turned the blender off and bravely drank down a healthy draught right from the jug. It seemed to help. Despite the green mustache on his upper lip, the hand that poured the rest of it into a champagne flute was noticeably steadier. He took another sip, then ripped out the heart of my fat, happy plans for the future by telling me that there weren't enough funds left in the construction account to finish the job.

Wind-driven snow, icicles hanging from eaves, and slush-filled roads loomed ahead.

The bank, Monk said, was sending over a set of duplicate account records. They, too, were worried about their investment. It suddenly dawned on me how that could actually work to our benefit, depending on what I found in the foreman's lock-up at the job site. It was a slim hope but a receipt for a warehouse full of appliances and fixtures, an elevator waiting to be delivered, could make a significant difference between a go or a no. If the bankers were sufficiently motivated (read: on-the hook) I might be able to formulate a plan they would agree to...maybe. Hopefully, this DEA nonsense would be nothing but a memory by the time we were ready to get down to the physical work. I wondered what incentives I might have to offer my potential foremen to keep them interested and on-call in the interim?

Promising to have a contract drawn up and ready to sign before the end of the day, Monk escorted me to the office door. When he solemnly shook my hand with both of his, sincerely thanking me for being a good friend, the wet glistening in his eyes, more than the blobs of green foam at the corners of his mouth, made me feel a little queasy. The mantle of Savior is not one I wear comfortably. I've enough crosses to bear without adding another. This was supposed to be a business arrangement, nothing more. I really did want to believe that.

It was well after eleven when I arrived at the condo. The parking area was empty, which let me breathe a little easier. After my last encounter with Duffy I had mixed feelings about another confrontation with the soon-to-be ex-foreman. The place was still a disaster waiting to happen but this time I was prepared. Heavy boots, gloves, and work clothes, a four-foot 'key' in my hand, I crossed the courtyard and entered the building shell. The crowbar gave me quick access to the second floor lock-up, where I discovered a small fortune in new power tools, many of them still in unopened boxes. Across the back wall, under a makeshift plywood table covered with smeared and stained layout sheets, were half a dozen plastic milk crates, each stuffed with bundles of blue, yellow and pink paper: bills, invoices, and orders; it was the history I had hoped to find. An hour later, my van was loaded with booty, and there was still no sign of crew, foreman, or for that matter, anyone else. Except for the sound of someone practicing the flute inside the sprawling Spanish split-level next door, the neighborhood appeared devoid of life. Perhaps, I began to hope the evildoers had all been arrested, America was again safe for the future, and we could now move forward into an era of prosperity.

Armed with clipboard and tape measure, I locked the van then reentered the gray, concrete tumor. A plan to reestablish control of the runaway project had started to take shape the night before. Being a devout proponent of the measure-twice-cut-once school, I wanted to check several key items before committing to any particular course of action.

It was a little before one in the afternoon when, with dozens of pages filled with notes and measurements, I'd begun to feel fairly confident I could make it work. Most of the critical construction had been well executed, until that one point in time when everything had suddenly come to a screeching halt. The *why*, I now understood, or thought I did. *How,* I wondered, had the shut-it-down order been communicated on that fateful day? Perhaps Duffy, with his gift for diplomacy, had been the bearer of bad tidings? Standing inside the dim gray halls, I could almost hear the sounds of voices shouting, tools dropping, and car doors slamming as crews reacted angrily to having their livelihood suddenly cut off.

Making my way down from the third floor, I heard a couple of loud bangs in the distance, then another, followed by a low tubercular growl; the sound of an engine badly in need of a new muffler and spark plugs. With a sudden premonition of a storm approaching, I exited the building in time to witness Duffy & Co. un-assing themselves from the same battered blue pickup I'd noticed the day before.

Catching sight of me, Duffy hollered: "The fuck 're you doin' here?" Puffing himself up for the benefit of his 'four horsemen' each of whom was a walking argument for retroactive abortion, he snarled, "I tol' you before to git."

When he stamped his foot to emphasize his point, it twisted on a chunk of concrete and he lurched drunkenly trying to keep his balance. Ever considerate of another's tender feelings, I tried not to laugh aloud. Besides, drunk or not, they stood squarely between me and the un-complicated departure I had hoped to achieve.

"Seein' how you're so fuckin' stupid, 'looks like I'm gonna have to teach you a lesson...."

Duffy turned to wink at his audience leering in anticipation of the forthcoming spectacle. That was my opening: I put a grin of pleasant surprise on my face, as if having discovered a long-lost friend, and walked straight toward him. Seeing my advance, one of the 'horsemen', Pestilence, I think, alerted Duffy.

"Look what I found!" I said, tossing the clipboard to him as he turned.

Reacting, without stopping to think, he caught it.

Staring stupidly at the pages of notes, Duffy's confusion allowed me to close the distance between us before he could suspect my intent. By the time he caught on I was too close.

His hands were rising defensively when I suddenly spiraled down. Pivoting, I uncoiled, exploding upward, driving a hard elbow deep into his soggy gut that was followed with a sharply executed back-fist that mashed his nose and cracked him smartly between the eyes. Duffy's legs melted. He dropped without uttering a sound. Calmly, quickly as I could, I picked up my clipboard, walked directly past his stunned crew, and got into the van.

Fear and adrenaline were vibrating my body so hard that I had to grip the wheel tightly to steady my shaking hands. I watched the frozen tableau behind me in the side mirror become smaller then disappear.

*   *   *

CHAPTER 10

Wednesday, October 15, 1997:

Early the following morning, I lingered over a third cup of coffee, scanning the morning paper; one of the few I'd looked at since returning from the mountains. If I hadn't been killing time, waiting until Monk got into the office before heading downtown, I might have stayed blissfully, perhaps indefinitely ignorant.

A name in bold print halfway down the left-hand column caught my eye. The item, evidently a follow-up to a previous article, made a brief reference to the continuing "...temporary closure of the Stock Island impound docks..." before reporting on the upcoming sentencing of the *former* Deputy Marshal.

Apparently, while I was learning to soar above the mountains, Ronald Schott had been involved in a different kind of high. Caught using the government impound docks to receive, store and distribute contraband; Customs agents reportedly seized over a hundred kilos of cocaine, along with various case-lots of illegal weaponry and military ordnance.

That, I reasoned, must have been the shake-up Charlie had mentioned in his phone message. Score one, I thought, for the good guys. If the rumors of treatment accorded to fallen officers of the law in the penitentiaries were only half-true.... I smirked, thinking Ronny-boy might go into prison a tight-end, imagining that it wouldn't be long before he became a wide-receiver, which was only fitting for a man who prided himself on being such a pain in the ass.

An internal roaring, like a high-pressure boiler leak, boiled the laughter out of my mind.

Below the fold, an item noted that the Coast Guard had officially called off its search for survivors. The Key West salvage barge, *Jawa,* evidently destroyed by an explosion at sea, had been reported en route to Andros Island. The cause of the mishap was thought to have been due to improperly stored flammable materials.

Even though the paper had carried these events as separate items, I had no difficulty connecting the dots.

A flash flood of emotions careened through the fragile canyons of my sanity. I stood without knowing why. The crash of shattering crockery came to me as if from far away. Why, I wondered had no one mentioned this to me?

         *   *   *

**Dark house, by which once more I stand
Here in the long unlovely street,
Doors, where my heart was used to beat
So quickly, waiting for a hand.**

- Alfred, Lord Tennyson

CHAPTER 11

A solitary Heron groomed the front lawn of Charlie's house. How had I come to be there, I wondered? I looked around. I didn't remember walking but I must have; the van was nowhere to be seen.

Hushed echoes of laughter and long-forgotten conversations lingered in the dark corners of the front porch. The key in my hand seemed to pull me forward. The gate on the white picket fence whined in protest. From habit, my foot scuffed the high spot on the third flagstone inside the gate. The white bird froze. Its brilliant black eyes watched me as I crossed to the house. I paused at the bottom step. Turning, I waved my arms at the still white shape.

"Yah-h!"

Normally wary, instead of flying off all a-squawk and a-flutter, it stood still as a statue, looking at me with an unearthly intelligence in those hard discerning orbs. A sudden gust of cold wind ruffled my hair and brought tears to my eyes. When I wiped them away the Heron was gone. I'd heard no sound of flapping wings. Had it been really there or was it something else?

A chill shivered my spine.

The front door creaked open. Stale air, smelling slightly of Old Spice, the heavy after-shave Charlie favored, beckoned me inside. On my left a rainbow of colored canvas and plastic go-caps hung from the row of bleached shark jaws mounted down one side of the shotgun hallway that ran the length of the house. The sun-faded Detroit Tigers cap, Charlie's favorite, was missing from its customary place "in the

Tiger's Mouth" next to the back door. Cartilage, teeth, and memories were all that remained of the fourteen-footer, who'd taken an active interest in us during one of our last salvage operations. I could almost hear his voice: "Raising a disintegrating helicopter off the bottom with nothing but raw nerve and a pair of leaky flotation bags, or any of a hundred other insane pursuits we invent as an alternative to working behind a desk..." Charlie had wryly quipped to our corporate client, after the aircraft was aboard and we were skinning the pesky shark on deck, "...is a lot like being in the mouth of a tiger. It's a choice we make in order to test our mortality."

Charlie had put himself into the mouths of one or another kind of tiger most of his life. The last one had eaten him whole, in one explosive bite. Along with him a big piece of my salvaged life had been blown to bits, and nothing, not even thoughts of the living hell the ex-Deputy would face, could help ease the pain.

I took a pair of mugs down from the pegs above the sink and placed them on the huge butcher's block that dominated the back wall of the kitchen. Running my hand over the scarred surface I remembered the gestured insults, traded ten fathoms below the surface, as we struggled to liberate it from the galley of a sunken freighter. Whim or not, once Charlie decided something was worth salvaging he was single-minded in his campaign. I was living proof of his determination.

The kettle moaned. Its cry echoed the hoarse, scalding shriek of the banshee crying in my mind.

A large, familiar outline permanently dented the leather easy chair in the front room. On the mantle, next to a mahogany and brass sextant, a picture framed from a single piece of Lignum Vitae showed Charlie and me on the barge, grinning broadly, as we posed in front of the helicopter freshly raised from the Gulf of Mexico.

Surrounded by the ghosts of our adventures, I set the teapot and two mugs on the coffee table made from a brassbound deck hatch then I touched the play button on the stereo. I tried to draw solace and strength from the familiar surroundings, but felt only implacable loss and an ache deep in my soul. While Miles Davis plainted through the mournful intricacies of *Sketches of Spain,* I filled our mugs with herbal tea clinked mine against his, took a sip, sat back, and let the room blur.

"Honor," I could hear Charlie preaching, in one of his favorite rants, "used to be our highest ambition. Today it's winning the lottery, or a new car...getting something for nothing. We lost something, kid, something of real value and I don't know if we can ever get it back."

The world had indeed lost something of value.

Friendships that had once been were gone, carried on for a short time in the hearts of the survivors until they too were gone. Leaving *what* as a legacy? I was a better, richer person for having known someone like Charlie. Would others, I pondered, ever find cause to feel that about me?

Shadows grew long. Their hard edges softened and dimmed as day yielded into night.

*   *   *

CHAPTER 12

WESTBOUND, SOMEWHERE OVER THE GULF OF MEXICO...

Thursday, October 23, 1997, 14:41 EST:

"The soul of a people lives in that which their country gives to the world. To purity..." Colonel Betancourt's stomach turned in recollection of the words he had spoken only the night before. The terrible lie inherent in the toast he was required to offer at the Officers Club dinners, where tailoring and genteel conversation often counted above ability, was particularly distasteful as he reflected on the kind of "purity" that these abominable missions represented. "...the purest sugar, the finest cigars..." he had said then, with a practiced turn towards Claudia Maria, General Ramos' wife, as he raised his glass to her before adding, "...and the most beautiful women in the world..."

Empty words reaffirming national pride in this leaky rowboat of a country, were what guaranteed advancement and generated the perquisites that made the difference between a mere career and a lifestyle. Pausing dramatically, he had raised his glass to the flag, swallowed the last of his self-respect, and finished saying: "...ladies, gentlemen, to Cuba!"

Soon, he promised, he would remove this foul stain from the soul of his people and in so doing cleanse his own.

*   *   *

CHAPTER 13

Thursday, October 16, 1997:

Two in the morning, it was pitch-black and roosters were crowing from the treetops. When I finally said goodbye to the Rock, I wouldn't miss the posses of wild chickens that brazenly prowl the length and breadth of Bahama Village, a part of the island I'd come to think of as "The Land of the Screaming Chickens."

Prior to coming to Key West I'd always thought that roosters only crowed at daybreak. Not so in this Tropical wonderland, where the descendents of the tough fighting cocks of Hemingway's days, announced themselves twenty fours hours a day, every day. Protected by a quaint city ordinance, they were spreading over the whole of the island—another good reason to leave, but that wasn't what was keeping me awake. Everything kept going round and round in my head. Within the whirls and turns I began to see that a puzzle lay hidden, a few of the pieces had already begun to take shape:

With the amount of heat drawn by Ronny Schott's arrest, the drop-off point for inbound drug shipments would, logically, have to be relocated, if they were to continue. Like the impound dock on the Atlantic side of the Island, the Fleming Bay condo site was easily accessible by road and water, yet sufficiently remote enough for such clandestine activities. The logistics were ideal, and with Kiley's "accidental" demise it *had* to be connected.

Possibly, Kiley had tried to play with the big dogs in the tall grass and had paid the price. Schott and Duffy, at best, were stooges, so it stood to reason that whoever killed Kiley was likely responsible for the explosion that destroyed the salvage barge. Maybe—*probably*—Charlie'd seen something he wasn't supposed to. Whatever the reason, I made up my mind, if these assholes were going to fall, I was going to be part of the push.

Later that morning, red-eyed and feeling the full weight of my commitment to the unknown, I told Monk he could count me in and that I was ready to sign the contract.

"Wonderful! And, shame on me." Monk alternately beamed and apologized, throwing his arm around my shoulders, walking me down to the opposite end of the gaudy pink corridor from his office. "What with talking to the bank and everything else, I simply haven't had a moment to myself to proof our agreement."

We stopped outside the last of the three untenanted offices, which had been relegated to the storage of superfluous furniture and files, pending the addition of associates. Monk positively sparkled with delight as he unlocked the door and stepped aside for me to enter. No time had been wasted in obtaining Kiley's records, or in installing them and me into our new home. All of the junk had been cleared out and what remained was a clean work area complete with desk, chair, and a good reading lamp.

"Oh, and these are for you."

With great ceremony he presented me with a set of keys then withdrew a clutch of papers from an inside pocket. Two envelopes slipped to the floor. I picked them up.

"I'm meeting with a client in Louisiana," he offered, taking one, clearly an airline ticket. The other, a plain white envelope, I noticed, had my name on it. At Monk's insistence, I opened it and discovered a draft of our limited partnership agreement.

Tapping the airline envelope thoughtfully against the cleft in his chin, he added, "I should be back early next week. The moment I return, we'll fine tune all the 'weasel words' and have our contract registered. You have my word on it."

Monk's disarming smile was once more locked firmly in place. Despite the uncertain state of his affairs he seemed to have found a new strength which enabled him to carry on. Mentally rubbing my thumb and fingers together, I was pleased with myself for having had a hand in his renewed good cheer and resolve, if only I could do the same for me.

When the last of the milk crates I'd liberated from the lock-up was added to the row of cardboard file boxes from Kiley's office, the sheer bulk of the task that lay before me seemed almost overwhelming. A tremendous amount of time and energy would need to be invested: Every piece of paper had to be read, checked on, noted and sorted out before we could take another step. There was no guarantee that it wouldn't be a total waste of time. I'd seen hundreds of better beginnings come to naught. Any of a thousand-and-one details could kill the job before another nail could be driven, so it was with a mixture of excitement and trepidation that I approached what I had begun to think of as The Great Wall of Shine-Ola, and opened the first folder.

In one of Kiley's files, I discovered a document outlining how the house and property had initially been obtained. The inappropriately-named Malcolm Strong, one of Monk's now-and-then playmates and a notoriously dissolute black sheep belonging to one of the older Key West families, had deeded the Fleming Bay property to a holding company owned jointly by Monk and Kiley. The deal promised Strong not only a third of the revenue profits but a newly renovated and maintenance-free condo complete with all of the latest modern conveniences, on what had once been the cornerstone of his family's estate. Copies of the black sheep's financial statements and tax returns, stapled to the agreement, indicated that other than the property—the maintenance of which ate up most of the five-figure trust fund annuity—he was living on the barest vapors of his inheritance aboard *Indulgence*, the shabby cabin cruiser berthed at the end of the pier.

Another question answered.

The details of the company's charter showed Kiley and Monk held all of the voting shares between them, with Kiley in control of fifty-one percent. A series of bills of sale, each for one dollar, recorded the transference of the total assets to another holding company, then from that one to another and again and again *ad nauseum*. In an agreement with the last-named corporate shell, which probably existed only in Kiley's mind, any restitution or return of property rights Malcom-the-fleeced might have sought from his shearers were effectively negated. Thanks to a clever little *quit claim* clause, the golden ball of wool was now irrevocably in Monk's pocket.

I made a mental note to carefully go over the fine print in my own contract before signing.

*   *   *

CHAPTER 14

WESTBOUND, SOMEWHERE OVER THE GULF OF MEXICO...

Thursday, October 23, 1997, 16:09 EST:

Colonel Betancourt compared his wristwatch to the plane's chronometer, which showed over a three and a half-minute variance. As he calculated the remaining hours and minutes of his life, the Rolex GMT Master, a gift from his employer, which showed comparative Greenwich Mean Time, was so accurate that it was said that the American astronauts used it exclusively. When one schedules one's death, he considered, it is a comfort to be on time.

"Shoddy, incompetence..." the words, spoken earlier that afternoon by the American, as he toured the Russian aircraft that would carry his terrible cargo, still echoed in Betancourt's mind. "Proletarian mentality," he'd added the final denunciation, unmindful of the implied insult to the men who risked their lives to do his bidding.

A bubble of gas, a memento of the rich lunch he had eaten too quickly, burned its way up from the Colonel's uneasy stomach. The American's negative assessments of his country's erstwhile saviors, he admitted, *had* occupied much of his own thinking since the USSR's ignoble departure from Cuba and its subsequent disintegration.

Politicians and politics were to be avoided whenever possible; politicians lied and their lies made no sense. As a military man he preferred dealing with real over conceptual, with function over form.

Though there was not the slightest hint of elegance to be found anywhere in his aircraft, flying it was one of his few pleasures.

Backfire, he mused with a grimace, stifling another sour belch, the
Tupolev Tu-22M2, NATO reporting name, Backfire, *was* a perfect
metaphor for the barren Communist legacy, thanks to Fidel's having
embraced a political ideology that was not only foolish but one that
still burdened his people.

Impoverished, desperate for money—any money, no matter what
the cost in human life and degradation—to prop up Castro's faltering
empire, these deals with the American were considered a necessary
evil, a political expediency. Colonel Betancourt had argued with himself, since first learning the true nature of these secret flights; he was
only a small piece of a much larger machine. How like the rationale of
the German officers protesting at the War Crimes tribunal they were
only following orders, his conscience often chided in the quiet hours
when he could not sleep. Would there be a Nuremberg for him one
day? Perhaps, if not in this world then what of the next?

*   *   *

CHAPTER 15

Tuesday, October 21, 1997:

Tuesday morning, after five days—mostly fourteen and sixteen hour days—on a steady diet of coffee and paper, I was ready to talk to Monk.

Explaining how, by eliminating a number of unnecessary and expensive cosmetic elements on the original plans, and with over forty-seven thousand dollars of materials and fixtures I had located in supplier warehouses—no elevator, though—I figured we could finish the project with only another six hundred thousand. Monk looked a little fragile until I explained to him that according to the consensus of several real estate appraisers I'd spoken to, and based on current and projected market values, we stood to clear almost a million dollars when the units sold...and those were conservative estimates. Probably, the profits might easily exceed $1.2 million. I'd seen a couple of ways to economize even further, providing I had a free hand and could call in one or two favors.

Less than half of the bank's initial investment had actually gone into building the existing shell, which meant approximately four-hundred ninety thousand had been diverted out of the original one million dollar budget. This was a little unnerving. Though half a mil' may be a lot of money to the average person, I couldn't reconcile that in terms of a purported "major" drug shipment. From what I'd heard about smuggling in the Florida Keys, $500K was chump-change.

Since Monk had plenty on his plate, without any additional distractions, I saw no need to confuse the issue. Keeping my speculations to myself, I suggested that, since we had to maintain Kiley's dirtbags on the payroll to accommodate the parameters of the ongoing investigation then, maybe, we could invoice for the extra expense.

Monk barked a loud sharp laugh, agreeing to put it to the DEA agent whose arrival in the outer office had been signaled only moments earlier. "You are so perfectly audacious." Standing, he chuckled mischievously. "I just *love* the devious way your mind works. You would've made a good lawyer."

I ignored the insult he had intended as a compliment and remained seated looking at my copy of our contract, still on his desktop.

Catching my intent Monk's expression changed to one of focused sincerity. "I'll see to the revisions you suggested, earliest..." Glowing with an inner radiance, his right hand fully extended, the left held high, poised and ready, he came around his desk ready to gather me into an embrace. "...and that's a promise..."

Instead of warm and fuzzy, my thoughts were on the cold uncharted waters that lay before us. There were a myriad of ways a venture like this could veer off course, sink, or be eaten whole by predators.

"...Partner...."

I saw emotion welling up in his eyes. To prevent having to endure one of Monk's patented *abrazzo* hugs I shook his right hand with both of mine then turned, diverting his momentum into carrying us toward the door.

When Monk attempted an introduction to Agent Whidden, for the second time, I watched in amazement at the casual arrogance as the same gray man nodded slightly before brushing past my outstretched hand. He quick-stepped across the imitation Persian carpet, set his attaché case on top of Monk's desk, opened it, and waited for Monk to attend him.

Shaking his head at the man's sheer audacity then winking, to show me he had everything under control, Monk squeezed my hand, turned, took a deep breath, squared his shoulders, and went forth to do battle.

*   *   *

CHAPTER 16

"How do you get a lawyer out of a tree?"

I stopped at Rosa's desk under the pretext of harmless flirtation. Monk's secretary and office manager shared her boss's penchant for self-deprecating legal-profession humor.

I pretended to think of a response, continuing my appraisal of the G-man, as Monk's door slowly closed. Other than a brusque manner, bordering on rudeness, he was so overwhelmingly unremarkable that his only distinguishing characteristic was that he seemed to have no distinguishing characteristics at all. Rosa, on the other hand, had two outstanding attributes: a pair of beautifully shaped dancer's legs and one very large husband.

Life, I opined, is seldom fair.

The few stolen moments of assessment added nothing to my knowledge of Monk's visitor. I shrugged another kind of ignorance to Rosa.

"Cut the rope."

I made an appropriately appreciative grimace, shaking my head in disparagement. Rosa's lusty laughter, replete with images of trees ripe with attorneys swaying in the breeze, ushered me through the louvered mahogany saloon doors and down the hallway to my office. Once inside, I acknowledged the seed of doubt that had begun to take root. There was something wrong about Agent Whidden, something I didn't like but nothing I could put my finger on. Chalking it up to a natural aversion to bad mannered bureaucrats, I set aside my misgivings then fielded the first of a series of callbacks.

After the fifth affirmative from key suppliers, sub-contractors and, thankfully, the City Planning Department on clearances and permits, I began to think that, just maybe, the project might actually happen. All we had to do now was sell the bank on the idea that throwing good-money-after-bad was the smart thing to do and we were in business.

About half-past one Monk called to invite me to lunch. I was a little surprised when I entered the lurid pink parlor and saw that Agent Whidden would be joining us. Though perfunctory, this time my introduction was accepted. His handshake was tepid and somewhat oily. I resisted the impulse to pull a bandana from my pocket and wipe my hand. Monk, I noted, seemed in good spirits though somewhat distracted. The small talk he initiated on the way downstairs indicated that he had other things on his mind. I was curious, but it had nothing to do with his suggestions on landscaping the condo site with Royals, Queens, and espaliered Traveler palms.

Pink rental mopeds, bleating shrilly, buzzed in around and through the crawl of people and vehicles that filled Duval Street to over-flowing. Rock 'n roll, reggae and rap, rattled eyeballs and shattered eardrums. Vendor's carts, surrounded by tight knots of buyers, added the rich aromas of conch fritters frying and perfumed sun-block to the damp-coat smell of someone's singing lunch. We avoided the spray, as one of the staff hosed the vomit off the sidewalk in front of the bar next door, and went around the bottleneck of baked, burned, and lotioned lushes, each waiting their turn to guzzle and spew away their vacations.

Monk's monologue, which now focused on the local sights, gave me a further opportunity to observe the enigmatic Agent Whidden. Iron-gray hair, cut short, as befitted an ex-military officer, which is how I'd begun to perceive him. In height, build, and most respects, he was average. He would probably have made a good hit man, save for his eyes—he went to great pains to avoid giving anyone a clear view into them—they were unsettlingly pale, almost a transparent gray.

Watching him, as we listened to Monk's narrative, I got the distinct impression of an icy-cold fire burning deep inside the G-man.

Clang-a-lang, a-lang!

Deceptively pure and free of pollution, the shiny black smokestack on the tour train engine, sailed high above the black smear of diesel smoke pumping out from under the plywood skirting gaily painted with rail wheels. We paused for the linked boxes of gawking tourists, cameras whirring and clicking as they trundled past, before crossing the street.

Real estate attorney that he was, location was everything to Monk. Feeling that the right setting was essential to establish the proper tone of every conversation, he invariably stage-managed his "important" meetings. During the course of our association, I'd gotten used to seeing him choose a variety of the island's beauty spots as a backdrop for business; Monk sold beauty to make money. His brand-new, antique suite of offices was meant to be just such a place. Where, I wondered, were we going, and *what* was he selling? Had something bad transpired in the office with Whidden? Was Monk trying to soften the blow?

Our destination, I discovered, was a small Cuban bistro around the corner in the relative quiet of a side street. Seated outside at one of four tables made by laying large wire spools on their sides, his cheeks a-bulge with Paella and sweet Cuban bread, Monk was oblivious to the overt stares of street-people appraising our potential for table scraps or handouts. (As a matter of course, half of my sandwich would be left behind. I remembered, too well, what down and out had felt like.)

We discussed the project, its completion and our mutual, though tacit, participation in the government's master plan. Monk impressed me when he courageously raised the issue of compensation. I relaxed slightly as Whidden graciously conceded payroll responsibility.

Clang-a-lang!

Another tour train chugged by in the street. At the same moment another bell was sounding, an alarum that only I could hear. Whidden had agreed too easily. There should have been some resistance, if only for form's sake, to making restitution for our carrying Duffy's crew. I began to catch the strong, brown aroma of a con. I glanced at Monk as he nodded encouragingly and in all the right places, giving me a sly we-got-it wink out of the corner of his eye. He appeared to be buying the lie, whatever it was. DEA Agent Michael Whidden, I sensed, was playing some kind of high-stakes poker game and there figured to be plenty of wild cards in his hand. I had no idea what they were.

While listening to the part about doing our bit for flag, country and justice, I made sure to look as if I, too, believed what I was being told, and followed Monk's lead by inserting the appropriate sounds and nods on cue.

Once the conversation deteriorated into trivialities, Whidden made a not-so-small production out of checking his watch. Understanding that everything we were meant to hear had been said, I was glad to make my excuses and leave.

*   *   *

Quis custodiet ipsos custodes?
(Who shall watch the watchers themselves?)

- Juvenal

CHAPTER 17

Television sets flickered like chromatic fireflies in the darkness accompanied by erratic spurts of music and canned laughter, as gusts of wind whipped palm fronds and rattled jalousie shutters.

On our left water slapped beach and breakwater alike, gurgling hollowly under the cantilevered houses and houseboat moorings where there was insufficient land beside the road to support foundations. A prickling sensation riffled the hairs on my arms and stippled the flesh at the back of my neck. The air was charged with the first electrical taste of a storm front moving north from Cuba. I felt its breath hot, humid and heavy against my skin.

"This is insane!" The rational, logical part of my brain whined. The determined part gave no heed; commanding my muscles to dig in a little deeper, push a little harder.

Left...right...left.... Steady resistance and the push-pull rhythm gave me something, someplace to direct my grief for Charlie's death. At least I'm doing something, I thought, it was no small comfort to know that I wasn't the only nut in the shell.

A new, almost frightening version of Tony had metamorphosed before my eyes earlier that afternoon when I summarized the events of the last week for him. The amiable Life's-a-Beach attitude had winked out in an instant, replaced by a graver, more serious Tony than I had ever before seen, as if a 'violence switch' had been thrown inside him.

Eyes glinting with a dangerous light, emanating not only the capacity to annihilate and destroy but the will to so do, he told me, "life's gotten rather boring lately, 'think I'll go out there and watch the watchers watch 'til something happens."

I was so impressed by the simplicity and directness of his plan that I was compelled to invite myself along. Elementary mathematics (two heads were better than one) along with my refusal to take no for an answer, had settled the issue. It was obvious that he considered me a loose cannon and, as such, something that would need keeping an eye on but I was determined to be in on the action. I hadn't cared what he thought as long as I got to go, nor had I missed the look of disappointment, as he watched me pull into the parking lot behind the gym just after sunset. The you-don't-know-what-you're-getting-into tone had been clear in his voice when he asked: "You're sure about this?"

Kneeling in the dark in a patched and dirty canvas kayak, being devoured by swarms of mosquitoes and no-see-ums, I questioned the sanity of my decision. Behind me, Tony was a silent and ominous presence. He hadn't spoken a word since leaving the dock.

We paralleled the finger of land leading out to the job site until it crooked and turned to point west. Moving clear of its shelter, into the boat channel that cut through the shallows, the wind found and quickly pushed us out into the bay where, thankfully, the cloud of bloodthirsty insects was left behind. A black outline, blacker than the surrounding night, loomed out of the darkness ahead. One of a sprinkling of modest and sometimes ruinous residences anchored in the bay, the houseboat was about the size of a one-car garage. With a commanding view of water and road access to the building site, we were going to be in a perfect position to see what, if anything, might happen.

We glided downwind then turned to make our approach from the lee side. No sooner had the kayak kissed the barge than Tony was out and onto the deck in a single fluid motion. I steadied the kayak until he had unloaded the two heavy black canvas bags then it was my turn.

All I had to do was hold onto the handrail, lean forward, unfold and extract both legs at the same time, and step out. It sounded easy enough. I started to extricate myself but found that my kneeling position, during the paddle out to the houseboat, had stemmed the circulation in my legs. Both knees locked, the muscles began cramping painfully as blood flooded back into the constricted vessels. The kayak began drifting from the houseboat. Stuck half-in and half-out, I let go of the railing, so I could lower myself back inside, but I'd neglected to let go the paddle with my other hand. My weight pinned the handgrip, grinding my trapped fingers, painfully against the hull. I leaned forward, to free my hand, which started the kayak wobbling from side to side. It quickly picked up momentum and started to swing wider and wider, like a pendulum. Feeling it rolling, inexorably, out from under me; panicking, frantically grabbing for something—anything—to hold onto, I held my breath and closed my eyes as I passed the point of no return.

Hands gripped the front of my jacket and I was unceremoniously hauled aboard the houseboat like so much baggage. I felt as graceful as a brick though almost half as clever. Unnerved, I looked on as Tony recovered the capsized kayak. Managing to rouse myself, to give him a hand bringing it on deck where it could drain, all the while rolling "Cherry" —evidently my new name and one I had justly earned— around in my mind. Tony made no further reference to my ineptitude other than a bemused headshake, which more eloquently than words reinforced the I-told-you-so look in his eyes. Rattled, I stayed outside for a few moments, holding on to the railing as I tried to regain some of my can-do attitude.

My near dunking, plus the sight of the wall-mounted shotgun and M-16 when I entered the single-room houseboat, started me thinking that I might, indeed, be way out of my depth.

Seeing how he was sealing the window facing our target, I took the offered roll of duct tape and garbage bags and continued on the other two.

Tony placed a card table squarely in front of the sealed window, measured and cut a vertical slit about twelve inches long, then started assembling an array of components from one of the two black carryall bags.

Mounted on a gimbaled tripod, the Starlite telescopic night-sight was an alien and impressive looking apparatus to the uninitiated (me). Able to electronically gather and intensify even the smallest amount of ambient light, it was designed to provide an almost daylight clarity to even the darkest nights. Coupled to a long-barreled shotgun micro-phone, the device bore a startling resemblance to a B-grade, sci-fi movie ray gun. Always fascinated by gadgets, I could hardly wait to get my hands on the new toy.

In the heavy, airless room during the long vigil that followed, I quickly grew to hate the thing with a passion. Sweat collected in the rubber lens cups and stung my eyes, and it wasn't long before my neck muscles were shrieking from the enforced posture necessary to sweep the terrain, while compensating for the rocking motion of the houseboat.

The one-hour shifts Tony had suggested—that I'd considered ridiculously easy—crawled by torturously, each second's passage, more excruciating than the last. The one-hour rest periods, if you could call them that, were just long enough to tantalize the mind with its need for wonderful, beautiful, uninterrupted sleep. I began to think the night would never end.

Shortly before daybreak, the sound of a boat gently colliding with the barge roused me from a restive doze. A few moments later two very large silhouettes obscured the virgin daylight. 'Dugout' Doug accompanied by his shadow, Sarge, a thickly muscled Rottweiler, filled the open doorway.

As plans went ours was simple: Doug would maintain surveillance during the day while Tony and I took care of our regular business until it was time for us to, again, split the night shift...but for how long?

*   *   *

CHAPTER 18

Wednesday, October 22, 1997:

After one long, futile and virtually sleepless night, the no-longer thrilling prospect of spending how many more such evenings sat heavy on my shoulders. Talons of a leaden vulture called Doubt were buried deep in the throbbing muscles of my neck, as I forced myself to concentrate on budgets and coordination charts for materials and crew scheduling. The numbers and dates kept scrolling from left to right then switching to roll back right to left, flowing in my mind, endlessly scanning from one end of the peninsula to the other then back again, over and over—

"I'm going home..."

Rosa's voice on the intercom woke me from a dream in which I had been tied to a huge pendulum, slowly swinging back and forth over a dizzyingly bottomless black pit filled with unknown horrors.

"...and you should too."

I heard concern in her voice, a small, warm sound that reminded me of the hole in the center of my life. In an instant, I was transported to a place where the rain blew in cold waves from the Gulf and fell, drip-drip-dripping eternally from the white featureless face of a broken marble angel in a New Orleans cemetery.

*   *   *

CHAPTER 19

WESTBOUND, SOMEWHERE OVER THE GULF OF MEXICO...

Thursday, October 23, 1997 21:14 EST:

The faint smear of purple above the western horizon faded to black, as the TU-95 began its long descent down below the operating levels of shore-based radar, where its course would change onto the second, shortest, and most critical leg of the triangular flight plan. Only down-looking technology could find the modified heavy bomber from that point on. There was no possibility of that happening; for the next three hours there would be a hole in the cordon of radar surrounding the Florida Keys. The pattern of US Navy balloon-deployed arrays and satellite coverage had been manipulated by the people whose cargo was being carried to allow a narrow corridor—the coordinates were clearly marked on the electronic flight screen. It would be perceived as an oversight and would not be noticed for another hour, nor would it be corrected until well after the Colonel's mission had been completed, it had been just so on all of the previous flights.

Sickened to his heart by the crimes against humanity these flights represented, all committed in the name of his beloved Cuba, the aristocratic, slightly predatory angles of Colonel Betancourt's face appeared unmarked by the inner turmoil.

Stealing a sidelong glance at the man in the co-pilot's seat, the blunt peasant features of General Arcadio Ramos were as serene as stone. For all the emotion his old friend and commander showed, as they skimmed just above the wave tops near certain death, he could have been sitting behind his polished desk reading an inventory report.

More than anything, Colonel Betancourt regretted the necessity of having to kill his comrade and the solitary crewman aboard, but he had made up his mind and it must be so.

* * *

CHAPTER 20

Wednesday, October 22, 1997:

Shortly after sunset we relieved Doug, who elected to stay on board. He communicated this by rolling onto his bunk and becoming instantly inert. Thinking back to the first time I'd seen him, in and outside the gym exchanging occasional nods and grunts with others, I don't think I'd heard him use more than two or three syllables at any given time. Possessing a marked similarity in size and demeanor to a Kodiak bear, he neither inspired repartee nor required a large vocabulary to make his intentions understood. Normally gregarious and engaging, Tony hadn't been half as talkative during the almost-twelve hours of our first surveillance; from the moment we met at the dock, I knew our second night promised more of the same.

It was during his master's downtime that Sarge decided to have a closer look at the stranger in his home. I had gotten the sense that Tony was old news, and as such, tolerated, though just barely. Tony and Sarge, I'd noticed, seemed to avoid being in the same space at the same time in an unconscious choreography of personal preference or dislike, tempered by mutual respect. I, on the other hand, as new meat, was fair game and the object of Sarge's intense scrutiny from the instant he first came through the door on the previous morning and found me sitting on a cot in the main room. After I dared to show up on the following evening, I was aware of his eyes following my every move. I knew it was coming but unsure of when and how it would happen. Fortunately, I knew enough about dogs to let him initiate the first contact.

A little before false dawn, I heard a soft snort, felt a puff of air on my skin, and a cold wet muzzle brushed my hand. A moment later, the solid presence of Sarge's weight pressed up against the side of my chair. I showed my gratitude for his having accepted my being there by keeping my movements slow and my voice positive, as I let my fingers softly ruffle the thick fur behind his ears. My friendly overtures were rewarded by having the hundred-plus pounds of Rottweiler come to rest full against my leg.

"Likes ya."

Doug was awake.

I translated his comment to mean: "My misanthropic companion, who usually prefers to intimidate and dominate, rather than fraternize, seems to have graced you with his approval. How marvelous."

Sarge yawned hugely; sounding like a rusty gate swinging shut. My jaw cracked and ears popped in sympathetic response.

"Needs ta run...."

In response to what must have been for Doug an excessively verbose observation, since he was staying aboard for the daylight vigil, it was only fair that I offered to let Sarge accompany me landward.

Doug's one nod signaled his compliance.

*   *   *

CHAPTER 21

EASTBOUND, SOMEWHERE OVER THE GULF OF MEXICO...

Thursday, October 23, 1997 22:44 EST:

The muted lights on the console betrayed not the slightest trace of the treacherous resolve burning inside Colonel Betancourt when their plane crossed the invisible line, committing an illegal incursion into the sovereign air space of a foreign nation, the United States.

Betancourt's thoughts went to his family, as he again weighed the recriminations his mother, aunt, and brother would probably endure against the degradation of humanity that was a certainty, should this hellish cargo be allowed to continue unchecked to its destination.

Tonight, he vowed, he would send a message to his country and to the world that would be impossible to ignore.

*   *   *

Birds of calm sit brooding on the charmed wave.

- John Milton

CHAPTER 22

GULF OF MEXICO...

Thursday, October 23, 1997 22:51 EST:

As if to measure the rise and fall of some primeval watery giant's respiration, two rigid inflatable speedboats rode the lazy lift of the five-foot groundswell before plunging headlong into the following troughs. Though, safely out of standard shipping channels, contrary to Maritime Law no running lights were displayed nor was there a sound to be heard, save for the sibilant whisper of water rushing past the non-reflective black skin above the fiberglass hulls. Only the phosphorescent sparkle of microscopic life, churned up in the soft gurgle of their wakes, marked their passage. Softly painted by the faint double flash of a distant lighthouse, two groups of unmoving silhouettes were barely perceptible in the pitch-dark night.

First Team Leader, Lt. Patrick Fife peeled back the cover from his diver's watch.

"Should've..." The thought had given birth to the word, which remained unvoiced as twelve blackened faces turned as one towards the West where an intermittent whine, hardly louder than a mosquito's, had come into being and was growing steadily in volume. Lt. Fife unclipped a small device from his harness and depressed a button twice, once short; the second sustained.

*   *   *

CHAPTER 23

SOMEWHERE OVER THE GULF OF MEXICO...

Thursday, October 23, 1997 22:51 EST:

Amid the array of dials and gauges on the console in the cockpit of the Backfire bomber, a tiny red light blinked once, quickly then came on a second time, longer. Colonel Betancourt's eyes confirmed speed and position. They were on target. Several seconds elapsed before the long-short pattern repeated itself. The intervals between the flashes gradually decreased. The Colonel saw General Ramos' mouth curve into a slow private smile, as the senior officer reached forward and with a small flourish, as if having just signed a manifesto of great moment, toggled a switch adjacent to the blinking light.

A yellow bulb flashed brightly against the matte black background on the crew chief's console in the waist of the aircraft. A wild, high-pitched shriek grew louder until it was almost deafening, as Flight Sergeant Ernesto Edelmira operated a hand crank to open a hatch in the belly of the modified bomber. Glistening and deadly, the water was close enough for the Sergeant to perceive the texture of its ponderous rolling motion as it flickered below in tight sharp ridges. Edelmira, the lone crewman, stared at the dizzying rush then shut his eyes for a moment in silent prayer—he resisted crossing himself. When he opened his eyes again, he noticed the frequency of the flashing amber light on his console had increased. He watched until it became a steady glow. His hand was already on the jettison release handle, anticipating the moment when the amber would wink out and the green light, directly below, went on.

Colonel Betancourt steadied his hands on the control wheel. In a matter of moments they would be on top of the pickup boat. If he timed it right, he could take them all out. One hard push forward and it would all be over. All over, that is, for him—this far inside the American waters the wreckage was sure to be found. When the nature of their cargo was discovered it would be sure to spark an international incident. The world had to know. The world *would* know, he would see to that. GRANMA International, the State news and propaganda organ would, no doubt, parrot the official Party line denouncing him as a rogue and a criminal while absolving the military and Cuban government of complicity or culpability.

Located beside the indicator on the console, which showed the opened hatch, the amber light meant the cargo had yet to be jettisoned.

The beacon signal was growing stronger.

*　　*　　*

CHAPTER 24

Thursday, October 23, 1997:

The day passed in a blur of phone calls, budgeting, plotting and planning. Things were starting to come together. I became involved in following leads—who was where and doing what?—juggling schedules, and preparing my 'maybe' lists. I needn't have worried about Sarge's fitting in or becoming bored. Independent and adaptable, when he saw that I was going to be anchored to the ringing thing on my desk, he used the time to satisfy his curiosity about his new surroundings. Mostly, I found him visiting Rosa, who he had charmed so thoroughly and with such ease that she responded with trilling and cooing noises whenever she saw him, and at lunchtime, treated him to a heaping plate of *paella* take-out from the Cuban cafe around the corner. Lucky dog! I had had to pay dearly for the dinky little collection of shredded lettuce and cherry tomatoes that was meant to pass for a proper meal. Other than great slurpings and mastications, Sarge, like Doug, hardly made a sound unless one counted the low rumbling growl that stopped me in mid-filch when I tried for one of the four slabs of sweet and buttery Cuban bread on his plate.

Late that afternoon, our walk in the park was cut short by the hard sting of raindrops that sent local and tourist alike scurrying for cover. The sky darkened as a long deep line of somber gray rolled in, thickened, and formed a low black ceiling that covered the island in a mourning cloak so thick that nightfall became only a minor variation in the already pervasive darkness.

We left Tony's station wagon and raced across the parking lot to the kayak; the tempest's passion had grown and with such fury that it was sheer madness to be outside, let alone persevering in what was proving a hopeless mission. Even the heavens seemed to be telling us how ridiculous we were.

Docking had been a groin-tightening experience, despite a safe, speedy passage. We were so thoroughly soaked it was as if we'd swum from the shore. Vibration thrummed beneath our feet, as the house-boat, buffeted by twenty-plus mile-an-hour gusts, strained at its anchor lines.

Twice, earlier, I hung up on Tony's, "Ironworks...?" Every time I'd tried to utter the words that would free me from this insanity and let me get back to some semblance of normalcy, I heard Charlie expound on his fundamental principles of stick-to-itiveness and honor: "Agree to do something, you better be prepared to see it through to the bitter end. Quit once, and the next time something difficult comes at you, you'll give up. Pretty soon you stop trying altogether."

"If you know you've made a bad deal and you're going to lose your shirt, why bother?" I remembered having asked him.

"Peace of mind...I never regretted something I did, only what I didn't, and I don't want to look back and say, I shoulda,' or if only, maybe I coulda,' 'cause it'll be too damn' late. The guy in the mirror knows a quitter when he sees one, once he gets those what-if hooks into you he don't ever let up. Take what life gives you and don't worry about it. Just do the best you can."

I was doing my best but nothing much was happening to justify the effort. The only results our round-the-clock vigil had produced so far were a growing stack of empty pizza, Chinese, and other assorted fast-food containers, and an uneasy feeling that something was terribly wrong: our vigil had shown no signs of government observation or any other activity whatsoever, unless you counted Doug's terse notations, recording the time and location of the morning mail deliveries to the other twenty-four houses scattered along the lane. Every one of those innocuous comings and goings and their times, were all duly recorded on a yellow legal pad. The gaps in between were accented with such keen observations as: "Jack-shit" and "More Jack-shit".

Clearly, Doug was similarly unenthusiastic with our progress or lack thereof, and though Tony and Sarge expressed no opinion one way or the other, I was beginning to feel like Chicken Little. The rolling barrage of thunder that accompanied the erratic bursts of rain hammering the tin roof mocked my resolve and reinforced my doubts. Literally, the sky *was* falling but no one besides me seemed to care one way or another.

*   *   *

CHAPTER 25

SOMEWHERE OVER THE GULF OF MEXICO...

Thursday, October 23, 1997, 22:52 EST:

Located beside the indicator, showing the still opened hatch, the amber light on the console meant that the cargo had yet to be jettisoned. The moment had arrived. It was now or never. In spite of the air conditioning turned to full, Colonel Betancourt could feel the slow prickle of sweat creeping down his sides. He tightened his grip on the control wheel, said a prayer, took in a deep breath and....

"So, my friend, are we to die by your hand on *this* trip?" Ramos' soft laughter caressed the Colonel's ears. "Will you kill us all tonight by crashing us into the ocean, hmm?"

The Colonel's face burned hot, the icy looseness of cowardice invaded his bowels, a familiar tremor infected his hands when he felt General Ramos taking control of the wheel.

"Tell me, Jorge, did we die magnificently in your imaginings? Were you buried with honors? Was I castigated by CNN?" A robust rumble of sardonic laughter filled the cockpit.

Despite the hot, tears trickling down his face, Colonel Betancourt nodded then smiled contritely at his old comrade-in-arms.

"Come, old friend, we will go home, smoke our cigars, drink too much, and speak of the battles of our youth, of missing friends and enemies as we watch the sun rise from the veranda while Maria frets and proclaims us both crazy. It is a shame that seasoned birds of war, such as we, must grow old as carrier pigeons."

* * *

CHAPTER 26

THE GULF OF MEXICO...

Thursday, October 23, 1997, 22:55 EST:

Only the eternal rush and flow of the great undulating swells broke the silence in the aftermath of the aircraft that screamed past overhead. Four dark bundles tumbled down out of the sky. No parachutes were deployed to slow their descent. The tiny salvo of splashes was insignificant in the vast emptiness. Beneath the surface, weight and saturation carried the four bundles deeper into the salty depths. Located under porous panels in the rip-stop fabric of each pack, a redundancy of sensors, responding to pressure and the saline content of the water, triggered four small compressed air cylinders each one inflating an external bladder. Less than a minute later, sixteen buoys broke the surface, where, confirming the new environment, yet another series of sensors triggered four tiny transmitters, which began broadcasting an electronic pulse over a narrow and very low frequency (VLF) band.

"Got it!"

Though the words were uttered barely above a murmur, Lt. Fife knew, instantly, he'd made a mistake and castigated himself for yet another mission slip, even before the dimly silhouetted heads of the team turned in unison in his direction.

The team had frequently tried to impress upon the inexperienced young Lieutenant that the hard-learned disciplines of the SEAL's were nothing to be taken lightly nor casually disregarded.

Knowing another lesson would be arranged before long, and when he least expected it, Fife shuddered, remembering the last. The broken nose and cracked ribs sustained in a training exercise had taken two months to heal and a further three weeks before he could take a deep breath without feeling nauseous.

Whisper-quiet, sound-suppressed electric motors impelled the black vessels across the watery dunescape towards the four floating bundles.

*   *   *

When the waves are round me breaking,
As I pace the deck alone...

- Paradise Lost, John Milton

CHAPTER 27

A little after three in the morning, having finished my shift, I was outside under the leeward eave, wrapped in a thin blanket, shivering, miserable. The combination of noise and strain, plus the damp, rank stench that pervaded the cabin, made sleep impossible and had given me a pounding headache. While waiting for the aspirin to take effect, I was giving quite a bit of thought to calling the whole thing off. Was there a reason, I wondered, for the story Monk and I had been given by Agent Whidden? Because, nothing we'd been told seemed to make any sense.

I was massaging the ache from my neck when a chance flash of lightning painted a featureless black hump on the water in the boat channel, just beyond the northwest fringe of houseboats. The electrical surge generated by the storm had knocked out the city's lights—an all-too regular occurrence—everywhere was pitch-dark except for a wide track of red and green channel markers that curved away to my left. In that searingly bright fraction of an instant, I thought I'd seen the shape of a man, in mid-backward fall, suspended just above the water. I blinked, rubbed my eyes, strained for a second glimpse but my night vision was burned by the lightning, all that remained was a strobe-like afterimage floating against a backdrop of black. In my excitement, I rounded the corner and was staggered by a blast of rain driven almost horizontally across the water-slick deck, only the railing saved me from slipping overboard.

"A diver," I gasped, fumbling the door latch open, "I, I think there's a—"

"It's on!" Tony barked.

Without a word, Doug was off the bunk and on the move. My mood changed from one of excitement to uncertainty when I caught a glimpse of what looked like a machine pistol slung over his shoulder as he tugged on a cammo' poncho. Within seconds, he was in the kayak and boring straight into the teeth of the wind, heading shore-ward.

"What and where?"

Inside, Tony opened what I'd initially mistaken for a bass guitar case and was snapping together components that quickly became the most lethal looking rifle I'd ever seen.

Shocked, I wanted to say something, but couldn't find the words.

"Again! What and where...?"

The sharp command snapped me out of my astonishment. I told him exactly what I'd seen.

Tony slapped in a magazine, jacked a round into the chamber, switched on the bulky mass of a light-gathering sniper scope, stood in the open doorway, and scanned the beach.

My guilty secret, smuggled aboard and hidden under the pillow on my cot, in light of the sudden appearance of this awesome arsenal, was a minor transgression at best.

"They're on the beach."

Curiosity got the better of me. I rushed to the neckbreaker.

Compensating for the pitch and roll, I ranged the scope across the beach in front of the job site. Nothing! On the next scan, a two-legged piece of shadowy black detached itself from one of the pilings and I found them. Tony continued describing, aloud, what I was seeing. I was puzzled why?

"Four—count four—units...Mac-10s and AR-15s...two flankers: One's covering the condo...Two has the road...Three and Four are at the water's edge, they're digging a hole in the sand. I count four—four bundles going in the hole...it's marked...a white plastic pail...Three and Four are back in the water...Flankers One and Two are pulling back...."

It hadn't taken a minute from the time they'd hit the beach until they'd disappeared back under the inky surface of the bay, but that minute had seemed like an eternity. Shortly after, I thought I heard the faint burbling of a motor through a hole in the howling winds, but I couldn't see anything through the rolling and plunging scatter of houseboats and pleasure craft. The sound wasn't repeated.

If not for the taste of the saltwater on my face and the shivering reality of sodden clothing, I might have sworn I'd dreamed the whole thing.

I was still trying to assimilate what had just happened when Tony, once again started speaking in the same terse observer-style he had used only moments before. That's when I understood his commentary had not been directed at me, he'd been cueing Doug. After several moments spent fighting the buck and roll of the houseboat, I found Doug when he broke cover and moved from one place of concealment to another. He'd stop, motionless under his camouflage cover, and become a clump of dirt, a pile of refuse, or part of a bush. His pauses ranged anywhere up to five minutes between moves while a steady narrative of observations and directions flowed around me.

The last move left Doug exposed as he reached the sand-filled 5-gallon pail marking the spot near the water's edge. He unearthed the four dark bundles then returned the burial site to its original condition. With the packs slung over one arm, he moved back in a line parallel to his approach. His retreat was every bit as painstaking and deliberate as his advance. Half an hour later—the sky at its blackest and only the now-distant glimmers of lightning providing any relief—I saw Doug push off from shore. Tony continued to scan shoreline and water.

Grumbling murmurs of thunder were fading away leaving only the hiss and sizzle of a drenching downpour in its wake. I was glad of the relative darkness afforded by the shielded red light, intended to preserve night-vision, which was mostly blocked by the bulk of Doug's body as he entered the houseboat, afraid of what I might see in their eyes when they remembered my presence. Tony maintained his sniper-scoped vigil at the door while I cowered in the shadows. The muted, bell-like chime of diving gear being taken from a storage closet helped set the stage for the next act in their script, a script that had been written in my absence and probably rehearsed in their past.

I had the sudden, sickening realization that I was alone in a tiny houseboat with a pair of trained killers. Tony, a known drug smuggler, was acknowledged a very dangerous man; there was illegal weaponry everywhere and a quantity of contraband that had either directly or in-directly claimed at least two lives, one of whom was the best friend I'd ever known. What did I really know about Tony? This was his world not mine.

Over the few short years I'd been on the Rock, whenever Tony or Doug's name came up in conversation, I'd heard any number of wild, hairy adventures ascribed to them. How many of those legendary exploits credited to them were embellishments, pure flights of fancy, or understatements, mere snippets of a larger, darker truth?

My insides clenched like a fist. Was I also expendable?

Inch by inch, I snaked my hand under the pillow on my cot. The heft of the army-issue Colt .45 gave me some measure of reassurance despite being surrounded by their high-tech arsenal. I wasn't completely sure why I'd bothered taking it from Charlie's house then smuggling it aboard. Later, I'd been too embarrassed to disclose its existence. At that moment, I was mighty glad I had kept it secret.

Tony continued to monitor the shoreline. Doug was busy opening the packs he'd brought on board.

I could take them out right then and there.

What if I was wrong?

Terrified and fascinated, I couldn't stop myself from watching as Doug extracted two rectangular canisters from each backpack. The black stenciling on the camouflage exteriors listed the contents: FIRST AID, RADIO, and two labeled as EXPLOSIVES. After wrapping and zip-locking each of the eight containers inside extra waterproofing he resealed them in their original packs.

I heard the gurgle and slap of water grow louder. Still standing by the door, Tony had hauled on a rope lifting up a large hatch set flush into the deck. Charlie's gun felt suddenly slippery in my hand when I recognized the clunk and clatter of weightlifting plates being moved about in a far corner of the room. The dim red light filled the gloom with an eeriness that twisted my nerves several notches tighter.

What if I wasn't wrong?

*　　　*　　　*

**The condition of man... is a condition
of war of everyone against everyone.**

- Thamas Hobbes

CHAPTER 28

Doug sat on the hatch coaming, his feet in the water; he shrugged a scuba tank on over his clothing. After, and to my relief, he double-checked the shackled connections from each pack to a medium-sized weight-lifting plate. Then, marked only by an explosion of bubbles tinted bloody by the tiny red light, he was gone.

"'Magazine's empty but if holding on to that antique makes you feel better, knock yourself out," Tony said, wrapping another hitch, locking the hatch rope onto a wall cleat.

"What now, do I mysteriously disappear too?" I asked, marginally relaxing my grip on the pistol. "Or am I going to turn up like Kiley, in someone's swimming pool?"

He leaned, one hand against the open deck hatch, looking down into the play of light on water. Reflection cast malevolent shadows twisting over the broad planes of his face.

"Look—"

"No! You look! I thought you were on the level—I trusted you."

Tony moved back into the shadows by the doorway, where he stood silently, staring out into the night. Without turning, he began speaking. He seemed almost to be talking to himself.

"I know some of the moves tonight are a shock—"

"Some...?!" I sputtered.

"—but what you're thinking is dead wrong."

"Then why? Why not just call the cops? None of this, this, this snatch-and-grab you and Doug just did was necessary unless, unless you've got another reason."

"It was the only thing I could do. I don't want that shipment to go any further—"

"Right...."

Tight-lipped, he turned, recognizing the skepticism etched on my face, he confessed: "I admit it, I walked the walk and lived the life and, yeah, I made a lot of dough smuggling dope but that was then and I didn't know any better. I quit. Believe me, I had to—"

"Believe you? Why? Because you say I should?" I was almost as angry as I was scared—I was terrified.

"Just hear me out. Will you do me that much?" his voice trembled with emotion. Without waiting for a response he continued: "I've killed...too many—too much...in 'Nam and after, but every one of those people had a weapon and was trying to kill me. That's something I can live with, but letting that shit ruin more lives when I can prevent it...?

"Goddammit!" he cried out, half rage and half in anguish, as he pointed towards the open hatch. "I lost my family because of that, that fucking poison."

Suddenly, he threw the front door shut with a violence that shook the walls. Then he leaned forward, his outstretched hands flat against the heavy wood. His head hung his face in shadows. He seemed to be fighting some inner demons. The air was thick with tension. When he turned to face me the soft red light gave an alien cast to his tortured features. His voice was little shaky.

"There is a reason for tonight: by taking control we remove the chance of those drugs getting on the street to damage any more lives. And don't you ever forget Charlie was a friend of mine, too. You and I both know something's wrong with the story you were told."

He seemed to wrestle with a difficult decision before continuing.

"Something else you don't know is, I came down to see you the other day and I got a close look at the guy you and your lawyer-friend were hangin' with. You don't know who or what you're dealing with. I do. His name is Whitefield, or it was when I knew him in the Nam. First time I saw him he was a "control" with Special Operations Group, a Company man—CIA. And, you'd best believe me when I say he is one dipped-in-blood, ice-cold, mother-fucking monster."

A chill finger of fear traced its way down the center of my spine. I could see it in Tony's eyes as he mentally moved half a world away and into different time and another reality.

"I was a member of a twelve man A-team. We were returning from a black-op, a 'strat recon' [strategic reconnaissance] on a report of heavy troop buildup in the Tri-Border area of Laos, Cambodia and Nam. It was near midnight and we were movin' fast, too fast. We overran the rear guard of what must have been a full company of NVA regulars. We tried to back-pedal, but no-go. We'd penetrated their position too deeply, and before we knew what was happening we were in-the-shit and fighting for our lives. We split up, tried to RTB [return to base] individually, hoping at least one of us would be able to 'Escape & Evade' to get our target information back to headquarters for a strike mission."

The rain beating on the tin roof and the wind moaning through the cracks lent an unnerving undertone to his account. I could hear it in his voice and almost feel the jungle, the panic, and the turmoil that had surrounded him.

"I was low runnin' when suddenly the ground wasn't there. I went ass-over-teakettle down into some kind of culvert, thick with brush; the bottom was knee-deep with mud and runoff. So, with all hell breaking loose above and around me, I half-ran, half-crawled along that gully until it dead-ended on me. I damn near broke my neck when I hit a wall of tree roots. I felt a hollow space behind the roots. Who-or whatever had been living there wasn't home when I dived in, so I pulled the hole in after me and waited. One of the hardest things I've ever done; sitting there, listening to—"

I looked away as he tried to find the words and failed.

"Sometime during the next day—I must have passed out because I didn't wake up until the morning of the day after. Two days! When I left my hole there was nothing: No trace of the enemy. Nothing! When I began heading toward our Forward Operations Base I found what was left of my team."

Though curious, I was thankful he hadn't elaborated on whatever it was he'd found. My respite was short-lived.

"We'd been...five of my, my team..." He struggled, searching for a way to say it, "...they'd been taken prisoner. Their hands were still tied behind their backs...where they lay...the flies...the smell...it...they hadn't died quickly. There was nothing, nothing I could do for them, other than complete our mission."

The horror was clearly stamped on his face. It was something I wished I hadn't seen.

"When I reached base I reported their position in my debriefing then tried to move on, put it behind me, but I couldn't. I spent the next three days in Saigon staying drunk while the strike mission, Operation Prairie Fire, went down. And when I got back...Man, it was like I didn't exist. Nobody wanted to get too close. Like some of my bad joss, luck, whatever, might rub off. Instead of doing what I was trained for, and getting some payback, they had me assigned to the 'ops' tent, shuffling papers.

"I was hangin' loose one day, watchin' the war pass me by, not really doing nothing about nothing, getting wasted and just trying not to feel, when I got rapping with Hammerhead, a guy I knew from a LRRPS [Long Range Reconnaissance Patrol] unit who was returning from the field. He'd been free ranging in the same area, heard our firefight seen the capture, the mutilations and the executions. He said Whitefield had been there with the NVA and several Asians dressed in civilian bush gear. When he told me that that sonofabitch personally oversaw their interrogations and gave the execution orders himself, I almost went crazy—I was closer to those guys than my own family—but I knew that where we were wasn't the place to do anything about it. If our previous boss hadn't gone and gotten himself whacked in a chopper crash then there would've been no problem, but the new company commander's nose was buried so far up the ass of the Company spooks that ran most of our ops he couldn't see daylight without a periscope. We figured we had to go over his head if anything was gonna get done. Hammerhead was up for a week's R&R, so he volunteered to go to the JAG [Judge Advocate General] office in Saigon."

I could almost fill in the rest of the story.

"A week went by, then another and another, and no word, no-thing, so I figured they were building a case. When it stretched into a month, and still fuck all, I knew something was wrong, but I didn't know what 'til I saw Hammerhead's name listed on a transmission notifying unit command that he'd gone over-the-hill in Saigon and was now on an MP wanted list. When I saw that I went ape-shit. It took five guys to haul me off Mr.-fucking-Whitefield before I had a chance to rip out his throat."

That might have explained the few faint scars I'd noticed buried in Whidden's bushy eyebrows and lurking under his shirt collar.

"Next thing I knew, I was in LBJ, [Long Binh Jail] then on a plane back to the States. I was moving so fast my eyeballs were spinning and my feet hardly touched the ground. I spent the last four months of my tour restrained in isolation in the base hospital at Bragg [Fort Bragg] where I got a medical discharge then I was out and on the street. And, let me tell you, back on this side, in-the-world, nobody wanted to know nothing about nothing."

I could see the pain and confusion. Tony had been right there all over again and hurting bad or else he'd given one hell of a convincing performance. I didn't know which.

"Several years later, I heard some rumors through some of my, ah, associates about a cartel of CIA, ARVN and NVA brass, who'd been involved in running large-scale heroin shipments out of the Golden Triangle into the good ol' U.S. of A. I had a pretty good idea who their point man was, but he was protected on both ends. End of story.

"I've had to live with the knowledge that I walked away from my responsibility, twice. And every time I wake up in the middle of the night seeing my team...the torn scraps of their dicks and balls stuffed into their mouths...their eyes staring at me...accusing.... Maybe, this is my way to finally do something about it."

I shivered involuntarily at the thought of having eaten lunch with the creature Tony'd described. Intuitively, I felt Whitefield/Whidden eminently capable of having committed such crimes. The question was, had he? Even further out of my depth, treading water was becoming damned hard.

"That still doesn't explain not just calling the police," I protested weakly.

"I have my reasons," he said quickly with a cold fury that chilled my heart.

"Right now, there are three people you can trust and two of them are in this room. If that's not good enough...."

My interpretation of his unspoken "tough shit" pointed to certain death, mine, should I choose a contrary course. I got the very bad feeling that, considering my tenuous position, I might've pushed things farther than I should.

"Your only ticket out, if we're all going to survive," he continued in a tightly controlled voice, nodding toward the slap of water in the open hatchway, "is down there. I couldn't tell you about plan B before and I'm not real happy with you being in this deep now."

That made it unanimous.

"I knew you'd be safer if you didn't know anything, but I didn't know how to exclude you. You can be awful' hardheaded when you want to. Tell me I'm wrong; could you've kept your cool if you knew before what I just told you, or that we were going to bag their shit?"

I opened my mouth to respond.

"You'd've lit up like a pinball machine, and instead of talking right now we'd probably be fighting a losing battle for our lives."

I nodded my head in agreement. There was nothing I could do or say at this point other than appear to go along. What Tony was saying sounded right, but it either was based on conjecture or fantasy. Perhaps he really believed he was some sort of avenging angel for something that may or may not have happened twenty years ago. Perhaps he'd overdosed on Agent Orange or that medical discharge he'd been given was a Section-8 and he was nutty as a bag of trail mix. I didn't know and I didn't care. The only thing I wanted was off that houseboat alive and I would say or do anything to be free.

"Here's the deal," he drew it out, "we go back to our lives like everything's normal, only we continue our stake-out here. I want to see who shows up and what they do when they miss their shit before we decide on a course of action. Remember our lives are going to depend on the profiles we show. And, uh, leave the piece here. You don't normally carry a gun and you couldn't not be aware of it. Hell, you might just as well wear a sign."

All I could do was nod compliance.

An uneasy silence descended on the room, broken only by Doug's return. Whether he noticed or not, I didn't know. I was beyond caring. He simply rolled onto his bunk and went to sleep. Shortly before first light we left Doug to hold down the fort while we put in our respective appearances on land.

*   *   *

CHAPTER 29

The system had pretty well wrung itself out by sunrise, Gradually, more and more clear than cloud was showing in the sky. I hoped it was a positive omen. After the night I'd experienced I needed one.

As agreed, I'd left the Dodge parked on a crowded residential side street a few blocks from the main road the night before—it seemed like a thousand years ago—Tony'd then met and ferried me to the private dock in one of an assortment of unobtrusive looking 'conch-cruisers' that fit into the neighborhood.

The most convincing argument on Tony's behalf was that I was still alive to watch him drive off after having dropped me by my van. It felt good to be out and breathing in the fresh air again; it felt good just to be breathing.

Within seconds of his departure, my hands started to shake so violently it took me several tries before I was able to insert the key into the lock. Sarge, who'd bunked down in the van overnight, anxiously watched me from his perch on the passenger seat. His stump was working overtime in a welcoming wave. Sensing my anxiety, as I climbed aboard, he stood between the seats before resting his head on my knee in an effort to show his concern and support. He then looked up at me, so serenely confident in my ability to drive home and give him breakfast that it seemed like the only logical thing to do. Clearly, Sarge understood priorities.

*   *   *

**If you your lips would keep from slips
Of five things have a care:
To whom you speak, of whom you speak,
And how, and when, and where.**

- Anonymous

CHAPTER 30

It was shortly after seven-thirty; Doug's muscle-bound dog was in the kitchen making noises with his food that sounded like a triple-X-rated soundtrack. Judging by Monk's groan, I'd succeeded in awakening him. I suppose I could have waited for office hours, but my nerves were so frayed that I felt compelled to give him a blow-by-blow of the previous evening's activities, including Tony's wartime saga and speculations on Whidden/Whitefield's real intentions.

Then, when I asked if he'd see to having the contents of my house packed up and made ready to ship while I left town and found a place to hide in northern Georgia, he made the appropriate lawyer sounds that meant 'chill out.' He then reminded me of my promise to help him out on the condo project. He allayed my fears by suggesting that the safest place to be might be as close to Tony and Doug as I could get. His tone was positive and reassuring, exactly what I needed to hear.

He explained, "They let you go free, so they must think you're going to continue to go along. All you have to do is keep an eye on them until I can arrange to have the proper authorities check out this 'Whitefield' character to see if there's any truth to Amundsen's allegations, then arrange to take them and the drugs into custody."

Relief and vindication flooded through me.

"I'm going to need you do me a small favor in return."

Naturally, I agreed.

"Have Rosa reschedule my daybook morning appointments to the afternoon. I'll need to talk to a few people right away about your, ah, situation. I'll probably have some good news for you by the end of business today. Until then, we have a project to get back on track. And remember: not a word to anyone. Okay, buddy?"

Showering and dressing for the day I noticed that I had become considerably lighter in spirit. Maybe confession *is* good for the soul. Regardless, I knew that with an officer of the court and trusted friend on my side, I didn't feel like the Lone Ranger anymore.

While the rest of the day rolled by uneventfully, and the specter of a decades old Vietnam War ghost retreated into the darker recesses of my anxiety closet, I managed to lose myself in the project schedules.

Rosa tapped and came in. Stroking and caressing Sarge, she asked if I needed her to do anything for me before she closed the offices for the day. I bit my tongue, knowing she would neither comply with my request, nor would Sarge have allowed me to assume his place beneath her hands.

"No, nothing thanks." I arched my back and groaned. "I'm beat. Give me a sec' and I'll walk you out."

Rosa normally took work home over the weekend. Ever the gentleman, I carried her stack of file folders along with my own. On the way to her car she remarked that Monk hadn't made it in to the office all day, nor had he bothered to call. This was news to me since. I was at the far end of the floor, secluded from the daily comings and goings. Rosa was by turns worried about him and irritated that she'd had to cancel and reschedule his appointments twice that day. I kidded her that punctuality had never been one of Monk's faults then offered to stop at his place on my way home, to make sure he was okay. She had a radiant smile and used it at full power in thanks.

Faithfully, I cruised by Monk's place. Seeing his car gone from it's parking spot, I decided not to stop. It was best that Rosa figured Monk merely guilty of skipping out on a Friday; a natural assumption with the good weather that followed in the wake of last night's bluster. High billowy clouds supporting a bright turquoise sky, as fragrant winds swept the island with the kind of invigorating freshness that drove insanely high real estate prices even higher, were an inducement to play hooky. There'd been several times previously, on just such a day, when Monk, admitting to having "stalked the wild bonefish," as he liked to call it, had surrendered to temptation.

I figured the real reason for his absence, most likely in light of my morning breast cleaning he'd devoted himself to taking care of my situation with the "few people" he'd mentioned and it had probably run longer than expected. I knew he'd contact me as soon as he had something to report, so it was with a buoyant sense of anticipation that I headed home to feed Sarge and get ready for the night ahead. I was positive there would be a message on my machine. That was it! It'd be just like 'The Monk' to keep it out of the office and away from Mr. Whitefield/Whidden's prying. Keeping me out of harm's way. What a guy! But, when I got there...nothing; nobody loved me, knew me, or wanted to talk to me.

Reluctantly, I choked down some food and prepared myself for the long night ahead. There'd be word from Monk waiting for me in the morning, of that I was certain and that surety gave me the strength to see through the rest of the insanity my life had become.

Waiting for Sarge to complete his investigation of the mango tree in my yard, I opened the journal for the "tumor." When I first began supervising projects for Monk, recording a job's progress from start to finish allowed me to see things more objectively and, occasionally, had eliminated costly mistakes due to oversight. A shelf in my home office carried dozens of the slim volumes. After Whidden tried snowing Monk and me, during his lunchtime story theater, I began adding these "outside" circumstances to the project log. Exactly why, I'm not sure; no one but me would probably ever see it. Tracing the chain of events, if nothing else helped a little by getting it out of my system and down on paper. Half the notebook, backward from the last page, I reserved for questions. Almost two full pages, so far, but with too few answers.

My watch beeped its seven-thirty signal, so I tucked the notebook into a folio of road maps under the passenger seat, hustled Sarge on board and backed out of my driveway.

Since the Maxi-van was a little too conspicuous to appear again and again in the tiny Fleming Bay parking lot, I made for one of our "neutral" locations on the side streets, where I would wait for another of Tony's seemingly endless string of rusting and innocuous-looking 'beaters' he had access to, thanks to his part ownership of a small used car lot. Tony organized our rendezvous sites and routes daily, so we could more easily check for tailing vehicles along the way. In the wake of the previous night's escapades I'd almost driven from one end of the island to the other to elude the sinister black Crown Victoria that tailed me through half a dozen turns and filled my head with visions of arrest, incarceration, or worse. Finally, I pulled over and prepared to accept the consequences. It turned out to be only a young fellow curious about my bumper stickers advertising hang gliding, so it was almost sunset when I arrived. Tony accepted my excuses with nothing more than a quizzical grin and the now-familiar headshake. Whatever thoughts he may have had about my paranoid behavior, thankfully, he kept to himself.

Sitting on a musty, mildewed blanket, surrounded by heavy cheese and spice smells emanating from three grease-stained bags on the back seat, breathing burnt motor oil coming up through the rusted-out floor, my stomach was doing flip-flops before we'd gone a block.

Paranoia or not, as I pulled on the bright yellow baseball cap and sunglasses Tony'd brought for me, I couldn't help thinking of how my disguise, should I fail to return from the houseboat tonight, could work to my disadvantage. No one would remember seeing anything other than a couple of guys heading out toward one of the dozens of houseboat moorings in a kayak; very boring, very mundane...and very, very convenient.

Confiding in Monk was my one slim safety line and I would cling to it for all I was worth.

*   *   *

**Whither depart the souls of the brave that die in the battle,
Die in the lost, lost fight, for the cause that perishes with
them?**

- Arthur Hugh Clough

CHAPTER 31

I took the bags of food and left Tony to finish mooring
the kayak.

"That's odd," I said, to no one in particular. The cabin door was
slightly ajar. The opening was framed from within by a soft red glow.
My hands were full, I tried toeing the door open further but it wouldn't
budge, so I put my shoulder against it and pushed. Something scraped
against the wooden deck, the door shifted, caught for a moment, then
swung free and I stumbled inside. Something metallic rolled unevenly
across the floorboards then spiraled round and spun to a stop almost at
my feet: a lens ring from the spotting scope.

"How did—?" I began. Looking up, I saw Doug. His eyes stared
at me blankly. The chair to which he'd been tied stood squarely in the
middle of the room. A gaping leer grinned at me from below his chin.
The front of his chest was a mass of blood.

My heart froze. I went cold as ice. Tony was at my side even as
the bags dropped from my hands. In the same instant, he pulled me off
my feet to one side as he dropped to the deck. Off balance, I landed on
top of something hard. Grunting aloud with the pain, I tried to roll off
whatever I'd fallen on but I was stuck half in, half out of the doorway
and couldn't move. Reaching under me my fingers identified the con-
tours of Charlie's pistol.

Knife in hand, Tony lay motionless except for his head, which
traversed side-to-side like a deck gun seeking a target. I tapped him on
the arm to show what I'd found, and as he looked back, I saw his eyes
widen. I turned back and in the red glow from inside the cabin saw the

dim outline of a diver rise from the open hatch, in his hand was what looked like Doug's machine pistol wrapped in clear plastic. Without thinking, I stuck my hand out and jerked the .45's trigger. The report was deafening. In the split-second illumination of the muzzle flash, blood and glass erupted from the center of the diver's mask.

Virtually blind and deaf from the gunshot, a vice-like grip on my arm yanked me off the deck. Seconds later all the air left my lungs as cold water closed over my head.

Desperately, my diaphragm humping, urgently pleading for air, I tried to free myself, as I was dragged down, ever deeper. Then I felt something being mashed against my lips. Locking my teeth together, I averted my head and tried to push it away and break for the surface. When my fingers felt the shape of a regulator mouthpiece, I stopped struggling and greedily sucked in a beautiful, sweet draught of life-giving air.

In a flash of comprehension I realized Tony, seeing the one sure escape route, had carried us after our would-be assassin who was now providing us with the means to sustain our lives.

So much for paranoia, someone *was* trying to kill us.

I was shivering so badly from fear that I was scarcely able to pass the regulator as we swam with the current, our passive accomplice between us. Before the combination of shock and cold leeched all of the strength from my body and numbed my mind, I found the valve and deflated his Buoyancy Compensator vest. By reducing the pocket of air, we were able to use his weight and equipment to counteract our natural buoyancy and remain submerged, but for how long? Time had no meaning beneath the surface, except every moment carried us a little further away from danger.

When the air started to run out—it might have been ten minutes or twenty—I found then released our dead companion's weight belt and we began our ascent. What we would find waiting for us was anyone's guess.

The night air felt icy-cold after our immersion. I tensed against the imminent spray of bullets. No gunfire, no boats, no lights, there was nothing anywhere near us, only the steady hiss of rain on the water. We had survived...so far.

Checking our bearings from the red and green channel markers and the nearest landmarks, we'd traveled about a mile and a half from the houseboat, east around the Navy base. We were in clear water maybe half a mile out from the peripheral Sea Walk that circles most of the island. I was about to suggest that we swim towards the neon marking the shopping mall, when....

WHUMP!

A red and black flare spangled with white flashes shot through my brain. Something had slammed into me, hard, right where I'd fallen onto Charlie's pistol. Crippling pain radiated outward from the point of impact.

Shark! Instantly, the image came full-blown into my mind. We were hugging a dead body between us and had left a blood-trail over a mile wide. —A short flirtation with shark hunting, off the Marquesas south of Key West, had left me with a profound fear and an abiding respect for these awesome feeding machines whom I'd seen lunge at crew half an hour after they'd been shot three times in the brain and bled dry.

"Sh-shark! There's a shark in the water," I stuttered and gasped through the pain, fear, and cold. Comprehending, Tony pushed us away from the dead diver. Knowing that sharks are drawn by sound, and that our best protection from attack lay in making a minimum of noise, silently, we side-stroked toward the shore.

Forced to take it slow and steady, I took comfort from the .45 in my belt. Unsure whether the gun would actually fire after having been underwater, I was thankful I'd managed to hang onto it just the same.

Queasiness and relief lurched through me when I heard the ominous splashes behind us. Better he than me, I thought. Though our unknown assailant had tried to kill us, he'd saved our lives, twice.

Before long it became possible to walk as the water shallowed to waist- then knee-depth. Between the chill from the wind-driven rain and water temperature in the 60s, over and above the nervous drain on my system, I could barely put one foot in front of the other. We had to get dry and soon, if not we stood a good chance of succumbing to hypothermia.

Coughing out the mouthful of water I'd inhaled, I remembered too late the narrow boat channel dredged to provide access to the hotel marina adjacent the Sea Walk. We swam the few strokes across the deep trough and pulled ourselves up into one of the thick stands of mangrove that dot the periphery of the island. There, between violent fits of shivering, amid the foul stench of stagnant water and garbage surrounding the root systems, we caught our breath. Directly across from us was the Iron Works, I could almost feel how delicious the sauna room was going to be after a long hot shower. I would have made a beeline for the gym had Tony not restrained me.

A dark vehicle was parked in the middle of the lot near the gym. Conspicuous, not only because it was the sole vehicle at the opposite end of the plaza from the movie theater, but because of the two shapes in the front seat.

"Like a couple 'a tarbabies," Tony quoted Uncle Remus, "...they jes' sat there 'n' didn't do 'nuffin'."

Evidently, someone had wanted to make sure.

*   *   *

Tar-baby ain't sayin' nuthin',
and Brer Fox, he lay low.

- Joel Chandler Harris

CHAPTER 32

Wanting to put as much distance as possible between ourselves and whoever was after us, we reached the relative safety of a quiet residential side street. When it became obvious that we weren't heading toward the van, I started to ask why. A fierce glare and cutting gesture shut me up.

Tony was right! We had to be careful. The diver would be missed, but when? We had no way of telling when they might actively begin searching for us, or if they hadn't already. Good thing, I thought, we were late getting out to the barge. Probably that and dumb luck, were the only reasons why we were still alive. Twice, we took cover when a car happened along the same street, neither fitted the image of a search in-progress. They hadn't sounded the alarm yet, but they were sure to before long. Who, I wondered, were "they?"

Inside bougainvillea-covered privacy walls surrounding a modest house in an unremarkable neighborhood, we practiced "listening to the night" and "being very still."

Other than the whine of mosquitoes and distant buzzing sounds that came from somewhere in the house, in response to Tony's rapid jabs at a call button, the night was blessedly quiet. The porch light came on. Someone looked through a barred view port in the door. The metal trap clacked shut. A moment passed then I thought I heard a sibilant curse from inside before the overhead light was extinguished and the door was unlocked. Tony started forward as it opened until a small fist holding a key, almost as if it was a weapon, about an inch in front of his nose stopped him dead in his tracks. The features of the blanket-wrapped figure inside the doorway were indistinct. Not a word was spoken, but the body language was clear. We weren't welcome.

"'Guestroom's out back," Tony murmured to me, taking the key from the fist before leading the way around the side and across the back lawn toward a small structure that had probably begun life as a garage.

Once inside, I suddenly began shivering. Violent tremors shook me, rattling my bones; my vision went black. I felt myself falling.

I came to lying on something soft, wrapped in something dry, but feeling like I might never get warm again. Someone, someplace was making kitchen noises. Another spasm of shivering rattled my cage and as I began to fade, a warm, sweet smell filled my senses. I opened my eyes as Tony helped me sit up. Pressing a large hot mug into my hands, he guided it to my mouth. Liquid fire blazed a path down my throat, lighting a friendly, familiar furnace deep in my belly. Instantly, the shakes vanished replaced by the radiant glow of wellbeing.

Judging by the various materials and works-in-progress we were, apparently, in a self-contained apartment that was being used as the work/storage space of some kind of an artist; someone who lived an economic and uncluttered existence. I sensed being in a place of peace and privacy.

Watching Tony expertly disassemble the pistol I'd clung to so tenaciously, placing the parts in a neat row on a coffee table between us, I tried not to think of how good the rum had tasted, perversely wanting more while regretting what I'd consumed.

"I lied," Tony said simply, working oil into the mechanism and testing the slide, when I picked up the magazine and saw the row of bullets.

Stunned and embarrassed by how easily I'd been out-bluffed I decided to let it slide, there were more pressing issues; staying alive for one. Back and forth, we discussed what to do next but there was too much we didn't know for us to develop any sort of a plan. We did agree that holing up in a converted garage—comfortable though it was—with no transportation and no information, was not much of an option.

*   *   *

A feeling of sadness and longing,
That is not akin to pain,
And resembles sorrow only
As the mist resembles the rain.

- Henry Wadsworth Longfellow

CHAPTER 33

Dressed in clothing, still warm from the dryer, under a borrowed slicker against the rain, I tried not to think about how good the receding glow of rum inside me felt while trudging west through Mid-town. The image of Sarge patiently waiting for me to return—something I couldn't or wouldn't let slide—had goaded me into volunteering to fetch the van. At first Tony's agreeing right off had surprised me until I remembered Sarge's behavior towards him in the houseboat. Clearly, Tony had not forgotten.

There had been another reason for my wanting to go: Pinned above the sun-visor was a set of keys left over from shelf building and water-damage repair sessions at Monk's ocean-view apartment. To some extent the truth of Tony's assertions had been vindicated under fire, but I shared neither our intended destination nor my reasons for wanting to see Monk. I knew he would resist but, like it or not, I'd made up my mind that's where we were going. As Tony had already observed, I *can* be awful' hardheaded when I want.

The van blended into the quiet neighborhood under the dripping canopy of two Royal Poincianas. The rain had slackened to a fine drizzly mist and fat drops fell irregularly from the giant seedpods and branches, popping hollowly on the metal roof. Under a leaky rain gutter, a steady dribble-drabble filled the sag of a plastic tarpaulin draped over a pair of mopeds, while a community of frogs discussed the advantages of traditional over man-made ponds.

The springs creaked and the van rocked slightly as Sarge moved to the driver's side. He stared down at me, his stubby tail twitching hello, before stepping down between the seats and allowing me to enter. I climbed inside, thanking him for the courtesy by softly scratching a favorite spot behind his right ear. Sarge leaned into me, savoring my touch, giving me his trust. Heartsick with the knowledge that he was now fully my responsibility, I wondered, uneasily, how he was going to react when he realized that his master wasn't ever going to show up again? Sarge grunted a big sigh that seemed to shake his body like a sob. I closed my eyes and saw Doug, seated in his death chair, his silent, eternal accusation of an unfair world demanding I do the right thing.

I started the engine.

*   *   *

...and in trust I have found treason

- Queen Elizabeth I

CHAPTER 34

Since the front seat was already occupied, Tony wisely opted for the carpeted middle cargo area. Predictably he objected when I told him where we were heading until I added another torque to an already over-stretched truth, by mentioning Monk's absence from the office all day. Equating that with the likelihood of the place being vacant, Tony agreed.

Tony and Monk were the only people I could trust. In addition to shedding a little light on agent Whidden/Whitefield, there was a chance that Monk's contacts in the State Attorney's office might be able to help sort this mess out. We'd jumped into the middle of something we'd no right to, and two lives had paid the price for our meddling. Self-defense or not, I was responsible for killing someone.

Having directly taken a human life shook me to my soul.

Only two windows in the apartment complex showed any light, given the late hour and the number of retirees in residence, everything appeared normal. Monk's sporty convertible, I could see, was absent from its assigned slot.

I tapped in the code on the keypad. The aluminum gates glided quietly open on greased tracks. Tony held the pistol ready, scanning the dripping shadows on either side. The white noise of the Atlantic Ocean became clearer, as we rolled on down to the last building above the beach. We crossed the parking lot on foot then took the elevator to the sixth floor. I unlocked the door to Monk's penthouse apartment, stepped inside and turned on the lights.

Chaos! It was as if the thunderstorm that assaulted the island had been spawned in Monk's apartment.

"Amateurs," Tony whispered, reading my mind, as he scanned the destruction. "Whoever did this was more interested in trashing the place than stealing anything."

To me, it looked like someone had been searching for something but hadn't been very particular how they went about it; I guessed the *what,* but drew a blank on the *who*?

Sarge moved under my hand. The vibration of his silent growl sent a shiver of gooseflesh up my arm and down my spine. When he moved through the wreckage toward the master bedroom, I followed. Tony was right beside me, the .45 in a two-handed grip, ready for whatever lay on the other side of the closed door. I didn't want to do it, in spite of my reluctance; I saw my hand reaching for the knob.

Blood had thickened, drying into dark streaks down the arms of the figure with the silver-taped face, covering his body and forming two large scabs on the carpet under his feet. Wide bands of duct tape covered his eyes and mouth. Nylon cable-ties had been used to crucify Monk, securing him to the massive bulk of the Universal Gym that dominated the mirrored corner of his large bedroom. Whatever torture Monk had been through had caused him to lose control of his bowels. His emerald green silk pyjamas were rags and the carpet below him was fouled. I struggled to control my gag reflex from the stench, as I bore his weight while Tony cut him free with his pocketknife. Each wrist and ankle had been cinched tight around a second nylon band that fastened him to the heavy weight-training machinery.

We lowered Monk onto the shredded king-size mattress lying on the floor. Grotesquely swollen, the purple-black discoloration showed the circulation to his hands and feet had been dangerously arrested. I took the pocketknife and began cutting through the primary ties. The nylon was so deeply buried into the abused flesh as to be almost invisible. I tried to be gentle when I worked the blade under the tough plastic, but Tony had to help restrain Monk as he began thrashing about unconsciously. I knew I was responsible for his suffering. Whatever torture he had endured had been directly caused by my/our actions. The muffled moans and pleas to the terrible phantom tormentors in Monk's mind broke my heart. Tony seemed to take it in stride. I hated and envied his apparent calm when he suggested I hold off on cutting until he'd checked to see if he could find something to ease Monk's pain.

From the sounds of broken glass and grit underfoot the bathroom had not escaped the general ransacking either. When he returned, his business-as-usual attitude was still firmly in place. He applied rubbing alcohol to ease the silver duct tape from Monk's face then forced a couple Nembutal into his mouth then washed the sleeping pills down with vodka from a miniature he'd found somewhere. Contrary to medical standards, I prayed it would help speed the onset of blessed unconsciousness.

We held a hurried council of war amid the wreckage of Japanese décor in the living room. Since Monk had been left alive he was probably due for a return visit, we agreed, so this was not a safe place. My house would also be out of the question; chances were it had or would soon receive a similar treatment. It stood to reason, I offered, Tony's was unsafe too. My fears were greeted with skepticism, until I explained about having told Monk about our stakeout and subsequent acquisition of the contraband shipment.

Two cold blue lasers savaged me. His eyes never left mine, as I retreated into the bedroom. Barely audible, I heard Sarge growl when Tony came in after me.

Monk was snoring softly, so I set about cutting him free.

"I'm sorry, but you guys scared the crap out of me when you took the, the—I didn't know what else to do."

Tony didn't have to state the obvious. I saw the answer smolder accusingly in his eyes; heard the two words "trust me" unspoken, as he said, "We can thrash that out...later. Right now, we better 'di di mau' and get the hell out of here, fast."

I see that Tony was severely pissed at me, but he was right in that this was neither the time nor the place for that particular discussion.

"Charlie's," I suggested, as he helped me clean and bandage the wounds.

Tony looked at me, hard, searching for signs of further deception or conspiracy; something I'd never felt from him before.

"His sister," I added, pulling a set of sweats and a sweater out of a dresser, "isn't due in from Virginia for the funeral for another week. The place should be safe for a day or two."

Tony quickly weighed the known and unknown, as he helped dress Monk against the affects of shock. My trustworthiness, I'm sure, was part of the equation. He nodded once then stood and turned his back to me, signaling, "end of discussion."

The noise of the distant motor spooling up, when Tony pushed the call button, sounded a silent warning. We'd left the car at the top floor and, though the doors had closed, it hadn't descended after we'd exited. Only someone signaling from a lower floor would have caused it to move. It was after three in the morning and the likelihood of one of Monk's neighbors using it at that hour was unlikely. When I alerted him to this, Tony instantly grasped the implication. The length of time it was taking to reach us meant the car had been on or near the ground level. If it was Monk's tormentors returning, we were trapped.

Back to the wall, offering the least possible target, Tony stood to one side of the elevator. Ready for action, he held the pistol in a double-handed grip about chest-high. Opposite him, my hands gripped the sharkskin hilt-wrappings of the Katana from Monk's collection that I'd rescued from the chaos, prepared to use the long samurai sword for diversion or defense. Behind me and insensible, Monk was watched over by Sarge.

The whirring slowed to a stop. After a pause, the doors bumped open. Bright and sterile, the empty car mocked my fears. The interior beckoned. Escape was imminent. The doors started to close. Tony struck the bumper, causing them to roll open again.

"Stepping in there'll be like sticking our heads in a noose...if there's a welcoming party in the lobby, and—"

"The fire stairs," I countered, moving to lift Monk to my shoulder.

"Cool yer jets," Tony cautioned, his hand on my arm, controlling me. "Anyone's down there, that'll be covered too."

He suddenly became very still, held a cautioning finger to his lips then pointed over my head. I got a sinking feeling that an axe was poised above me about to fall. Reaching into the car, he threw the emergency-stop switch, and directed me to use the sword to raise the escape hatch on top of the car, while he covered it with the .45. Tony'd seen a third alternative and recognized the possibility of a threat, in case someone else had thought of it too.

They hadn't.

Grabbing the frame, Tony pulled himself up into a sitting position on top of the car with a single fluid motion. I passed the weapons up first, then Monk, followed by one very concerned Rottweiler. This had to be an unsettling experience for Sarge, but he bore the indignity with composure.

Using the tip of the long sword I reached down and flicked the switch back, immediately the doors closed, the motor whirred and we began our descent. In the darkened shaft, while supporting Monk, I gentled Sarge with soft scratches behind the ear. Ever vigilant, Tony had taken a position opposite me so that he could cover the hatch with the pistol.

Approaching the ground floor, where there was no telling what waited for us, my heart leapt into my throat! A corner of Monk's sweater disappeared under the edge of the hatch. I grabbed it and tugged. Caught fast, it refused to come loose.

The motor droned to a stop. A moment later the doors rumbled apart. After what seemed an eternity, a relay clicked shut and the doors started to close. I reached for the hatch. Sarge's growl beside my ear was scarcely audible. I froze. My hand had just touched the trapdoor handle when the doors below abruptly stopped and rolled open again. The car below us rocked as an indeterminate number of people quickly entered. I heard the scratchy crackle and rasp of radio static followed by a series of electronic squawks.

The police! I thought, feeling almost faint with relief, it was short-lived.

"Set a field of fire..." one of the passengers below us ordered, as the car began its ascent, "...stand ready at both rear exits."

There were two answering squawks.

"Rearguard...fan out below the balcony. Look sharp!"

There was another acknowledging squawk then all was deathly silent, save for the whir of the lifting motor. Any moment now, I was sure, someone would look up, see the dangling corner of Monk's sweater, and bullets would start punching holes under our feet. A hot flush of panic made me squirm. A tiny dribble of sweat rolled from my hairline down between my eyebrows and along the length of my nose, where it hung from the tip, dangling maddeningly. The drop of sweat fell, and I felt it spatter on the back of my outstretched hand, followed by another and a third. I became aware of the pounding thud of blood hammering inside my ears.

The motor whined to a stop at the top floor. The doors opened and the passengers below stealthily ex-filtrated the car.

When the doors below closed, I let go the breath I'd unconsciously been holding. Lifting the hatch, I retrieved the end of Monk's sweater. Tony never lost his survival perspective for a moment, he pulled it wide, and used my sword to stab the L button sending the car once again down its five-story descent.

First down through the hatchway, I was trembling so badly that my legs were scarcely able to support me. Blinded by the glare of the overhead lights, after the gloom in the shaft atop the car, I winced as I reached up. Sarge, uncomplaining, came next followed by Monk's dead weight. The car once again neared its destination; we flattened ourselves against the walls and prepared to meet the unknown.

The doors rolled open. The small lobby was empty, the only motion was from the swirl of moths batting and fluttering futilely against the frosted glass panels covering the fluorescent lights.

With Monk over my shoulder and Sarge at my side, I hid in the dripping shadows of the bushes framing the lobby entrance, waiting; watching as Tony glided noiselessly from shadow to shadow towards the van. So skillfully did he use the night that I quickly lost sight of him. After a minute or so, I noticed the slow, unlit approach of the Maxi-van. Nearing the entrance he slipped the van into neutral, to avoid triggering the brake lights. I moved from our hiding place and bundled Monk in through the already opened side door. Leaving one ajar, I ran ahead to manually open the front gate. Efficiently flanking me, Sarge kept pace. Tony followed using only the idling engine for momentum. Moments later, the van ghosted through the open gate and out into the street. I didn't begin to relax until we'd left the main road, performed several complex series of turns and were over half a mile away.

*   *   *

**When we remember we are all mad,
the mysteries of life disappear and
life stands explained.**

- Mark Twain

CHAPTER 35

The sum total of our weaponry was limited to the six remaining bullets in the .45 pistol and one antique sword.

Astutely, Tony suggested that without any substantial increase in firepower we didn't stand a chance against our opposition, however many they were.

"You think?" I agreed sourly.

Since I had no intention of liberating whatever arms might still remain in Doug's houseboat I grudgingly asked what he had in mind. In that moment, picking the two words historically responsible for most of the world's problems would have been easy. Coincidentally, they were the same two words I'd imagined hearing in Monk's apartment, in Tony's silent indictment of my betrayal.

"Trust me," was all he said.

We detoured off Flagler Avenue, the east-west road bisecting the island lengthwise, then headed toward the Ironworks. About two blocks shy of the gym, Tony executed a right then an immediate hard left, entering the vast labyrinthine Stadium Mobile Home Park. We wove our way through the maze of aluminum-lined cul-de-sacs and crescents, coasting to a stop beside a pedestrian gate in the chain-link fence facing the rear of the shopping center.

Wanting to be sure the focus of attention was elsewhere, before stepping into what could easily prove to be another trap, we stood in the dripping shadows of a prosperous Ficus tree directly across from the Iron Works for about fifteen minutes or so, though it seemed a lot longer. Then, casually but quickly, Tony crossed to the back door of the gym and was inside almost immediately.

Standing there alone, on the brink of a nervous breakdown; in fact, I think I may have even promised myself one if only we could figure out how to stop these people—whoever they were—from trying to kill us.

A series of pinpoint flashes from the blackened interior of the gym caught my attention. Believing them to be a signal from Tony, carefully and with a copied cool I didn't feel, I crossed the street. Sarge, unbidden, stayed where he was. I envied him.

Midway across the deserted street, as I knew would happen, I walked into a blistering hail of bullets that tore my body to pieces and flung me to the asphalt like a broken toy; Tony must be laying somewhere inside the gym, either dead or incapacitated and in the hands of his captors.

On the verge of bolting and running off screaming into the night, I blinked my eyes free of the hallucination and continued towards the ominously darkened doorway. I chalked the psychotic delusion up to a combination of nerves and a reconstituted LSD episode from some idiotic part of my misspent youth.

The assault rifle in Tony's hands was a lethally reassuring sight. I grunted at the unexpected weight of the dark canvas bag he tossed at me; it must've weighed seventy to eighty pounds; he'd handled it like it was nothing. Tony slipped another duffel over his own shoulder before returning Charlie's Colt .45 to me. I had to stuff it down my pants in order to accept the assault rifle he thrust into my hands. Evidently, it was meant to be mine. Ignorant of automatic weapons, but assuming it was loaded, I wondered what I had to do to fire it.

The armory being pulled out of thin air was undoubtedly a legacy of his smuggling days, which gave me a little deeper insight into Tony's shadowy past, but in no way helped me achieve a peaceful and serene state of mind. Though I still wasn't all that convinced about how pure an agenda he carried, at least he was arming me instead of trying to kill me. That was something in his favor.

After pausing to adjust what appeared to be a small pair of binoculars ending in a single lens, which he attached to a pivoting headset and put on, Tony reached back into the shadowy opening hidden behind a false wall in the last shower stall, and extracted yet another canvas bag and a rifle. Like the one on the houseboat, it was fitted with a bulky sniper scope. At this point it wouldn't have surprised me if he'd driven through the wall in a tank.

Lowering the optics into place, clicking on the headset, he took his time checking the area outside. Then, as calmly as its possible to be—loaded down with a ton of illicit weaponry—we crossed to the trailer park. Sarge quietly fell into step on our return to the van.

After being out in the clear morning air, fresh and clean from rainfall, the ambience in the van had all the charm of a septic tank. The drop sheet I'd used to cover Monk helped to contain some of the smell, but even with all the windows open I was still on the verge of losing it.

Sarge, always the clear thinker, in a display of superior intellect sat with his head out the passenger window.

I doused the canvas tarp with the last of a bottle of car deodorant.

"Somebody back there shit a pine tree?" Tony yelled over his shoulder. He laughed wildly then leaned his head into the draft from his own open window.

I smiled weakly, neither appreciating his humor nor the even bigger mess I'd created for everyone, feeling about as alone as I'd ever been.

*   *   *

**In nature there are neither rewards nor punishments
—there are consequences.**

- Robert Green Ingersoll

CHAPTER 36

Other than an intermittent buzz coming from a nearby pole-transformer and the softly gurgling rainwater running into sewer grates, the neighborhood appeared untroubled, asleep in its innocence. Somewhere, a few blocks away, rap music rolled past and vanished into the distance. At the end of the block we stood cloaked by shadows in dense tropical foliage, hidden from view behind a boxed all-weather shrine dedicated to a gilded Santa in a Cubano garden. A frangipani tree drenched the air above us with the sweet scent of candy canes. Across the street, two houses down, the same one light I'd left on in the living room several days ago still burned in Charlie's house.

Something, some sixth sense, prevented me from making any move from our place of concealment. We were lucky to have gotten out of Monk's alive, and the idea of jumping into another kind of frying pan rendered me immobile. I could feel the moisture soaking into my feet. My immobility wasn't doing Monk any good. We needed someplace safer, somewhere less accessible.

"'Doesn't feel right." I whispered.

Tony gave me a funny look followed by a short nod of agreement then abruptly turned back the way we'd came. It took me a moment to catch up to them. Tony and Sarge were both as silent as shadows, as we made our way back to the van. Try as I might, I couldn't move as quietly or find the easy predatory rhythm they both used so effortlessly. Repeatedly, I tripped and snapped things underfoot. Once, I stepped into something that I didn't want to know what it was. I was like a kid playing at a man's game, insecure and scared, reluctant to do anything lest it bring ridicule and derision. If I couldn't learn the rules of this very real and very deadly game, the penalties promised to be severe.

*   *   *

**We find not much in ourselves to admire,
we are always privately wanting to be like somebody else.
If everybody was satisfied with himself there would be no
heroes.**

- Mark Twain

CHAPTER 37

The peripheral design of Key West's roads funnels out-bound traffic through a natural bottleneck at the last stoplight before crossing the Cow Key Channel Bridge east to Stock Island and the upper Keys. If anyone wanted to intercept a vehicle attempting to flee the Rock the three-way traffic triangle would be the perfect place.

Still yawning, the driver of the van with the Ontario license plates was probably trying to get a jump on the Island Highway traffic. Like most early departures, probably, his plan was to pass through Miami before the turnpike circus cranked up to full insanity. Scrupulously obeying all the traffic signs, he seemed intent on placating the unseen minions of law and order who were surely lying in wait.

Tony snugged us in behind him hoping, by following his every move, to foster the impression of two families returning home from a shared holiday. At four in the morning, ours were virtually the only two non-commercial vehicles on the road. The effect of our shadow-tag on the people in front could have them imagining dread images of highway piracy or a rolling undercover police trap intent on dogging their progress until they made that fatal error which would result in unspeakable horrors.

We rode out the facade and, and if there was a sentinel we didn't see him, nor he, us. Once we cleared the far side of the bridge and entered Stock Island without ambush or alarm, I began to relax my grip on the rifle. The relief from our designated convoy leader was audible when Tony eased over and slowed to enter the warren of side streets; his acceleration was immediate and hard. Silently, I warned him to slow down; about four to five hundred yards further on, right before a long, straight stretch where the speed limit ramps-up from local to highway, was an empty lot with large bushy stands of scrub where the Florida Highway Patrol liked to set early morning radar traps.

*   *   *

CHAPTER 38

The padlock opened with a meaty click, silencing the waves of cricket song. Sound seemed magnified out of proportion by the intense surrounding stillness emanating from the mangroves, as I unwound the clanking length of heavy chain and swung back the gate for Tony. I made sure to slide the locked chain back around to the same position I'd found it, before getting in and directing us across the open plain toward our new base of operations. Despite the *NO ENTRY* signage, no one had bothered changing the locks on the front gate or the Judas-door of the one-time Commissary building, nor, apparently, had anyone ever oiled the springs. The raucous screech and twanging caused my shoulders to flinch protectively up to my ears, a condition that was becoming all too frequent.

We carried Monk inside and laid him on a surplus army stretcher. Still out of it, he appeared to be resting and his color didn't look too terribly bad by flashlight. Taking charge, Tony sent me to bring in the rest of our gear before heading toward a pallet stacked with first-aid kits to see what he could find.

With the yard closed to general access and Deputy Marshal Schott in jail, I had no way of telling if anyone might be prowling around during the day. Inside the warehouse we'd be okay, but what to do about the van? Since we were going to spend the night, or longer, it needed to be well out of sight. The large rollup door sported a new set of locks, so that was out. I wondered. What to do?

Towards the end of the tiny peninsula a row of ancient hulks sat in varying stages of attitude and decomposition, they'd been there for years. The rotting hull of the Captain Butch, an outdated long-liner, still stood, semi-upright supported by a series of obliquely angled 4 by 4 wooden shores. The stern, which pointed towards the mangroves verging on the shallow southern shore, was an open and gaping wound where the whole transom below decks had been removed to allow easy access for the cannibalization of the engine and prop-shaft fittings. Carefully by flashlight, the tires of the van bumping softly over the partially buried wooden ribs, I got almost amidships near the empty engine mounts with only a few scratches and scrapes. Close to six feet of hull extended beyond the rear of the sixteen-foot Maxi-van. For the second time that night I was thankful I'd procrastinated in removing the drop sheets from the van after Monk's office renovation. Draped over a crossbeam, completely screening the rear of the vehicle, the unusually repellent aromas clinging to it, thanks to Monk, might deter any but the most curious.

Feeling quite satisfied with my improvised garage; I was jogging back to the main building, not paying much attention to my immediate surroundings, on my way to report my cleverness to Tony. Suddenly, I came to an immediate stop. Firmly rooted to the ground, a cry of pain rising into my throat seemed to change shape while still a whimper until it became a high-pitched animal squeal. Consciousness shut down before a massive wave of pain. When I found I could think again, I was on my side, lying with my face in the dirt just inches away from my rifle. Cautiously, I reached down. My fingers found fully an inch of steel poking up through the tongue and laces of my Reeboks.

"No-oo." I groaned through tightly clenched teeth.

There were, I didn't know how many people out there trying to kill us, my best friend was injured, perhaps critically, and I'd managed to effectively take myself out through sheer stupidity.

"I...don't...need...this." The gritted words of self-recrimination didn't help much. Each movement shot burning arrows directly into my brain, as I dragged the assault rifle to me. Holding the barrel, I positioned the butt-plate against the long piece of plywood to which I'd become attached, took a couple of ragged breaths then placed my right foot onto the board in front of the pulsing mass of pain at the end of my left leg. Steeling my nerves, I took one last deep breath, held it and pushed down. My muscles vibrated. Sweat stung my eyes. I thought my lungs were going to burst.

Slowly...it felt like it was never going to end...I couldn't believe the sensations as millimeter after excruciating millimeter of the spike unsheathed itself from my flesh. Finally, as if from far away, I heard the clatter as the board fell free. Totally spent, I lay there gasping for breath; my body was bathed in sweat; the night air was chill and icily delicious. I shivered then began to tremble. I knew I had to get going or risk passing out. Nothing wanted to function. Deliberately, each move planned in advance then, through sheer willpower, I forced my limbs to comply, and crawled forward.

When Tony found me I was on my hands and knees and still some distance from the building. He half-carried me inside and lowered me into a chair. I saw him reach for an open first-aid kit, surrounded by the contents of several others, when the first rolling wave of nausea hit and washed over me.

Shock!

I'd had a similar experience once before when I was a kid at the beach and I'd stepped on a broken pop bottle under the sand. I'd nearly fainted then. This time I did.

*   *   *

There is no man so friendless
but what he can find a friend
sincere enough to tell him
disagreeable truths.

- Edward George Bulwer-Lytton, Baron Lytton

CHAPTER 39

Crunch....

Hot breath tickled my nose and drowned my face in a smell of fishy garbage. Sarge's nose was almost touching mine as he stared down intently into my eyes. I combined a friendly ruffling of his ears with a gentle, but firm, pushing away, wondering if dogs could be trained to use mouthwash.

Sarge 'hmmphed' softly at my ridiculous thought. I moved my arm into a sliver of light peeping through a loose overlap in the corrugated building skin. My watch read a little before 9:30. I'd slept-fainted for nearly five hours. I covered my eyes with my arm. Sleep pulled me back down into a soft dark place.

Crunch....

I rolled my eyes around, trying to identify the sounds that had yanked me back to consciousness. Sarge was staring intently at the outside wall directly beside me.

Crunch....

Footsteps, outside the building, were coming closer. Still tucked under my belt, the solid weight of the .45 rested lethally heavy on my stomach. I withdrew it and used both hands to quietly thumb back the hammer.

The footsteps stopped. Someone was right on the other side of the wall! I held my breath.

There was a sharp *tap* followed by a liquid *ploop* then a protracted *spattering* before the footsteps continued on at a leisurely pace in the direction of the government office, a weather-beaten Airstream trailer up on blocks near the rusting bulk tanks beside the main gate.

The pulse thudding in my ears, from having held my breath was echoed by the reverberation of raw pain from my left foot. The attempt I'd made at sitting up was no longer the issue, not crying aloud was.

"Pretty bad?"

I could only nod through the tears flooding my eyes.

Tony hunkered down beside me holding the Kalashnikov in both hands like a staff, the rifle-butt on the floor by my head, his chin resting heavily on his forearm. The word "haggard" came to mind. For the first time since I had met him he looked every one of his fifty-five years...and then some.

Then I got it! He'd stood guard over me all night.

I felt fairly useless and inept, and those were my good points.

"Just the one guard," he said, chuckling softly. "Not what I'd call the ambitious type. Three rounds since he got here; just down to the end of the breakwater and back. No deviations. No inspections. No interest. 'Smelled coffee brewing after he got here, about eight. Since then the only thing on his mind has been recycling water into the ocean."

I would've *killed* for some of that coffee. That, and a handful of painkillers. I immediately regretted my choice of words.

"The van...?" I croaked. There was something about the van. What was it? I couldn't think.

"'S Okay where it is. 'Can't be seen unless you know what you're looking for...and where to look. Good thinking, sticking it inside that boat. 'Didn't find where you'd hid it 'til almost sunup. 'Swept the tire tracks clear 'n weighted down the tarp so's the wind wouldn't move it. Otherwise, you done pretty good."

Amazing! I'd actually done something right.

"'Got Monk cleaned up a bit 'n sank what was left of his pajamas off the dock...."

He paused as if deciding on whether or not to continue. I wished he hadn't.

"Looks like he was tortured...pretty bad. 'Found some puncture marks when I cleaned him up...one of these was stuck in him."

The small object he dug from his shirt pocket resembled a large airgun dart. He dropped it into my hand. A broken stub of red plastic wire with a few fine strands of copper protruded from the blunt end. The pointy end was studded with tiny barbs.

"What is it?"

Tony took it from me, held it up in front of his face, and examined it closely.

"'Know what a 'Taser' is?" he said, lifting his eyes to meet mine.

"Some kind of stun gun, isn't it?"

"'Stands for Tom Swift's Electric Rifle."

I felt my left eyebrow stretch upwards in disbelief.

"It really is."

"Sure, and I'll still respect you in the morning."

He grunted a laugh before going on to explain how, originally developed to combat sky-jackings, the device was actually patterned on an idea from the old Tom Swift boys-adventure books. Largely due to the advent of metal detectors it had never been implemented by air security, so the inventor ended up marketing it as a non-lethal personal defense system.

"One variety, this type," he said, "shoots a pair of small electrodes attached to the handset by wire." He held the tiny dart between thumb and forefinger then spread them apart. The probe dangled from the end of his finger.

"'Figure, judging by the marks on him, they must'a used at least three of those things. 'Probably goosed him using the charging triggers until he either told them what they wanted or lost his marbles."

He waggled his finger. It hung on like an obscene electronic tick.

They left this one behind."

Tony must have thought I wanted to know as much about this technology as possible. Elaborating, he added that it was an adaptation of a torture principle developed by the Nazis, used later by the North Koreans, and lastly by both sides in "the 'Nam." He went on to say that these non-lethal devices usually ranged from 50- to 100,000-volts each, and there were ways of modifying them to cause excruciating pain instead of merely knocking someone down and rendering them helpless, as they were designed to do.

"Combined force of two or three of these things could probably scramble your brains pretty good."

I shuddered at the insane idea: A portable electroshock therapy unit, the perfect gift for those hard-to-please in-laws.

"The lights are on but nobody's home," he said, looking over at Monk, tapping the side of his head with a grimy finger. "'Hard to say how many times they lit him up, but Monk ain't right...physically he's sort of awake, but that's about all."

If Tony and Doug hadn't stolen those bags in the first place there would have been no reason for any of this. If only I'd kept my big mouth shut and resisted the impulse to bare my soul, Monk would never have been harmed. Consumed by my guilt-driven desire for vengeance, I silently swore to effect a full measure of payback for the suffering he'd been forced to endure.

"When yer up to it, I liberated some food stores. We got crackers, sardines and tap-hot instant coffee."

I made a sour face. "I caught a whiff of the sardines already, but I'll take some of that coffee."

"'You allergic to penicillin?" I shook my head, and he fished out a plastic pill bottle from a breast pocket.

"They're Monk's—interesting life style—'found a few jars of 'em at his place. 'Made up a couple improvised field kits last night with some of the stuff in here," he said, pointing to a stack of rifled first aid kits spread over one of the nearby work benches. "Oughta be able to handle just about anything shy of major surgery."

Not saying anything, I palmed and swallowed the bitter pills, washing them down with a draught of the tap-warm and vile-tasting brew. Tony looked at me expectantly, waiting. I was still thinking about my responsibility for Monk's condition. The silence, stretched, became taut.

"Why'd you guys take their stuff? Real reason." There, I'd said it. "Doug's dead, Monk may as well be. Dammit, we almost were, twice."

"You're either deaf or stupid," he said curtly. "I explained all this to you on the houseboat." He shrugged showing there was nothing else to be said on the subject.

"So we sit in the dark like a couple of mushrooms...?" No need to complete the analogy. It must have been pretty obvious I didn't believe him.

"First thing you can do is stop feeling sorry for yourself. The guy you aced last night could've killed us...he had to have been first-rate to have taken out Doug. Accept it or not, you saved our tails last night...I won't forget *that*."

His acknowledgement carried an undertone of rage. I was puzzled then the penny dropped. Most of the time I seem to wander around in a confused state with occasional flashes of intelligence, but I clearly understood his meaning.

"Maybe, I shouldn't have said anything to Monk," I capitulated, but what was I supposed to think?"

"That's your problem. I told you the truth. It's up to you to make up your own mind. But, know this: right now, understanding who and what we're dealing with is a whole-helluva lot more important than arguing about who did what and why."

I couldn't argue with that kind of logic, so I did us both a favor and shut my mouth. Tony sat on the edge of a cot adjacent to mine. He looked beat.

"Indulge me, just for a moment," he said, unable to resist picking at it, "whoever's behind this may have limited numbers...to make sure that all bases were covered last night...they might've used some local talent at Monk's."

"You mean the way the place was torn up?" What he was saying made sense, in a perverted kind of way. It had been bothering me and, bizarre as it sounded, I kept coming up with the same name.

"That was your basic dirt-bag level. The people on the beach and in the elevator wouldn't trash a place like that, and they wouldn't drink on the job. There were a lot of empties lying around, along with what looked like a home-made crack pipe and a couple of roaches."

I clearly remembered the devastation, and other than the kicked-in portrait of the General, which I thought showed a modicum of good sense, it had reeked of mindless vandalism.

"'From what you've told me about Duffy and his crew, 'sounds about their speed." Tony leaned back against a steel girder, watching me, looking for a confirmation.

I nodded slowly. Tony'd made the same connection.

"If Whitefield's conducting this, and it feels like him, it doesn't figure. If nothing else, he's a professional."

He was right! Something didn't fit. Try as I might, I couldn't make any sense out of it either.

Tony stifled a yawn, then continued. "'Figure our best bet is to move the stuff to some place we *can* control...where Doug hid it in the bay's too vulnerable...then, we can use it as bait or ransom."

Yawning, Tony set the assault rifle down on the cot beside him. Without the weapon in his hands he seemed to shrink several sizes. I could see he was fading fast. His eyes dropped shut, the sound of his breathing slowed, and the muscles in his face relaxed. I'd thought he was fast asleep until, eyes still shut, he began speaking.

"Whitefield's our number-one concern," he drawled. "'Knowing what he's capable of, we gotta start thinking about long-term insurance for ourselves, something against any kinda comebacks."

I didn't know what to say. After a moment Tony began snoring. Sarge trotted over to where I lay. After a long, silent minute of just standing and looking down at me, he dropped smoothly into a Sphinx-like position, then rested his head on my right leg. I stroked him, burying my fingers into the thick black fur at the back of his neck. He gave a deep, heart-felt sigh and closed his eyes. Within moments he was asleep, so, while they slept, I worried.

*   *   *

CHAPTER 40

Shadow patterns crept across the walls, marking the passage of time as morning stretched into afternoon. The enforced inactivity was getting to me, making me restless. Tony awakened, checked Monk's and my bandages, doled out the penicillin, and laid back down on the mattress, he seemed unable or unwilling to return to sleep; so, when asked, he began my weapons instruction. While I was shown how to dismantle, reassemble, clean, oil, and clear jams, Sarge yawned hugely, rolled over, grunted, and slept on.

Tony was a walking encyclopaedia of death. Intuitively, I knew that if we were both to survive I would need all the martial knowledge I could absorb, so I listened intently as he talked about basic tactics like flanking, fields of fire, covering fire and several simple methods of silent killing.

Despite the relative cool of the nascent tropical winter, the metal skin of the building soon absorbed and was radiating enough of the sun's energy to turn the warehouse into a low-grade sauna. Monk was heating up, too, with fever. I was becoming increasingly concerned about the condition of his wounds, which were not healing. The raw lacerations caused by the plastic bonds on his wrists and ankles wept steadily. Though we'd managed to force more penicillin into him and a fair quantity of water, it became apparent that it wasn't going to be enough. He was in serious trouble and the enforced delay in getting him proper care wasn't helping.

"We're not going to do anyone any good locked up or dead," Tony repeated again and again, patiently, irritatingly, reiterating the simple necessity of our waiting for the cover of night before moving and the importance of his being free to go after our "insurance policy." Then, and only then, would I be allowed to tend to Monk's needs.

Tonight, I silently vowed to my unconscious friend, I'd get him to the emergency ward and figure some way to get him safely admitted. His condition would raise too many questions and red flags to simply carry him in through the front door. I needed a plan but couldn't think of one.

Later, after a meager lunch, Tony insisted we use our down time to assess the contents of the vast warehouse, to see what there was that could serve our needs. Stacked on pallets and racks, on either side of four aisles running the length of the hundred and fifty-foot building, were groupings of equipment, parts, and assorted bits and pieces. From marine fittings to emergency pumps and gasoline generators, there was something of everything housed under the sheet metal roof.

Charlie was—*had been* organized. Surrounded with the harvest of the work he loved, I missed him more deeply than ever. I'd helped him amass a good quantity of these strange odds and ends; the storage layout was largely due to our joint planning.

"Primacord. All-ll ri-ight!" Tony crowed in a whisper, almost doing a victory dance, as he pulled one of several spools of detonation cord from the locker Charlie'd used to secure hazardous materials.

"Grab ten of those empty paint cans, and bring 'em over." My foot was aching like somebody'd used it for an anvil, but I limped over and set them down beside a row of five-gallon plastic pails filled with nuts, bolts, and assorted metal fasteners. Tony cut the Primacord into ten sections, each about eight feet in length, and while I scooped handfuls of fittings and fasteners into the cans, he laid in tight curls of the waxy cord.

"I get *what* we're doing, but *why?*" Curiosity had gotten the better of me.

"'Poor man's claymores." He saw the confused look on my face.

"Booby traps, child. Det-cord's used to ignite bigger explosives, but it'll do the job. Look, we may need a door we can slam shut behind us in a hurry if someone's on our tails. These little gems could make the difference between us surviving or not."

The purpose behind the ropes, hooks, spools of wire, and pulley blocks he'd assembled was fairly obvious, but some of the stuff made no sense at all, at first.

The sound of the guard's pickup truck had long since vanished down the roadway before Tony deemed it safe enough for us to get on with constructing our escape route.

I watched from below as he scaled a steel girder leading up into the system of open beams, where, with easy confidence, he walked the narrow flanges overhead while I hobbled underneath tying the deadly pails to the lines he lowered. Then came the tricky part, connecting them to the electrical system. I found then killed the appropriate breakers, so that Tony could connect the explosives to the wiring junctions. When he was finished there were still two pails left, one each designated for the rear exit and the small Judas-gate in the bay door. He assured me they'd "make dandy burglar alarms."

I shuddered. "Dandy" was not the first word that came to mind, when I thought of what case-hardened steel shrapnel could do to a human body.

Having rigged a simple knife-switch in such a way that the circuit would close when the door was opened, the last thing we'd do on our way out would be connect a couple marine batteries to the remaining two charges, making them independent of the main system. I didn't like the thought of leaving armed explosive devices behind us until I thought about finding Doug's body in the houseboat. That made it a little easier but not by much.

While Tony picked over the diving gear, Sarge accompanied me outside.

Looking west at the dying rays of the sun, my mind's eye saw the daily ritual at the Mallory Docks. I'd often smirked at the foolishness of tourists and locals alike who gathered, reverently, to observe the solar event as if the sun couldn't properly set unless duly witnessed; some straining for a glimpse of the signature of a perfect pelagic sunset, the elusive "emerald flash". I would have given a lot to be one of those fools right then, wondering what were the odds of my seeing another sunset.

Under a concealing wrap of canvas, used to disguise the telltale features of the assault rifle, I eased the selector switch down two clicks, from safety to semi-auto, then started across the compound.

Each step was a painful reminder of my carelessness the night before. Nearing the improvised garage I noticed Sarge had stopped to inspect a thick strip of plywood bristling with a row of sixteen-penny nails. My stomach did a quick tilt.

"Come on, I see it."

Sarge looked up then turned his attention back to one noticeably darker nail. He gave the blood-streaked point a final sniff then looked up at me before ambling over to walk at my side. Characteristic of my normal outside-the-box sense of humor, this prompted a spontaneous, albeit queasy, chuckle.

"If you're so smart, where were you last night?"

No sooner had the words left my mouth than that final image of Doug filled my thoughts. No doubt, had Sarge been with his owner instead of with me, Doug might still be alive.

Sometimes, lately it seemed much too frequently, I say things so monumentally stupid that I wish I hadn't spoken.

After carefully scanning the mangroves at the water's edge, I limped around the shelter, checking for any signs of tampering while Sarge patiently sat by the tarp, yawning as he waited for me to get on with it. Satisfied by my own observations and reinforced by Sarge's tacit approval, I retrieved the van, hung the concealing tarp back in place, and headed for the warehouse.

With our weapons and three sets of BC's and air tanks stowed in the center cargo area, Tony and I carefully loaded Monk aboard the sleeping deck in the rear of the van. He seemed to be resting but his face was hot to the touch, too hot.

The padlock snapped shut with a heavy bronze *chunk*, so with the gates behind us securely locked; the unknown looming ahead, I looked back at the comparative quiet of the boat yard and sighed.

Swinging up into the driver's chair, I became aware of a thrilling blend of excitement and dread stirring inside of me. Maybe, I thought, what I was experiencing was a preliminary shot of adrenaline, a taste of things to come.

* * *

And Time, a maniac scattering dust,
And Life, a Fury slinging flame.

- Alfred, Lord Tennyson

CHAPTER 41

I eased over and pulled to the side of the road. Wearing a wet suit under a baggy pair of coveralls, in preparation for his part of the night's maneuvers, Tony was screened from view by the bulk of the van's large body as he exited from the side cargo doors. I heard the small avalanches of dirt and gravel that preceded him down to where he cached a dry change of clothes at the base of the Cow Key Bridge. It was the make-for point he'd selected earlier. In case I was delayed or taken out, he wouldn't be wandering around wearing a rubber suit. I didn't much care for the sentiment, but I understood the logic.

Several minutes later, when we entered the Garrison Bight drive-around, I was pleased to note that none of the crew hands hanging around the charter boat docks had given us more than a passing glance. Their attention, now that their day clients had gone, was more inner directed. I'd caught an errant whiff of ganja emanating from the group as we rolled past heading down to the far end of the parking lot. I pulled into the last space beside the channel narrows, the cargo doors faced the water. We were well into the heavy shadow of the two-lane arch overhead that led down to Old Town.

Tony stripped off the coveralls then finished applying a black, non-glare compound to his face, neck, and the backs of his hands. He climbed over the low stone wall and lowered himself into the water. I handed down scuba gear along with a CO_2-powered spear gun and spare shafts; the shark-feeding episode was still fresh in both of our minds.

Having rehearsed our basic and contingency plans to the extent that we knew each other's timetable by heart, there were no farewells. One moment he was there, then there was only a track of bubbles disappearing in the distance.

*　　　*　　　*

CHAPTER 42

Owing to an almost obsessive attention to detail, the time he'd spent poring over the harbor charts earlier that afternoon at the warehouse, allowed Tony a relatively direct and unimpeded passage through the narrow strait that joined the Garrison Bight harbor to Fleming Bay. Aided by an ebb tide, it was a fast trip, despite the burden of two extra scuba outfits. After twenty minutes he stopped swimming, removed his mask before surfacing to check his bearings. The extra caution, perhaps, wasn't necessary but Tony Amundsen hadn't survived the countless shit storms life had thrown at him by not understanding the rules attendant to Murphy's Law or scrupulously following them. He checked position. Finding he'd drifted a little, thanks to the same current that aided our escape on the previous night, he sank with hardly a ripple to mark his passing. The surface exposure had been so limited anyone looking might have confused the minimal disturbance with a harbor Tarpon breaking the skin of the water.

Replacing and clearing his mask beneath the surface, Tony moved unerringly toward the outermost fringe of houseboat moorings.

The repository for the contraband had been selected with care. Almost a thousand yards away from Doug's floating mausoleum, close to Rat Key, the small hump of land in the middle of the bay, was the burned out hulk of another houseboat. All that was left were a few jagged and blackened timbers stabbing up out of the water; it was a two-year-old relic of a teenage rave party that had gotten way out of control. A County Commissioner's son, so the story went, who was responsible for the unauthorized use and destruction of someone's floating vacation home, had received merely a slap on the wrist. Word was that he was currently studying Political Science at Gainesville, no doubt intending to carry on the family tradition.

Bleeding air from his vest, Tony sank slowly to the bottom then turned on his diving light for the first time. It took a few minutes to find, then secure a safety line to one of the anchor blocks, and swim in ever widening spirals to the end of the rope. The "tetherball" technique allowed him to quickly locate the debris that had fallen through the burned-out remains above. The bundles were supposed to be stashed inside the refrigerator. In the murky light, Tony could see the freezer was empty. Keeping a little to one side, using the tip of his spear gun, he prodded the bottom door open. A green blur exploded forward. Tony grinned around his mouthpiece, appreciating Doug's delicate sense of humor. The resident moray eel sulked in one corner as Tony hooked the packs out at the end of a spear-shaft. Using the last of the air in his tank, Tony unshackled the packs from the weights, secured them to one of the spare air tank harnesses, then changed into the reserve. He inflated the Buoyancy Compensator vests until both he and the contraband were sufficiently weightless to be carried off with the current, allowing him to conserve energy and air.

*   *   *

CHAPTER 43

Chloroform, disinfectant and mortality, nothing else, thank goodness, smells quite like a hospital. The stink made my nostrils twitch and filled my mind with the jumbled memories of a place and time that haunts my dreams still. I pushed the demons back into their box and made a quick survey of the barren halls of medicine. The emergency ward of the small private hospital was vacant, as were the adjoining passageways. Only the admissions desk was occupied; the nurse was comfortably busy simultaneously chatting on the telephone and sorting files. Loafing in an anteroom watching a football game on a small TV, while inhaling a box of gooey donuts, was a spongy looking white-haired guy in a green rent-a-cop uniform; he appeared to have his agenda locked down, so I was fairly confident he wouldn't be interfering with mine.

I peeked around the corner and found what I was looking for; three gurneys and two wheelchairs stood unattended against the wall near the entrance. Perfect! This was going to be easier than I'd dared hope. Everything I wanted to do would be well out of anyone's line of sight.

I'd parked the van adjacent to, but not directly in front of the emergency entrance to simplify unloading Monk, figuring all I'd need were a few seconds grace to get him inside. Someone would be bound to find him before too long and get him the care and attention he needed. I sneaked one of the wheeled tables out into the parking lot easily enough, but I was forced to go slower than I'd wanted; anything other than a dead crawl over the coarse blacktop started the wheels jiggling, and set the gurney to ringing and clanging like a Chinese cymbal parade. Added to that, each left footstep was fast becoming an ordeal.

Monk was insensible and therefore uncomplaining when I tried to shift him aboard, by the same token he was more awkward than I'd anticipated. I started to sweat as my efforts to move him onto the gurney were frustrated by the dead weight of his flaccid body; like trying to balance a hundred-and-fifty-pound bag of Jell-O.

"Yo, lemme give you some help," a rapidly approaching voice called out from behind me. I was bent over holding Monk around the chest, his head faced back over my left shoulder, in the direction of the lit entrance. I forced myself to continue my efforts without showing any trace of the panic that clutched at my heart. I turned slightly and saw a male nurse tucking the pack and a loose cigarette into his pocket as he approached.

Presumably, having snuck out for a quick smoke, he was now all business and heading right for me. I wanted to run so badly it hurt, and it would have; each time I put my weight on my left foot I saw stars. Instead, I grunted my assent nodding as I made a production of almost losing the gurney, as I tried to lift Monk aboard.

Training asserting itself; he caught the frame as it started to roll away and steadied it with his foot as he took hold of Monk's legs and lifted. I managed to keep my back towards him as I stabilized the other set of wheels. Together, we shifted Monk onto the padded top.

"What's wrong with him?" he asked, moving closer and lifting Monk's eyelid.

"He's got a bad fever, I think. I'm going to park out of the way. I'll be right back. Can you get someone to look at him right away? Please?" I said, climbing into the van, hopefully misdirecting his attention.

In long-sleeved sweats, Monk's suspicious looking wounds might escape notice long enough for me to make my escape. Otherwise, I would probably end up trying to answer some awkward questions. The guard I'd seen inside might have borne more than a passing resemblance to the Pillsbury Doughboy, but the gun on his belt made him someone I wanted to avoid at all costs.

Ever so carefully, I eased the van back out of the emergency zone, all the while watching the nurse out of the corner of my eye. The instant he turned his back to wheel Monk inside, I drove down to the street and accelerated off to keep my next appointment.

*   *   *

CHAPTER 44

Tony surfaced several hundred yards offshore. Scouting the area around the Cow Key Bridge, everything appeared normal; no shadows with guns lurked in the bushes or under the concrete span. The matte-black headgear and face-dark gave off no reflection as he ventured closer. About fifty yards short of the bridge footings he stopped. Treading water, the Buoyancy Compensator helped him hold position with a minimum of effort with only his head exposed, as he maintained a comfortable shore watch waiting for me to arrive at our rendezvous.

*   *   *

O wad some Power the giftie gie us
To see oursels as ithers see us!
It wad frae monie a blunder free us

- To a louse, Robert Burns

CHAPTER 45

I'd pulled the big van well over to the side of the road just beyond the horizontal guardrails after the bridge span. The side cargo door was unlocked and left an inch or two ajar for Tony. I was in front of the open hood wearing *the look*, which every man—no matter how mechanically incompetent—has used a variation of at one time or another. Simply, it declares to one and all: "I have almost figured out which of the thousand-odd parts is responsible for my being here and am about to make that critical adjustment that will rectify the problem, so don't bother to stop and offer help because I have the situation well under control." It's something only another man would accept at face value, and a generous woman might pretend to believe.

If I hadn't been expecting the tiny spark from the water it would have gone unnoticed. I gave an answering flash with the Mini Mag-lite concealed under my arms, which were crossed in serious automotive contemplation.

There is something about the combination of red and blue flashing lights that causes an immediate reflection on one's sins, a rapid drain of confidence, and an overwhelming sense of impending doom.

Either I was a pathetic actor, or I had unknowingly adopted the appearance of someone needing an immediate interface with a servant of the public, because, within seconds of hearing Tony move up the embankment from the water and into the bushes next to the van, a passing Monroe County Sheriff's car slowed, pulled over, and backed up in front of the Dodge.

"Watch out!" I hissed desperately, hoping Tony would hear. "Cops!"

I foresaw my own imminent arrest on a variety of charges ranging from murder to smuggling. Perhaps, I hadn't been half as clever as I'd thought when I'd left Monk at the hospital. My head swirled with all of the mistakes I'd made and laws I'd broken, my shoulders automatically slumped in surrender. At the very least I was guilty of manslaughter and transporting a small armory in the van. All the possible excuses I could use to explain my involvement and innocence sounded like so much bad fiction. I had to get a grip. My imagination was making things worse than they already were, or so I thought until the door swung wide.

"Oh no!" I whispered under my breath.

I watched the officer get out, in stages, dwarfing the patrol car. He was every bad joke about red-necked sheriffs come to life, and then some. The last time I'd seen anything that looked that big it was hovering over the Macy's New Year's Day parade. The size 16-plus cowboy boots and wide-brimmed Stetson did nothing to diminish the impression. He was big all over, even his head, which looked like the leftovers from a Hallowe'en party gone wrong, being roughly the same shape and size as a Jack-o'-lantern. Bright blue eyes squinted out from his creased and seamed pumpkin-head. The squint, if it was a home-grown attempt to emulate Dirty Harry, worked. I *was* intimidated.

Gravel crunched under his boots as he approached. The closer he came, the greater my feeling of being trapped.

"What's goin' on, heah?"

Blossoms of perspiration exploded all over my body.

"It wasn't my faul—" I blurted.

Fool! My mind hollered. Why not just hold out your wrists for the cuffs?

"... uh, it, it just stopped—I think it maybe, uh, overheated."

"Y'all want me to call you a tow?"

What a dope I was to panic; he was buying it. My fear sweat turned clammy and squirmed maddeningly down under my shirt.

"No!" I said, sounding a little too anxious. "That's okay, I, uh, it'll probably start if I just let it cool down a bit, I'm just heading to my, um, to my girlfriend's place...it's only a few blocks away."

'Nice touch,' I congratulated myself, overlooking the mumbles and stutters.

A muffled thump came from inside the van, as it rocked.

My heart stopped! The cop had noticed it, too.

"Somebody in there with you? That your gal?"

I could hear him asking me questions but I didn't know what to say, so I said nothing.

Suspicious, his cop sensors twitching and quivering, his little eyes squinted even tighter as he ushered me away from traffic to the offside of the van. His hand rested on his pistol butt. The restraining strap, I noticed, was off and dangling. The gun was just barely in its holster.

My first impulse had been to cut and run, but the standard issue Clint- Eastwood firearm at his side rendered running a moot point. Did I really want to "make his day"? I didn't think so either.

'Okay, dummy,' the contemptuous critic in my mind demanded, 'explain the guy in the diving suit, the weapons, and don't forget to mention the dripping bags of drugs.'

Shit. Shit! SHIT! I couldn't believe it. Why had Tony risked sneaking on board? No! He was smarter than that. Sarge! It must have been Sarge moving around in there, but I couldn't open the doors. There were weapons and God-knows-what under only a loose cover. What am I going to do? My mind or what was left of it refused to cooperate.

"I, uh—"

'Brilliant, just brilliant,' chimed the critic.

"I asked y'all, 'you got anyone in there...?'"

"It's uh, my, m-my dog," I finally managed to stammer out.

"Y'all move down to where I can see you 'n' grab aholt of your veehicle...

I leaned against the van, as much to steady my shaking knees as to comply.

"...both hands, SIR."

Facing the van, I assumed the position as ordered. Keeping one eye on me, he reached up and began to ease the side door open.

Like a jack-in-the-box from Hell, Sarge's snarling jaws roared out within inches of his face.

"Sarge! No-oo!" I shouted.

The gun was out of the holster as he back-pedaled rapidly, skittering over the loose gravel. The cop looked totally freaked. He looked ready to kill.

"Please! No! Don't shoot! He won't hurt you."

Having come to rest with his butt against the guardrail, he was traversing his long-barreled pistol—it looked big enough to be a deck gun—back and forth from Sarge to myself, narrowing focus, centering on me as I edged over to stand between Sarge and that huge cannon. No way I was going to let Sarge get hurt on account of my stupidity. Suddenly, the cop's huge shoulders began quivering. I watched in horror, as the tremors spread over the rest of his body, like the slow-motion onset of an earthquake.

'Ohhh no-o-o,' I wailed inside. I knew he was going to kill me.

The cop's mouth became a raw scar twisting across his face—he could've scared barracudas out of the water. Then, from someplace way down deep inside of his vast belly, a braying nasal laugh came hooting out.

"Hyunh—Hyunh—Hyunh. Boy...you don't know how close you got to gettin' that dog of yourn shot? That'd be a 'dum' shame, I-tell-you-what. 'Cause he's a good looker.

"Look-a-here," he said, laughter still in his voice, "whyn't you try starting your rig 'n' if it still don't work, I'll give you a lift over to your gal's place, and see y'all get a tow. Go on now, give her a try." He said, holstering the cannon, laughing: "'He won't hurt you,' Hyunh—Hyunh."

No longer trusting my mouth; there was no telling what might come out of it next, I nodded my agreement. Taking as much time as possible I closed the side door, gimped around to the front of the van on shaky legs, closed the hood then climbed up into the driver's seat. Stalling, hoping against hope that he'd leave.

Please! I begged, go for donuts; get an urgent call...anything.

Hands on his hips, he waited. There was no mistaking his intent; I couldn't delay any longer without his offering any more assistance. I turned the key and started the engine then honked and waved my thanks. He came over beside my door, a neutral smile on his face.

Listening to the engine, he said, "'Sounds okay. You go on ahead, I'll be right behind, 'case you have any problems on the way," then walked back to his patrol car, got in, honked and flashed his lights.

I edged out onto the road. He merged right behind and began to follow. But, where could I go? Maybe, I could pick a house at random and try to bluff it out, maybe ask to borrow the phone?

'Yeah, right, with a cop car sitting out in front,' agreed the cynic.

"Now what?" I asked myself aloud.

"Turn right then make another right at the second street after the stop sign." Tony's voice came through the curtains behind the front seat.

"What're you doing to me? There's a cop right on my tail. What am I gonna do?"

"Turn here...then right, there...there you go...now up ahead—over there in front of that green Audi...park there then get out natural-like, like you belong here. This's my—Marisha's—my ex's place. Just walk on in like you own the joint. She never locks her doors. I'll be in to explain as soon as he splits. You better hurry before that cop decides you're not real. And remember: act natural."

*　　　*　　　*

Necessity is the mother of taking chances.

- Roughing It, Mark Twain

CHAPTER 46

I'd done a lot of strange things in my time and this was right up there with the best of them. There was a slight movement of curtains at the window, as I walked through the front gate of the two-story split-level and came up the walk. A moment later, the front door swung open; a tall, attractive, big-boned woman stepped out. I became keenly aware of her full lips and the long sweep of her thick honey-blond hair as the gap between us narrowed. Her eyes widened when she began to realize that (a) I was a complete stranger, and (b) I had no intention of stopping to introduce myself before attempting to sell her a vacuum cleaner, a set of encyclopaedias, or ask if she'd found Jesus.

I put my arms around her, tightly pinning hers to her sides, and kissed her full on her gorgeous mouth, which had begun to open in protest. Using my momentum, before she could react, I moved both of us inside the house then released her to pull the door shut behind me. The loud slam of the door coincided with the annihilating slam of a hard knee into my groin.

"Tony's—" I gasped, my insides turned to water, my legs melted, and cold beads of sweat popped out on my forehead; crushing pain only a heartbeat away "—in the car." The words whistled out as I sank to the floor.

When I dared open my eyes again, the first thing I saw through a blur of tears was the black hole of a gun barrel right in front of my nose. Two angry blue eyes were directly above the sight on the barrel.

Having guns pointed at me was getting to be a bad habit; one I wanted to avoid.

"Alright, asshole, who the fuck do you think you're supposed to be?"

Hark! The fair young flower speaks.

Who *did* I think I was, I wondered? Before I could begin to come up with an answer, a large hand clamped over her mouth as another closed over her gun hand, twisting it up and away from my face. Without letting go of the gun, Tony pulled the fighting, kicking, wild-cat into the living room then spun her around and down onto the couch. She made a grab for a heavy ashtray, to slam into his head, but his grip on her captive hand prevented her from reaching it. Instantly, she turned ready to launch herself at her captor, nails ready to scratch and claw, until she saw who it was and stopped. Breathing heavily, her attitude tense and belligerent, she wrenched her hand free.

Tony seemed to inspire a desire for distance in those who knew him closely. Similar to Sarge, when he sat she removed herself to the maximum distance allowed by the couch.

Directly across from me, I thought I saw the shadow of a smirk flit across her features as I tenderly eased myself into a sitting position in the hallway. Back against the wall, legs spread wide, I listened to Tony's condensed version of the last few days that caused us to be there. It was a good thing he'd kept hold of the gun because she wasn't accepting any part of it. When he paused at the end of his narrative, Marisha leaned forward and unloaded a solid roundhouse left to the side of his head that rocked him. She stood, looking down on him with utter contempt, then left, ostensibly to check on the children who'd started calling out from another part of the house. I wasn't entirely sure she hadn't gone for another gun and wouldn't come back blazing away. Since, Tony'd already displayed an uncanny ability to produce a wide assortment of weaponry at a moment's notice, maybe, I wondered if that ability didn't extend to his ex-wife.

The side of Tony's face, already starting to swell, glared hotly in the hallway light when he came over to where I was, and offered to help me up. Not sure that "up" is where I wanted to be, I feebly waved him off.

"Damn you...!" Marisha was back, and with all the ferocity of a wild she-bear protecting her cubs from bestially-inclined sodomites. Fortunately, I'd noted, she carried no firearms.

"I told you I didn't want you *'dropping in'* whenever you feel like it. Now you're messing around with that shit again...after you swore up and down you were through. You stupid sonuva—! Where the hell d'you come off bringing that kind of trouble into my home again? What the fuck's wrong with you? Is your head buried that far up your ass? 'You trying get the kids sent to a foster home? I knew you were crazy, but you've set a new record, buster. And, if that's not bad enough, this no-good, shit-for-brains, lowlife *friend* of yours, forces his way into *my* house, and tries to rape me...."

"I'm not a 'lowlife,'" I protested silently.

As the decibel level and her fury approached critical mass, I decided that inside was perhaps not the best place to be. Gingerly, I rolled onto my hands and knees then carefully made my way through the kitchen and out the back door. Once outside, thanks to the aid and support of a friendly handrail, I practiced breathing and standing at the same time. My respite was short-lived. Coincident with the screen door clacking shut behind me, a hand grabbed my upper arm, as Tony pulled me down the garden path. I wondered, as I struggled to keep up, if I would ever walk normally again.

*   *   *

If, of all sound words of tongue and pen,
The saddest are, "It might have been,"
More sad are these we daily see:
"It is, but hadn't ought to be!"

- Francis Brett Hart

CHAPTER 47

The air was sweet with the fragrance of night-blooming jasmine from the overgrown hedge bordering the neighboring yards. After a half-hour standing, hidden in a small stand of banana trees about eighty feet from the house, I had almost completed the evolutionary process of achieving a fully vertical (the word 'erect' never entered my mind) position. I didn't mind the inactivity. Standing still, after Marisha's tender attentions to my manhood, was my idea of having a good time.

Tony, I hoped, was using the time to evaluate the validity of her accusations. I could only guess at how much our coming here had cost him. He still cared deeply for her that much had been clear, because of that the scathing rebukes she'd used to lash him had hit their mark. That there was more than a little truth in her charges, would only add to the sting of what was apparently an old and familiar knife twisting in a wound that might never heal. Those who have once shared a great love know exactly how and where to slip the blade to achieve the most damage with the least effort.

I soon began to feel awkward, as if intruding on the privacy of his thoughts, so I made my way up past the side of the house to the street. Mercifully, the Sheriff's car was gone and Marisha stayed inside.

Sarge and I waited for close to an hour before Tony joined us. Presumably, he'd arrived at some sort of truce with his past. Though, just for the briefest of moments, while driving away, I'd thought I'd seen the glisten of a tear sliding down his face before he twisted around to look backwards. When he turned back again and there was no sign, I thought maybe I'd imagined it.

*　　*　　*

CHAPTER 48

We were nearing the fork in the road that led to the fishing docks on one side and down the long road past the wreckers to the impound docks on the other where, by mutual consent, the driving lights were extinguished and the NVGs switched on.

There were no such things as shadows in this strange luminous world. There were only varying grades of cool bluish-green. Almost like being underwater, everything took on an unearthly glaucous hue except for the blurry, eye-scorching flares of the waterfront security lights. Though the distorted depth perception of the Night Vision optics precipitated a creeping headache after only a few minutes' exposure, Tony insisted they gave us an edge we needed. It was an edge I was about to appreciate.

Once locked inside the impound yard I dropped Tony, carrying the four backpacks, at the warehouse then stowed the van inside the improvised boat-hull garage. I'd only just keyed the engine off and was about to turn and move toward the rear doors when Sarge suddenly gripped my wrist in his mouth and clamped down, hard. Something was wrong, besides my being in danger of losing an arm. I froze and, the instant I did, he released me. Sarge had wanted my complete attention and he'd gotten it. Spiders of fear skittered over my nerve endings. What had he heard? Was there an unknown threat? Everything had seemed secure as I'd driven across the yard.

"What is it, Sarge? What is it, boy?" I asked softly, feeling like an idiot, like I expected him to answer.

Sarge moved to the rear of the van and waited for me to open the door for him. As soon as he jumped down, he went into his sphinx-like position then looked back at me over his shoulder. I picked up the AK-47. If he wanted to play follow-my-leader who was I to argue? Sarge'd been consistent in making the right moves even if I hadn't. The worst I could do, I figured, would be to make a fool of myself. And since I'd been doing that with considerable regularity, once more, I figured, wasn't going to make much difference.

Sarge trotted off at an angle, down toward the mangroves along the northern shoreline on the right where he waited for me. Following him was painful, but I was surprisingly quieter than I'd previously thought myself capable.

He'd stopped in the outer fringe and was steadily staring at the far end of the row of deteriorating boat hulls, which had been obscured by the bulk of our improvised garage. I didn't see anything, but I took the precaution of fitting the blocky sound suppressor onto the barrel.

Silence, I was learning, was a good thing.

A low grumble of thunder next to my ear caused me to look up. About seventy yards away, I saw a piece of one of the smaller derelict boats break off and assume human form as it ran towards the make-shift garage, angling in to get behind us. I sent Sarge off along our intended path, and he made an unusual amount of noise to mark his progress: wooden *thunks*, scrapes, scuffling gravel and the metallic rattle of a tin can, as it bounced along the coral. When I heard him rustling his way through another large stand of mangroves, further along the shoreline, I saw our shadow figure slip from cover and make directly for my place of concealment.

Stealthily, steadily, he came closer; his focus was intent on the direction Sarge had taken. He wasn't wearing light-gathering optics and the meager amount of illumination from the thinly horned quarter moon gave little assistance to the naked eye. I could hear his breathing when he stopped directly opposite me. He began to move forward until the uncompromising pressure of the silenced muzzle, hard against his throat, instantly froze him in place.

"Talk to me," I whispered harshly, then eased the gun barrel back slightly. The stunned expression of fear slithered into a cunning, sly expression almost hidden below the brim of his canvas hat. I saw, clearly, as a jade-green hand slowly reached for the darker green hilt of a knife strapped blade-up in a shoulder sheath worn under an army field jacket. It was a practiced and natural movement; if I hadn't been wearing the NVGs I would have been blind to his intent and probably dead within the next few seconds.

A flat, toneless bark, not much louder than dropping a book onto a table, was followed by a pinging ring as the ejected cartridge struck and bounced in progressively smaller hops across the ground. Part of the hand he'd been leaning on had disintegrated behind a spray of fragments. Crumpling into a trembling protective huddle over the bits of flesh that were still attached to his wrist where his thumb had been, he keened a horribly stifled, choking rasp. The real pain that would start him howling and wailing was, for the moment, buried under a numbing blanket of shock. I jammed the barrel into his face, breaking several teeth. This time I got his full attention.

"Talk or die, asshole...last chance!" I hissed. I'd recognized him when the denim hat had fallen off. One of Duffy's playmates from the job site. This was probably one of the animals that had brutalized Monk and trashed his apartment. These guys, here; now; it explained much.

I took his knife from the sheath then questioned him. His answers confirmed my suspicions and fears; Sarge and I were outnumbered, outgunned, and the clock was ticking. A muffled squawk came from his jacket. I patted the pockets and found a half-pint of liquor and a cheap 2- way radio, not much larger than a pack of cigarettes. An idea began to take shape.

Once I'd determined he had little left to tell me I encouraged him, with his own blade tight against his throat, to radio for help from one of his fellow sentries. The story I gave him involved his stepping on a nail and being unable to free himself. Not original but plausible, and the pain in his voice transmitted well. When I saw another figure detach itself from the shadows behind a storage building and head towards our position, I thanked him then returned his knife.

The killing was getting easier, especially when I thought of Doug and Charlie and Monk.

The second sentry responded to my waving from a bent over position by the scrub bush. The fractional moonlight showed him only my general shape and movement; I was hunched over as if in pain, trying to look as if I was concentrating on an impaled foot—no great stretch of my imagination or limited acting ability. I watched his approach from under the brim of my borrowed hat and recognized him as another of the four Horsemen from the construction site; Famine, I thought. I moaned loudly as he clapped a hand on my shoulder, called me a clumsy fuck-up, and asked after the whereabouts of my quarry.

Twisting my torso from its bent posture, I pivoted quickly. The expression on his face blanked with incomprehension as the killing-knife entered the soft delta of flesh just above the Adam's apple and drove upward into his brain. A quick left-right pivot of the hilt scrambled his brains and flooded my hand with a warm glut of blood while greasing the blade for easy withdrawal. I caught his body as it started to fall and lowered it quietly to the ground where it gave a few desultory twitches and kicks, then nothing.

Along with how to kill efficiently with a knife, "...the secret," Tony'd instructed me, "to moving with relative impunity through virtually any situation..." was acting relaxed, like you belonged.

Calmly—outwardly that is—I moved openly in the same direction Sarge had taken. As I was about the same size as the last sentry, with his baseball cap perched on my head and wearing his dark jacket, I could pass for him until I was too close for it to make a difference. I'd regretted leaving the sound-suppressed assault rifle behind because even in the faint moonlight the distinctive shape of the 30-round banana-clip might easily give me away. Instead, I carried the pump-action shotgun belonging to the late-Famine in one hand; the long-bladed killing-knife was held close to my leg in the other. For back up, the familiar weight of Charlie's Colt .45 was tucked under my belt.

A chillingly vicious rumble stiffened the hairs at the back of my neck. I discovered Sarge standing above the head of the third sentinel, Pestilence, who lay flat on his back softly blubbering and shivering in terror.

After questioning and finding him a cipher with nothing to add to my information pool, I killed him.

It was done nonchalantly, indifferently. I was wiping the knife clean on his clothing when a sudden clench of nausea caught my very core and threatened to turn me inside out, as I lost the meager contents of my stomach. I wasn't the cold-blooded killer I'd thought I needed to be. My tongue was thick with the rank and coppery taste of fear, death and vomit; my knees were wobbly from the intensity of my reaction; an invisible shaft of heat in my left foot throbbed and pounded in sync with a blinding pulse behind my eyes. Not only was I sickened by what I had turned into, but deeply terrified of what lay ahead. Only the knowledge of Duffy's potential for brutality spurred me onward.

Together, Sarge and I crept around the periphery of the yard to the channel-side of the warehouse. I wedged a wooden pallet to block the rear door then moved around to the front. Only Duffy and one of his crew, my interrogations had confirmed, remained inside with their prisoner. With my capture all but assured they were supposedly waiting for the imminent arrival of the "Big Boss," so I probably didn't have much time to do whatever it was that I was going to do.

*   *   *

CHAPTER 49

The borrowed field jacket muffled the snick-snick of easing a round into the pistol's chamber. Having come to a decision about how to proceed, I'd stood the shotgun against the wall then removed my goggles to let my eyes adjust to the night. For what I had in mind, they'd be more a hindrance than help. When I took them off my vision tilted and so did my equilibrium. I hunkered down on one knee to avoid falling over. My face was sweat-soaked and my heart thundered inside my chest.

Time, salt corrosion, and rust had coarsened the corrugated sheet metal with barnacles of decay. Its texture was rough to the touch as I leaned against the warehouse and tried to catch my breath. My mouth was foul with the taste of bile accented with the metallic tang of terror.

Sarge whimpered softly, reminding me that there wasn't any time for self-indulgence. I nodded my head in agreement. Sarge looked at me as if I was losing my mind. He wasn't far off the mark, I decided.

Holding his collar, I gave it a quick shake to get his attention then pointed to the door, and gave a forward tug towards the building.

"Ready!" I whispered close to his ear, hoping he'd gotten the idea.

Sarge cocked his head to one side, looking intently at me like I was from another planet, or maybe a pork chop in disguise.

"We got him! We got him!" I mumbled into the radio then switched it off and put it down.

Seconds later, a vibrating growl began under my fingers, where they rested in Sarge's neck fur, which was closely followed by the sharp grate of a latch being slipped then the juicy twang of oiled springs. The Judas-door began to open. Sarge's muscles bunched and tightened. My hands were suddenly slick with sweat. I wiped them on my pants leg. When I reached back for Sarge, he was gone. Just then, Duffy's large, lump of an accomplice, shotgun in hand, stepped out into the yard. He stopped and turned his back to me to hold the door for someone behind him to step through. I reached for my shotgun. In my nervousness, I knocked it over. It fell with a rattling clatter. The instant he began to turn in search of the cause of the noise I'd made, he was blown off his feet, blasted backwards by a flying black and tan block of muscle that exploded into his chest. Quickly, I angled out and away from the building, pulling the pistol and holding it two-handed as I hobbled in a low shooter's stance.

The timing couldn't have been better. Duffy had been caught in mid-step, half-in and half-out of the door when Sarge took out his man. Duffy tried to hold the door open for light, so he could find the dropped shotgun; his attention was centered on his accomplice and the large Rottweiler viciously mauling him. I drew a bead on where his heart should be and started to exert a slow, even pressure on the trigger. With only seconds to live, Duffy fumbled in the dirt for the weapon. The moment he straightened up he would die. My hands began shaking. I didn't think I could do this. Suddenly, Duffy flew forward, his face plowed a trench in the hard coral. Right behind him, trailing pieces of yellow rope from his wrists, Tony stepped directly into my line of fire.

"Move!"

Eyes glaring with a cold fire, a feral snarl twisting his mouth into a savage mask, Tony spun to face me. Immediately, understanding what had happened, he reined in the killer-ego. Stepping aside, he never lost track of Duffy, who lay motionless face down in the dirt.

Guarded by Sarge, the untidy lump of an accomplice lay nearby, unconscious or unmoving from either concussion or fright.

Realizing I was still holding the pistol with an almost desperate ferocity, I relaxed my grip. As my arm dropped to my side, Duffy's outstretched hands suddenly darted for the shotgun. The roar of the Colt sledge-hammered the air. A spray of dust and coral exploded less than an inch in front of his fingers. He let out a yelp and quickly pulled his hands back and covered his head.

The expression on Tony's face was a mixture of admiration and approval, as he softly applauded my marksmanship.

I didn't let him know that I'd been aiming for Duffy's head.

* * *

**The more I see of men,
the better I like dogs.**

- Mme. Roland

CHAPTER 50

"Fatboy brought all kindsa goodies," Tony drawled, pulling a fistful of cable-ties from a cheap plastic gym bag. "Some of the stuff," he threw me an odd look, which I couldn't decipher, "might look kinda familiar," he said, before whizzing it across the concrete floor to where I was standing sentry. I waited until he had secured both our prisoners' hands before kicking over the bag and toeing through the contents.

Besides a large bundle of nylon cable ties, identical to those I'd found buried deep in Monk's flesh, which I'd expected, I wasn't surprised to find an economy-size plastic jug of Jack Daniels, a baggie stuffed with green buds, and a couple packs of rolling papers. Duffy and the boys liked to party. No wonder they'd been so easy to take, I thought, upending the gym bag. Party indeed! The missing Wazikashi, the short companion sword to the one I'd found at Monk's, spilled out along with four Taser stun guns with spares and several expended cartridges. One of them was missing an electrode. My anger screwed a couple of notches tighter.

Tony had Duffy hung by his ankles from a chain-fall hook. His unconscious accomplice dangled beside him, upside down, about a foot above the floor.

In one of the zippered side pouches was a set of cheap nunchakus, several large alligator clips with long wire leads, the purpose of which I could only guess, and a very large pair of tin cutters. I held up the metal shears.

"What're these for...?"

Tony stopped hoisting, leaving Duffy semi-inverted, head and shoulders still on the deck, as he described, in a very off-hand way, how Duffy'd bragged that he was going to use it to cut off our fingers then our toes, slowly, one-by-one.

My grip on the rifle stock tightened.

"Oh, yeah...!" Tony added, as if appreciating Duffy's playfulness. "Chubby-guts here's got a real *different* sense of humor. 'Said he was saving snippin' off our tongues and dicks for last." In my mind, I heard Monk's heart-rending pleas when we'd found him insensible and blindly begging his tormentors for mercy.

"He's a funny guy." The words, inadequate to what I was feeling, came out in a hoarse growl. Duffy twisted his head around to look at me. I hoped he'd give me an excuse to pull the trigger. For once, he wisely kept his comments to himself.

Sarge, who'd remained beside me, trotted directly towards Duffy, whose eyes became very large; fear shone bright in them as the powerful beast he'd seen mauling his companion drew steadily closer. Sarge stopped beside the defenseless man's head and looked down at him for the longest moment. I wondered what he was going to do. Tony, who was closer but not close enough to stop whatever was about to happen, was watching intently. Then Sarge lazily turned, cocked a hind leg, and loosed a steaming wet stream squarely into Duffy's face.

It started softly with Tony, not much more than a cough at first, then a grudging chuckle, but it built quickly and I couldn't help following suit. Within moments, the two of us were howling so hard, tears streamed from our eyes. I needed to lean against the desk to keep from falling over. Accidentally, or on purpose, Sarge had defused a potentially ugly situation and I loved him for it.

Most of what Duffy told us was uninformed, stupid, or just plain bullshit but he had talked long and desperately. Throughout, Sarge sat staring down at him; although the implicit threat of our using the Tasers on him and his humiliatingly vulnerable position was probably enough to convince him of our sincerity, I gave a lot of the credit to Sarge's not-so subtle canine intimidation.

It was almost more from what wasn't said than what was, that Tony and I sifted out a few kernels of real information; those details, coupled with what we had already surmised, caused more pieces of the puzzle to fall into place.

*   *   *

CHAPTER 51

Duffy, an erstwhile distributor of drugs to street-level dealers and a facilitator of strong-arm collections from defaulters for Morton Kiley, confessed that Deputy Marshal Schott had been Kiley's business partner. Several weeks after Schott's arrest Kiley'd introduced Duffy to Whidden, telling him to regard the quiet gray man as the boss in the event of his temporary absence. Then, several months later, when Kiley'd become permanently absent Whidden instructed Duffy to pick up the next drop.

Entrusted to handle the initial access to a shipment all on his own, Duffy'd thought he was moving up and, maybe, about to replace Kiley. The next morning, when he attempted to carry out his orders, there was no shipment only a five-gallon pail half-filled with sand on the beach. Duffy tried to cover how scared he must've been that the blame and accountability for the missing shipment would fall squarely on his head. He said Whidden had acted almost as if he'd expected it, before letting on that Monk, Kiley's silent partner and the only other person who knew the schedule and whereabouts of the drop, had probably gone into business for himself.

My face burned hot under the glare Tony flashed at me when that nugget popped out. Whidden, Duffy continued, then ordered him and his wrecking crew to pay Monk a visit at home.

"The lawyer," Duffy said, "musta had some set a' balls on him, else he thought we was totally stupid not to think we wasn't gonna figure out it was him. The asshole invites us in like we was buds or something."

I kept my attention focused on Duffy, not wanting to see what was in Tony's eyes.

After taking Monk prisoner, Duffy continued, he called Whidden who brought over the "bag of toys" and personally directed Monk's interrogation. My mind recoiled from the savage imagery that Duffy's words painted; I began to appreciate Tony's Vietnam revelations.

"When the lawyer starts to crack," Duffy said, almost smirking, "and Mr. Whidden invites us out of the room to—he says—'sample Rothschild hospitality' as I was goin' out I heard him call you two by name."

Most likely sensing he was going to be shut out again, I guessed Duffy became motivated to going for it on his own. Probably, instead of staying with Monk as he had been instructed, as soon as Whidden left, Duffy'd torqued Monk's bonds tighter, so he and his friends could go visiting, in the hopes of catching one or other of us with the goods. That was strike one. After waiting for us to show up at our respective residences, when he'd returned to Monk's place and found Monk gone. Strike two. Duffy'd probably wet himself. Hoping to soften the blow over Monk's disappearance, he called Whidden and let on that he'd overheard my name mentioned as he was leaving the room, then— conveniently after Whidden left—remembered who I was. In an effort to show initiative, and that he was capable of taking care of business, presumably, Duffy' said he tried to find me and recover the missing goods; although, unsuccessfully. Whether out of desperation or flawed memory circuits, Duffy'd grasped at the impound dock as the place I would make for, and Whidden, probably thinking to get these loose cannons out of the way, had gone along with his setting up an ambush for us.

Ironically, unfortunately for Duffy, he had guessed right.

Duffy confirmed how he and his crew had only just arrived, and had been about to try breaking in to the building, when I'd delivered Tony and the backpacks right into his hands.

Remembering the claymores we'd left, I thought it was a shame we hadn't tarried a little longer at Marisha's.

Taken by surprise, Tony had little alternative but to disarm the booby traps before entering the warehouse to wait for my inevitable capture. That was when Duffy, now in possession of the packs and the authors of his embarrassment, decided he was going to have a little fun with us and keep it all for himself. He'd told the others that the "Big

Boss" had been called—the fool even lied to his own troops. And that, as they say, was strike three.

Having learned all there was for the moment Tony suggested we take a break. While he gathered up Duffy's goodies and stowed them in Charlie's office, I found myself looking down on the sorry pair of thugs and thinking about the end they'd had in store for us. I wondered who had done what to Monk's damaged body and how they'd felt—if they were capable of feeling anything at all—while they were torturing him? It was a unique perspective, to be in custody of someone who has no qualms about inflicting physical violence and cold-blooded murder, especially since I was their intended next victim. Monk's complicity, however, was jarring; these creatures didn't surprise me; they were acting true to form, but Monk? I'd trusted, confided in him, and had long considered him a friend and benefactor. Was Duffy lying about that, too? Although I doubted Duffy had the ability to recognize the truth if it was right in front of him, he wasn't capable of telling that convincing or complicated a lie.

I smelled a familiar smell.

Looking around I saw Tony had fired up a joint he'd rolled out of Duffy's stash. He took a deep hit, held it, took another then, seeing me watching, offered it. I shook my head. He shrugged and took another hit. I wasn't sure how I felt about Tony smoking dope. I'd sworn off everything several years earlier, and was uncomfortable about falling into old patterns. Quite honestly, it scared me. I was scared that I might like it too much. As much to satisfy my curiosity as to occupy my thoughts with something other than the tantalizingly seductive aroma of high-grade marijuana, I stood one of the backpacks on Charlie's desk and undid the straps.

There'd been no opportunity to really examine them onboard the houseboat. Too many other things had been going on that night. My main concern then had been whether or not I was going to be joining them, weighted down, on the bottom of the bay. Since then, for one reason or another, they had been lurking in the back of my mind.

Inside one backpack were two rectangular canisters, roughly 16 inches tall by 10 inches wide and 6 inches thick. I figured there was about half a cubic foot of storage space in each. Unintentional, I'm sure, but as Freudian-slips went it wasn't far off the mark: The black stenciling on the camouflage exterior indicated the canister I opened contained 'EXPLOSIVES'.

Tony was curious, too. He watched as I stacked seven shrink-wrapped white kilo bricks on the desk. I'd expected that; the tight row of fat cigar tubes below the bottom bricks, I hadn't.

A voice from long ago cheered, "...Peruvian dancing dust!" I knew the dangers; had seen them firsthand, knew the cost. 'I can resist that,' a frail, little voice pathetically pleaded in my mind.

"The white block's're 'coke'," he informed me absently as he picked up one of the tubes.

"You think...?"

Tony looked up from the tube and grinned, though it was mostly out of charity. My gibes had lost much of their zing In light of Monk's duplicity, not to mention my own dubious status as someone worthy of his trust.

Pure crystal clarity! In the insane chaos my reality had become, I craved it. My nostrils quivered in anticipation. I could almost taste the sharp medicinal tang trickling down the back of my throat.

"Look at this...."

My fingers stopped toying with the sealed edge on the brick I'd been unconsciously fondling.

Under the manufacturer's ornate emblem blue script on the satiny aluminum tube proclaimed, in Spanish, the name and type of cigar. Inside, instead of a prime hand-rolled leaf El-Robusto, were two lumpy cling-plastic twists twined together. Unfurled, each revealed a glittering row of diamonds.

My eyebrows lifted and Tony whistled long, low and tunelessly.

"'Five stones per roll, two rolls," he quickly calculated, "if the others are the same that could put count up to two hundred stones in each canister, times eight. 'Say sixteen hundred stones averaging two to three carats each. 'Figure fifteen thousand a stone, conservatively..." He looked me in the eye; his own were twinkling brightly, "...call it $25 million, and that's probably way low.

"How you like being a millionaire, sport?"

The test was there, hidden behind his words. Or, was it a test?

"This isn't what this was supposed to—"

What had we gotten into? I felt the water level of our situation swiftly rising higher.

*   *   *

But when we in our viciousness grow hard, —
O misery on't!— the wise gods seel our eyes;
In our own filth drop our clear judgments; make us
Adore our errors; laugh at's while we strut
To our confusion.

- Anthony and Cleopatra, William Shakespeare

CHAPTER 52

Assigned to stand guard over our prisoners while Tony hid the packs somewhere outside. I'd tried not to follow the crystalline glitter under the plastic, as he returned all seven bricks of cocaine to the canister and resealed it. He'd been gone about fifteen minutes, time enough for me to have mentally flipped a coin, drawn straws, and played scissors-paper-rock several dozen times over. Was Tony really stashing the drugs? He could just as easily take off and leave me hanging. Maybe I should do the same? I'd disappeared before; I could do it again. There were only two living witnesses, both of whom were helpless, and I had a gun.

My thumb seemed to have a mind of its own as it played with the selector switch on the assault rifle; clicking it from safety on the top, down one notch to full auto, and then one more down to single shot, then back up again. Duffy and his partner were awake now but silent; duct tape over the mouth can have that effect. They watched every gesture. I could see them cringe at each click. Had there been any sudden movements, regardless of their defenselessness, I wasn't so sure what my reaction might be. Or, maybe I was.

With what they'd done to Monk, and the tender mercies they'd intended to bestow upon us, I began to comprehend the dynamics involving so-called war criminals accused of shooting prisoners, who "attempted to escape."

A wet spattering sound intruded on my thoughts.

Tony stood just outside the door; water dripped onto the concrete apron. I didn't know how long he'd been watching before I'd become aware of him. He looked more seriously pissed than he had when he'd found out I'd been feeding Monk our full agenda. Wordlessly, he stepped inside and squelched over to where I stood.

"If it means that fucking much to you," he said mistaking my intent, before tearing the rifle from my grip, "then go the-fuck ahead, but do it close in. And, you'd better be real sure about your reasons; you won't be able to lie to yourself once it's done." With that said, he picked up Charlie's .45 pistol from the desk, grabbed my wrist and jammed the gun into my hand hard enough to send shock waves up to my shoulder.

Our two captives started yammering and squalling through their taped gags.

Almost as if in a dream, I pulled back the slide, heard the hammer cock. —It was very loud.— A round slicked itself into the chamber. I let the slide slip forward. The pistol felt as if it weighed a ton.

They were shrieking, their faces red with the effort, their eyes bulging with terror.

I aimed down at Duffy's head. Slowly, I took up the pressure on the trigger.

Their futile attempts to evade the gun barrel set the chains overhead rattling and clanging. My arm started trembling. I took a step closer to steady my aim. A sudden ammoniac stink hit my senses like a rock. Duffy's bladder had let loose. The clatter-clash of the chains assaulted my sanity. Sweat ran hot into my eyes. My heart pounded under my ribs. I couldn't seem to catch my breath. I looked at Tony. His face was carved in stone. Slowly, I lowered the gun. Frustration ran hot down my cheeks. I un-cocked the hammer and slammed the pistol down onto the desk in disgust.

"I gotta get out of here," I said, as much to myself as anyone else. My voice, thick, shook with emotion. Sarge followed me outside. He stood beside me and leaned his weight against my good leg. I was ashamed of myself. I hadn't been able to pull the trigger. How could doing the right thing feel so wrong?

The door twanged open behind me. I didn't turn. Instead, I moved off across the yard at a fast hobble. After a few seconds, Tony caught up and walked wordlessly at my side. He was content to merely rest his hand on my shoulder. Injury soon got the better of attitude; I gimped to a stop by the boat dock and stared out into a night that was only slightly less dark than my thoughts. He chose that moment to break the silence that stood between us like a wall.

"You made the right choice. Congratulations, on rejoining the human race."

I nodded my acknowledgement not trusting myself to speak.

"Just 'cause you didn't kill those two doesn't mean you get to take a vacation from thinking."

The blank expression on my face prompted an explanation.

"We still have to deal with the three body-counts you and Sarge racked up. Don't think I'm not impressed or grateful for what you did, 'cause I am. That took a lot of guts and determination. But, you're responsible for them, too.

C'mon...." He gently steered us towards the shoreline. "You can start by hauling your *people* down here," he said, as we neared the water. "I'll grab us some chains and weights."

He and Sarge left me to my grisly chore.

* * *

CHAPTER 53

While dragging the three dead bodies—my burdens—across the coral yard, I began to understand there *was* a difference between these and the two inside. Maybe, it was like Tony'd tried to explain to me that night in the houseboat; it was kill or be killed. These guys had been trying to kill me and they'd had a chance, sort of. Only I would know how it had really gone down. Intuitively, I began to see that had I yielded to my murderous impulses toward Duffy and his accomplice, those actions would have tormented me for the rest of my life.

I dropped the last corpse by the other two. When I turned to head back to the warehouse I saw Tony coming towards me. Slung over one arm were several long wraps of chain, in his hands he carried fins and masks.

From a pile of construction litter in a nearby part of the yard, we carried back four concrete blocks, which we fastened to the corpses before dragging them out past the gentle surf line. About fifty feet from shore was as far out as we'd deemed safe, not having forgotten the dinner party we'd precipitated during our Friday night swim. We were almost a third of the way to the steel barge Charlie'd grounded in ten to twelve feet of water to use for heavy equipment storage. The barge was a popular hangout for an assorted community of ravenous reef dwellers; there'd soon be little left of them. Recycling Florida Keys-style. I shuddered.

It was shortly after two in the morning when we passed by the dog track and turned south, heading back toward Key West.

From our interrogation of Duffy, we'd concluded that our little farce—the cleverly disguised trips to and from the houseboat—must have been performed for an attentive audience. Duffy claimed to have seen Whidden entering one of the motel units located at the mouth of the narrow lane, which led out to the construction site. The motel faced out onto Fleming Bay.

I no longer believed in coincidences.

*   *   *

CHAPTER 54

My reason for requesting one of three rooms facing the main thoroughfare wasn't needed. 'Jabba', whose eyes kept returning to the television set behind the check-in counter, intent on following the late-night talk-show antics of Lesbians-trapped-in-the-bodies-of-married-men, simply agreed.

The van was in the far corner of the rear parking lot, effectively hidden from view of the street by a large utility building. Tony wanted to "scout out the terrain across the street" before joining me upstairs

I confirmed which room I'd been able to get.

A smallish pre-formed concrete box; impersonal, depressing and geared to the utilitarian. I'd been in a thousand rooms like this while travelling with the bands—several lifetimes ago, it seemed—and they hadn't improved in the interim. It was perfect for our needs; the front window offered a direct line-of-sight to the motel rooms where Duffy said he saw Whidden.

Enthused by having taken the initiative, excited by our proximity to the opposing forces, if the 'intel' we gathered from Duffy was still valid, I wondered if we might have the beginning of another of Tony's edges. Unsure what it would look like and what we were going to do with that "edge", if and when we got it, I twisted the blinds shut before turning on the lights.

After assembling a twin to the Starlite scope we'd used on the houseboat, as requested, I laid out the remaining contents of the bag. A couple of new wrinkles had been added.

A cumbersome looking laser-guided shotgun microphone, which I didn't touch, would be attached to a small amplifier used to power the signal to a Nagra voice-operated tape recorder. Tony said this would allow us to more than maintain visual surveillance; since the invisible beam could read sound vibrations on the surface of window glass across the street we could eavesdrop on conversations within the target room, and the Nagra would keep a record. With our forces reduced by a third, this would let us review and appraise any information we might otherwise have missed through sleep or absence. Also, we might now be able to start building the "insurance policy" Tony believed/ hoped could allow us to live out a normal life span.

Previously, I'd never aspired to normalcy, right then it sounded pretty nice—though, clutching-at-straws was the image that came to mind, thanks to my critical demon weighing our chances of survival.

"Enough!" I promised the Blue Boy, as I strengthened my resolve, vowing to be courageous. The figure in the Gainsborough print over the bed seemed unimpressed. Imagining the antics he'd undoubtedly been witness to, mine must have seemed pathetic by comparison.

My heart stopped, my hand scrabbled for the pistol on the table; a soft scratching at the door had interrupted my resolve strengthening.

Shielded by the frame, I eased the door open with my right while holding the gun correctly in my left hand at waist level. I now carried a nine-millimeter Beretta fitted with a stubby sound-suppressor; the Colt .45, Tony'd said, was too much of a dinosaur. He figured I might have need of the extra eight rounds in the magazine, not to mention the relative anonymity of a silencer—my ears were still ringing from the last shot I'd fired with Charlie's hand cannon.

Tony nodded his approval at my applied lessons in the fine art of door opening. Once inside, he confessed that the reconnaissance of the motel across the street had yielded no evidence of Whidden or anything unusual. Seeing where I'd left off, he set about completing the assembly of our surveillance system.

*   *   *

CHAPTER 55

A half-pot of instant coffee remained on the warmer in the micro-kitchen. I controlled my urge-to-hurl long enough to take another sip from my cup. I'd logged close to an hour and a half on the new neckbreaker. Other than a mishmash of mindless ads and movie-dialogue from the rooms I'd sampled—all broken up and interspersed with the rumbling vibration of passing vehicles—I'd found no sign of Whidden. However, according to, "I saw you looking at those young girls" Judy from New Jersey, her husband, George "Oh, horseshit!" was exceedingly guilty of enjoying their vacation considerably more than she thought was necessary, and she was exacting her retribution. His "But, baby..." pleadings for forgiveness and sexual favors were infinitely more sincere than the TV programs I'd sampled in some of the rooms; I gave him eight points out of a possible ten for credibility.

My eavesdropping was essential; their convenient drama was used solely to adjust and balance the audio levels; the smirk on my face was purely coincidental.

"I'll take next shift."

Tony slipped the second headset around his neck and jacked in. He gave me a funny look when he heard the substance of my subjects' conversation, then took a long pull at his coffee. I shuddered on his behalf, marveling at his tolerance or lack of taste buds.

"Want me to wake you if anything happens?"

"Uh-uh." I shook my head; the only thing I wanted was down, as I rubbed my eyes sending a blaze of phosphenes kaleidoscoping across the inside of my eyelids.

My mind was awhirl with the bizarre impressions of the last few hours. While waiting for some long overdue sleep, I understood that my conscience would not accept these latest burdens without comment

Shifting my focus from the chill embrace of the bodies I'd sunk near the barge, I took a long, deep breath, exhaled, relaxed my body then mentally stepped off the launch ramp. The imaginary A-frame lifted from my shoulders as the sudden clutch of gravity pulled at me. The rush of air speed increased before I sheared away from the cliff face then angled off into a gentle, drifting glide.

*　　　*　　　*

CHAPTER 56

Seconds later—it seemed like I'd only just put my head down—I was awake. A hard hand was firmly clamped over my mouth. Tony watched carefully until satisfied he'd seen coherence in my eyes then he looked over his shoulder. I followed the direction of his eyes and heard a tapping at the door. At his insistence I'd booked in as a single, therefore I had to be the one to answer.

"Yeah, what's up?" I mumbled, wading toward the door, the sleep thick around my legs, heavy in my voice.

"I clean the room," a Spanish voice replied, "lazy Anglo" implicit in her tone.

"No, ah, come tomorrow, I got in late."

"You know, you got a card for the door knob. You use the card I don' wake you. That's what we got the card for. You got to use the card. How I supposed to know if you don' use the card?"

I reached through—Tony stood about five feet away; his Beretta held chest-high in a two-handed combat grip—offering a timid smile at her faintly mustachioed scowl, while I fumbled the card onto the doorknob. The chubby maid, a flush of disapproval in her cheeks, turned her stiffly-held back and propelled a cart piled high with linens and cleansers down the balcony. I heard mutterings; dark imprecations on all stupid people, of whom, I'm sure, I was leading the league.

"Sorry, I didn't think." Tony apologized and laughed softly.

I waved it off and stumbled toward the coffee machine and the quarter-full pot. I drank a long, steaming draught and shuddered at the rankness of the stagnant brew. Irrespective of how badly it tasted, I soon felt some synapses began to sputter and spark back to life.

"Let me get a shower 'n' I'll call down and see about getting a stop on our housekeeping."

Instead, Tony suggested I go down later in person and talk to the desk manager. "Apologize for upsetting the maid and drop a ten—no, make it a twenty on him to, ah, let's say, to compensate the maid for the trouble. She'll never see it, and you'll never see her again, I guarantee it."

The hot water helped loosen things up a bit. I noticed the swelling in my foot was down considerably, only the immediate area around the puncture was still sore. I was gaining back some of my mobility but it would be a while, I hoped, before I'd run any foot races.

"Find anything last night?" I called out from the bathroom while toweling off. "Will George ever have sex with Judy again?" The lack of any chuckles, groans, or otherwise response, got my attention. I poked my head around the door. Tony's expression was pretty bleak.

"Look, you'd better sit down. It isn't good, but it answers a lot of questions."

I wrapped the towel around me and sat at the tiny table, the rancid coffee in front of me forgotten for the moment.

"Whidden's not staying at the motel."

I felt a sense of futility and wasted effort but that couldn't account for the gravity of his tone.

"I think what we've got is a six-man SEAL-team, I'm pretty sure it's the same bunch from the beach."

"Not circus horns and fresh fish? You mean 'SEALs', like in the military?"

Tony nodded.

"There's a lot of Navy around here. You can't be sure they're the same ones?"

"It fits. Think about it...."

I started to say something.

Tony gave me a dangerous look. "No! I mean *really* think about it."

I did, and suddenly it made sense; Tony's initial evaluation of the clandestine landing tactics we'd observed had been on the money. With Whidden's wartime history, his connections and his seniority he could manipulate the military into providing selected personnel subject to his authority. Then, the enormity of it all hit me. The scenario was both frightening and believable: Whidden, with a plausible story and under the auspices of the DEA (the biggest drug-oriented organization in the world), could co-opt any police or government agency around the world and use them, unwittingly, to aid rather than interdict drug shipments. As such, Whidden could be one hell of an ally to any of the cartels. I wondered how high up the ladder the corruption spread. The implications were staggering.

"We can't win," I said, seeing the hopelessness of our position. "We've declared war on the government."

"Wrong; *he* has. Check out the tape; these boys are not real happy with 'Mr. White, that's the name he's using with them. —They have a few of their own names for him."

They weren't alone.

"According to the troops, this was supposed to have been a simple training Op, involving," he paused to effect the proper jargon, "'deep water rendezvous/retrieval of air-delivered materiel' and 'clandestine re-supply on hostile terrain'."

Responding to my apparent skepticism Tony held up his hands forestalling commentary, saying, "Yeah, the military really do talk like that."

"You don't think they're in on the, the drugs and diamonds?"

"No. From what they said, I don't think so. The stenciling on the canisters were probably there to fool these guys instead of any other reason I can think of, but I could be wrong. Listen up, there's more: 'Fearless Leader,' one of their nicer names for White, volunteered them to effect action in—now this is really *outside*—'the surgical removal' of homicidal, druggies in a hostage-taking scenario."

I didn't see the connection. It must have showed on my face.

"Uh, a prominent lawyer was being held prisoner...? There was no one home when they went calling...? The place was trashed...? Any of this sound familiar yet?"

I could only nod my head. The full impact, improbable as this sounded, rendered me speechless.

Surgical removal...? Reflexively, I gulped the last swallow of my coffee then choked. Not only was it sour and vile-tasting but stone cold.

"Don't get yourself all uncunted," he drawled, "'t'ain't as bad as it sounds."

He was right. It sounded worse than "bad" to me.

"The team was told it was a SIM." Off my puzzled look, he elucidated, "a SIM-ulated operation, designed as a possible real-life scenario, meant for training purposes."

I nodded mutely, understanding how it would have gone down: faced with Duffy and his fun-loving gun-toting crew, and their likely response, they would be taken out in the ensuing firefight. Whidden could have the know-how and the credentials to effect a cover-up.

"A few of the lads don't completely swallow the scenario or that it was about training, especially when there was no one home, but these puppies're trained to do what they're told."

My look of skepticism prompted his informing me that SEALs are often used for 'Black Ops' and their training affirms tacit accept-ance of whatever cover stories they're given.

"Plausible deniability" he said, covers a multitude of sins. Mr. White," which is how he now referred to Whidden, "and a few others' are probably operating way out on a limb; all we gotta do is document his moves, get the evidence to someone in authority, they'll take the fall, and we'll be in the clear."

What he meant was: all we had to do was *stay alive* long enough to get evidence, find someone we could *trust* who could do something about it, get it to them and *hope* we are in the clear. Piece of cake.

"I flagged the tape where they came in, use the Walkman to listen to it, but first check—"

I interrupted, "—check the recorder before I pull the tape, because there might be something going on. Right?"

"You know the drill. Good! There's a pack of spare cassettes in my bag. Load a fresh one just in case." The last bit was muffled by the covers Tony pulled over his head before rolling over and going to sleep.

I slipped the headset on and jacked in. Nada. These folks probably operated under cover of darkness, and like all good night-stalkers they used the daytime to recharge their batteries. I traded tapes, tagged it #1, zeroed the counter, hit rewind on the Walkman, found the flagged number then clicked the play button.

The click and rattle of a door being unlocked was my introduction to a series of disgruntled assessments of the "Op" [operation] and White/Whidden's abilities, or rather, the lack thereof.

Grumbling is a time-honored tradition in the military. I'm pretty sure the Roman Legion must have had its share of malcontents who groused about their commanders and any of the myriad details that plague a soldier's life.

The basic bones of contention were, as Tony had reported: cabin fever, due to the protracted nature of what was meant to be a "routine training op" but more importantly, the lack of liberty in a "wild pussy-haven" like Key West.

Instead of doing my own grumbling, I decided to visit Sarge. It seemed like a good excuse for a change of scenery, besides it would give Tony a little privacy. Also, I had some things on my mind that needed thinking about. I quietly let myself out. The do-not-disturb sign was still on the doorknob.

Head bent to one side, welding a telephone to his shoulder, the Day Manager, a goggle-eyed, round-shouldered 'Gollum' slithered the $20-bill off the counter with the speed of a three-card monte dealer. He accepted my apology for having misplaced the room key that was safely in my pocket. When he spoke, it was prefaced and concluded with a bout of swallowing, which caused his Adam's apple to jiggle obscenely. I thanked him politely and walked out into the sunshine, with his assurance that I would remain undisturbed until such time as I requested housekeeping service.

*   *   *

CHAPTER 57

Only one block away from North Roosevelt Boulevard, one of the primary peripheral roads, was the fringe of a quiet middle-class neighborhood. I herded Sarge to a small park. Upon entering, he immediately sat and looked up at me expectantly.

"What is it fella?" I couldn't think for a second, then I made the connection. I ruffled his ears, made as if I was throwing a ball and said, "Go on!"

One, or perhaps the combination of all three must have contained the secret key, because he tore off in a flurry of leaves and grass clippings. As he raced around the full perimeter of the park at top speed, the only thing missing was the Indy-500 sound effects. A bright, sunshiny crispness prevailed; the wind blew fresh and clean out of the east. I sat on a bench, leaned back, closed my eyes, and took a deep breath of the sweet air. Similar to northern autumns, it was brisk for Key West this early in Season. It was a great day to be alive.

Shattering, full-blown images of my killings swarmed up through my mind with a fury that left me weak and devastated. I wasn't a killer, not where it counted, and I didn't know how to handle it or even knew if I was strong enough. I couldn't seem to catch my breath; the weight was crushing; none of this should ever have happened—

"Sarge, get down."

It's hard to wallow in guilt when the slobbering tongue of reality slides across one's face.

Sometimes the simplest approach is the best. Apparently, that's the way Sarge looked at life. A powerful bond was growing between us. He owned a large part of me, and there was no way I was going to let him down. I vowed that once we were clear, *if* we got clear of this insanity, I was going to make sure he'd never want for anything.

He seemed to be grinning at the future I had in store for him, and by the way he looked up at me, coincident with my thoughts of finding him a harem to proliferate his progeny, I was almost convinced of a psychic link. Temporarily or not, Sarge had helped yank me out of my depression. For that small blessing I was grateful.

*   *   *

**When a person cannot deceive himself
the chances are against his being able to
deceive other people.**

- **Mark Twain**

CHAPTER 58

Around me a world still existed where people moved freely without fear of torture and death, once I returned to the motel an inescapably impossible situation demanding I deal with it lest it deal with me would define my reality.

To perpetuate the fiction of normalcy—it wasn't much of an excuse, but I didn't need a very good one because the longer I could delay my return to that small room and the necessity for my being there, I could prolong the illusion that all was well—I completed two full bags of serious provisioning at the local market. Sarge, a patient statue on the sidewalk outside, was perfect company throughout our excursion, undemanding and acquiescent. Though once back in the van, I winced at the serious consideration he gave to the huge joint bone I'd bought for him. The awesome power in his jaws and flashing teeth, as he steadily reduced it to so many small fragments, was daunting. Not for the first time, I was glad he was on our side.

After a little fresh air, exercise, and exorcism, I wasn't ready but I was resigned to dealing with the 'problem' again. That is, until I entered the motel room and found myself looking into the business end of a silenced pistol barrel.

I was beginning to hate guns. Even more, the anxiety that came from having one pointed at me but I said nothing. It was a necessary evil, I supposed. Acceptance was something Tony seemed to expect from me, but that didn't mean I had to like it.

I tossed Tony the spare room key and dropped the morning paper on the table, on my way to stock the under-counter fridge. Four hours of uninterrupted sleep, I noticed had been something he had really needed. There was color in his face again—other than gray—and his pale wolf's eyes were beginning to show considerably more white than red surrounding the icy blue.

"Key's section of the *Herald*," I mumbled around a sweet carrot slathered with fresh-ground peanut butter. "Check the piece about vandalism; note the addresses."

Monk's, mine, even Tony's had been listed in the article. Luckily, I'd guessed right when we'd skipped going home. My fictional reason for an open-ended motel stay was now firmly based in fact; I had spoken to Gollum of renovations; according to the newspaper they'd been extensive, though not the kind I'd had in mind.

"Says here," Tony looked up from the paper, one eyebrow raised above a lop-sided smirk, "'the police were unable to provide comment other than to state: the incidents may have been related?' 'Ya think?" he added derisively.

I feigned indifference as the room around me lurched sickeningly. Bitter memories of New Orleans, the last time I saw Nicole, swarmed up, it was only through conscious effort that I was able to remain in the present.

Not a huge fan of the police I considered their expertise, beyond legendary donut consumption, confined to ambiguous speculation and hollow promises; that is, when they weren't actively working for the other side.

"Any suggestions?" I asked, surprised my voice had not betrayed the almost overwhelming onslaught of anger and sorrow.

Tony had, but he made me wait for an answer until he'd poured himself a fresh cup of real coffee, to which he added three heaping spoons of white death, before loading a plate with a respectably heart-unfriendly mound of blood-rare roast beef and imported Ementhaller cheese. Sitting at the table, his plate before him untouched for the moment, he looked me in the eye.

"'About time we stopped being reactive."

"Okay...?" I'd been entertaining similar ideas myself, but hadn't known what to do about them.

"'Quickest way out," he said, chomping down a mouthful of food, his eyes still locked with mine, probably to see the effect when he swallowed and said, "we're gonna snatch White."

That I hadn't considered.

"What happened to collecting evidence? 'Snatch White!' Are you nuts?"

"Nope..." he mumbled around another mouthful, then swallowed, "...trying to stay alive. We take him and we cut off the head. I don't want six guys with guns getting in our way, and I'd be willing to bet these boys won't precipitate any moves on their own. Most likely, when they figure something's wrong, they won't try to contact the local law; they'll have a secondary control to call to get themselves pulled out or sidelined, that'll give us breathing space."

"'Most likely; you'd be willing to bet?' Well, that makes me feel a whole hell of a lot better. What if you're wrong?"

"Then we'll be dead or in a jail cell."

He'd said it simply, directly; the teasing edge of a smirk flirted with the corner of his mouth.

"Know what I like about your sense of humor...?

He looked at me, expectantly, waiting.

"And that is...?"

I paused, "...Can't think of a thing." The punch line was delivered with little humor.

"Ha-ha-ha." His monotone laughter had even less. "I'm not joking; I'm gonna take White, with or without you."

"You're serious?"

He didn't say a word. His steady, unflinching gaze said it all.

"But, golly-gee-whillikers, I've never kidnapped anyone before," I said mordantly.

"You never killed anyone before, but that didn't stop you," he said in an iron voice.

I felt like I'd been doused in cold water.

"Thanks a lot. I really needed that."

"Getting pissy with me, 'n copping an attitude isn't going to make this go away. 'Best chance we're gonna have is by us doing something positive, and doing it first."

I searched his face for uncertainty but found only determination. He was right and I knew it. Also, it hurt to admit that I did sound "pissy."

"Okay, okay." I capitulated, "What, exactly, do we do?"

"Wait'n listen. 'Best case scenario: somebody over there mentions where he is; worst, we follow them when they leave and hope to get lucky. We're about due for a break."

Long overdue, I thought. Wisely, I kept that observation to myself.

"Did you make a note of the 1800 hours call the kid from Texas mentioned?"

I nodded. His nasal twang had been as distinctive and obvious to me as the group's varying degrees of respect for his authority.

"Then we might as well conserve our energy for the night ahead, could be a long one."

Tony pulled the headset from the recorder, bumped the speaker volume up a bit and made himself comfortable on his bed. He seemed content to laze away the dregs of the afternoon listening to ratcheting snores of our opposite numbers highlighted by the occasional noise of a toilet flushing, overlaid by the constant rumble and swish of traffic buzzing through the laser-guided microphone.

*   *   *

CHAPTER 59

A little after four—Tony'd set the alarm for five-thirty lest we doze off—I gave up counting the holes in the acoustic ceiling tiles. Deciding to wait it out in the van, Sarge favored me with a brief display of affection until he noticed I had arrived empty-handed, so he got out to stretch his legs a little; mostly the hind one it seemed.

Reclining on the thick carpeting, a couple of cushions behind my back, windows open to cool breezes in the shade of a massive Banyan tree was a big improvement on the bleak and soulless concrete motel room.

After reading my previous entry, I began jotting down the latest series of events in my project journal when Sarge, having completed an in-depth inspection of the local plant life, reentered the van and lay beside me. I'd been staring at a blank page for several minutes before I realized what I wanted was to have the last week back so I could tell Monk: "Sorry not interested. No can do. Send my mail to Georgia."

Briefly, I considered firing up the Maxi-van and heading for the highway, but that really wasn't an option. I'd run away too many times before; I was too tired to run any more. There really *was* no way out, as Tony had pointed out, except forward.

Sarge whuffed a two-note sigh, which sounded to me like, "Damn Right!" that coincided exactly with my own conclusions.

Although I didn't feel any better about the situation, the onus of what I was doing and about to do was, perhaps, a little more tolerable for having allowed myself the choice between facing it or skipping.

I gave up any pretense of finding answers to the last in a growing postscript of questions in my record of events—most of the earlier ones still defied solution—before returning my scribblings to their hiding place; content just to watch the shadows lengthen as the sun glided down toward the Gulf of Mexico. Approving my decision, Sarge grunted, yawned then rested his massive wedge-shaped head on my lap. His weight and presence were both reassuring and dependent at the same time.

A moment or two before any sound reached my ears I felt Sarge tense, an inaudible growl vibrated against my leg alerting me to a potential danger. Though he appeared dead to the world, I could feel his muscles, like steel springs, coiled like a sprinter waiting to explode from the blocks at the starting gun.

When Tony identified himself, as he approached, Sarge relaxed a little but I kept the pistol ready at my side until I could determine that all was truly well. There'd been too many surprises as of late for me to totally ease off.

"They're saddling up." Tony placed an equipment bag on the floor beside me then got in. He chuckled softly before adding, "First stop's McD's, and there was a lot of whining about that. Three wanted to hold out for Wendy's until the team leader cast the deciding vote. 'Less we end this stand-off soon these boys are going to lose their trim figures off this fast-food diet."

I appreciated Tony's attempt to interject some playfulness into the situation; without his positive attitude we would never have gotten this far. I smiled politely at the effort rather than the comment.

"I think I know where they're going afterwards, but, we better follow them anyway, just to be on the safe side." Tony offered.

"My thoughts exactly."

With some coaxing and a little bribery, I convinced Sarge to cede Tony front-seat privileges; something I would not have contemplated trying several days earlier.

We spotted the "A-team" (Tony's sobriquet for our opposing force) as they pulled out of the parking lot in a matching pair of shiny, new Toyota Landcruisers. My grumbling remark about government budgets and tax-dollars-at-work, earned a snort from Tony. I waited until they were well past before joining the northbound flow, settling in about five cars back, safely anonymous in the Sunday afternoon traffic while Tony ran down the most recent chatter picked up from our listening post.

"Point Delta" he said, "is where Mr. White's supposed to meet the boys, care to guess where that might be?"

"Not really." Feeling the tension building inside, I wasn't in any mood for games, guessing or otherwise. Just trailing these guys was twisting my insides into knots.

"Here's something you might be interested in: One of them," he said tipping his head back to point his chin at our quarry, "was talking about that piece in the paper; he thinks the 'vandals' were the ones involved with kidnapping and wasting the lawyer."

"'Wasting'?" Another twist to the knots was added. "Monk isn't dead, is he?"

"No, leastways, I don't think so. But he would have been if Duffy hadn't gone tear-assing after us on Friday night and stuck around like he was supposed to."

"But, why?" It hadn't made any sense when Tony'd first suggested that, and it made even less the second time around. "He knew we had his stuff. With them gone, how does that get it back?"

"This is a small town. Right?" He patiently asked like a tolerant adult about to explain something to a backward child.

"The fuck's that got to do with anything?"

"Plenty. You and I, thanks to Monk, are known quantities, right?

"Okay, but—" a hot flush burned my ears at the reminder.

"Just hear me out... "

I nodded for him to continue.

Dramatically waggling his fingers like a puppet-master, he said, "White's got the full resources of the DEA right there at his fingertips. Finding us'd be child's play, if we tried to make a run for it. Right now his major concern's gotta be damage control."

"But, the diamonds, there's millions, what would stop us from—?"

Again, he adopted the parental tone I was quickly learning to hate.

"'Ever tried to sell a diamond, Sparky?"

Sparky? When had I become a 'Sparky'?

I shook my head. "No, but—"

"Ri-i-ight! Believe me, partner, t'ain't that easy. Whatcha gonna do? Fill the gas tank and take your change in Slim Jims and Turkey

Jerky? Barter for butter 'n eggs in a grocery store? Pawnshops, jewelry stores, right? Forget it. 'Soon as you tried to pass the first stone, no pun intended, the trail would start. Believe me it takes a lot more than luck, it takes some serious connections; 'specially if you can't prove you're the legal owner."

This was something else I hadn't considered.

"Then what are we supposed to do?"

Pointing down the road he said, "Exactly what we're doing, ride herd on these boys 'til we find White, figure a way to take him, and do it. Then, and only then, do we stand a chance of getting outta this jackpot."

Tony'd obviously given our predicament a lot more thought than I had, seen more and in directions I hadn't known existed.

"White's probably dancing as fast as he can right now to justify keeping the A-team on station, and to prevent them from finding out what they're really doing here. Acceptance of cover stories has its limits, even for troops trained to swallow whoppers."

"They did their job when they brought the load in, why's he still need them if we're going to be so easy to find?"

"That's the point!" he crowed extending an index finger into the air.

My blank look of incomprehension caused him to snicker.

"'See, you and me, we've put him right in the middle. Whoever's pulling White's strings can't be too tickled with his performance thus far. We've got what he wants and we've already caused him serious delay. 'Not like some neighbor who forgets to return your lawnmower, something with that much value gets missed real quick. Every minute we're on the loose makes White look worse. That equals pressure and pressure causes people to make mistakes"

Tony shrugged expressively. "Any mistake he makes has gotta be an advantage for us. Just like Monk and Kiley, Duffy represents a loose end that White'd love to eliminate, but so long as he believes there's even a chance he might find us and his goods, he'll give Duffy his head. 'Sides it'd save him from having to come back later to try to pick up our trail. Less chance of any other complications that way and he'll look better to his higher-ups. Betcha, he'd give his left nut to wrap this up right here and now."

What Tony was saying began to make a lot of sense to me.

"Duffy's got no idea how valuable he is," he continued. "Lucky too; if it weren't for that greedy streak of his he'd be nothing but a bad memory."

I got a cautioning look as I booted us through the last trace of a yellow light in order to keep our targets in sight. I grinned in apology; the last thing we needed was to be stopped by an ambitious traffic cop.

"Yup, 'beginning to look like there just might be a light at the end of the tunnel."

"One thing I don't get. How do we use Duffy to our advantage?"

"We don't." Tony clicked the seat back to its last position, stretched his legs, then continued. "Like I said, Duffy's a loose end, not knowing where he is keeps White off balance, and that, my friend, makes it a little easier to do what we need to. Taking White's the key to buying time, and time's what we need to survive. Duffy's our ace. We keep him as our hole-card."

"I'm still not a hundred percent on this but, okay. Are there any other surprises you haven't told me about?"

He cocked an eyebrow at me, while considering how to respond to my question. I didn't have long to wait for an answer.

"There is one thing I haven't been able to figure: that diver; the other night, these guys don't act like they've lost anyone. And, there's no way in hell Duffy's bunch could have handled Doug. Nope, I'm beginning to smell an independent in the woodpile."

I almost creamed a sunburned tourist on a moped, when he sped out in front of me, just as the meaning of Tony's last comment became clear.

Maybe that light at the end of the tunnel, Tony'd mentioned, was really a freight train heading right for us.

I'd already begun to decelerate when the brake lights on the Land-cruisers flashed moments before they entered below the golden arches. I drove into the Food-N-Fuel self-serve on the adjacent lot and pulled up to the pumps near the fence separating the two businesses in time to see two trios of clean-cut young men approaching the restaurant's front doors. Though differently colored, their pastel polo shirts and casual slacks were worn almost like uniforms. They were a team and they moved with an unconscious awareness of each other, like components of the same machine.

I finished topping off the fuel tank when, after several minutes, they were back outside, bags in hand and heading for a grouping of concrete picnic tables on the far side of the building.

"I want to get in closer," Tony said, taking out a pair of binoculars and reaching for the door handle, just as I was climbing up into the driver's seat.

When I asked why, he grumped, "Get me close enough and you'll find out."

The question was plain to see in my expression.

"I want to watch them," he added.

My suggestion, of there being better hobbies like bird watching or stamp collecting, earned me a look recommending I forgo comedy as a career.

"There might be a way." Acting on memory, I drove down to the next hotel then headed through to the rear exit, turned then doubled back through a recent subdivision of modest cinder-block bungalows, each on its own minuscule lot. A requisite number of palms and bougainvillea had been installed to soften the Spartan ambiance of the low-rise neighborhood, comprised mostly of starters and retirement villas, distinguishable only by the presence or absence of plastic yard toys. Visible at the end of a cul-de-sac, directly opposite the burger palace, one house still featured a for-sale sign in the yard. From the looks of the place—the concrete in the driveway was virginal and the grounds were devoid of landscaping—it'd never been occupied. Probably, I reasoned it took a special type of person to truly appreciate the daily allure of tallying up yet another billion served.

I parked in the partial shade of a supported coconut palm. Our elevated position inside the van gave us a clear view of the A-team occupying both outside tables.

"Perfect."

Amazing! I'd done something right. I basked in Tony's praise.

He reached into the electronics bag, extracted the tape recorder and set it on the engine cover between us. Raising the binoculars, he steadied his aim, adjusted focus, and immediately began speaking.

"...wring the 30-weight out of your sausage..."

It took me a second or two to catch on. The soft whirring of the voice-activated recorder was my clue; lip-reading. It was fascinating and at the same time very disconcerting to see how someone could so easily steal a distant conversation.

"Know thine enemy," Tony said, by way of an explanation, as we learned about two of our opposing numbers: Patrick, the wiry freckle-faced team leader, with thinning coppery-red hair and blue eyes, that were probably a legacy of his Irish genetics, appeared an easygoing sort. Though a little intimidated by some of the others, he seemed to take it well when his teammates jokingly referred to him as "Barney O'Fife." The shortest and, by appearance, the oldest of the group, "Duke" with a heavy five-o'clock shadow and blocky Mediterranean features, we gathered was a fairly recent addition to the team. A surly creature, either by choice or consensus, he sat somewhat apart from the group, where he puffed out clouds of foul cigar smoke and responded only minimally to the others.

Although fragmented, we were able to glean a few usable pieces of information, predominantly their tactical strategy. Tony'd parroted aloud that White had ordered them, "to secure and assume a perimeter surveillance at Point Delta where they would RDV."

According to Tony's worst-case scenario, which was about to come true, all we had to do was follow them to their rendezvous and watch.

*   *   *

CHAPTER 60

We backtracked to North Roosevelt Boulevard, waited until our targets passed then locked-in about five cars behind them on the main artery and comfortably held position.

An icy finger of worry touched me when they eased over and took the left fork of the triangle, to the Cow Key Channel Bridge. —I'd imagined Monk's apartment might be the designated rendezvous.— Worry grew into a sick feeling below my heart when they took the first right after the bridge. That road led down into the same residential area I'd entered the night before.

Tony's anxiety was palpable.

Was the "Point Delta" he'd jokingly referred to his estranged family's home? Were they about to be the focus of White's attention?

"No!" I shouted silently, trying to will them into going anywhere but there.

That I'd placed Tony's children, any children, at risk horrified me; it was something I couldn't allow to happen; I would refuse nothing to protect them.

"They're lost."

I immediately pulled to the side and parked.

"Or, they're checking for anyone following." I offered.

"Down a dead-end street? Get straight."

When we saw them returning, we slumped below the dashboard. I held my breath as they approached. Sarge regarded us as if we were both mildly insane. In unison, we breathed a sigh of relief when they continued back past Marisha's street. I suppose it was inevitable that they would take the road leading out to the salvage yard. I'd forgotten about Duffy's report to White mentioning it as his objective. Because there was no covering traffic I dropped back almost two blocks; close enough to see but far enough to be anonymous, I hoped. Ahead, the second set of lights slowed, as the lead vehicle turned right and picked up speed then was followed by the second.

"'Told ya!" Tony sounded pleased enough for both of us. Even though he hadn't, I should have guessed their destination.

On its left, the road leading to the impound docks shouldered by the back end of the old Berenson's Greyhound Dog Track. On the right was an empty block of undeveloped land that eventually gave over to mangroves by the water's edge. The first hundred yards of the lot was clear except for a few feathery Dutch Pines amid wild clumps of scrub brush. Used initially for extra parking for the racing events no one had bothered to develop this large expanse after the track folded, so it defaulted into a neighborhood dump. Corpses of wrecked cars, a dead mobile home, the hollowed carapace of a school bus, and defunct appliances of all shapes, sorts and sizes dotted the landscape. All were in varying stages of cannibalism, deterioration, and decomposition. Over the years, I'd seen a host of derelicts slowly melt down to nothing but bare bones.

I slowed and turned right on the near side of the vacant lot, paralleling the A-team until they'd passed the auto wreckers, rounded the curve and were out of sight. Since there was only one road, to or from the impound docks, we had only to wait until Mr. White showed then follow wherever he led.

The neighborhood consisted mostly of single- and double-wides raised up on foundation blocks, each on its own tiny but heavily foliaged lot. Near the end of the second block, on our left, the vacant lot was given over to use as a parking lot for trailers, boats, and camper bodies up on stands. A temporary observation post; with plenty of camouflage and natural cover, it was perfect. I U-turned, nosed in front of a trailer next to some scrub, and turned off the engine.

I heard the rasp of a lighter, saw the muted flare, smelled the pungent aroma, and rolled down my window. I refused the proffered joint and kept my thoughts to myself.

Outside, a contingent of tree frogs and crickets began a twilight conference on the addictive habits of humans, as we slipped into a quiet introspection waiting for our quarry to make an appearance.

My attention shifted to the stainless steel marine shackle that hung from the ignition key. I smiled at the memories carried in that silvery bit of metal.

*   *   *

The secret sympathy,
The silver link, the silver tie,
Which heart to heart, and mind to mind,
In body and in soul can bind.

- Sir Walter Scott

CHAPTER 61

There was one more of the seven ballast sections to be salvaged; our labors over the previous four days had netted us about three and a half tons of solid lead, which represented a nice bit of pocket change on the scrap metal market. The remaining section promised to be difficult, but Charlie'd made up his mind he was going to have it.

I'd begun to notice, during my short apprenticeship, when Charlie made up his mind on anything then that "anything," whatever it was, would happen, one way or another.

During a storm several days earlier, a large sailboat had grounded on the Eastern Dry Rocks reef; the severe pounding it had taken had literally broken it to pieces. We'd gone out to salvage those pieces and—though considerably different in shape and size—the last section was the same unimpressive lead-gray color as the others. The previous slabs were about 10 inches square, 8 feet in length, all with a rough-cast surface. The last—the section containing the drop-keel—was about 8 feet wide and tapered gracefully down to a point, nearly 10 feet in length it was some 12 inches at its thickest. Covered with a smooth fiberglass shell, it bore a striking similarity to a shark's fin.

Seeing that the only purchase available to lift it off the bottom, since the main pinion-hole fitting had been shattered, was a small stainless shackle used for the cable hoist, I'd suggested that it might only be fiberglass, nothing more. —I knew that lifting this 'pig' represented a lot of effort. It could get pretty scary, trying to control x-amount of tonnage with so much smooth surface.

"Flinching can be habit forming;" I remember him saying, "whatever comes at you deal with it." Knowing that it was probably my fear speaking, Charlie focused his energy on could-we-do-it? and in doing so, reinforced a positive perspective. He believed there was another piece of solid lead core, similar to the rest of our salvage, just waiting to see if we could take it. I'd had to admit that he might have a point since its weight had been impossible to move with the tools at hand. So, a-salvaging we went.

After considerable effort, we excavated two channels in the coarse sand and pebbled ocean floor sufficient to work a pair of heavy lifting straps underneath. To these we chained large reinforced neoprene air bags, and clipped them together with adjustable straps into a make-shift harness. Then, came the moment of truth. Each of us carrying a spare air tank, we moved from bag to bag carefully alternating the fill to ensure the whole rig came up evenly. Any error in judgement; off it would slip and we'd be back to square one. To say nothing of the time lost retrieving the lifting bags and equipment, which more often than not, once freed of their load, would drift away.

Charlie'd told me that everything was twice as difficult under-water; he was wrong, it was ten times harder. If we hadn't have been forty feet below the surface I would've been covered in sweat.

Once the salvage bags were fully inflated and the keel section was positively balanced near the surface, we checked the purchases, rigged it for travel, hooked the array to a towline, and at dead slow brought it into port with the utility boat. By the time we'd reached the dock and had our lines secured there was no light left in the day. Wisely, Charlie elected to wait for morning before attempting to raise it with the deck crane.

First thing on the following day, with the drop-keel dripping and heavy on the dock I started in on the fiberglass sheath. Only, once the shell was breached, the interior proved not to be the saleable base metal we'd counted on. The boat builder had used the shell as a mold, and filled it with nothing more valuable than concrete. The only yield after a whole day's labor was the stainless steel shackle used to attach the cable that raised and lowered the drop-section.

This had been one of our first salvage jobs together, so for Charlie was largely an unknown quantity. I remembered searching his face for a clue to how he was going to react to this monumental waste of time, energy and effort. Carefully, he unfastened the shiny shackle. He then held it up to the light, turning it first one way then another, as if it were a rare gem. He wore a straight face throughout. I was totally baffled.

Finally, he looked at me and proclaimed with authority: "This shackle's too valuable to sell, for what we got invested. 'Think I'm going to keep this one."

A dead silence followed; the kind one usually associates with the eye of a hurricane. I'd almost opened my mouth to question his sanity. When I caught the slight twinkle in the corner of his eye, I understood what he'd meant about 'dealing' with whatever comes at you.

Charlie made that shackle into a key-chain, and on it he hung access to everything he owned, boats, buildings; the work, which he gave to me as a symbol of the trust and friendship I'd earned. When he'd referred to it as the most valuable shackle he'd ever seen he wasn't far wrong. I valued few possessions higher.

Then it came to me. I sat bolt upright in horror.

"A boat!"

We had been sitting in the van complacently, waiting for close to twenty minutes. There'd been no traffic on the road since we'd arrived. White had scheduled the rendezvous for over five minutes earlier. He hadn't impressed me as someone who'd be late to his own party.

"What if he's coming by water?"

Tony's features mirrored an instantaneous grasp of my meaning then quicksilvered into an angry scowl of self-recrimination.

"Wait here. If they split before I get back, trail them. I'll meet or call you back at the motel."

Off at a trot, he was around the corner and out of sight. Sarge, visibly upset—a patch of furrows wrinkled his forehead as he watched Tony run—displayed an unusual amount of restraint in not giving chase. I petted him generously, reinforcing his good behavior. He accepted my praise with his normal equanimity, as he invaded the now-vacant front seat daintily as a Mongol horde.

The soft mask of settling night brought the disturbing awareness that I was sitting safe and snug while Tony was somewhere out in the night, probably putting himself at risk.

*   *   *

"For the Angel of Death spread his wings on the blast,
And breathed in the face of the foe as he pass'd;
And the eyes of the sleepers wax'd deadly and chill,
And their hearts but once heaved, and for ever grew still!"

- The Destruction of Sennacherib, Lord Byron,

CHAPTER 62

Beyond establishing a new personal record for looking at my watch, the vigil yielded little until shortly after six-thirty when I noticed a glimmer of light in the night sky about where I imagined the warehouse was located, followed almost immediately by a flat, concussive: *Whammp! s*o faint as to be almost unheard, it startled me.

I'd heard explosives before; though muted by distance it could be nothing else. I saw a vague glow of yellow and red rise above the distant trees, brighten then slowly fade. A superior smirk began, at the idea of catching one or more of our tormentors unawares, until I remembered Duffy and his partner lying there, helpless. It had been right in front of me all this time and I'd subconsciously rejected the probability. No! It wasn't probability, it was a certainty that this would happen, and I hadn't given it a thought.

My body went cold. I started shivering.

Sarge dropped down between the seats next to me. I leaned over and hugged him. In return he gave me the unqualified comfort of his presence.

The glare of headlights painted the sky, back-lighting the trees with movement. Seconds later, the Landcruisers tore down the road, past the dog track. Sliding into the cross street, they raced back toward town. I waited until the second passed then followed.

The trailing vehicle was at the far end of the block and turning on to the main highway when I entered the street. The green light died, yellow glared its warning. I held my breath, jammed the pedal down, and went for it. Engine roaring, I pushed the Maxi-van unmercifully. The light changed from amber to red as I'd reached the intersection. Juddering into a four-wheel drift, I felt the driver's side unloading, the wheels began to lift. Screeching across four lanes, to the far shoulder of the divided highway, the world became a blur of motion, headlights, shrieks of tortured rubber, car horns, and metallic crunches. I was almost in the ditch before the van stabilized and got it pointed towards Key West. I flinched at the chaos filling the rearview mirror but dared not stop, putting distance between me and the snarl I'd caused.

Slaloming through the flow of traffic heading into town, I only just managed to keep the Landcruiser in sight. Predictably, they pulled into their motel parking lot.

Back in our room, I slipped the headset on; our focus on the target window, the truncated shout: "—therfucker!" blared loud in my ears. Backing the volume down, I remembered to switch on the recorder.

These boys were hurting. Having lost two of their number, during a forced entry into the warehouse, they were severely pissed because "Mister-fucking-White," who'd showed up late, had nixed their going in after their dead.

Somehow, the initial blast had touched off a secondary and much larger explosion, which had lifted the roof off the building causing the whole structure to collapse on itself.

"That's it! We're outta here right-fucking-now," a voice quavering with fear and emotion roared. Their program was a total bust, morale was in shambles. By default of rank, Duke was the new leader having succeeded Patrick (AKA Barney O'Fife), now "Missing In Action."

Probably a KIA, I thought morosely.

The phone in their room rang. I heard the rage and defiance deteriorate into an angry grumble of yes-sirs and no-sirs. Doubtless, the riot act was being read to the new team leader. Duke was no match for whomever it was on the other end of the line. The remainder of the crew, picking up on the harsh realities relevant to their position in the command structure, sank into sulky silences broken only by occasional expletives on the incestuous predilections and dubious parentage of all officers.

I'd just started brewing a fresh pot of coffee, more to occupy my hands than anything else, when the phone rang.

"Are our friends broadcasting?"

I briefly relayed my observations.

"Come to the Pier House. I'll meet you in the north parking lot."

I asked if I should leave the listening post on automatic.

"'Better bring the gear," he suggested. "I think we're gonna need it."

*   *   *

**I do not see them here; but after death
God knows I know the faces I shall see,
Each one a murdered self, with low last breath.
'I am thyself,—what hast thou done to me?'
'And I—and I—thyself', (lo! Each one saith.)
'And thou thyself to all eternity!'**

- Dante Gabriel Rossetti

CHAPTER 63

The pricey beachfront hotel complex occupied almost a full city block. Its convoluted sprawl dominated the western foot of Duval Street, the heart of Key West's party central district. I navigated the narrow in-town streets clogged with tourists and locals, the closer I got the more people-dense it became.

To vacationers, Old Town must seem quaint and magical, as if created expressly for their amusement by some Disney-like hand. Stoplights and crosswalks were solely for decoration, as everyone apparently believed because everyday rules simply did not apply when on holiday. To add to the festive air eccentric locals, some wobbling in and out of traffic on luridly painted bicycles—though, not as wholesome as Mickey or Goofy—were almost as amusing especially when fleshed out with early birds costumed in anticipation of the Fantasy Fest street parade. It was, after all, Sunday night. Any old day of the week, just being 'On the Rock' can be reason enough to propel the island's self-proclaimed court jesters into the public eye, but weekends tended to jam the sidewalks to overflowing. Now that the dinner hour had come and gone, it was officially *Happy Hour,* until sometime around four the following morning.

Twice, I'd had to jam on the brakes to avoid acquiring a drunken hood ornament; the second, glassy-eyed, camera poised to capture some Kodak moment, stepped off the curb, directly in front of me. In recognition of my not having run him down, he generously bestowed

upon me a look of total disbelief supported by a righteously indignant
sneer that questioned why someone would dare use such picturesque
streets to merely drive upon. Then, having put me in my place, he set
his Big Gulp-sized cocktail at his feet, bravely turned his back, as he
framed then captured a perfect shot of a floodlit tropical mansion with
his trusty camera. No doubt, this would be the substance of many an
alcohol-fueled saga, in which he 'noble tourist' bested me 'bandy-
legged local'.

Waiting for him to redefine photographic genius, while two cabs
whipped around me, the words of a burned-out, alcoholic, carpenter I'd
once, unsuccessfully, tried to rehabilitate came to mind. Fuzzy Mike,
so called because of his particular outlook on life, used to hold forth
how wonderful the world would be if, on one day each year, murders
were permissible.

Having snapped his photo, the sunburned Ansel Adams picked up
his drink and decided to bawl me out. As he approached I rolled up the
window, partly to avert his sprayed invective, mostly to prevent Sarge
from chewing his face off. Murder Day, I reckoned, had some merit.

My vision blurred, Duffy's face was superimposed on the front of
the tourist's head.

Cars behind me honked. Sarge barked.

Startled, I looked around. The tourist, back on the sidewalk, his
face his own again, flipped me an elaborate bird, turned and was
swallowed inside the seductive interior of a bar. I wanted to follow.
We'd buy rounds for each other, become friends for life, or until the
place closed. I licked my lips. Thinking of the cool, easy slide of
oblivion down my constricted throat, I swallowed in reflex.

*   *   *

CHAPTER 64

Tony waved me down when I entered the parking lot. I noticed his hair was wet and his clothes different from earlier. He got in. Directing us to the VIP parking area he explained how a Jet Ski and a dry change had been obtained from a *"friend"* who lived close to where we'd parked. The quick acceleration, small size and shallow draft of the agile watercraft had allowed Tony to get close enough to see the explosions, the damage, the resulting confusion, and, most importantly, to follow White in his subsequent retreat without being seen.

"We have," Tony read aloud from the glossy brochure, "'a delightful suite overlooking the confluence of the Atlantic Ocean and the Gulf of Mexico.'" Grinning a wicked grin, he added, "and we have a most interesting neighbor."

It was good to see him in a positive frame of mind. I wondered if he saw faces changing in front of his eyes.

"Did you hear the secondary, after the 'frags' went off?"

I solemnly nodded.

He got my drift immediately.

"Yeah, that was a rough way to go but it musta' been quick. Don't forget about Monk and those metal shears. No one forced Duffy to come after us. He didn't have to be there."

I'd given up making similar rationalizations because they hadn't helped. I was trying not to think about well-stocked mini-bars in hotel suites.

"Chill out, partner. You can beat on yourself if you want but it won't do nothing 'cept help every asshole that's tries to fuck with your reality. 'Let you in on a little secret; it comes down to them or me? I'm gonna bust my hump making damn sure it's gonna be them.

"Next time you're in a kill-or-be-killed thing, and you hesitate because of this, you're dead! Think about it, Sport, death by distraction is still dead. Now, let's do this thing."

I nodded again. There was nothing I could say. I knew he was right, but that didn't make it any easier. I would have to make my own peace when these new demons came calling.

We carried our bags to a row of luxury units fronting the private beach. On the winding path through lush tropical foliage, two sun-bronzed, spa-toned men, arm-in-arm and wobbling a little smiled and nodded toothy "hello's" to us. One, I noticed, winked at Tony. His partner smacked him lightly, chastising, "Bitch!"

Tony laughed lightly, telling him, "I'm taken, sweetie." while I tried to look suitably jealous.

We were just another couple, checking in to Paradise.

Inside, the penthouse apartment was awash in a palette of trendy mauve tones sufficient to induce dizziness and a protracted bout of vomiting in all but the very blind.

"How much did this set you back?"

"Don't ask," was the terse reply.

I swallowed my gag reflex then laid out the audio equipment on the dining table. Hearing the soft rumble of sliding glass doors, I saw Tony step out onto the terrace overlooking the private beach. I willed myself to ignore the perfectly aligned rows of shiny little bottles on stepped and mirrored shelving. The key lay on the table right in front of me. I swallowed the lump of sand in my throat and concentrated on assembling the surveillance gear.

A few minutes later, I'd finished Tony and still had not returned, so I went looking for him. The veranda was empty. I was on the verge of calling out when I caught sight of him backing out of the dense foliage of the potted privacy jungle separating our from next door's balcony. He went inside and I followed. Carefully, Tony paced off ten steps where he directed me to stand before returning outside. Moments later he appeared at the sliding door and signaled me to move back a little. We repeated this sequence until I found myself opposite a color-washed ink sketch of a Key West harbor scene, in—you guessed it—mauve. The dark mauve aluminum frame was screwed to the pale mauve wall in an effort to deter theft, whereas good taste alone should have sufficed.

Tony used a screwdriver accessory to remove the objet d'art then gently tapped the wall with the base of his pocketknife until he found an appealing spot. Plunging the blade into the sheet rock, he chewed out a rough circle of wall about ten inches in diameter. I directed a narrow beam from my penlight into the gaping wound as he carefully scraped a narrow hole almost through to the paper inside the wall of the adjoining suite.

Unnecessarily, he held a finger to his lips as he signed for me to bring the electronics bag. He slipped the sponge-rubber condom off the microphone. Twice, he tried fitting the mike head in the small hole, each time slightly widening the excavation until it fit snugly. A couple of strips of masking tape set it in place. Next, he switched on the recorder, adjusting gain and tone on the tiny amplifier.

I pulled on the spare headset, plugged in, and heard White saying, "...stop being part of the problem, and start being part of the solution. Another foul-up like tonight and I'll have the lot of you guarding snow shovels at a weather station on the Bering Straits."

I couldn't hear the response, if there was one it must have been brief because White continued almost uninterrupted. "Fife and Lewis went against orders. The team was supposed to secure the perimeter, only. I gave specific orders for a reason. You should have prevented them—"

There must have been an attempted rebuttal.

"That's not germane, you were inserted into the team to ensure the delivery would be completed, so far you've done nothing but screw up. Tonight, will serve as a lesson to you on the consequences of ignoring orders. A lesson I want everyone to take to heart. Be at Point Alpha tomorrow, at 1600 hours. You have until then to grow a pair of balls. And, if you bother me one more time without good reason, you're on the next transport north. Do not doubt that I will make it my personal mission to see that you won't be coming back. Do I make myself lucid?"

A reply must not have been essential because the phone crashing into its cradle buried the needles of the VU meters into the red. I looked at Tony who looked knowingly at me and nodded. He seemed, like me, to be thinking, "Uh huh."

The handset clattered again when White picked it up then began tapping in a long distance call. For some reason, I sensed this could be something hot. Tony paid close attention to the needle movement recording the tones; they could be decoded. If White was about to check in with his boss, we needed to know where this call was going. I wondered, and not for the second time, just how far up the chain of command the corruption spread.

The tenor of this conversation was substantially different from the last.

"Angel?" White asked diffidently.

Something in my memory banks twitched at the name, but my mnemonic retrieval system found nothing. Yet, I had the disturbing feeling that the name should mean something.

After a pause he identified himself: "White. Yes, sir, I know—"

He seemed to be on the taking end of a severe reprimand.

I grinned.

"I'm very close to concluding this phase of the operation.... Two assets were withdrawn."

"*Withdrawn?*" I stopped grinning.

"They precipitated the action themselves. The incident was fully contained, and with plausible deni—

"No, there was no local participation involved.... Two more days on site should see this resolved.... Yes, sir; I'll apprise you soonest of any further developments."

This time the phone was cradled quite gently.

"That's it. Let's grab the son of a bitch." I whispered angrily.

"We are. Assume he's armed. And, here...." He handed me the Beretta I'd left on the table by the electronics gear when I'd set it up. "Stop leaving your weapon lying around. Keep it with you!"

I acknowledged the rebuke. He'd been right, I wasn't used to carrying a gun, nor was it my aspiration.

*   *   *

**Force, and fraud, are in war
the two cardinal virtues.**

- Thomas Hobbes

CHAPTER 65

Like all good plans, ours was the ultimate in simplicity: we'd surround the other guy.

After counting off sixty seconds on my watch, I slipped over the rail set into the top of the concrete wall and crouched in the shadows of the potted palms on White's terrace. Luck, I noticed, was with us for a change. The patio door was open. Another twenty seconds passed. I heard a knock at White's door. Wearing slacks and a shirt, he entered from another room carrying a hand towel. He paused to take a small pistol from a holster under his jacket on a chair. Draping the towel over his gun hand he queried his visitor as he neared the door. I couldn't make out the muffled response, it must have been enough to make him curious yet sufficiently innocuous so not to have raised any suspicions. He dropped the towel onto a side table, transferred the gun to his left hand and slipped it under his belt at the small of his back. Not completely taken in by whatever he'd heard, he continued to hold it by the grip. Standing partially behind the door, he reached to open it with his right hand. That was the moment I chose to act.

As the door swung open I stepped into the room and pointed my pistol at him.

"Police! Freeze! You're under arrest."

The kid in the blue and red uniform stood framed in the doorway. Blood drained from his face, his mouth gaped wide in shock. The flat box flew out of the red insulated sleeve and whirled through the air when White grabbed the kid's outstretched arm then wheeled him around in front, using him as a shield. A strangled squawk came from the boy's mouth as White's arm tightened around his slender throat. The kid's eyes were large with terror and frantically darting in every direction.

Time seemed to slow with the molasses texture of inevitability as White's gun swung toward me. His face was cold with determination. I saw the barest hint of a grim smile flicker when he recognized me. A lethal glint shone in his gray killer's eyes. He knew I was a dead man.

I froze.

White's eyes shot wide open, his head arched back, the pizza boy sailed towards me propelled by White's body. A pile-driving shoulder block, laid about waist high from behind, cut White in half and sent both of them flying into the room. The gun spun out of White's hand as he crashed into the heavy bureau then fell hard to the floor where he lay, writhing, gasping like a fish out of water.

Grease dripped from the inverted pizza box.

Tony rolled White over, straddled his back, put a restraining hold on his wrists and started reading him his rights in a workman-like portrayal of a police officer.

I snapped out of my daze. Taking my cue, I helped the kid up, thanking, congratulating him for being of service in apprehending a criminal, asking him if he was okay, all the while escorting him out of the suite. His eyes were round with astonishment and shock, but otherwise, he seemed not too worse for his experience. I walked him back to his delivery vehicle where I had him write his name and address on a slip of paper. When I paid him for the ruined pizza, I sternly warned him against saying anything about the case for twenty-four hours, because he was going to be a very important material witness and we needed to preserve his original impressions for his testimony.

Between nervous gulping and wide-eyed "Wows" and "Yes-sirs" he stammered a promise not to say a word. I figured he couldn't wait to get back and brag about how he'd single-handedly helped catch Public Enemy number one. Watching him drive out of the lot, I figured—according to the ads—we had "less than thirty minutes, guaranteed" before we had to be gone, but where?

Tony'd stripped White of his shoelaces and used them to fashion a serviceable behind-the-back, finger and thumb restraint. Our guest was clearly not impressed with Tony's craft skills. The blood suffusion in his face, as he scourged us with a predictable menu of threats, showed a dangerously high cholesterol level. Refusing to settle down, a short clinical tap Tony delivered to the occipital region of his skull, which I saw as a merciful attempt to save him from further anxiety, caused him to instantly go limp. He appeared to be smiling peacefully, as he lay on the floor.

We quickly gave the room a going over, scooping everything into White's suitcase. After taking his luggage to the van, I returned to our own unit where Tony had already stowed the electronics away and replaced the artwork on the wall. He accompanied me on a "dummy check" of the adjoining suite. The rooms looked exactly as before, except for the small stain on the carpet. Before leaving, Tony called down and asked to be read back the number of the long distance call he'd placed a few minutes ago.

I was impressed; a lot easier than duplicating recorded beeps.

He jotted the number down, thanked the operator then pocketed the whole pad of hotel stationery. We then toweled off any surface we might have touched. Having read enough spy-versus-spy fiction, I understood why.

If only this *was* fiction, I wished.

Linking arms around White, we hustled him between us, down the stairs and through the parking lot to the van. Keeping up a light patter, like two friends helping a pal who'd had a little too much of a good time, hoping to deflect attention from the unconscious guy between us. I expected us to be stopped any moment by a roving security patrol, but we made it without incident.

Tony left me on guard, saying, "Just in case...." before heading back to make a final walk-through of both units. Also, 'just in case' my pistol lay in my lap, under my jacket, where I could reach it quickly. One of the A-team, or any of a hundred other catastrophes, might show up uninvited. Sarge, I noticed, didn't seem to mind one way or another as he happily munched the cheesy mess of pizza while keeping one eye on our new best friend.

Tappety tap tap!

Immediately, Sarge's rumbling grumble was directly behind my right arm. I slowly turned my head and found myself face-to-face with the flirtatious member of the sun-bronzed couple we'd met earlier.

"Leaving, so soon?"

When I rolled the window down, he put his hands on the window frame.

Teasing, he said, "Don't tell me we scared you and your good-looking, *friend*, away?"

Without looking, I pushed back at Sarge, while trying to think of a suitably unprovocative reply. Sarge resisted. I persisted. Grudgingly, he conceded another couple of inches. I felt my jacket sliding to the floor between my legs.

"I'm Todd..."

I looked down.

"...and *you're* shy."

The Beretta glistened lethally. It was in plain sight.

"That is so-o-o endearing."

Todd leaned forward, his head inclining inside the open window, as if he meant to rest his head on my arm on the doorframe. Perhaps, he wanted to gaze up into my eyes. Most likely he would try to see if Tony was in the back, or check on the state of my arousal. What he *was* going to see was either the gun in my lap or an unconscious guy sprawled in back with a pizza-faced Rottweiler waiting to rip into him.

Todd's head made contact with my forearm, a dreamy look in his eyes, his teeth parted to show the tip of his tongue. For a moment I fantasized slamming the barrel into his mouth, wondering if it would leave a gun-shaped hole in his grin before the orthodontist-perfect teeth crackled and fell like Wile E. Coyote's. Slowly, Todd reached up to caress my cheek. His grin broadened as I slid my hand up his arm, cupping his hand against my face. I found his thumb, then gripped it and pulled it down and away from me. He let out a sharp yelp and rose up on tiptoes. Pushing down, in opposition to the natural action of the joint, I levered his elbow on the doorframe causing him to rise up even higher smacking the top of his head sharply into the window frame. When I let go he stumbled back holding his injured hand and head, excoriating me with a fiery string of unladylike and uncomplimentary revilement before lurching down the beach path where he almost collided with Tony.

Irritatingly insidious flirt or not I'd hurt someone. Needlessly causing pain, delighting in using a dirty trick—calling it cleverness. Probably, I could've found another way to thwart his prying but I'd resorted to violence; it was an easy solution that required little or no thought; talk about instant gratification. I should have known better but I thought I needed to put on a tough, smart front to impress Tony. In reality, I think I might have been trying to impress myself.

"Don't ask," I cautioned Tony when he got in.

I saw him weigh the sequence of gibes already on his tongue then, to his credit, let them drop.

"Okay, where to?" I asked, ignoring what might have been the lingering trace of a smirk, completely missing his clinical evaluation of my *tough, smart*-ness. "The dock? Whatever's left of it is out. The motel…?"

"Think that'd be pushing it just a tad, don't you?"

He was right. Being directly across the street from the A-team, with their abducted commander bound, gagged, and stuffed into a closet *was* pushing what little luck we had to the extreme.

"Hey…!"

Tony listened to my idea, a smile slowly growing.

*   *   *

Calling shapes and beckoning shadows dire,
And airy tongues that syllable men's names
On sands, and shores, and desert wildernesses.
These thoughts may startle well, but not astound
The virtuous mind, that ever walks attended
By a strong siding champion, Conscience.

- John Milton

CHAPTER 66

Flaccid strands of black and yellow crime-scene tape, if they were meant to keep anyone out, were a waste of perfectly good plastic. A couple of neighborhood kids were already using two of them as the basis for an intricate game of tag, while another was zooming about trailing several streamers in a modified Super Hero cape. Tony detached the strands across the driveway and opened the gates. Once safely inside, hidden behind the high fence capped on all sides by a thick spiny spread of bougainvillea, I began to breathe a little easier. Sarge explored the grounds while we carried our unconscious prisoner into the shop.

When I first became involved in construction, on Monk's behalf, I had the garage converted into a soundproofed workshop. That same baffling and insulation, used to muffle heavy power-tools, allowing work to continue well after dark without disturbing the neighborhood, was about to serve another more sinister purpose.

Tony went out to retrieve the Nagra and the rest of Duffy's bag of tricks, affording Sarge the opportunity to slip inside past the closing door. I had almost finished replacing the improvised shoe-lace bonds from our supply of nylon cable-ties, using them to secure him to the base of a cast-iron table saw, when I noticed Sarge edging closer. I stopped what I was doing to watch. After giving White a couple of tentative sniffs Sarge *whuffed* once, derisively, then went over near the door where he found a soft piece of concrete floor to lie on.

His assessment of our new friend pretty well matched my own. Even without his superior canine sense of smell, there was enough of a repellent sourness emanating from our guest that I was compelled to finish quickly and join Sarge near the door. There I wondered what sequence of events could conspire to create such a creature.

Unconscious, his legs sprawled wide, back slumped against the heavy table saw; I looked for some outward indication of the history of carnage and devastation accredited to him, but found none. He looked like a copier salesman or an accountant snoozing off the effects of an office party; in a word: harmless. Resting, chin on knees, I stroked Sarge who, I noticed, never took his eyes from the inert Mr. White.

Fixing the tape recorder against the rip fence above White's head with a bit of masking tape, Tony clicked on voice-activation mode. A few minutes later, when White, who had already begun to make noises and show signs of regaining consciousness, went uncharacteristically quiet, Tony dropped Duffy's kit bag on the floor near him and began noisily rummaging through its contents. Curiosity got the better of White; he began sneaking peeks. I could see that he recognized the bag, probably knew what it contained and that meant he must have a good idea what might be in store for him. Tony stopped scrabbling, evidently having found what he'd been looking for then pulled out one of the modified Tasers. He stepped back, pointed its flat rectangular face at White, there was an instant and violent reaction.

Eyes wide, head shaking, "No!" White jerked and wiggled madly trying to shrink out of the way. Sarge was on his feet, growling; his fur bristled. I held his collar to restrain him.

A pneumatic *phffutting*-sound announced a pair of tiny probes that shot out and buried themselves into White's chest and abdomen. Each trailed a fine wire connecting it to the handset. White was frantic. Tony's almost casual caress of the trigger switch caused White's body to spasm and arch almost off the floor. Alarmed by the sudden and violent reaction, I was on my feet. Sarge, equally startled, emitted a concerned noise and backed half-a-step behind me. Tony seemed frozen by the spectacle. White's face crimsoned and his eyes rolled back until only the whites showed. A soupy substance began trickling from his nostrils. His face was turning purple. He couldn't breathe. Before Tony could move, I jumped forward and ripped the tape from White's mouth. Immediately, he covered himself with the contents of his stomach. My motivation, I'm ashamed to admit, was not wholly humanitarian. We needed to find out what he knew. He could yell and shout as much as he wished inside the soundproofed garage but he had to be alive in order to tell us what we wanted. Asphyxiating in his own vomit, much as he may have deserved such a nasty end, wasn't going to help our situation.

White's mouth moved silently, like a fish out of water, trying to pull air into his lungs. He gasped. Then wheezing in little grunts he started to take in a little air. Slowly, too slowly for my liking, his breathing and color returned to normal. The hatred in his eyes was still there, now tempered with fear and something else. An ammoniac stink filled the air a moment before a stain began to spread, darkening the concrete under him.

"Don't worry, I'll help you," I said with concern.

White looked up at me, half-expectantly when I reached down behind the table saw, as if hoping I might free him from his bonds. Bringing out a five-gallon pail, I covered the mess sprinkling on and around him with handfuls of sweet-smelling sawdust.

"There, all better now." Feeling terribly clever I resisted patting him on the head, only just.

Our guest didn't look overly pleased.

Tony turned his head and grunted something, which I thought might have been a laugh. When he turned back, I saw my petty callousness appraised in his flat glare. The mean-spirited grin melted from my face. Instantly, I was chilled despite the now almost stifling atmosphere in the garage. Chastened, I drifted back to stand with Sarge by the door.

White's reaction, when Tony toggled the switch again, was more terrifying than the first; the next was even worse. White didn't even try to play the hero; he screamed long and loud his voice going hoarse as, again and again, Tony sent one pulsating shock after another jolting through him. There were no questions for White to deny and earn the punishment he was receiving; there was no resistance, only the nonstop ebb and flow of agony. Each barrage diminished my resolve and eroded my nerve. Having never been involved in anything even remotely like premeditated torture before, I couldn't stop thinking of Monk and how he'd been "lit up" and what it had done to him. I could only imagine what was happening inside White's mind, as he sank deeper and deeper into the abysmal depths of suffering, looking as if the very life force was being leeched from him.

Concerned that we might end up with another corpse on our hands, I caught Tony's eye, and nodded towards the door. After a very long pause, during which he leveled those penetrating eyes at me, thankfully, he nodded.

"Watch him!" I commanded, forcing strength into my voice where there was none; making it sound, for White's benefit, as though Sarge would know what I was talking about.

Resisting the impulse to run and keep running, I stopped outside where I greedily took in deep draughts of the sweetly fragrant night air. I hadn't realized just how oppressive the interior of the shop had become.

I heard the door close behind me.

"Remember what Monk looked like?" I whispered harshly, "I don't think he can stand much more—I can't stand much more of this."

My words hung, unanswered, in the air. I turned, fearing what I might see reflected in Tony's eyes. He gave me a long, cold look. I shrank inside.

"Do we have to jam him like this?" I could hear the pleading tone in my voice, so unlike the cool assurance I had felt when we began this exercise in terror scarcely half an hour earlier. "We're not even asking him anything? We're, we're...." I couldn't give what we were doing a name.

Perhaps, it was because I was showing signs of rejoining the human race, I thought I saw him thaw several degrees.

"If I can convince him that we have no qualms about torturing him to death, for the sheer thrill of it, he might say something I can get down on tape, something that'll help us." With that Tony turned to go back into the shop. I knew what that would mean to the man waiting inside; imagined what his return would mean if it was me in there.

"You had me convinced." There was an edge to my voice.

Tony stopped. He turned and gave my upper arm a hard squeeze. "I know how to do this."

My thoughts must have been obvious. He waited with me, silent, making no move to return inside. We stood on the narrow flag-stoned path that led from the shop to the kitchen door on the side of the house. Above us the thin, sharp horns of the Devil's moon cast its pale glint above the coppery glow of Mars. A velvet wind gave shadows movement.

"How about putting on a pot of coffee? We may have a long night in store." Then he added gently, "I *will* be careful."

I nodded, but before I could start for the house, Tony gave my shoulder a final squeeze.

"That's a promise."

"Thanks." I nodded again. The door closed behind me, leaving me alone with my thoughts.

*   *   *

CHAPTER 67

It had been several days since I'd been home and I was ready for a change of scene from the motel room, or so I thought.

The bulk of the damage inside was mostly confined to spillage, turning things over, and scattering books and papers. The contents of the fridge and cupboards covered the most of the kitchen floor and were alive with cockroaches, ants, and palmetto bugs. Judging by the smell, my visitors had been either unable to find, or understand the complicated workings of a toilet. Fortunately, my tabula rasa lifestyle, and having pared down preparatory to moving, gave little fuel to the efforts of vandals save for the walls, which were splashed and covered with obscene and some misspelled graffiti; they'd needed repainting for some time, I rationalized. Even the ground-in fecal footprint on the prized Ghiordes prayer rug I'd rescued from a thrift shop was a minor inconvenience. The only casualties were photographs of adventures shared with Charlie. The torn and crumpled mementos lay scattered about, though the memories remained untarnished and intact.

In the course of setting things right I located the base unit. A few minutes later the handset was discovered behind an overturned dresser. Until I was actually standing there, amid the wreckage, with the complete telephone in my hand, I hadn't understood that my quest had had a purpose.

*   *   *

**The voice so sweet, the words so fair,
As some soft chimed had stroked the air;
And though the sound were parted thence,
Still left an echo in the sense.**

- Ben Jonson

CHAPTER 68

Warm, sweet, and musical, with a hint of a husky purr that sent shivers a-tingling up my spine and bristled the fine hairs on the back of my neck, hers was a voice that reached out of the past from a place where bittersweet memories dwelt. It was so reminiscent of Nicole's that I almost cried from its familiarity.

Sounding as if she welcomed having the long night interrupted, the nurse on the night desk said she wasn't supposed to release any information. Craving the embrace of my dead love's voice, no matter what, I persisted, prolonging the experience. Through improvisation and invention, I convinced her that I was a relative, calling long distance—not a reporter as she'd first suspected—and a medical student, a fellow professional with whom she could be candid.

"Seeing how you're family and all," she supposed, "calling all the way from Oregon, I guess it'd be okay to tell you, though he isn't allowed visitors yet, your cousin is no longer in ICU..."

Once begun, as the conversation gathered momentum. I warmed myself in the familiar sound wrapped around words Nicole had never spoken, listening with only half an ear to what the woman was actually saying.

"...he's responding to treatment, and post-operative recovery is listed as satisfactory," she added, as if referring to his chart.

My hand moved with an exaggerated slowness. Her voice grew faint then was cut off as I replaced the phone in its cradle. To keep from going back into the shop and emptying my pistol into White's face I had to do something positive, so I immersed myself in a binge of cleaning while tears ran freely down my face.

Miraculously, a gift box containing a bottle of Napoleon brandy, a dusty and forgotten token of appreciation from Monk for one of the first "jobs well done" had somehow escaped the attention of Duffy's crew during their visitation. I found it under an overturned file caddy beneath a scatter of books and project papers strewn about my office. The box literally fell apart in my hands when I picked it up but the bottle was still intact and unopened. I placed it beside White's attaché case on top of my desk. The rest of the house was a mess but my office was soon squared away.

Often, seemingly of their own volition, while I cleared away and set things right, my eyes sought out the rich green shape on the back corner of my desk. The precise almost delicate folds of lead wrapping that sealed the cork drew me closer. The suede finish on the bottle soothed my fingertips. Raised golden script held a tacit promise of the treasure contained within and its effects on one's spirit. I swallowed a dry parchment swallow.

Outside, I heard the shop door open and close. My heart leapt into my throat. In a panic, I wanted to hide the bottle inside the desk drawer; it wouldn't fit. Tony and Sarge were right outside the kitchen door. I heard the knob turning. Fumbling, almost dropping it, I barely managed to return it to its place on the desk before Sarge's nails *tic-tic-ticked* across the kitchen tiles.

Sarge wanted petting; I was powerless to resist. A moment later Tony, cup in hand, appeared in the doorway.

"'Lookin' good," he nodded approvingly at the restored order, then raising a mug suggested, "'Take a break?"

After regaining my composure, I joined him in the kitchen, where, after adding enough sugar to improve the flavor of battery acid, he shook his head in the negative to my unspoken question, then headed for my office and White's briefcase. If he noticed the bottle of brandy on the desk he didn't mention it. I didn't give him the chance.

"Monk's alive."

The tone of my voice stopped him. He stood with his back to me, tense, listening.

"M-most of his arms and legs...nerve damage...gangrene...."

He turned and fixed me with an intense stare as the meaning hit home.

"They had to—"

The sustained silence started to deteriorate what little was left of my self-control. Up to that point I'd avoided dealing with it. The silence continued, Tony said nothing to dispel it. It soon became too much for me, I had to try and explain what was going on. I stared into the mug clasped between my hands, as if the answer was hidden in the impenetrable black depths, but the words wouldn't come.

"I've, I've been trying to make sense out of everything, everything that's happened—" I heard my voice rising in pitch, edging towards hysteria, so I shut my mouth around a large gulp of coffee, searing the back of my throat.

"You're not the Lone Ranger," he said gently, coming closer. "Its been getting to me too, but you gotta remember, what's done is done, and ain't no changing that." He put a comforting hand on my shoulder. "'Best thing is to talk it out when we feel the pressure starting. Don't forget, there is an upside: We have their goods; more importantly, we have White. Believe it or not, I really think we might be able to pull this off. But I'm not going to say don't worry, 'cause that's so much happy horseshit. You'd better, 'cause you're gonna need that edge."

With that said, he gave my arm a soft jab then turned to the desk and White's attaché case. Unsnapping the locks he lifted the lid. I was about to ask what he meant, when there was a sharp *rap-rap-rap* at the front door. Automatically, my head turned. Sensing movement beside me, I looked back and saw the lid of the case falling shut. Tony's Beretta was already in his hand, he was bent low in a half-crouch and moving silently toward my unlit bedroom at the back of the house. He touched a finger to his lips, lifted it away and made a half-circling motion in the air then flashed five fingers twice. Another three raps, a little more insistent, came from the front door but I waited until he'd melted into the darkened interior of the bedroom before counting to ten.

*   *   *

CHAPTER 69

A squad car was parked in front of my house. Up and down the block some of the neighbors had gathered into loose knots of interest. Police visiting a Bahama Village residence, especially late at night, was a public event to be witnessed first-hand then shared at news-dissemination briefings in launderettes and corner stores over the following days. Tabloids have nothing on these local news-gatherers; each is skilled in recalling relevant items that may never have happened in order to prove conjectures and hypotheses of things that perhaps never would. It was entertainment and communication in the traditional manner. There were no drums to beat, nor signal fires to light; word of mouth was the media. Soon, the story would grow and take on a life of its own until eclipsed by one more lurid, compelling and current.

In the wake of the recent vandalism in my home, it stood to reason that someone in the neighborhood would be on the lookout for my return. Thus, the police visit. I was an idiot not to have taken this into account when I suggested we hide out there. Stuck between a hard place of my own fashioning and a rock with a badge and gun, I had no option but to play it out.

The officer turned from his observation of the stacked debris and overloaded garbage containers; he was fairly young, in his mid-to-late twenties. His trim, Tom Cruise-like good looks, infectious grin, and courteous manner were in direct contrast to my idea of the typical cop. Apparently, he hadn't become jaded, corrupted, or callused by the constant contact with the assholes of the world, yet.

I invited him in then gave a cheery wave to the local Press Corps, who immediately began to fragment into small conversational clusters.

Evidently, unfortunately for the assembled audience, there were to be no fireworks tonight. Though, I'm sure every move, word or gesture I'd ever made since arriving here would be collectively taken out, dusted off, and closely examined in order to determine what had really transpired. If nothing came of it, then a reporter would probably be delegated and sent around to interview me under the guise of "just dropping by to say how-ya-doin." The Rock may have been many things, but it was, above all else, a very small town. In small towns the Unofficial Press Corps never sleeps.

Officer Joe Murphy commiserated with me over the damages. Strangely, I found myself actually believing him—a new experience for me in dealing with law enforcement types. I imagined the usual police station humps, seemingly the rule rather than the exception, giving him the tedious chores like calling on absentee victims while saving themselves for the excitement and danger of cracking important cases; cases of Twinkies and do-nuts, most likely.

He had, he said, been trying to reach me for several days, and had taken to periodically driving by in the hope of finding me home. He was on his way back to the station at the end of his shift when he received an anonymous call from my next-door neighbors reporting my return. I invented a vague shopping trip to Miami in answer to his circumspect query of my whereabouts. White's luggage, standing in the hall by the entrance to my office, added verisimilitude to the lie.

He gave me a case-file number and a victims rights brochure; they would help, he said, in dealing with the insurance companies. —In one of my more brilliant financial maneuvers, believing I had little to interest any self-respecting burglar, I'd never bothered with insurance.

Fidgeting with a broom, indicating my need to get back to the reclamation of my home, he took the hint. Unable to hide his revulsion; the unmistakable odors of human waste and rotted food that permeated the house may have helped curtail a lengthy conversation, probably loaded with questions I was ill-prepared and unwilling to answer. I saw him to the door and thanked him for his consideration, mentally wishing him luck; mostly in finding a new line of work before he succumbed to the case-hardening and morals-twisting process that seemed to me to be a major and inevitable component of his profession. There had been a refreshing openness about him that I'd liked, and I found myself wishing he not lose it.

The patrol car had faded into the distance when Tony stepped back inside, his gun again in its holster. The call-by, he allowed, in light of the break-in and the neighborhood, was only to be expected and nothing to be overly concerned about, for the moment. I confessed my own negative opinion of police forces in general, when I received no dispute, added. "I can't help feeling sorry for that guy, he doesn't seem to fit the mold; every cop I've met could care less about the victim. He seemed different. I actually believed him."

Tony barked a short bitter laugh. "Give him time, he'll come around."

Intuition told me he was mistaken but I shrugged it off. When it came to being a shrewd judge of character my batting average, as of late, had fallen far below 1.000. Besides a discussion of a young cop's questionable lack of apathy really wasn't that important, there were more immediate problems we had to deal with, like survival.

Tony opened White's attaché case and began carefully examining the contents. I could stack books and sort papers anytime. I pulled up a director's chair still missing the canvas back panel. We catalogued the contents: A diplomatic passport, inappropriately, made out in the name: Whitelaw, read like a world tour; the most recent stamps were from South Africa, Israel, the Netherlands and a host of South and Central American countries including Bolivia and Peru. Quite a few visits were to Switzerland.

White's official status was a perfect mask for his clandestine affairs, but we found nothing to document any wrongdoing. The papers in the file sections mostly consisted of correspondence to and from various police and government agencies. Though some were in a foreign language, they appeared innocuous. A bundle of pens and pencils looked promising, but when examined carefully were just pens and pencils. Everything was consistent with the appearance of a travelling government functionary, including an odd assortment of airport claim check receipts, a large calculator, and a small laminated calendar card. We looked, poked, prodded and disassembled the attaché case to no avail. The answer had to be there somewhere but there was nothing out of the ordinary. If it *was* there, then I was either too tired or stupid to see it.

Someone once said: The only thing good about beating your head against a brick wall is how good it feels when you stop. I took that sage advice and stopped.

When I looked in on White, I took the precaution of slipping a couple of Monk's remaining Nembutal into his mouth. As I re-taped it shut the look in his eyes was pure venom. I shivered inwardly at the promise they held in store for me. So unnerved by the glimpse of raw hatred, I decided to add another nylon tie to each wrist and found he'd almost succeeded in chafing through the existing restraints. He was obviously going to require full-time observation. After securing a new pair of cable-ties to each wrist, I brought in a padded mover's quilt for Sarge to sleep on and an overloaded food dish as compensation for having to be shut in with White. As he plowed through his second dinner of the night, I noticed that he appeared to be taking his confinement with both forbearance and dignity. I gave Sarge a scratch behind the ear then a cheery wink to White before locking them both in.

Tony looked up from his examination of case and contents when I reported my findings and the safeguards I'd taken. He expressed appreciation for my thoroughness, but I didn't feel thorough; tired, vulnerable and very fragile; yes. Also, the inside of my eyelids felt raw and gritty and I was starting to see double.

*   *   *

Oh why did I awake?
When shall I sleep again?

- Alfred Edward Housman

CHAPTER 70

Reluctantly, I awakened from a tragic dream; one I had had more times than I could remember—though, I hadn't experienced it in almost a year. In it a beautiful raven-haired woman had lain in my arms. She cried softly as I tried to soothe her. The tragedy was in waking up without her by my side. The events of the last few days rolled in relentlessly replacing whatever warm remnants I'd carried from my sleep with a cold sense of disconnection to what and where I wanted my life to be. My uneasiness was partially dispelled by the knowledge that we had captured and now controlled the key to our survival and by the tantalizingly nutty smell of freshly brewed coffee, which drew me into the kitchen where I found an almost full pot of Cuban espresso warming on the stove.

The waking-up process almost complete, I wandered from room to room, sipping from my steaming cup, reacquainting myself with my little home—for however long I'd have it as my own. In the morning light the degradations the cottage had suffered were not as apparent as the night before. Other than a damp towel in the bathroom, there were no signs of recent human habitation. My search for Tony led me to the workshop. Despite my budding hatred of guns, I carried the Beretta loaded, cocked and ready in my hand. The events since finding Doug's mutilated body had irrevocably changed me. I doubted I'd ever be able to go through a closed door again without anticipating either a threat or some unknown or horror lying in wait.

Three pairs of eyes looked up at my entrance. Sarge, always the clear thinker, seeing no reason to be inside any longer than absolutely necessary, pushed past White to get out. He seemed to make a point of roughly jostling him aside. Knowing what I knew, I wouldn't have blamed him if he'd chewed White's head off.

"So, do we kill the son of a bitch now, or wait 'til after breakfast?"

Tony, who'd gotten up to follow Sarge outside, looked me in the eye. He tried and only just succeeded in keeping a straight face. White, too, looked at me but he showed no appreciation of my attempt at humor. —I wasn't completely sure humor is what I'd intended— I saw uncertainty, a fleeting shadow of something approaching vulnerability in those inhumanly pale eyes until he quickly turned his gaze away lest I catch a glimpse of the inner workings of his mind.

If, as the poets would have us believe, the eyes are truly the windows of the soul, then White had no soul. His actions, to date, had me convinced.

I sat on the edge of the big workbench and studied our captive. Intriguing, in the way people are drawn to the snake exhibit in a zoo; it was like looking at a particularly loathsome species: fascinating, cold-blooded and deadly. I tried to figure out what made this creature tick. He killed with no compunction; lied and cheated with every breath he drew. Why, I asked myself, should something like this be allowed to live? When I'd tried to execute Duffy, I was prevented by something in me that recognized worth. However small, Duffy had had worth, but in this monster I saw nothing redeeming whatsoever. I looked at the pistol in my hand. I knew I was getting close to the abyss; to the point where there would be no pulling back. I could stop this while it was still an intellectual exercise, so I placed the gun on the bench then hunkered down in front of him. Eye-to-eye, I was, close enough to hear him breathing. Beads of perspiration spotted White's hairline and a tic started below his right eye. He was unnerved by my scrutiny. Perversely, I enjoyed his discomfort, but it served no real purpose other than pandering to some morbid, sadistic thrill, so I checked his restraints, found them intact, retrieved my pistol then left.

"Anything?"

Tony was in the breakfast nook close to the kitchen door nursing a coffee. He'd left me alone with White. I appreciated the trust but left my acknowledgment unspoken. I gave him an edited version of my observations.

Tony nodded. "First thing this morning, when I looked in on him, he was still pretty fucked-up; probably a combination of shock, stress and barbiturates. I managed to get him to talking a bit, before he came to—"

He hesitated. I saw him eye me strangely, struggling, then, having made up his mind, he continued.

"In addition to being in on the dope deal with Kiley, I think Monk might've been responsible for Kiley's death."

I didn't respond. It felt like there was a second bullet. I was right.

"You're not going to like this, but he was either out of his head or he was wasn't as far gone as I thought and he was jerking my chain, I think Monk had Kiley's guy, Deputy Schott, rig the bomb on Charlie's barge."

Mind reeling, I went into my office, grabbed the bottle of brandy, broke the seal and took a long pull. Gasping, coughing as the liquid fire burned its way down my throat, I sagged into my chair. I hadn't been a drinker for five years, since Charlie helped me resurrect my life, but right then I needed a jolt. I felt like I was going to need a lot of jolts, and maybe there weren't ever going to be enough jolts to stop the shrieking inside of my head.

After prying my fingers from the bottle, Tony dumped an unwholesomely large slug into my mug and topped it off with coffee. I heard him pouring the rest of it down the kitchen sink. I wanted to curse him for the waste but part of me, the part Charlie'd helped to rebuild, recognized the act as one of kindness and clear-thinking; with the kind of snarl we were caught in, a drunk with a gun was a liability.

*   *   *

CHAPTER 71

Key West is a very small town; because of the disparate and dubious nature of many of its citizens, it resembles a Rubik's cube of cells, cliques and circuits. All interlocking and interdependent yet each one is separate, distinct in its own right. Reds may associate with blues, yellows and greens but only within certain limits. Charlie and Tony had each let on that they knew the other; I sensed a shared past, but neither would elaborate beyond saying that they traveled in different circles. Tony had delivered the news of Monk's complicity in Charlie's death as gravely as if he had lost a close member of his own family. Unlike me, he was keeping things in perspective: Charlie was dead, nothing was going to bring him back, but that didn't make it easier to bear.

I picked up the calculator from White's briefcase, playing with it, something for my hands to do, to occupy my attention and a diversion away from my dark thoughts.

"That's odd?" I thought aloud.

The calculator, when I'd turned it on, flashed a please-return-to-owner message on the tiny screen along with a 1-800-number. None of the keys would function. What, at first glance, I'd mistaken for a calculator, appeared to be some kind of tiny computer. I fiddled and diddled it, and when all else failed, read the instruction manual on the fold-up lid. Nothing seemed to work except the flashing message.

Other than a nodding acquaintance, from a distance, computers and I had very little in common. I showed it to Tony, who also toyed with it unsuccessfully. Perhaps, I suspected, we already held the key to our survival.

"I'm going out for a bit, Tony said, taking the mini-computer with him. "There's someone I want to check this out. You okay keeping an eye on things 'til I get back?"

A little time would let me wrestle with my demons in private.

"I'm fine." I lied.

*   *   *

CHAPTER 72

With the house to myself I filled my cup, resisting the temptation to go out and get another bottle. Tony needed and trusted me to keep myself together. If I couldn't stay straight for myself I could do it for him, but I couldn't stop thinking how wrong I'd been about Monk. Lying and cheating I could understand, sort of—he was a lawyer—but a party to pre-meditated murder?

"Good morning, law offices of Montgomery Rothschild, how may I help you?"

Vastly different from her normal voice, which could melt stone and make a grown man sigh, Rosa affected an off-putting nasal whine, reminiscent of receptionists and telephone operators the world over.

"Hello, Sweetheart." I said in a passable Bogart growl; a standing joke, which never failed to elicit a giggle, though, my heart really wasn't in it today. Something Monk had said, or I thought he'd said, had been bothering me.

"Last week when Monk went out of town, where did he go?"

"New Orleans, why?"

Most of the coffee in my mouth went back in the cup; the rest I choked on as the gasp of air carried it into my lungs. Rosa waited until I'd stopped coughing and was able to breathe again.

Her voice dropped, "'funny you should ask, because the man he went to see has been waiting in the outer office since ten this morning. Monk hasn't been in or called. I don't know what to tell him. You haven't seen him, have you?"

"Listen," I whispered urgently between coughs, "whatever you do don't look at the guy. Turn and look out the front window."

"Wha—?"

"Please, just shut up for a second and do it. Are you turned away? Can he see you?"

"Yes—I mean, no. Why?"

"Just listen; is he a big fellow, around six-four or five, about three hundred pounds, looks like a walrus with a bad comb-over and a beard?"

"Why, yes. How did—? You're starting to scare me."

The urgency in my voice was getting through to her.

"Now, so he can hear you, but not too loud, I want you to pretend this is a normal call, uh, say I'm the guy you get office supplies from; just make it seem normal. Can you do that?"

"Thank you, but I'm having dinner with my husband tonight, and he wouldn't appreciate my standing him up."

I cringed at her improvisation.

"I'll still need those supplies Wednesday morning, they are going to be here first thing Wednesday, aren't they?" Then in a conspiratorial whisper, "How was that?"

"Great, you should have been a movie star." I lied. "Listen, as soon as he leaves I want you to call me at home. Now hang up and go back to what you were doing before I called, and remember, whatever you do, don't pay any attention to him when you hang up. Wait for him to get bored. Treat him like you would any other peon waiting to see 'El Bosso'. Got it?"

She agreed.

"Good. One last thing: before he leaves, try, but not too hard, to get a phone number or find out where he's staying. Now hang up, and remember, be cool."

I had a strong feeling of déjà vu, as if I'd traveled full circle and would never escape my past. I was shaken. This wasn't jumping to conclusions or imaginary shadows; it was real. My nerves were so badly frayed I almost dove under the desk when the phone rang. It was Tony.

"He's here! L'Angousette's here!" I burst out when I heard his voice. "It's no coincidence. He's in Monk's office, right now! What are we going to do?"

"First thing *you're* going to do is calm down."

"Okay-okay-okay, I'm calm." I heard the barely contained frenzy in my voice. "Now, what are we going to do?"

"'We' are going to tell me what you're talking about—Lang-goo-what?"

Briefly and dispassionately as I could, I told him about the events prior to my last Mardi Gras in New Orleans leading up to the confrontation I'd had with my former business partner before I ended up in Key West. Tony listened without interrupting.

"We got more bad news partner," he said. "My, uh, computer guy drew a blank on this, it's something he's never seen before. 'Says he'll keep trying, but doesn't think it's possible to get inside without zapping the data. Nice try but no cigar. Now, about your French buddy, are you absolutely sure it's him?"

I repeated the conversation with Rosa and her confirmation of my description of Monk's visitor.

"How about I tail him, he suggested, "he's never seen me."

I couldn't think. "Good idea." I agreed; any idea sounded good.

"Any chance of him leaving before I get there?"

"Rosa said he's been there since ten' he might wait for Monk until lunchtime. 'Figure about twenty minutes from now. I'm waiting for her to call back as soon as he leaves. She doesn't know about Monk. I've got to tell her." That was a conversation I was not looking forward to having.

"On my way."

After fifteen minutes of stewing and sweating, I heard the van outside. Concealing the loaded pistol behind my back, I met Tony at the gate.

"Traffic! The engine's overheating and Downtown's jammed with snowbirds. I'll move and blend in better on two wheels." Tony threw me the keys, as he headed for the bicycle rack.

"Hang at one of the sidewalk bars across from the office, he won't be hard to spot. Watch your back," I cautioned, twirling the lock's dial so Tony could memorize the combination, "he usually travels in a pack." I gave him a description of Gordo, L'Angousette's enforcer—a pack unto himself—before sending him off towards Duval Street. He was around the corner and out of sight in seconds.

Everything was in motion, kind of.

I checked to make sure White was still there. In a compromise to his request I brought in the portable toilet from the van. I kept the pistol trained on him throughout, not really caring if my presence inhibited his performance. As soon as he'd finished, I reattached his free hand to the saw base and checked the other ties.

Though he didn't really want to be coaxed back inside, Sarge complied. The look he gave me, as I closed the door, was poignant.

*   *   *

**The only trouble is, we cannot understand
what is happening to our neighbours.**

- Joseph Chamberlain I

CHAPTER 73

Rap-itty-rap-rap...ding dong!

Pistol in hand, held down and out of sight behind my leg, I opened the door.

"How-ya-doin'?" Phillip and Arlene, my usually dour next-door neighbors, said as one, before laughing at each other for their synchronicity, welcoming me home me with huge, toothy grins—the first display of their dental work they'd favored me with in the three years I'd been living next door.

After the events of the last week, my return to the neighborhood had probably eclipsed their customary diet of soap operas and tabloids as a potential source of entertainment.

Fending them off, twice, as they tried to edge their way past me, I dropped any pretense of good manners.

"There's a difference," I grumped, "between neighborly and nosy, and you just crossed the line. Go home, leave me alone, and mind your own business!" I shut the front door in their faces and locked it, sliding the deadbolt home with a substantial *Clack!*

I watched their shapes through the tiny frosted-glass rainbow. They stood on the porch for another moment or two, maybe, in case I had a change of heart, before shaking their heads at each other; Arlene saying, none too softly, "Boy's done lost his mind."

Phillip's "Uh huh!" signaled they had done all they could and it was time to leave.

*   *   *

Like one, that on a lonesome road
Doth walk in fear and dread,
And having once turned round walks on,
And turns no more his head;
Because he knows, a frightful fiend
Doth close behind him tread.

- Samuel Taylor Coleridge

CHAPTER 74

Get busy! Do something! The little voice in my mind commanded. After an indeterminate number of minutes in my office, sweating and staring at the misspelled obscenities smeared on the walls, waiting for the phone to ring while trying not to think of the time I'd spent in 'The Big Easy' I wasn't having much luck. Like footsteps in an ever-tightening spiral, pulling me back, it was all there again right in front of me, just as clear and frightening as if the intervening years had been nothing more than a crazy interlude. I'd thought I'd succeeded in putting the ashes of my life in New Orleans far behind me, but the tape loop of that last Mardi Gras played over and over in my mind; each image etched in my memory clear and sharp-edged as the irrevocably shattered fragments of a mirror.

My imagination conjured up a nightmarish variety of conclusions to my final scenario with Bobby, each more lurid than the last.

I used to scoff at *film noir* movie plots for being overly dramatic and unrealistic; now, caught in the inextricable machinations of a past I had thought I'd escaped, I wasn't so sure.

Shortly before noon, when the phone finally rang, I was a wreck.

Rosa told me that L'Angousette had just left. He'd gone, she said, without leaving his number, saying he planned to be back after lunch, if not then he would call on the following morning. She added that two men had come in to collect him and they'd left together. She remarked that they'd been extremely deferential towards him. I wasn't surprised;

L'Angousette was powerful and dangerous, demanding and receiving the respect due a feudal warlord.

"They were the most intimidating people I've ever seen. I don't know what I would have said if they'd questioned me. I, I'm just glad they're gone. I've been on nines and tens all morning wondering where Monk is. Someone from the police called, twice, wanting to speak to him about a break-in at the condo, and you-know-who has been threatening to come back down here from West Palm if she doesn't hear from him 'not now, but right now.'" Her mimicry of the General's signature demand for promptness was uncannily accurate.

Silently, I counted to ten then suggested she close up the office and go to lunch. "After," I added, "give the hospital a call to see how Monk's doing and if he needs anything." Deserving of his fate or not, Rosa needed to know.

The sharp intake of breath was prelude to a flurry of questions.

Briefly, I explained that Monk might have been involved in some unspecified activities concerning his business with L'Angousette and it would be in both his and Rosa's best interests if his whereabouts were kept entre-nous; no one else needed to know where he was at present, especially the General. There were enough loose cannons rolling on deck without adding another who could, and probably would, point the finger at me if; only because she envied my friendship with her son. —Because Monk had spent most of his life trying to live up to her expectations, he confided in her much too much. That she knew of my involvement with the condo-site and the contraband, I had to assume, was a given. That kind of aggravation I could do without.

I also suggested to Rosa, that it would be a good idea if she had the business calls routed to her home and stay clear of the office for at least a week. Although, nothing of this severity had ever happened before, she'd been witness to a few less-than-honorable events in Monk's past, and was well aware of the part I'd played in getting him off the hook on the last occasion. Rosa was smart enough to recognize the logic of my warnings coupled with my reluctance to discuss the reasons for Monk's hospitalization; it took me a moment to realize I was talking into an empty phone.

Okay, maybe I was a coward, but hospitals, I rationalized, are more experienced when it comes to breaking really bad news.

The temperature rose, as the hour hand dragged towards one o'clock. Several times I'd reached for and almost picked up the phone to call Louisiana, but there was no one there I could talk to, not anymore. I was cradling the phone in my lap with my hand resting on the receiver. The shrill jangle startled me.

Tony gasped, "He's at the same motel as the A-team."

That meant almost a two-mile car chase on bicycle; no wonder he was out of breath. Were White and L'Angousette in this together? I wondered.

I promised to bring the surveillance gear with me then hung up. Two of the dwindling supply of sleeping pills went into White's mouth before the application of a fresh band of duct tape over his mouth. His eyes flashed sheer, undiluted hatred. Letting it affect me, I listened to the loathsome little voice inside my head. (As species go, we humans are not really all that nice of an example). It was wrong and contrary to all the rules of common decency, but I couldn't resist rattling his cage, as I pocketed the tape recorder, saying, "We won't need a record of what's going to happen next."

Leaning down, I whispered in his ear that he'd just been given a lethal dosage and Sarge was going to be disposing of much of the evidence because I didn't expect to be back for at least a week to ten days. He tried not to show it, but I'd succeeded in scraping twenty-grit across a broad horizon of raw nerves.

I patted Sarge on my way out and wished him, "*Bon-appetite.*"

Phillip and Arlene sat rocking and fanning themselves on the front porch of their house, no longer smiling or making any pretense of not intently monitoring my every action. I closed and locked the driveway gates then gave them a big friendly wave and drove off.

*   *   *

He saw a Lawyer killing a viper
On a dunghill hard by his own stable;
And the Devil smiled, for it put him in mind
Of Cain and his brother, Abel.

- Samuel Taylor Coleridge

CHAPTER 75

Tony flagged me down on North Roosevelt Boulevard about a block away from the motel. I pulled into a remote parking slot in back of the Taco Bell.

"I couldn't believe it when they went there." He said, indicating the motel, as he wrestled the bike through the cargo doors. "For about half a second I thought they might be going to join up with or take on the A-team." He got in, closed the side door and came through to the front. He looked uneasy. "I never used to believe in coincidences before."

"Don't start now." I growled. "Remember Doug?" I'd been giving a lot of thought to coincidences before and during the drive over. I'd come to a conclusion that brought a bitter flavor to my words.

"Explain yourself." There was a dangerous edge to his voice.

"Think about it: we've being going around in circles trying to figure what...?"

There was a moment of silence. Then he got my meaning.

"Son of a bitch! He was right on top of us all the time. The A-team didn't pick up on us. He did!" Tony's eyes slitted tight with malice. Desire for immediate and wholesale destruction rolled off him in waves. "It was Monk playing both ends against the middle. I didn't think the greedy little fuck-spot was that devious. I don't give a good goddamn what you say, he deserves everything he got. Doug was a hell of a good man, too good to—"

Emotion choked Tony's words off. I knew what he wanted to say. His thoughts were not far from my own: When Monk insisted I return to the houseboat that last night to "keep an eye on things" while he contacted the proper authorities, he had purposively set me up to be killed with Doug and Tony,

"Let's see if we can locate their room and listen in?" I suggested.

Tony didn't say a word. He got out of the van with the electronics bag over his shoulder and set off, head down, towards the motel.

I gave a casual salute to the desk manager as I picked up the room key. As usual, a telephone welded Gollum's ear to his shoulder. He'd seemed a little nervous and twitchy, but I didn't pay much attention to him or to the way his beady little eyes followed me through the lobby. My adrenaline yo-yo was on the upswing again, if I'd been a little looser, I might have been a tad more observant.

Hindsight can be a wonderful thing.

The do-not-disturb sign was still in place. From the airless stink and rumpled bedding the room had remained undisturbed. Most of the equipment, I saw, was already assembled and set up on the table by the window. The recorder was connected to the signal amplifier, I could hear the small motor whirring.

I froze in my tracks.

There is something compelling about looking down the barrel of a gun that the human body instinctively interprets as a signal to cease activity. If he'd taken any notice of my growing resentment he hadn't shown it. Holstering the gun, Tony checked down the balcony both ways then locked the door behind me, and returned to the electronics surveillance station. I suppose he felt I should be taking his armed reception in stride. I still hadn't moved. He gave an imperceptible nudge to one of the aim-adjustment screws on the laser sight then, looking over his shoulder, held out a second headset and waved me forward to the table.

"French!"

He was right but he was wrong. I hadn't heard the rolling lazy slide of pure Cajun spoken in nearly five years. Outside of a few words it was just as incomprehensible to me now as it had been then, another brick wall. I looked at Tony expecting to see confusion. He grinned wolfishly, answering my shrug, saying, "I picked up enough in 'Nam to get a handle on this little coon-ass tet-a-tet."

"Wasn't what used to be French Indo-China European French?"

Allowing that they *were* substantially different languages, he then explained how, after serving almost two tours with a quartet of Cajun boys followed by time spent roaming the backwater maze of Louisiana bayous with two former members of his first team, who'd rotated out before disaster struck, he'd acquired a certain grasp of the language.

I presumed he was referring to his smuggling period.

"I won't pretend to be fluent, but I can probably get pretty close to the flav-or ob dis gumb-o," he said in a pure Big Easy dialect before turning his attention back to the headset where he made a couple fine adjustments to the alignment settings.

With nothing for me to do, I decided to raid the fridge; there had been little left at the house fit to eat. My face was wrapped around one end of a huge sandwich when I returned. Tony looked up and gave me a pleading look reminiscent of one of Sarge's better efforts. I presented him with an extended middle finger. Good-naturedly, he threatened me with a fist until I reached into the micro-kitchen and handed him an identical twin to the hero that was saving my own life.

His spit-in-the-devil's-eye grin after our pantomimed trading of insults warmed and gave me a small insight and understanding of the nature of friendships shared by comrades who have undergone battle together. A shrink might call it, male bonding; or a feminist, a 'dick thing'. Whatever it was, it gave me the strength to face more of the same deadly shit because, though I knew my knees would be shaking and my laundry stained, there was someone there to share the terror. Somehow that made it a little less scary. In a perverse way, it also made me acutely aware of the loneliness I'd carried for such a very long time.

*   *   *

"Yet each man kills the thing he loves,
By each let this be heard,
Some do it with a bitter look,
Some with a flattering word,
The coward does it with a kiss,
The brave man with a sword!"

- The Ballad of Reading Gaol, Oscar Wilde

CHAPTER 76

It had only been six years—it doesn't sound like much, if you say it fast—but it seemed like a lifetime since I'd lost Nicole. I'd learned a lot about being alone in that time.

It was near the beginning of '82 when I first came in contact with L'Angousette. He'd had a thing for Nicole that predated my arrival in town by several years. It was a sick and twisted 'thing' as I discovered one hot and rainy night. The beginning of the end started earlier that afternoon when she refused his invitation to be the star of his stable of nightclub performers and had security escort him out of her dressing room. When she'd gone on stage later that night, instead of the usual dollar-stuffing antics of her admirers, a gang of L'Angousette's goons had peppered her mercilessly with a hail of quarters and half-dollars. Responding to a call from the club manager, I found her in a backstage bathroom crying, her trembling body covered in angry welts.

Predictably, I reacted hot and hard.

Two days later I woke up in the hospital with a concussion, a pair of obnoxious detectives in my face, and my mind a total blank. The last thing I'd remembered was looking for blood: L'Angousette's. I'd been found, I was told, passed out behind the wheel of a wrecked car. The charge was drunk driving—I had stopped drinking six months before and, as a favor to Nicole, hadn't touched a drop since. When the lab records, which would have proved my innocence, couldn't be located I was given a suspended sentence.

Three months later my woman was dead.

I had been on the road with a new band and it was several days before word caught up to me. Arriving at New Orleans International, I was taken into custody by the same detectives who'd interrogated me in the hospital. They tried their damnedest but they couldn't discredit my alibi. The findings of the inquest were the very best that money could buy; it was, no doubt, L'Angousette's money. The ruling was death by accident owing to a faulty fuel line.

The explosion that destroyed my new Cadillac had come within days of her last refusal to sell the agency to L'Angousette for ten cents on the dollar (his idea of a fair price). The blast had taken off the front half of our house and left a three-foot crater where the car had stood. That I'd borrowed her powder-blue Lincoln instead of using the Caddy', simply because hers had had a full tank and I'd been too lazy to stop for a fill, was a burden I would carry with me until my dying day.

How many times, I have wished I could make that choice again and choose differently.

My third arrest came on the day of her funeral. I could still feel a residue of the rage; remembering how I'd looked up from her almost empty coffin, thinking I was hallucinating, seeing three pink stretch limousines enter the cemetery. Bobby'd put his arm around me, and Denis, her cousin, called my name distracting my attention. I heard car doors open, turned and saw L'Angousette, resplendent in a matching pink suit, a fat Havana cigar in his mouth, making a grand entrance. Following him, a full entourage; probably some of the creatures who'd tormented her that night, all decked-out in their party finery; talking, joking amongst themselves as if attending a festival.

Snake-eyed crazy, when I went straight at L'Angousette with a gravedigger's shovel, I was beaten into unconsciousness.

It really wasn't any surprise when L'Angousette cut the business out from under me through Bobby's addictions. Now, he was back again. I supposed that in some weird and perverted way our lives *were* fated to be inextricably intertwined.

When will it end? I wondered. *How* will it end?

*   *   *

In time of war,
the first casualty is truth.

- Boake Carter

CHAPTER 77

The constant weight under my arm and slight restriction of movement was wearying. I was glad of any excuse to take the shoulder holster off, if only for a little while—it wasn't actually the weight of the gun; it was the idea that was tiresome. A gun was a tool, a tool of death. I needed such tools now, but I craved a time when they would be unnecessary.

Tools, Charlie had instructed me time and again, if they're to be of any use, need maintenance. Tony would approve, so I used my time positively to break down, clean and reassemble the Beretta, trying not to think of loneliness and death and war.

The only war I'd known wasn't anything like the kind Tony had experienced—mine had been a small, violent conflict six years earlier in Louisiana. Only, after losing the first battle, when cowardice had prevailed I'd deserted the field and gone into hiding seeking exile in oblivion.

*   *   *

CHAPTER 78

"Yes-s-s!"

I looked up from the almost-assembled pistol in my hands. Tony was making that odd gesture, peculiar to armchair quarterbacks when a goal is scored that resembled pulling open an imaginary drawer.

"What...?" I heard the emptiness. My voice sounded hollow, devoid of life, drained from the descent into the dark well of my past, its waters slimed over with regret, soured with loss. But for those too few desperately happy memories, I was saddened, thinking I might never feel anything again except hatred and terror.

"The frogs are pissed! Seems everyone has vanished; their man, thanks to you; and Monk, thanks to Duffy and White, but they don't know who or how or where."

Tony sounded so positive, so on top of what was happening, I envied and hated him in the same moment. I remember thinking that if it weren't for him, I'd be dead; he had focus. I had never felt so lost.

"One opinion holds their guy's gone into business for himself but two of 'em—I think one's a relative—aren't buying that theory. They think Monk must've aced their pal and split with the goods. Basically it's a circle jerk; they're going 'round and 'round and getting no place at all."

I was glad to hear everything was not sweetness and light in the Camp Langouste. Anything that gave him grief was fine by me, but I didn't see how that made much of a difference to us.

"The boss isn't thrilled having to referee his four soldiers. They're distracted and a little off-balance. Now'd be the perfect time to spring a trap." He paused, looked at me, chuckled, asked, "You got any traps on ya?" then winked.

He'd posed the question as a joke but I wasn't laughing. Instead, I was listening to the venomous little voice in my head; the same voice that liked to play mind games with our prisoner. It had, it seemed, the aptitude for other things.

"Someone said, 'Revenge is a dish that should be served cold.'"

Tony looked at me, as an icy presence inside of my mind shaped itself into a keen blade paring everything down to the barest details. I felt more in control of my emotions than I'd been since this craziness had begun. The problem-solving abilities Charlie'd helped me discover inside myself were adapting to the situation. Suddenly, I began to grasp the mindset of what Tony'd tried explaining that first morning in the warehouse, when he'd talked about combat strategies; overlapping fields of fire and flanking maneuvers. Like the sequence of steps in a salvage job, there was a logic to these things.

"I just may. How'd you like to use your Cajunese to make an anonymous phone call from a *friend*?"

Tony looked at me, like I'd taken leave of my senses.

"You made some reference to loose cannons a while ago, maybe it's time we started thinking and acting like one. They have a man missing, they can't find Monk and what they're most interested in, the drug shipment, has gone stray."

Tony inched forward, elbows on knees, chin resting on fists.

"And just how, do you see any of that as helping us?"

"Something you told me about Napoleon not stopping his enemies when they were making mistakes. Why can't we help them make the mistakes we want?"

Tony smiled. It was not a pleasant sight.

"Tell them Monk double-crossed them, killed their man after he took out Kiley and kept the shipment for himself; we know where they can find it and him...for a price. L'Angousette'll respond to that; he'd sell his mother if the deal was right, and to his mind everyone else thinks the same way. Doing it in Cajun'll just help confuse the issue."

"One thing I'm not getting."

"Yes...?"

"Just exactly why, do you want to go and fuck with these puppies when we're this close to defusing this thing once the A-team finds itself without a leader and stands down?"

I ignored the almost-touching finger and thumb Tony held in front of my nose.

"White's probably only after the diamonds, these guys want the coke, and L'Angousette's involvement makes this a different thing."

"Maybe for you"

"If Doug was here he'd say it was all part of the same thing."

Tony became very still.

"That's a cheap shot. So's trying to use this as payback for something that went down with you-all in New Orleans. Using Doug, to get me into it is, is, it's low."

"Yeah, you're right. I really see the difference between this and your Vietnam vendetta with White-whatever-the-fuck-his-name-is."

If looks could've killed, I'd have been splattered over four walls and part of the ceiling. The atmosphere in that small concrete box of a room pulsed with things said that could never be unsaid. I let Tony wallow in silence for as long as he needed. It took ten long minutes before he would meet my eyes.

"You're right."

He'd dragged those two words up from some place deep inside, I could see that he'd paid a stiff price to admit it to me.

"Go ahead:" He sat back in his chair arms crossed, legs stretched out, one ankle over the other. He was going to make me work for it, and he didn't intend on being easily impressed. "Lay it out."

I took a breath. "We exploit the suspicion in their ranks to stop them from initiating any action on their own and channel them in the direction we want, thus eliminating them as part of the larger equation until we can use them to our own purposes, like White used Duffy. And, while we're taking the initiative—now that we have a lead to White's boss—I think we should see what lies in that direction."

"You're right out there, y'know?" his tone, implying severe brain damage on my part.

"After hearing the way White was kissing up on the phone last night, we might be able to get his boys working for instead of against us, too."

Tony looked at me with a puzzled smirk on his face. I continued quickly, cutting off the unspoken questions.

"Think about it for a second. You said it yourself: White has screwed up. Right?"

"Agreed—"

"Okay, the head man can't be very happy with the mess. This was supposed to be a covert operation. Right?"

He nodded, not at all sure where I was going with this, or if it was going to make sense.

(That made two of us.)

"Here's the deal: we approach his boss direct and he orders the A-team to go after the New Orleans drug dealers who have captured Mr. White. In turn, we guarantee White will be eliminated in the rescue attempt."

Tony's eyebrows drew close together, hooding those two piercing, almost transparent blue-gray eyes, which stared intently at me as if I'd suggested we play Russian Roulette with a machine gun. Shaking his head, he started to stand. With a calm I didn't feel, I gestured him back down.

"White's become an embarrassment, made mistakes, too many to trust anymore. His operation is in danger of being exposed. If the bad guys waste White, the DEA, by taking them out, lets White become hero; it's a win-win situation. I'm guessing White's boss isn't going to offer any resistance once he knows we hold all the cards, especially all of the sensitive data from White's computer note-book."

"One problem, bud, we couldn't get into the files."

"You know that and I know that." My insincere grin widened. "I'll promise not to tell if you will."

Tony sat dumfounded, he opened his mouth several times to say something then shut it, until, finally: "You said White was a hostage. Now, we're going to kill him to appease his boss?"

"It's the same trip White tried with Duffy at Monk's apartment," I said smugly. "We record the deal we make with White's boss and play it for White. I'm pretty sure he'll recognize his master's voice then realize he's dog meat if he doesn't play along with us. He has no alternative, so we give him one: Enough diamonds to dig a hole and hide in for the rest of his life. I'm sure he can find a way to liquidate those assets. In exchange he makes a full confession that names names and tells where the bodies are buried. That, is our insurance."

"You, my friend, are one crazy son of a bitch," Tony started chuckling. "Deceitful, too."

"I'll take those as compliments. Another thing, we'll need to let White see that we do have the shipment and we *accidentally* let slip its hiding place prior to our letting him go." That got Tony's attention.

"You want to explain that to this slow child, and why?" He sounded amused, eager to hear more. I think I'd impressed him a little with my audacity.

"A couple of reasons. First, let me answer your question with two of my own: Can you come up with some kind of storage container and dummy it up to look like it has the real stuff in it?"

"No problem. Why—?"

"Second, can you rig it to explode if someone tries to open it?"

I watched Tony's eyebrows climb up his forehead until they were lost in the tangle of black curls. Smiling cruelly, his mouth widened in comprehension.

"You're figuring, he tries to fuck us over, he'll go for the stash and take himself out. Is that it?"

I shrugged. "If we can't trust him to honor our deal he's a liability. We'll still have his testimony and you'll have your payback for 'Nam."

Tony's eyes glinted sharply at my mention of Vietnam, he kept whatever thoughts he'd had to himself.

"Say his boss sanction's his death; if he gets greedy he does our job for his people, or he either plays straight with us and gets golden. Bottom line: He screws himself or not, we can get what we need; what we want: Out. When it's over, if he's still alive, you can do whatever you please with him, with impunity."

Tony shook his head in amazement.

"Man, I have heard some cold-ass ideas in my time, but that one is way beyond frosty."

"No one voted me God. 'You don't like it? Feel free to come up with something else. I'm open to suggestions." He put both hands up, palms towards me in surrender.

"No; it's poetry, I love it. Just do me a favor," His mouth twisted into a rocky smile. "Stay on my side." The smile left his eyes. They bored into mine searching. Then, very slowly, he shook his head.

"Man, I'd hate to have you seriously pissed at me."

We chased the idea back and forth then, with a few variations, decided to go for it, at least far enough to test the waters to see if there was enough interest to justify developing the second part.

"The number White called from the hotel...?"

Tony slapped his pockets. Finding the note pad, he read: "Area code 202, Washington DC; no surprise there."

I gestured Tony do the honors. He handed the pad over, silently inclining his head to me, indicating: My shovel, my grave. I keyed in the numbers.

The phone was instantly picked up but no one spoke. In a passable imitation of White's raspy voice, I said, "Angel."

I waited for maybe a minute listening to a series of clicks then silence, another click, then a ring tone, mentally rehearsing my pitch.

Conflicting ideas played havoc. Countering every line of opposing strategy I tried to envision, finally, I resigned myself to keeping focus on the end goal and remaining sensitive and fluid to any means of achieving it. In other words: I'd wing it.

"Yes?" The voice was deep and mellifluous, resonant with power and control. The voice of a man accustomed to respect.

"You're expecting White, Whitefield, Whitelaw, whatever his name is, but he isn't avail—"

"I know of no one by any of those names," he interrupted. "You have reached a wrong number—"

"Fine, hang up, and tomorrow you'll read the first installment of the unknown Mr. White's journal in the Washington Post. There's an interesting segment devoted to Mr. Angelo Rossi, current chairman of the DEA."

I had just taken my first leap of faith. It was all or nothing—I'd read about Rossi's development of special task forces in the ongoing war on drugs, in the newspaper, and White's use of the single word "Angel," the night we'd snatched him from his hotel room had gnawed at a corner of my consciousness. The penny finally dropped sometime during Tony's report on the dissension in the French ranks. It was a long shot, an extremely long one. I speculated on what life might be like in Costa Rica if I'd guessed wrong.

Tony's face was a mixture of shock and disappointment. Whether or not he approved was something I would have to deal with after. For the moment, keeping focus on the entity on the other end of the line took precedence.

There was a long silence. I took that as encouragement.

"A small preview...?"

Leap of faith, the second: He could call my bluff or simply hang up and we would be back to square one.

Connecting the latest series of stamps in White's passport to the contents of the containers with the military markings, I put a storyteller's confidence into my voice.

"You'll like this: The trail, boys and girls, starts with diamonds, lots of diamonds from South Africa, it leads north through Europe, then all the way to the Caribbean, where they're hidden in a load of pure cocaine that's covertly delivered inside the United States by nonother than an officially sanctioned team of—"

"This," he interrupted me with his toffee-smooth voice," needs deliberation before any rash moves are precipitated."

Gotcha!

"Where, may I reach you?"

I guess he had to try.

"A number and a time..." I demanded, ignoring the question as if he hadn't spoken. Tony looked encouraged. The 302 exchange could mean Rossi's posh Georgetown residence, which had been mentioned in the newspaper article. "Midnight" meant we had a little over eight hours to fine-tune our plans. I said nothing further, simply hung up. I gave a circled thumb and forefinger-signaling success then handed the receiver to Tony.

"Your turn."

He regarded me silently, thoughtfully, for a long moment, snorted in amazement and shook his head. Still shaking it in disbelief, he entered the number for the motel across the street.

Amazement, or doubt? I didn't care. It felt good to be taking what I believed was a positive and very large step forward. I found myself looking forward to our next. This time the play would be on our turf, maybe on our terms.

In what sounded like a very bad Maurice Chevalier imitation, Tony asked to be connected to the room of Monsieur L'Angousette. When he was promptly put through, I was a little surprised that Langouste had registered under his own name.

The balance of the conversation was a total loss to me, so I got an apple from the fridge then shuffled through the stack of newspapers on the end of the bed.

"I'm not sure," Tony said, when he'd finished the call, "I think they bought enough to justify having made the effort. He wants to check a few details out before I call them back with a rendezvous."

Giving me a funny look—one that spoke volumes about not pulling fast ones on your teammates—he promised, "You and I have a few things of our own we need to talk about, too."

Tony pulled on the headset and was quickly engrossed by the nest of snakes we'd stirred up with our poking stick. His meaning had not been lost on me, I was going to be doing some fast-talking.

I opened the cabinet to toss the apple core into the garbage, a dozen cockroaches scattered eight ways from center. The place was a mess: paper plates, empty food containers everywhere, no wonder. Everything went into a pair of plastic garbage bags. Tony paid me only the briefest attention as I went out.

*   *   *

CHAPTER 79

Within seconds of tossing the two bags of trash into the dumpster, at the far end of the parking lot, two unmarked police cars with bubble-lights winking on their dash boards, screeched to a stop hemming me in front and rear. A pair of plain-clothes cops closed in on me, one from either side. The smaller of the two, a hard-faced, shaggy blonde, in his mid-forties, looked like the leader. Raising my hands in the universal I-give-up position, I turned to face him but before I had a chance to ask what was happening, the other one blind-sided me, slamming my face across the front of the nearest car. My world exploded in a flash of brilliant white and red. Blood sprayed across the hood and windshield. My arms were wrenched up behind me, higher than they were meant to go. A stunning hit in the kidneys paralyzed me, stifling my screams as handcuffs were slipped on and cinched so tightly they grated on the bones.

Another cop, who sounded like he would've preferred stomping through the trash with the two who were seizing the "evidence" from the "drop site", speed-Mirandized me. Then two pairs of hands picked me up from behind and I was thrown bodily across the rear seat with enough force to drive my head into the opposite door. My neck bones crackled like cereal in milk, but a lot louder. The trunk was slammed shut, someone rapped on the roof, and we tore out of the lot. My face was mashed into the door, while the dead-weight, plain-clothes cop sitting on the back of my legs responded to my every movement with love taps to the insides of my elbow joints with something hard that shot rockets into my brain along shrieking nerve paths.

We arrived at the police station where I was dragged from the car by a pair of beefy uniforms and hauled towards an unmarked door. My legs were dead from the knees down, and I heard rather than felt my feet clatter down a short flight of stairs. There was another shower of stars as my face was used to ram open a swinging door. Half-dragged, half-carried, I remember a dizzying rush down a darkened corridor. We turned at the end, at the second open doorway I was cannoned into a small room towards a table and two chairs. Hurtling through the air, I knew I was going to hit hard. I could do nothing to protect myself except tuck my chin into my chest and hope that the damage wouldn't be permanent.

*   *   *

**To believe yourself brave is to be brave;
it is the one only essential thing.**

- Joan of Arc, Mark Twain

CHAPTER 80

High up in the ceiling a bare bulb in a cage was the first thing I saw when I opened my left eye. My nose was solid with dried blood; I could feel the stiff wrap of its flow on my face, sealing my other eye shut, cementing a plug into my ear. My body ached. I was confused about where I was or what had happened. Then it came to me that I'd been arrested. But for what? Had someone found White in the workshop, or recognized me dropping off Monk at the hospital? Was Tony here too? Had he escaped? I'd been unconscious, but for how long? I had no way of knowing. I'd made several mistakes, that much was pretty obvious. I then made another; I tried to move.

Residual waves of agony were echoing through my body when the door opened. Three suits and two uniforms came in and stood over me.

I'd like to think that I withstood my trials in a manly fashion, the truth is I whimpered and blubbered pitifully. I was ready to confess to anything. I begged them not to hit me any more—no one had moved. The suit in charge was turning a bright red above his white shirt collar. I felt myself being lifted onto my feet. Tensing my stomach muscles, I tried to lock my legs firmly in front of my genitals; so far, the only part of me that didn't hurt. I closed my one good eye. Whatever was coming next I didn't want to see it.

Like forks of barbed wire, pain scored tracks up from my wrists as the cuffs were taken off. I opened my eye and looked at my tormentors in surprise.

"Please accept our sincere apologies. On behalf of the City, I can assure you that the, the *over-zealousness* of the officers involved will be looked into. You will, if you wish it, be escorted forthwith to the hospital for an examination." The head suit intoned his declaration with all of the profundity of a preacher, lacking only a pulpit from whence to expound. "Or, if you need transportation to—"

"What *is* this and *who* are you?"

Unfazed, Deputy Chief Mitchell Kennedy introduced himself to me with the gravitas of funeral director. He almost put an avuncular arm around my shoulders, thought better of it, then went on to tell me how the manager of the motel, civic-spirited citizen and all, believing I was involved in the distribution of controlled substances, subsequently reported his suspicions.

"In view of the, ah, how shall we put it, the *questionable* nature of the information, it seems our detectives may have been a trifle high-spirited in the performance of their duties. They were, perhaps a little preemptive in their actions? You certainly must know what a problem drug—"

"Is this what false arrest and police brutality are all about?" My mouth blurted, provoking, before my brain could muzzle it.

Kennedy's face went a few shades deeper, the red showing bright in contrast to the grilled-cheese dribbles of white hair that fringed his perspiration-shiny dome. Exasperation bracketed his tightly pinched mouth that grew tighter by the second. Feeling backed into a corner, he started to squirm. For a moment I enjoyed it until I remembered the things in which I *was* currently involved.

'Give the man a way out,' my voice of reason suggested. 'A little rhythm would go a long way.'

"Yes, Chief Kennedy, your boys got very enthusiastic, but if they really did think I was a drug dealer, then okay, I can understand that, I guess. What do I do to get out of here?"

When it became apparent that I meant to accept the apologies of the City, giving him a promotion in the bargain, the Deputy Chief's internal pressure gauge eased up, as did the tension in the room. No sooner was my intent clear than a pen and release form appeared, as if from nowhere. Also, as I signed, I noticed there were four witness signatures already on the document. I wondered if they came printed that way to save time?

*   *   *

Tender-handed stroke a nettle,
And it stings you for your pain;
Grasp it like a man of mettle,
And it soft as silk remains.

- Aaron Hill

CHAPTER 81

Out in the free world, locals and tourists alike; tie-died, Aloha-shirted and wildly costumed, added then subtracted themselves from one side of the narrow two-lane street to the other. Impulsively, unconsciously, it seemed; crossing when- and wherever they pleased, stopping, backing up, grinding the flow of traffic slower and slower, to create the stutter-stop called "the Duval Crawl."

"If it's Tourist Season can we shoot a few...?" The bumper sticker on the pickup truck ahead was representative of the attitudes of those residents whose lives and livelihoods were not perceived as immediately dependent upon the annual influx of snowbirds. The truth was the town would have dried up and blown away years before, if not for the disposable income that was dropped in town annually. Attitudes were superceded by latitudes, when it came to Winter People.

"What time is it?" Along with pistol and holster, I'd left my wristwatch sitting on the kitchen counter in the motel room. My driver, Officer Joe Murphy, the same cop who'd stopped by regarding the vandalism, had been starting his shift when he'd been volunteered to return me to the motel.

"Nearly quarter past seven," he checked.

Less than five hours remained in our time line. The moves Tony and I had initiated were, hopefully, still in motion.

"I'm really sorry about what happened to you. The last thing you need right now is more harassment."

"Isn't that a forbidden word: 'Harassment?'"

He laughed. It was a good clear laugh with no artifice.

"Tell me," I probed, "do you like being a cop? I mean, is this really what you want to do?" I was curious and felt that he might be willing to be candid. He was.

"With a name like Murphy," he said, affecting a thick brogue. "Tis either a policeman or a priest you're becomin'."

I smiled, encouraging without distracting, waiting; letting him fill the vacuum.

"Far back as I can remember, yeah; I've always wanted to make a difference. I like helping people."

"Sorry to say this, but you don't seem to be cop material." I was pursuing a thought that might be developing into an idea. Crazy? Most likely. Helpful to the present state of our affairs? Perhaps. Dangerous? Definitely!

"Thanks, I guess." He smiled a cautious smile that let me know I was treading on dangerous ground. "After what you ran into today I can see why you might say that, but—"

He showed an uncommon candor as he voiced his perceptions of what a police force could and should be, then he threw it right back at me. "Tell the truth, why'd you back off?"

I felt the flicker of his cop antenna, he was probing too, but for what purpose I couldn't tell.

"*That* is a very long story. Let's just say a big part of it was self-preservation." I laughed softly to defuse the harshness of that reality. Mainly, that's what I'd been feeling in the bowels of the police station, and a part-truth still reads like the truth.

"You may not know it but you have pretty good instincts," he said before his voice hardened. "The two who arrested you, have been up on charges before, and both times the complaints were *dropped*."

Apparently, Officer Murphy viewed abuse of power an insult and indictment on all honest police.

"I'd give anything—" he muttered to himself.

Beeping, bleating for attention—as much a way of life on the Rock as mosquitoes, and almost as pleasant—we were passed on both sides by a buzzing swarm of pink rental scooters. A dozen college kids, baked and burned, full of life and laughter zipped in and out threading their way through the 'Crawl'.

Thanks to an inconvenient little weather anomaly that had shot the temperatures well up into the nineties that afternoon, the street still wore the weight of the heat like a leaden mantle. Inside the patrol car, it was stifling. Wearing the bulky Kevlar vest under his uniform shirt Murphy must have been sweltering. What he'd been about to reveal floated heavily in the close confines of the patrol car. He'd opened up more than he'd intended. I could sympathize, but only a little, with his discomfort. He bought a moment fumbling in his shirt pocket.

"My card." The regulation 'City of' business cards were printed with a generic blank space for employees to write their names.

"High-class stationery," I joked to break the tension and give him a safe place to fall back. There was nothing to be gained by reminding him he'd already given me one a couple of nights before. I wanted to keep him talking. An idea—insane as it was—was starting to form. I wanted him to carry the conversational ball a little longer, until I could see its shape.

"Yeah, right." he said, humorously defensive. Then he tossed it back to me. "What are you working on now?"

I couldn't think for a moment. What do I say? Killing, kidnapping, extortion, hijacking...?

"Nothing much. Actually, I've been thinking about leaving."

"The Keys?"

"Mmm-hmm."

"Then what?"

"I'm not really sure; it's a lot like the song: '*I Still Haven't Found What I'm Looking For.*' I know, from experience, a lot of things that I don't want to do. So, I guess I'll keep trying a bit of everything until I find it. I think I'll know when it's the right thing."

I then distracted him, and gave myself a little breathing space, by pointing out a few of the renovated buildings I'd supervised.

Not having anticipated a philosophical discussion on life choices when I'd accepted the ride, I found myself liking this guy, wanting to open up to him. He reminded me in many ways of what Charlie might have been like as a young man; he had similar attitudes and ethics, and he was an easy person to talk to. Too easy, perhaps.

Already on a first-name basis, as the rough outline of a friendship was being defined, Murph' described how, as a kid, he'd grown up by learning boxing.

Chuckling when I'd asked, he reminisced, "'Almost made the Golden Gloves, 'til one night when somebody better, a whole lot better than me, turned my lights out."

Trading experience for experience, as I described my adventures in hang gliding he became enthusiastic. Immediately wanting to know everything about it; saying he had been curious about the sport for some time, and planned to "take a whack at it" either next year or maybe the following. I informed him that 'whack' was the term for an embarrassingly ungraceful nose-down crash landing; something to be avoided, especially in front of other pilots, who were only too happy to chorus: "Whack!" as loud as they could.

He laughed good-naturedly when I confessed I'd received a few of those landing field raspberries, which never failed to turn an afternoon of gliding tips into an evening of camaraderie around a barbecue, singing songs and getting to know good people. I imagined Murph' fitting right in with the gliding crowd. When I offered to give him several back issues of Hang Glider magazine and an official pilot training manual, that had somehow escaped vandalism, he was like a kid at Christmas.

At the motel, "where I was staying pending the reclamation of my home," I thanked him for the ride. Tapping his card in my shirt pocket, I promised to give him a call as soon as I found the magazines.

"Oh, you can tell the Chief to relax. I won't press charges, this time." Pretending to make light of the episode, I was testing the waters. "But if one of those guys shoots me, unless there's a very good reason, then all bets are off."

An awkward pause followed a charitable grin at my lame humor. "To be honest, I'd like you to reconsider." He paused again then came to a decision. 'Community'd be better with them off the force."

Bingo! That was the answer I'd been hoping for. All I had to do now was find Tony and sell him.

I told Murph' I'd think about it, before giving him a cheery wave goodbye for the benefit of Gollum, who'd been ogling my arrival with the concentration of a lapsed celibate at a nude beach.

*   *   *

CHAPTER 82

Not knowing what I might find, I unlocked the door. The privacy card, I noticed, was no longer on the knob. Stepping inside, I came to an abrupt stop. The solid, unrelenting pressure of a gun barrel behind my right ear became the sole point of my awareness. Just as suddenly as it had appeared it was gone. I heard the door slam shut behind me. Imagination running wild, I turned slowly.

Hip-shot, shoulder against the door, like a cowboy propping up a barn, Tony gave me a long look of appraisal. His mouth twisted into a lop-sided smirk. A gust of incredulity rolled up from a chuckle gained momentum and tumbled out in a full belly laugh.

Like those who find themselves the object of laughter, I failed to see what must have been pretty obvious. Holding his middle, as if it might burst, Tony indicated I go look in a mirror.

I stared at a stranger wearing a lurid raccoon mask of purples and blues around both eyes over a swollen red thing, which may or may not have been a nose. Above, blood-stiff clumps of hair poked out at odd angles. This guy, whoever he was, could haunt houses or frighten kids who refused to eat their vegetables.

I may not have liked it, but I couldn't help but see the humor, as I looked at my reflection for the first time since my arrest, while Tony cackled, hooted and almost fell over in the background. Probably, he was relieved at seeing me free and whole, more or less, and that was just his unique way of showing it.

"I thought for sure we were gone," Tony said between giggles. "The way you look, I'm not so sure you're not."

"Ho, ho, ho." Perhaps, he could have shown his relief a little less enthusiastically.

Gingerly, I stretched out on the bed. All I wanted was a soft place where I could feel sorry for myself, for about a year or two. No such luck; Tony wanted to talk.

"When you went out," he rattled on, stepping into the niche that served as a kitchen. "I saw you forgot your gun and I was gonna give you a lecture about leaving your weapon behind..." He paused, came back into the main room and generously added, "...lucky thing you did, so strike the lecture."

A small indulgence, for which I was grateful.

I tried a sip of the mint tea he handed me, wincing as the hot plastic touched a split lip. I put the mug on the night table to cool.

"What happened?" I'd been far too close to the trees—pinned under them was how it felt—to get much of a view of the forest.

"You mean when the bust of the century went down? Haw! Haw! It looked like a pack of monkeys trying to hump a beach ball. Cops! All over you, jumping in the Dumpster, tearing open garbage bags. It was really something."

Tony seemed to enjoy the comedic aspects of my arrest enough for both of us. Too beat to care one way or the other, I tried another sip of tea, it was still too hot. Hoping to avoid the rest of Tony's play-by-play, I carried the mug into the bathroom. It didn't work. He followed me in before I could lock the door.

"Soon as I saw what was going down, I stripped the room and got everything outta here before you'd cleared the parking lot. They really fucked up, not searching the room right off. Yup, the gods were truly smiling on us today."

I glanced at the mirror, to fix in mind what a blessing by smiling gods looked like.

One thing I've always liked about hotels is the endless supply of hot water. The hard spray kneaded the knots out of the muscles along the top of my shoulders and carried them on down the drain. While I worked two of the tiny bars of courtesy soap together vainly trying to generate a bubble, Tony sat on the john and listened to me over the hiss of the shower as I ran down the sequence of events following the "big motel dope bust." Then, I sketched out my plan.

"I like it," he said, with conspicuous delight, "and hate it. It's pure poetry, but everything's way too complicated already. There're prob'ly more ways this 'thing' can screw up than dogs have fleas, and that's without adding a whole new set of variables. You never heard of the KISS principle?" Tony persisted.

My silence encouraged him to explain: "Keep It Simple, Stupid,"

I dutifully grunted out what I hoped would pass for acceptance.

He wasn't going to go away—neither were the bad guys. Tony was adamant but I wasn't convinced; my gut said I was on the money.

Cleaned, dressed, and feeling slightly less folded and mutilated, I walked out onto the balcony and looked down beyond the small grove of shade trees on an empty expanse of asphalt. My heart sank.

My van! Did the cops impound it?"

"Relax. I got it when the Miami Vice finally remembered to check the room. It's stashed at Sis's place. We're in the conch-cruiser," he said, pointing out a decrepit-looking green Chevy. "'Better saddle up, we'll get you to the van, so I can do that thing."

*   *   *

**It is the province of knowledge to speak
and it is the privilege of wisdom to listen.**

- Oliver Wendell Holmes

CHAPTER 83

Sarge had already been locked in with White almost six hours—far beyond the call of duty. The workshop looked secure but the nine-millimeter was ready in my hand when I unlocked the door. This close to the end of the deadly game we were playing, I'd no desire to be caught off guard. Sarge barreled past me as soon as the door was opened. I guessed his intent; probably he was decorating the compost heap on the opposite side of the house.

"Sleep well?" There was no response, so I ripped open a corner of the tape over White's mouth; that widened his eyes.

"Want to go potty?"

The urgency of his need momentarily canceled his sullen look; still he refused to speak. Reviewing our agenda for the great deception plan, I freed one hand to facilitate White's toilet needs. 'We have plenty of time' I remember thinking, as a cloud of sawdust exploded into my face. Spitting, gasping in pain, backing away while frantically trying to clear my eyes, I heard violent tugging grunts from White then a wrenching of wood and metal as he tore the heavy saw loose from the extension table that attached it to the back wall.

Tiny needles of wood stabbed my eyes. I was helpless. Even if I knew where he was I couldn't shoot—the door was ajar, the sound suppressor was safely snapped into its pocket on the pistol harness hanging on a kitchen chair—the neighbors would be sure to hear it and they *would* report the gunfire.

I heard White's laborious approach as he dragged his two hundred-plus pound anchor closer. A hand clutched at the front of my loose polo shirt and missed getting a firm grip. Within seconds I'd be at his mercy. He grunted. I heard the saw screech a little closer. I was backed tight into the corner, a workbench pressed into my lower back on one side, the front wall of the garage hemmed me in on my right.

Trying to keep the pistol out of his reach and fend off his grasping claw at the same time, I kicked out blindly and was rewarded with a squeal of pain as my foot connected with what I hoped was his knee-cap. My body was tensed, anticipating how it would come, as he collected himself for his next assault. In the same instant he grabbed my shirt, an ominous, growling rumble of thunder approached from my left, accompanied by the clicking and scrabbling of claws on concrete. There was a sharp cry followed by a sudden tearing noise, I was pulled forward almost off my feet. Suddenly, White was no longer at my throat and I felt a draft of air on my chest where my shirtfront now hung in tatters.

"Call him off!" a strained voice squeaked from the floor, begging.

After several painful minutes, I'd restored enough of my eyesight to be able to see through a scratchy film of tears. White was on his back with Sarge above him, his neck fully engulfed by those powerful jaws. White's plaints were reduced to a feeble croak when Sarge, grumbling a deep baritone growl, flexed those awesome crushing muscles. Fascinated, I watched bloody streaks appear where Sarge's fangs indented and scored deeply on either side of his throat. White was dying in front of me I couldn't or wouldn't move. That was the moment Tony chose to show up. Grasping the situation at a glance, he immediately took charge.

Washing my eyes free of the remaining wood dust I castigated myself thoroughly, acutely aware of having almost jeopardized the whole operation, not to mention our lives, by being complacent. Day-dreaming when I should have been taking care of the business at hand; there was no excuse for having forgotten the risk potential in a snake like White. Could I resuscitate the cool calculating persona that had asserted itself when I'd dealt with his boss? I hoped I hadn't left it, along with my nerve, on the floor of the police interrogation cell.

Tony was in the workshop. The door was closed. I took a deep breath, let it out slowly then entered.

White's surly glint promised: "Next time."

I made my own silent promise to him, too.

When I saw what Tony was monkeying with on the workbench, at first I mistook it for a scuba tank. Then, as I came closer, I saw it was a little bigger. The outer shell featured welded-on eyes by which it could be easily anchored or carried. The threaded cap would make it both air and watertight when sealed. I suspected Tony'd probably had a few of these safety deposit boxes secreted around the Keys. Since I didn't ask and he didn't volunteer, I let it slide. What astounded me was the stack of plastic-wrapped packs and cigar tubes that covered the top of the workbench. Tony'd been busy. If I hadn't known better I would have sworn these were the same packets from the warehouse. They were identical. Were they the same? I wondered.

He made a show of carefully placing each bundle in the canister. He had White's undivided attention, too. As per our script, I asked him where we were going to stash it. He gave a significant look in White's direction shaking his head in the negative as if to say: 'Ot-nay in ont-fray of the erk-jay'. He then, took a crude map out of his pocket and pointed to the obligatory "X". Ignoring White—feeling his eyes hot upon our every move, examining every nuance, listening for any clue —I played off Tony's lead, nodding then placing the map on the bench before helping him load the rest of the packs into the container.

"Leaving the map and canister in there with him is like cooking a steak in front of a starving man." Tony said, once we were outside and the shop door closed. "You should have seen the look on his face when I put those cigar tubes on the bench." Tony added, chuckling dryly.

"I should have seen it before I put my mind in neutral." I replied bitterly.

"Hey, that's right, I forgot, you had an easy day. Yeah, it's all your fault," he went on sarcastically, adding, "there's an eraser on the end of a pencil, ya know why?" He paused for effect. "'Cause ain't nobody's perfect."

Sarge *whuffed*.

"Sorry," Tony addressed Sarge, "I stand corrected; you're perfect."

Sarge accepted the compliment before continuing his inspection of the base of a Frangipani tree.

"We're in this together and that means we cover each other, just in case we become human and fuck up. That's all—got it?"

I silently nodded. I valued Tony's unconditional acceptance of my strengths and weaknesses alike.

"There's something else needs doing."

If we hoped to survive the moves we were contemplating, we had to know our guest was secure and safe. The welded eyes attached to Tony's canister had given me an idea. "Watch my back," I asked, not fully trusting White—or myself alone with him.

During his attack White had torn the cast-iron table saw free from its extension table. A wreck of split, broken plywood and two-by-fours was all that remained of the cutting station. Once freed, he'd been able to drag the heavy saw over the polished concrete floor. In the few short minutes we'd been outside, White had backed the saw against the workbench and succeeded in quietly turning it over. He was smart enough to make it look like he hadn't been trying to see the map, which lay nearby on the bench.

"'Fool just don't give up!" Tony said in his twangy cowboy voice. Pretending to believe White's single intent had been to escape, Tony administered a sharp tap at the base of his skull with the butt of his pistol. White played his part admirably by rolling his eyes back and slipping unconsciously to the floor.

I brought a long, flat tool chest out from one of the cabinets under the workbench, removed a Ramset and a handful of shot-nails. From a bin of assorted hardware, I selected a heavy steel staple mounted to a flat plate with four holes. Designed as the male-half of a padlock hasp, it would adapt well to the purpose I had in mind. After shooting four case-hardened fasteners deep into the floor, anchoring the staple plate to the center of the workshop, I snipped the ties binding White's wrists to the upended saw and rolled him near the staple. Pulling his hands behind his back, I cinched two quarter-inch cable ties around each wrist. Two more ties were looped through them and the staple. Tony looked on in approval.

"Should've thought of that before," I said, outside, by way of an apology. I was still taking his almost escaping very personally.

"It's done now," he padlocked the shop behind us, "that's what counts. You learned a valuable lesson. Now, if your willing, let me give you another free of charge."

I waited, not quite knowing what to expect.

"Ease up."

I waited.

"That's all. Just 'ease up'."

"People, a lot of people with guns, are trying to kill us." I became hot. "'Ease up' that's your answer? Gee! Thanks."

"Listen. You want to get out of this thing alive you gotta divorce yourself emotionally. Don't worry how things are or aren't gonna turn out; they'll turn out the way they'll turn out without the worrying." He parodied Frank Zappa singing: "You gotta get out of it, before you get into it." Then, in a serious note, added, "I know you can do it. I've seen you in action. And, no, it ain't easy. This shit is no different from The Nam. The only way to win is to stay loose. Get outside yourself."

What happens, I wondered, if the door slams shut behind me while I'm outside? I decided to keep my irreverent thoughts to myself as I listened to Tony's voice of experience.

"You gotta get your mind around the idea that the other guy's only doing his job. You do yours, only better. Once you get that together everything kind of falls into place. Trust me."

"But, will you still respect me in the morning?" I joked trying to show that I was getting my perspective back. Of course, I was taking it personally, but seeing how Tony'd lived through more hairy times than I could guess at, and he seemed to be taking everything in stride, I resolved, like 'Cool Hand Luke', to get my mind right. Tony faked a jab, gave me a playful punch in the shoulder then headed inside the cottage. I followed.

We had adopted a working plan; it was already up and rolling but I couldn't leave it alone. Again, I suggested the logic behind involving Murphy. Probably, just to shut me up he again admitted that the idea had merit and conceded that maybe we could consider it as a fallback.

"It's too risky for plan A but it does appeal to me, on a personal level."

I shot him a questioning look, in return got a cryptic smile and a promise to elaborate at a later time.

"That's not going to fly, give...." I didn't need enigmatic sidestepping; we were making life and death decisions, everything had to be on the table.

"All right." He conceded, leaning back in the desk chair, picking up a mechanical drafting pencil. Sliding the lead in and out, absently playing with it, he explained. "Today you ran up against a couple of humps name of Gallagher and Eaton. You found out they're a matched pair of assholes, what you don't know is they've been trying to bust me for years."

I started to ask why he was against a little payback. Anticipating, he forestalled my interruption before I could say a word. "If you really want to know, shut your pie hole 'til I'm done, okay?"

I nodded.

"Those two wood pussies have been chiseling a piece out of every dealer and smuggler's action down here for years. They're *The Man*, the System, and they've made fucking with me a career. My only claim to fame has been; I'm the only one they could never catch or coerce into working for them, and it's driven 'em nuts. So, I've become an object lesson for their new talent. I couldn't tell you the number of times I've been hauled in for questioning, seen my home and business trashed under the auspices of a search warrant, or had my property seized and returned totaled. The real bitch of living in a small town is *everybody* knows your business, or they think they do. Nobody in City Hall will believe a 'smuggler' over a pair of super cops."

"You could've played the game like everybody else?" I wondered why he'd bothered to stay in town with that kind of harassment.

He paused for a long moment then asked me, "Why didn't you just leave the other night when Duffy and his crew grabbed me? You could have just 'played the game,' they had what they were after."

"Okay, okay," I conceded. "Point taken. Continue...."

"They finally succeeded in driving Marisha out of my life about two years ago. I couldn't blame her for leaving me; around-the-clock anonymous phone calls, threats, slashed tires; petty shit, but it finally got to her. Don't forget there're a couple of little kids to consider. Besides, even on a good day I'm no picnic to live with."

I thought about disagreeing but let that slide, too. His bullshit detector wouldn't have accepted it, besides I'd already earned enough disapproving looks without actively seeking more.

"Toughest thing I did—*had* to do," he corrected himself, "was let Marisha and the kids go. If anything ever happened to them it woulda ripped my heart out, I couldn't let anyone know that, couldn't let them become pawns in some pissing contest. I had to distance myself from them. I didn't have a choice, it was the only way I could make sure my kids are gonna grow up knowing both of their parents."

The little muscles in his jaws flexed reactively. I heard the anguish behind those words.

"With my family gone, I took a long hard look at what I was doing. The games weren't fun anymore. Making money couldn't justify the loss, so I quit. Think it made any difference? No how, no way!"

He paused then looked at something in the distance I couldn't see and hoped I never would.

I'd helped Tony clean up some damage in the gym less than a year ago. The place had been a mess of broken mirrors, slashed benches and pads when I'd arrived for my morning workout. At the time it was explained away as teenage vandalism. What he had been living with and subjected to, accounted for his ready access to the type of canister he'd brought for the phony drugs and diamonds; hard to get a search warrant for something buried in the ground or under water. What other resources, I wondered—and not for the first time—might he have?

"*If*, and it's a big if," Tony continued, pacing the room as he spoke, "we could get that pair of whores into the tail end of this thing and bag them, that would make some of the crap I've been through almost worthwhile. But don't be deceived, Ace, these guys are meat-eaters, and so far, we've been awful goddamn' lucky. 'Just a small part of the stuff we've done comes to light you and me are going to end up in a very small room for a very long time."

That was a comforting thought not unlike the notions I had entertained during my brief stay in the nether regions of the police station.

"We got some work to do and phone calls to make tonight. That's about as much future as I can handle right now. We're too short to start adding extras."

Tony stopped moving about the room. He stood squarely in front of me, his hand outstretched, offered to me—a rarity! Unlike most people, I couldn't remember ever having seen him perform this basic, simple human gesture before.

I took his hand. Silently, we drew strength from our commitment to seeing this insanity through to its conclusion. I couldn't look him in the eye knowing what I was about to do.

*   *   *

**A moment's insight is sometimes
worth a life's experience.**

- Oliver Wendell Holmes

CHAPTER 84

White was locked in the workshop, anesthetized, and watched over by Sarge, who I'm sure would have preferred hanging with us. Tony wanted to exchange his current "beater" on the way to the "concrete box," so we parted company at his sister's. Roughly twenty minutes later, the van was back in the lot and I was in the motel room, listening on the headset and waiting for him to show. The soft two-long-three-short knock announced his arrival.

Noting my armed and ready presence, Tony gave me a thumbs-up while I set the door locks. He then picked up the phone and, for the next few minutes outlined a succession of events and conditions that included a quarter of a million dollars and a drop location. That's what he was supposed to be doing. From the incomprehensible jabber, for all I knew, he could've been describing how to make Crème Brûlée. I tuned out and began the familiar ritual of brewing a pot of coffee.

I was drinking more coffee than ever, stronger, too. My craving was more, I supposed, for the heightened acuity it engendered than the flavor. Raising the cup to my mouth, seeing the ripples vibrate across the inky surface, I knew it was doing my nerves no good. Resolving to taper off at a later date I gave in and took a bracing draught, snickering to myself at the image of a man in front of a firing squad refusing the offer of a last cigarette because it was bad for his health.

Having agreed on a key exchange as our medium of transfer: Two keys would be passed using a taxi as a cutout, or courier, which would allow the rest of the moves to be handled safely over the telephone. Knowing in advance where and when, we could, in theory, control the arena. Though, lately, application and theory seemed to be possessed of mutual exclusivity.

"Twenty-four hours 'n counting," Tony said, standing, stretching, "your turn."

I took his chair, while he connected the voice-activated recorder to the receiver. I watched the tape wheels on the fresh cassette start to move as I tapped out the Georgetown number. My mouth was dry as sand; my heart beat rapidly. I blamed the caffeine. The coffee was guiltless. I closed my eyes to focus my attention; senses extending, probing like imaginary flight feathers seeking invisible air currents; the precipice was before me. There was an abbreviated ring and the phone was answered. I sensed the whisper of an updraft flowing up the face of the cliff.

"Yes?"

Careful, he was anxious but still cautious. I interpreted the speed of answering my call contrasting the carefully composed modulation of his voice in that one word. Feeling as if I'd taken the first footstep down the launch ramp; the glider's weight lifting off my shoulders; the empty, yawning abyss rushing towards me, I opened my eyes. In the mirror reflecting the room behind me, Tony's face appeared beside the mask I now wore. Crafted in New Orleans, to hide a broken heart and withered spirit, it promised everything was going well and according to plan. Alert to every nuance, Tony watched my reflection with an animal intensity that might have been unsettling, had he been looking at the man and not the mask.

"I have an offer for you; an extremely generous one, considering the circumstances."

No response; he was waiting for the stick.

An insight came to me. The shape of the problem, like seeing the invisible shape and path of a thermal, everything that had happened to us, what needed to be done, suddenly became clear. We had the tools: Tony's past, his training and abilities, and my own. I saw how they fit together. We could do this but not as planned. Trusting in nothing but instinct, committing myself to another kind of "Leap of Faith", I eased my pistol from the holster and held it under the table, ready.

"There are two conditions: First, the detached-service group your Mr. White's been running will be immediately recalled to duty with their original service branch."

"'The fuck're you doing?" Horrified, Tony'd mouthed the words in a furious whisper. He leaned forward to take the telephone from me.

I could only guess what this would do to him but there wasn't time to explain once I'd started off the precipice.

I swiveled. My gun pointed at him. He stiffened.

"Do not do this!" The command, though whispered, was clear. He held out his hand. 'The gun or the phone? Choose!'

I cocked the hammer; the sound loud in the room. Very slowly, he resumed his seat on the bed. Anger and disappointment showed in the hard set of his mouth. I couldn't look in his eyes and see my treachery reflected. The sound of Rossi's breathing into my ear, waiting, took precedence.

"Second; you will alert the local police to the presence of a drug smuggling operation in Key West. You'll be given the details at the appropriate time, which you will pass along. And, you will encourage them to have two specific officers in charge of the raid."

In spite of the inner turmoil, I was amazed that my voice sounded so calm and assured.

"In return for that and your immediate resignation—for personal reasons, shall we say? You will be allowed to gracefully retire. I'm sure you've generated sufficient wealth to allow you to live out the remainder of your years in comfort. Refuse, and the world will know what you are and what you've been doing to this country, and they'll read about it over breakfast. Do I make myself clear?"

"Yes." There was a note of weary resignation in that one syllable. Now, the carrot: "I also mentioned an offer: in exchange for your compliance I will arrange for the permanent—how did you say it the other night, 'withdrawal of an asset' wasn't it? Your Mr. White has become an embarrassment, wouldn't you say?"

I held my breath in apprehension. All or nothing! Had I been too greedy? The seconds stretched maddeningly. A door slammed several units away. Someone passing by on the Boulevard discovered that the horn in his or her car worked. Tony searched my face. Sweat prickled the back of my neck.

"Yes, and your offer is acceptable."

I pivoted the phone up and away from my mouth breathing for the first time in what seemed like an eternity. Tony eased slightly standing down from combat status. There would be an accounting, of that we were both certain.

"You'll hear from me within the next twenty-four hours. I'll give you the names of the officers and the location where the criminals will be holding Mr. White hostage."

"As neither they, nor Mr. *Whitelaw*," he said, correcting me for the record, "will survive. He will, of course, be honored for bravery and his devotion to duty."

Whatever else, Rossi was not a slow study. He knew full well how to manipulate events to his own advantage, even calamitous reversals. To him White was a pawn; pawns were expendable; best to turn their loss into a profit, no matter how small. Angelo Rossi was not just another Capitol Hill flesh-presser; he was a master string-puller and arm-twister. Was I deluding myself into believing that he could be whipped so easily and without a fight? What if he was playing with me in a vastly different game than the one I'd begun?

I noted the pronounced tremor in my hand when I un-cocked then placed the Beretta on the table beside the telephone. Tony leaned forward, both fists on the table beside me, then lowered his head level with mine.

"I know why," he growled, "but that don't excuse what you did." He picked up his headset and rudely gestured I vacate his chair. Before slipping the sponge covered speakers down over his ears, he said in a very quiet voice, "You ever pull a weapon on me again, you better be prepared to use it."

I turned away, silently promising, "*I will.*"

Tony focused on the doings across the road. I tried not to think of the consequences if I was wrong. All this plot, counter-plot stuff was giving me a headache and making my guts churn. I thought/hoped he would've been more supportive of my efforts to put a little justice into the world. None of this was going the way I wanted. The worst was still ahead; waiting, not knowing what moves were coming, and from what directions.

Little as I trusted White, I rated Rossi several levels lower on the evolutionary path from reptile to human. I'd left a few steps out in my negotiation with him when my subliminal alarm sounded. I considered trying to explain that to Tony. Probably, he'd just see it as some lame excuse for deviating from our plan; I couldn't let him know just how far.

It was almost two in the morning before Tony moved again. He switched tapes in the recorder then put down the headset and headed for the fridge. He recapped our French friends' debates, mostly with his back to me, around a standing meal of smoked meat and coleslaw.

He can still eat, I marveled, kneading my aching belly, trying to assess the damage my body had received, so far; wondering how much more punishment would come, how much more could I withstand?

"Even though they are deceitful bastards," he said flatly, turning his head to fix me with a steady look.

I met his eyes, wincing inwardly at the implication.

"They seem to be going along with the plan. The boss called one of his people in New Orleans. He's bringing the quarter 'mil' down by plane first thing tomorrow."

Tony made no further mention of my treachery. I was willing to let those dogs keep on sleeping; they could bite me later just as well.

"One of his crew—not the sharpest pencil in the box—wants to do us."

Why not? I mused, it seemed like everyone else did. What's one more? Outside, hidden within the Tour Guide's amplified voice, as a sightseeing bus rolled past, I imagined Loki laughing, placing another sprig of mistletoe onto our growing pile of discord.

"The one who wants us dead was kin to the diver you took out at the houseboat, and he's not buying White and Monk for that action. He figures we did it and wants off the leash so bad he can taste it. The big guy pulled rank and his boy seemed to snap to. I figure we're going to be straight up with the exception of that one soldier, he's the kind to keep on coming—Cajuns can be real cross-grained when it comes to blood vengeance."

Tony paused for a large leisurely stretch.

"Until he gets his hands on the 'merch', L'Angousette will make sure things go down the way we called them. He talks tough but he'll play ball—he knows what he wants.

"I know I might've stepped over the line with Rossi—"

I got a look, from Tony questioning "might've" with a hard slitting of his pale eyes, before heading to the kitchenette.

"—I know this guy likes to comes on like everybody's favorite uncle, but underneath he's the same kind of creature as White, maybe worse."

Tony turned his back and opened the fridge.

"Believe me, you don't know who or what you're dealing with."

Cranking up the energy to paste a half-smile on his face, Tony said nothing, then selected an apple and began sectioning it with a pocketknife.

I figured he was sulking. I couldn't blame him. What I'd done was two parts gut-reaction and one I-don't-know. I couldn't fully explain my reasons to him, or to myself. (It was like the good-news-bad-news joke about a busload of lawyers going over a cliff; everyone is killed, the bad news: two empty seats.) When Tony'd let on about Gallagher and Eaton—the pair who'd given me a 'tune-up'—and I saw a way to include them, I couldn't resist.

Still giving me the silent treatment, Tony elected to stay behind, to monitor the competition while I drove back to the house, ostensibly to retrieve the false 'drug stash' and look in on White. More important-ly, it would give me the opportunity to decide if I was really going to make the next series of moves.

*   *   *

I go to seek a great perhaps.

- Francois Rabelais

CHAPTER 85

Discovering I'd arrived empty-handed, Sarge barely paused long enough for a scratch behind the ears before heading to the back yard. White appeared unconscious; after the fun and games we'd had last time, I was in no mood to relax my guard even for an instant. I approached him cautiously and checked his bonds. They were secure. The new anchoring system was working. The plate was tight against the floor and there were no signs of chafing. Outside, I found Sarge patiently waiting beside the van intent on reclaiming his place in the mobile kennel, now that the dummy tank was onboard and had assured myself that White was under control.

"We all got to make sacrifices, little buddy," I apologized, as I topped up his food dish and ushered him back inside. Clearly, he was not pleased to be left behind, penned in again with White. If he could've spoken I had a fair notion what his comments might have been, as I shut him in. I considered myself fortunate he could not.

In my office, after several minutes glancing at the phone, trying to ignore the little voices in my head that refused to stay silent, I gathered enough nerve to do what I knew I was going to do the moment I'd left the motel. I hoped it was the right thing. Maybe, I thought—without believing it for a second—Tony would understand.

"Murphy, here."

"Hey. Sorry for calling so late"

"No problem. I just got off shift; this is afternoon for me. What's up?"

"'Just took a break from cleaning up and was wondering if you feel like shooting the breeze a bit?"

"If you don't mind coming over here. I'm about eight-nine blocks from you. No offense, but your place stinks." The laugh was friendly, and I accepted the insult the same way.

"Tell me about it," I agreed.

I called Tony to let him know where I was going. His response was predictable. He didn't like it, but he resigned himself to giving me enough rope. Gravely, he reminded me to play it slow and cool.

As if I would do otherwise.

I opted for the twenty-minute walk. After the last few days it felt good to get the blood pumping and the legs moving again. Except for occasional twinges, as long as I took it easy, my left foot was a little better. The rest of me, unfortunately, left something to be desired.

Key West wasn't all T-shirt shops, restaurants, and hotels. Though, most of the time it seemed that way. Once upon a time, it was safe to walk down almost any street downtown after dark. At worst you'd be greeted by some harmless drunk for no other reason than to say, 'how-ya-doin, maybe bum a smoke or a few pennies for a bottle of Mad Dog. With the advent and skyrocketing popularity of 'crack-cocaine' much of it from Miami, there'd been a steady increase of hedonistic and thrill-seeking tourists who would dare the fringe areas beyond the neon circus of Duval Street. A thriving population of ghouls competed to service this lucrative clientele through the sale of drugs, rental of clinically suspect companionship, or the occasional extraction of money by violence. Injuries were usually bumps and bruises with the odd knifing thrown in for good measure. The unofficial New Year's Eve firearms salute in the 'Village' was striving to become a nightly event, now that the Miami gangs had started playing in earnest for distribution rights to the Southernmost sales region. The tourist death toll, though nominal, was on the rise. Most were 'innocent bystanders' caught in the wake of a drive-by.

My path to the other side of Duval lay past a warren of lanes, alleys and dark hollows, home to an omnivorous species. The nocturnal cornucopia of goods and services, marketed by the future leaders of commerce, encouraged me to walk a little faster and nearer the center of the road, well away from the shadows. The street lamps in this area were shot out with such regularity that the city works crews had all but given up on promptly replacing them.

I began to doubt my decision to walk, but I'd gone too far to turn back. Duffy's set of nunchakus, camouflaged in a plastic bag, gave me a measure of confidence. Silently, I thanked Tony for having shown me how to use them.

I found the white Bahama-style house that matched the address; its paint was chipped and peeling, the staggering columns showed a building long in need of repair. Once, it'd been a comfortable single-family dwelling. Judging by the number of mailboxes tacked onto the porch wall, there were no less than eight separate residences.

"Up here," a voice from above called softly, considerate of the late hour. I stepped back to the sidewalk and looked up. Leaning over the second floor balcony railing, Joe Murphy, in shorts and a loose red Hawaiian shirt, pointed to the near side of the building.

"Stairs're around the corner, I'm the first on the right."

I waved and followed the path. Out of sight from above, I tucked the fighting sticks into a thick hedge of night-blooming jasmine near the stairs.

My nose wrinkled as I entered a narrow and dimly lit hallway on the second floor. Most old tenements and apartment buildings have a distinctive odor; this was no exception; fried pork, mothballs, and stale cigar smoke.

Murph's apartment, probably a bedroom at one time, had been reallocated into a common area surrounded by several tiny alcoves. From the comfortable and semi-organized mess that overlaid most of the horizontal surfaces, Murphy was a bachelor. The sole concessions to personal taste being mounted Opera posters on the walls and a decent stereo, surrounded by milk crates full of albums. The theatrical memorabilia were the only eye candy in an otherwise Spartan room.

"Good to see you." Murphy had reacted visibly to the battered condition of my face. The swelling and purple-yellow rainbow would get worse before it got better.

"You too."

I accepted the falsehood and a cold Perrier in exchange for the plastic bag.

The tiny apartment felt overcrowded with two people. I preferred close quarters for the conversation I planned, knowing I would give up a few points by negotiating on his home ground. It was an advantage that might give him the confidence to commit to the risky proposition I had in mind. Also, his place didn't have a hostage drugged, bound, and gagged in the next room, which might give me the confidence to be as candid as his response warranted, or to safely break it off if things started going in the wrong direction. Besides, as he'd already pointed out, it smelled a whole lot better.

Sitting across from me, on a hide-a-bed (now disguised as a sofa), he fanned the magazines across the scarred coffee table between us. From a comfortable and equally scarred oaken rocker, I watched the slow kaleidoscope of colored wing shapes as he turned the pages.

"Murph'...?" I set my drink on the end of the table.

Remembering my presence, he looked up from the centerfold of a glider in flight, an apologetic grin slipping comfortably into place.

"It's easy to get hung up on this stuff—" His grin ground to a halt when he perceived the gravity of my mood.

"I've got a, a proposition, something I'd like you to consider."

"What's that?" No grin, voice cautious, his cop radar warming up was beginning to focus.

"You recall our conversation about the, ah, the two assholes?"

I can be delicately circumspect when I want. He was all business.

"Sure. Why?"

"I may have a way of doing something about them but I need this conversation to be off the record, way off."

"You got it. Now, what's up?

A tickle of sweat began under each arm. I wanted to get up and run away. It was launch ramp time. Instead of away, I ran directly toward the precipice.

"Suppose there was a drug deal, a big drug deal, going down and Gallagher and Eaton heard about it, would they want or try to be in charge of the bust?"

The magazine lay forgotten on the small coffee table between us.

"And, do you think they'd be the kind of people who'd have any, say, creative thoughts regarding the amount of drugs that reached the evidence room?"

There's a moment of emptiness, of free falling, before glider and pilot achieve sufficient speed to convert a plunge to certain death into a graceful glide.

The moment stretched.

Fully a minute passed as he considered his response. Pinpricks of sweat, grown into trickles finger-walking maddening tracks down my sides were impossible to ignore. I wanted to squirm, or pick up the

Perrier bottle and pretend to examine the label, but couldn't. Every movement, every nuance was being examined and analyzed. Tony had been right.

What did I really know about this guy? He must be asking himself: What happened to just a couple of guys talking about sports? Does he see trouble or opportunity sitting across the table? He had to be wondering who just stepped into the ring? Was I, like that Golden Gloves boxer of so many years ago, also looking to turn his lights out?

Murph' countered to what surely must have been a sucker punch. "Yes-s-s, and it wouldn't surprise me. Who have you been talking to, and why do you want to know?"

The two secrets to surviving interviews, I'd heard a politician on television once remark, was to answer the question you wish had been asked and, when cornered, answer a question with a question.

"Do you know an honest cop would be willing to observe, record, and at the appropriate time take them into custody? And, would his testimony be enough to put them behind bars?"

"All this, of course, is hypothetical, right?"

"'Hypothetical.' Yeah." My voice cracked, betraying my emotions as I considered my efforts to stay alive described as an intellectual exercise. "But I need to know if that 'honest cop' exists."

Murphy delayed by going to the alcove kitchen. He pulled a fresh Perrier from the fridge; mine still sweated on the table. I dabbed under my shirt with a bandana. It came out dark.

"First," he asserted, "this 'honest cop' is going to need to know everything: background, who all's involved, and how you figure in it."

This is going well, a snide little voice chirped inside, as I absorbed the quick combination he threw at me.

Stalling, I took a healthy swig, letting the tiny bubbles abrade the back of my throat; several layers of residual heart swallowing were washed away.

"The only thing I can tell you is when and where, the rest is up to you."

Murphy studied me for a long moment then dropped his head and shook it. As he started to speak, he looked up. I could see anger.

"You're asking me to put my neck on the block while you sit on information I might need to stay alive? Right!"

I *was* asking a lot and offering very little. Logic and arguments aside, there was something that told me he was the right person. If I wanted him involved, I'd need to level with him, treat him like a member of the team, albeit a junior one. I dropped the circumspection and gave him a severely edited insight into the last week. He dedicated himself to listening with an intensity that precluded movement, even reducing the frequency of eye blinks to a degree I found disconcerting. I restrained myself from a soul baring commensurate to the attention he paid my narrative.

"I can see why you didn't want to press charges. They'd have been on your ass in a New-York second. There're a few blanks in your story. If I asked you for any clarification, would you be frank with me?"

"Yes, I'll be frank. Frank says: forget it."

He sipped his drink. His eyes drilled holes into mine. I wanted desperately to swallow.

"Accept it as I've laid it out or not. I've kept a few things back, but I'll make you a promise. If we survive—"

His eyes widened at my choice of words.

"Yes, I said, 'we' if you're in you make three; and my partner's not too keen on my trusting you. My instincts tell me you'll do the right thing, even if it wasn't technically, by-the-book legal.

"If we survive, I'll tell you everything from start to finish, nothing held back. But, only you, and no record of the conversation. There've been a few, irregularities involved with coming this far. If you include me in your report I'll be the anonymous—"

"CI," he corrected, "Confidential Informant."

"Whatever. I don't want any credit, shiny plaques, or a key to the city. I've gotten caught up in this, this thing and I only want to get out, hopefully in one piece and alive. Anything I tell you after will only be to satisfy your own curiosity."

I looked at my watch. I'd already been here too long. Murph' was motionless, waiting.

"I'm going to need a decision before I leave."

Had I misjudged? Had I blown up Tony's and my chances to get out of this situation, alerting the police in the bargain? Since he hadn't thrown me out the window or reached for the handcuffs...like the man said as he fell past the eightieth floor of the Empire State building, 'So far; so good.'

Murphy drank reflexively, occasionally looking at me. Then, with whatever information he'd gathered in that viewing, he retreated back to his decision-making process.

I scraped rows down the Perrier label with my thumbnail. My thoughts were drawn back to the first time I'd taken notice of those little green bottles.

*   *   *

Twice or thrice had I loved thee,
Before I knew thy face or name,

- John Donne

It was 1982; I was kicked back in a tiny bar watching an apathetic 40-something stripper grinding it out on the stage, that is, if you could call a sheet of plywood on top of two-by-fours a stage. I'd come in an hour earlier to wash the road out of my throat, and caught a fleeting glimpse of a naked angel disappearing behind a partition backstage. I'd felt like I'd been hit with a sledgehammer. Saying she was beautiful didn't come close to describing the sensuous perfection that briefly lit up the far corner of the seedy dive. After seeing her once, I couldn't leave until I saw her again, if only to convince myself that I hadn't been hallucinating; something I'd been doing quite a bit of at the time, attributable to the pharmacopoeia I'd been ingesting on almost a daily basis. When she again set foot on the stage, my world stopped. Until then, I'd never believed in love, let alone love at-first-sight. To be more accurate, what I'd felt was closer to lust than love, but it didn't matter; I was gone. Gone to a place I'd never been before and I wasn't coming back.

If thou remember'st not the slightest folly
That ever love did make thee run into,
Thou hast not lov'd.

- As You Like It, William Shakespeare

After, when she came out a side door dressed in street clothes, I couldn't tear my eyes from her dark beauty. I hadn't been able to move, let alone breathe during her performance. It was only after she'd left the stage that the room had returned to normal and once again became a grungy bar. She stopped for a moment to chat with the bartender. He looked over at me and said something to her, then sank below the bar, stood, and placed something in her hands. She turned, and carrying a pair of small green bottles, came directly to my table and sat down opposite me.

Man has his will, — but woman has her way.

- Oliver Wendell Holmes

It was, as if the air had suddenly solidified around me, I couldn't move, I couldn't speak; she'd stolen my heart without having said a word. Sitting silently across the table, the heat in her eyes burned into mine both teasing and promising. All the while, her fingers ran up and down her Perrier bottle in so explicit a manner as to leave no doubt of her intentions.

*　　　*　　　*

I shifted uncomfortably in the rocking chair, the bittersweet images of Nicole were always there, powerful, evocative, poised just beneath the surface waiting to tantalize my body and break my heart. I had loved and been loved in return. Maybe once, if you're lucky, is all you get in this lifetime. Reviewing my limited list of options should Murph' decline and become Officer Murphy again, I sighed inwardly. Everything I had was gone; what did it matter anymore?

Maybe a nice long, stay in a jail cell wouldn't be so bad after all? Would Tony forgive me?

Murph' snorted once, loudly, then said, "You got it. But, I'm going to need a minimum of two hours notice, and, there are two other guys. I want 'em in or I'm out. They'll be my responsibility," he said cutting off any objections I might offer. "I trust them."

I kept my face neutral as I reached forward to offer my hand, to seal our understanding. Murph' gave me a stony look, then responded with a firm, hard grip.

Maintaining the handshake longer than necessary, he increased the pressure, warning me: "This is going to cost, plenty. You'd better not be playing games."

Games!? I kept silent, my thoughts on what this "game" had cost: Doug, four men I'd personally killed, and four more indirectly. Monk was mutilated and crippled for life. My best friend, Charlie, was gone forever. Ice flooded through me, swelling blood vessels, tightening muscles, freezing my grip into a cold steel vice grinding tighter and tighter. Murph's eyes widened. Not wanting to give in, he tried not to show the pain.

"This is no '*game*'." My voice sounded to me like the groan of a damned soul, irrevocably doomed to loss and sorrow.

Taken aback by the surge of raw emotion. I think he sensed some of what was going on inside of me as he massaged feeling back into his hand.

"It better not be." He sounded shaken, "I'm betting my career on it."

"I'll be in touch within twenty-four hours."

At his suggestion, I would use a code name in case I had to go through police dispatch to make contact.

"A phone call from Sarge will be the signal to go."

*　　　*　　　*

To set the Cause above renown,
To love the game beyond the prize,
To honor, while you strike him down,
The foe that comes with fearless eyes:

- Sir Henry John Newbolt

CHAPTER 86

I'd unfairly exploited what might have become a good friendship. There were solid reasons for the lies, half-truths and manipulations; my conscience rejected the rationalizations as so many fabrications of convenience. Anger and self-loathing were my companions; they whispered harsh truths into my ears, muting the music and noise on Duval Street. Revelers, drunk, laughing and boisterous, flowing past, reinforced my separation from the rest of humanity.

Sarge bolted out of the shop, his headlong dash nearly knocked me over. Bad kidneys, I thought, until seconds later an abbreviated shout was followed by a crash. I gave a quick look at White—he lay on his side unmoving in a fetal curl—then ran toward the muted sound of a brawl coming from the back yard.

Three figures were engaged in a deadly spiral; a black-clad figure circled Sarge, tracking him with a matte-black pistol. His twin, on the ground, had hold of Sarge's collar, as he tried to steady the ferocious Rottweiler for his partner's shot while spinning on his back to avoid the flashing sharp fangs. The shooter was about five feet away. His back was to me. There was no conscious thought of what to do; I was already attacking. Even before I saw his finger begin to tighten on the trigger, the nunchaku flashed out from my hand, a rising, inward swing connected with the point of his wrist. The pistol went flying, accompanied by a yelp of pain. Rolling the chain-swung baton over the top of the figure eight, gaining momentum, his cry was cut off as the hard downstroke sharply nailed the outer corner of his eye socket. The sequence, completed within several tenths of a second was, to my perception, slowed to such a degree that time moved with a dreamlike viscosity.

The would-be shooter lay at my feet still as death. I picked up his pistol. It resembled my Beretta, though heavier. The other shadow-figure still wrestled with Sarge. The only sound, their wild thrashing, was underscored by Sarge's bone-chilling snarls. I couldn't keep the intruder sighted for more than a fraction of a second, so furious was their struggle.

"Sarge!" I hissed. "Enough!"

The instant Sarge released, the dark figure had twisted, reaching for the knife strapped to his calf. The silenced pistol-shot was the stuttering spit of a venomous snake, the recoil unexpectedly hard in my hand. He yanked his support hand away as a shower of chips exploded from the flagstone beside his fingers then quickly spinning away from me, he turned in the opposite direction. Stepping in, I used the doubled nunchaku handles in a stabbing strike to the base of his skull. He was out even as he began to melt to the ground. I heard a metallic clatter a moment later. He'd gone for a gun strapped under his left arm, and almost reached it.

I turned my attention to Sarge. He stood guard over Ninja #1, who offered no resistance as I patted him down and relieved him of his leg knife. When I pulled the knitted balaclava from his head, I wasn't surprised. The blood-spattered face of Duke, the new leader of White's A-team, lay unconscious.

Learning from my mistakes, I bound them, then took the time to shoot two new anchor staples into the concrete floor. Properly secured, I left Sarge on guard.

Evidently, things had been going too well. With Rossi's double-cross, if they knew enough to stake out my place and there were two of them here, the odds were good that the remaining two team members were at Tony's house; not the motel, I hoped.

Predictably, Tony was pissed, until I gave him the good news about Murphy's willingness to go along. When I suggested taking a crack at the two remaining A-team members, Tony nixed the idea. I didn't push it. Instead, I recommended dismantling our listening post and regrouping.

"Already on the way."

I spread a towel on my desk and placed the guns on it. Something about them had made me curious. According to the name-stamp, it *was* a Beretta, it resembled the one Tony had given me. There were several modifications: the barrel, minus the silencer, was ported with three holes on either side and extended maybe an inch or more beyond the muzzle slide. Below the barrel was a lever hinged to the forward part of the trigger guard. I couldn't figure out what it was for until I gripped it and discovered the thumb of my lever hand slipped naturally through the front of the elongated trigger guard.

Curiouser and curiouser. On the left side of the receiver were a cluster of three white dots above a single white dot, a notched dial bracketed the three.

Trading the gun for a flashlight, I retraced my steps to the garden. I recalled feeling only a single recoil, albeit a heavy one, when I fired the warning shot. There were two furrows scarring the flagstone walk, one higher than the next. By rough measure the third would've been just beyond the slab. My finger found a small hole between the stones. The dial made sense: single, safe, and rock 'n roll; it was some kind of machine pistol.

Back inside, I inspected the shoulder harness. Besides two spare magazines, in a slender sheath was something resembling a tiny golf putter maybe six or seven inches in length but hinged in the middle, fully extended it became a shoulder stock. A lock-slot was machined into the butt of the pistol to receive it. The level of equipment being used against us was improving.

Tony's conch-cruiser chugged to a stop in the driveway.

"We're running out of places to—" he stopped in mid-sentence, gaping at the fully assembled weapon in my hands.

"Where in hell—? The A-team." he concluded.

"Machine pistols," I informed him, having only just figured it out.

"Close, but better," he said, taking it; admiring the heft and the feel of it. "They're 93Rs, Rafficas. A rotary cam limits bursts to three rounds. 'Less chance of wasting ammo. Very effective—Mother-trucker! Two of them?"

Tony was so impressed with the weapons he immediately adopted the one he was holding as his own.

"Should we send a thank you note to Rossi?"

"Yeah. Look," he struggled with the words, "I've been guilty of treating you like an FNG [fucking new guy]. I hate to admit it, but you're holding your own. Some of your moves have been, inspired. 'Good thing."

"Is this where I'm supposed to say 'aw shucks' and scuff the floor or something."

His mood cooled appreciably.

"Don't get me wrong, I appreciate the sentiment, but we'd both be chilling big-time if Sarge hadn't bailed me—us—out, twice. He did the work. I only cleaned up. Here, you may need this."

Mollified, he accepted the harness, stripping off his own. I stuffed it into the desk drawer, while he adjusted the straps.

"The clips are bigger, they're what—eighteen, twenty?"

"Twenty—good guess. But, what we need right now is a new base of operations. Any ideas what to do with our *guests* now that the DEA's back in the game?"

We had been so very close to resolving our situation; this latest wrinkle had Tony plenty worried. We were running on pure nerve and adrenaline. There seemed little left in reserve. He looked beat. Not wanting to shatter my own illusions of resolve and fortitude, I decided not to risk a look in the mirror.

"I don't much like the idea of keeping watch on them and dealing with everything else at the same time."

The image of circus performers came to mind, as they maintained an ever-growing number of bowls and plates spinning on rods.

"Know where we can get our hands on a boat?"

Tony looked over from the fridge, where he had been inhaling milk directly from the jug. I saw a smile start in his eyes that reached his lips a second later. A large droplet of milk fell from his moustache.

"There's a thirty-six-foot cabin cruiser at the sub pens. That do?"

"Any diving gear on board?"

He paused for a moment. "Yeah...?"

"This might sound a little crazy, but I was thinking—how about the job site? Lots of places to hide things, phone and power lines in both structures, and a dock to the beach"

"Perfect!"

"I was thinking we could leave them tied up in the houseboat, then—"

"You shoulda quit at 'perfect,' " he mumbled, his cheeks stuffed with half a slab of cheese. "We can figure this stuff out while we load up," he nodded ominously toward the locked workshop, "before we get more company."

He was right. The comings and goings; the sounds of a fight; who knew what my neighbors had heard or seen, or what they might do. Tall fence and thick foliage, or not, we were center stage.

Once loaded, I decided to risk one last call.

The oily smooth voice answered on the first ring, "Yes?"

Awake and composed, at four-thirty in the morning; that told me a lot. Calls were expected. None, though, I was certain, from me.

"I'm conducting a survey: What's your favorite news progr—"

"I can promise—"

I hate being interrupted.

"See you on CNN."

*   *   *

The night has a thousand eyes,
And the day but one;
Yet the light of the bright world dies,
With the dying sun.

- Francis William Bourdillon

CHAPTER 87

Our arrival at the pleasure boat moorings, converted from World War II submarine pens, had gone unnoticed. There'd been neither guard nor curious onlooker around to get in the way, at quarter to five in the morning that was only to be expected. Nary a Rambo in the bunch, the security staff were an easygoing group who seemed to believe that Graveyard shift was the right time for an extra forty winks or another hand of cards before the day crew arrived.

The cabin cruiser Tony indicated, an Egg Harbor, appeared well built, trustworthy in foul weather, and in premium condition. Unlike many people, Tony took care of his toys.

The powerful diesels idled rhythmically in the cool morning air. Early fishing trips and their attendant noises were a small price for a live-aboard residence at any of the crowded docks, especially in-Season, therefore, normal.

We transferred our gear quickly and quietly. Ready to get under-way, Tony powered against the remaining spring line. When the stern warped away from the jetty, I untied the rope and tossed it onboard. The pitch of the diesels shifted then deepened; the propellers bit the still-black water, churning a soft fluorescent froth at the stern. By the time I reached the top of the jetty, the running lights had cleared the breakwater.

Minutes later, a lone pilgrim moving through the night, I guided the van towards our rendezvous. Down a side street, I saw the rotating yellow *blink/wink* atop a distant street sweeper as it wandered on its endless cycle. The naked Duval sidewalks were lonely and despondent at this hour, painting a sadder, grimmer "Night-hawks" than Hopper envisioned. Pools of harshly incandescent window displays and garish neon cast a surrealistic, brooding, nightmarish quality to the shops and trendy boutiques. Most of the ghouls and vampires had dispersed with the imminent sunrise. Only a few desperate creatures remained, skulking in doorways where shadows veiled and softened the skeletal ravages of their crystalline hunger.

*   *   *

CHAPTER 88

Of the two garages built into the ground level of the original house, one was jammed with construction materials; the other, with a broken lock, had been left vacant. I threaded the van between mounds of debris, squeezed it inside then ran the door down.

An interior doorway opened onto a polished marble foyer. The graceful sweep of a winding staircase led up to the main floor where I entered the ruins of a once-gracious, now-cavernous shell of the great room. The idea had been to install a bank of glass doors across the rear wall of the building facing the water. Four gaping twelve-foot wide holes—the middle two still held billowing sheets of plastic—faced the elements. Rain, trash and wind-driven sand grated underfoot as I crossed the tiled expanse. I picked up the phone in the kitchen, heard a dial tone then went back to one of the open holes to wait and watch.

False dawn announced the coming day, painting red against an indigo sky. Two speedboats, a pontoon 'party boat', a Hobie-cat, and the now-vacant live-aboard belonging to Monk's Black Sheep realty partner were still tied to the moorings; ours would blend right in.

Hearing the faraway hum, I picked my way down through the garbage heap towards the dock. Throttled back, the diesels were a low throaty idle in the no-wake zone, gave enough turns for maneuvering when crossing the Bight channel at the end of the point. When Tony shut down, to drift the last dozen or so yards to the pier, the silence became a physical presence; the smallest noises were magnified out of proportion, each carrying the threat of discovery. Exposed, vulnerable, standing out in the open on the end of the dock, I tried to look casual.

There was little reassurance in the weight of the heavy pistol under my jacket. My camouflage relied solely on Tony's truism: "...act like you belong, just business as usual."

An unexpected gurgle of laughter surprised me. My business-as-usual facade nearly dissolved into giggling when I straightened up from tying off the stern line and saw, splashed across the breadth of the boat's transom, in bright gold script, *Never Again III*. The name was insane yet so perfectly in-sync with all that had happened, was happening, and would, in all likelihood, continue happening to us.

We would remain on board, since the cover of night would make it easier to move our prisoners when and if necessary. Until then they would stay below decks in the bow section. Using heavy-gauge cable-ties, each man's left ankle was fastened to the next one's right. Their wrists—the team leader's, where I'd hit it, wasn't broken, though it was swollen to almost twice the size of his other—were doubled together behind them, cinched tight. All three G-men were now awake and in varying degrees of irritation and discomfort. Guessing the substance of the oblique eye signals flashing between them, I pictured the name on the transom.

Tony was close to exhaustion; visibly, every step was a labor, so I took the first shift. He climbed up the gangway to the wheelhouse, stretched out on a bench seat with a life vest for a pillow, and was instantly asleep. Below decks, Sarge had racked out, hogging the side berth opposite the galley, I had the gangway all to myself. The narrow steps, covered in hard ribbed tile made it impossible to get comfortable that would ensure I stay awake.

As the sun warmed the day, the crowded quarters below decks soon took on the closeness of a Turkish bath. Steam-heavy, the air was redolent with the fragrances of diesel fuel and sweat accented by the rattle of snores. Shortly after noon, looking rested, Tony relieved me. I'd had to use both hands to pull myself up the stairs to the wheelhouse and was asleep before my head touched my Day-Glo orange pillow.

*　　　*　　　*

Care-charmer Sleep, son of the sable Night,
Brother to Death, in silent darkness born:
Relieve my languish, and restore the light,
With dark forgetting of my care return,
And let the day be time enough to mourn
The shipwreck of my ill adventured youth:
Let waking eyes suffice to wail their scorn,
Without the torment of the night's untruth.

- Samuel Daniel

CHAPTER 89

She growled seductively, deeply in her throat, speaking my name. Hot breath, her husky voice next to my ear, a warm, sexual sound, sent a shivering thrill speeding over my flesh. Her lips; firm and full; teasingly, she refused to open her mouth under mine. Her athletic, resilient body twined sinuously around and on top of me holding, squeezing, grinding hard against me. I groaned with longing and anticipation, responding, feeling the urgent stirrings of tumescence grow until I was vibrating, hard and thrusting toward her, blind to everything but the raw sensuality of primeval rhythms. She held me tight, biting my shoulder, at first playfully then passionately. I tried wrestling her over. She was very strong and agile; resisting, she locked herself onto me even tighter. Caught up in the ferocious twisting and thrusting of her body, I tried to hold onto this sexual hurricane. Lifting my leg, I wrapped it around hers, groaning at the renewed contact of her body against me. I swung my arm back, to generate momentum to reverse our positions and gain control. A flash of pain exploded in my hand as it slammed into the bulkhead.

"Wake up." Tony's hand shook my shoulder.

"Enough. I'm awake," I groaned, "enough...." The ache in my hand slowly became a dull throb. My mind and body, replete with an empty post-dream depression, made more profound by the bittersweet memories of Nicole. I brushed the hot, wet regret from my eyes then disentangled the life jacket from between my legs.

I would carry her with me the rest of my life which, given recent events, promised to be not much longer.

*   *   *

CHAPTER 90

An eerie tone suffused the twilight. One slender, red ray of light reached out through bruised purple clouds, portending the arrival of another storm system. Pinpoints sparkled in the silhouetted skyline as day surrendered to encroaching darkness, bringing with it the cloaking anonymity of night.

From the dock, up the gentle incline of beach to the construction site, Tony and I picked a trail through the piles of debris. Duke, the de-facto leader, complained through his duct-tape gag, as did the larger man Tony carried. There'd be no breakfast today and I'm certain my shoulder in the middle of his gut was a poor substitute for an Egg Mc-something. Tony entered the building shell. By the time I reached the first floor landing he was out of sight, I was lagging far behind. Duke's weight felt like a ton pressing me down. On the second floor landing I had to lean against the wall to rest for a moment before continuing. Almost out of breath, doggedly, I pushed on. Each step became a goal that moved further and further away.

The ceiling on the third floor was unfinished; the overhead rafters, awaiting sheets of drywall that might never be applied, were exposed. For what Tony had in mind, they would do nicely. I kept watch as he bound their adjacent ankles together. The two SEALs seemed resigned to their fate, offering no resistance; both seemed a little less invincible. Based on my own recent experiences, I knew too well how easily a beating and physical restraint could induce feelings of helplessness.

Tony left for a few minutes, returning with several lengths of rope over his arm. Tossing one end over the beam that ran the length of the building, he fashioned a slip noose on the other end, then snugged it over their joined ankles. I gave a hand hoisting until only their heads and shoulders touched the floor. Suspended by the single rope, they resembled a peculiar letter W. I could see why Tony favored this method of restraint; inverted this way there was nothing they could do to free themselves.

He shook out the other piece of rope, cut it into two sections, each perhaps fifteen feet in length, which he tied in abbreviated hangmen's nooses. Aware of the significance of that knot, they complained into their gags as the nooses went around their necks, more so when he attached the other end of the lines to the open studs on the adjacent wall. I told them to rest easy; that they were merely to prevent them from trying to escape and that someone would release them within the next day or so. I was relieved to know that I'd told the truth when I saw Tony nodding in agreement.

*   *   *

**Still-born Silence! thou that art
Floodgate of the deeper heart.**

- Richard Flecknoe

CHAPTER 91

The diesels filled the wheelhouse with a wall of sound. I searched the zippered carryalls stowed in the access space between the engines. Finding the small pack, I slipped it into my jacket pocket, lowered the hatch in place, and went below for a visit with the black-hearted Mr. White.

Sarge looked up at me expectantly. I gave a friendly rumple to his ears. Seeing I hadn't smuggled him a T-bone, he grunted and went back into doze-mode. Judging by the pure malice White aimed at me, I figured he had yet to appreciate my boyish charm and whimsical sense of humor; we were even on that count.

The tape was cued; I placed the headset over his ears and turned it on. A slow but distinct change of expression showed; first disbelief transitioned into bloody revenge as the identity of the speaker then the content of the conversation became evident. I counted the numbers ticking by on the display then clicked the tape player off at the end of my conversation with Rossi.

The headset was still in place. White stayed silent while I spoke into the microphone. Our script, amplified by the little machine, would fill his mind. It might have had something to do with the band of duct tape covering his mouth, but I'm pretty sure that he would have chosen to keep his own counsel regardless.

Forty minutes, or so, later, with the boat safely riding at anchor, Tony and I were in the inflatable Zodiac racing across the mirror-flat water toward the storm clouds that lay dead ahead.

*   *   *

CHAPTER 92

The Blue Lagoon Motel is, as the name could imply, a motel that's been painted blue. Located on North Roosevelt Boulevard, a narrow boat-channel dredged to allow water access to the motel also supports a thriving kayak and Jet Ski rental business. Fully a third of the motel fronts a broad shallow expanse of water—the same shallow expanse Tony and I waded across several nights earlier. Technically speaking it isn't really a lagoon. However, since 'The Blue Dredged-Channel Motel' doesn't sound quite as picturesque, I gave the owners credit for picking a more inviting image. Image, perhaps more than anything else these days, is so very important.

Striding down the length of the dock, like Caesar through Gaul, a cigar clenched in his teeth, the Dock Master wore a pristine "Grateful Dead" T-shirt, threadbare chinos and a grizzled three-day beard. The scowl under the battered Yankees ball cap was one reserved for those who dared tie up to his dock without paying tribute. About to begin a practiced recitation of dock space fees on a per-foot basis (broken-down and simplified for congenitally stupid and substance-impaired tourists), he recognized Tony and changed gears in mid-blather. A ten-dollar bill earned us a crooked, yellow-fanged grin of appreciation and temporary moorage.

Outside the supermarket we took stock of our dwindling funds, which now amounted to some twelve dollars. I took the paper and left Tony with a handful of change for the payphone. A few minutes later I was back outside, most of my purchases securely tied in a plastic bag, waiting for Tony to finish up with Langouste.

"D'accord." Tony said and smiled. The smile of agreement died when he disconnected. I swapped a half-full tub of potato salad for the phone.

Murph' wasn't at home. I called the alternate number. The police operator took the message from "Sarge." I tried to ignore Tony's rolling eyes and I-told-you-so looks until the pay phone rang.

"We're on for tonight." I told Murph', smiling at Tony's nod of approval. "There *is* one small wrinkle."

"Ohhh...?"

I'd gotten a lot of practice deciphering monosyllabic responses. His reeked of skepticism.

"The *thing* will probably be going down on the water—a house-boat—will that be a problem for the 'assholes'?"

"No, not really," he said, confirming Tony's prediction of how he would respond to our sounding like we were making this up on the fly, in case Murphy was trying to second-guess us. "They've used both the police cruiser and their own boat on several raids I know of. Where's it going to happen, on 'The Row'?"

Houseboat Row? I thought, nice try but no cigar.

"I'll give you the location when it's definite. How about you, any problem with being on the water?" I asked.

There was a pause. I could almost hear the wheels spinning.

"I've got use of a fast boat, but it's going to cost me a favor. I—"

"Spend it."

"I'm starting to get a bad feeling about this."

I could feel Murph's mind changing.

"Either you're in or you're out. You got a problem with how it's going, fine. Stay-the-fuck out of the way and watch it on the news. See ya."

Beside me, Tony was flipping out. The potato salad foaming from his mouth made him look like a rabid vegetarian.

"WAIT!"

That's what I wanted to hear. If it hadn't happened—I didn't want to consider that alternative.

I counted to five in silence, letting him sweat.

"Go ahead," I drew out the words, sounding reluctant.

"It's going to take me some time to arrange this"

"How long?" I needed to keep the pressure on, make him commit to making this work.

"Three, maybe four hours."

I figured he was probably allowing himself a comfortable margin. Though it was well within our time frame, I didn't want him to become complacent. People try harder when they're under pressure.

"Start what you can," I said. "I won't be able to give you any more than fifteen or twenty minutes notice once we're rolling. It'll be that close. Can you do it?"

There was neither hesitation nor humor in his voice. "I'll have to, won't I?"

He gave me another number to call.

*   *   *

CHAPTER 93

The cabin cruiser loomed ahead, a silent white wedge floating serenely in sky-purple water. Something was terribly wrong. I voiced my concerns to Tony while unlocking the toolbox.

Covered by the noise of the idling outboard, as Tony fended off and motored astern, I moved quietly across the forward deck to the clear Lexan hatch. In the cabin below me, White appeared not to have moved during our absence. He could be playing the 'tethered-goat'.

My nerves were bowstrings. I scratched softly on the deck. White spun, looking up. Seeing me he looked away. Sarge's massive wedge-shaped head edge around the corner. I relaxed a little after checking White's bonds, finding them still intact. The malevolence, that I'd come to expect, I noticed, was absent. Like standing with both feet firmly planted in the air, only too well I remembered how it felt when I learned that Monk had knowingly sent me into a trap I was not meant to survive.

Despite White's apparent dejection, I checked the rest of the boat but found nothing amiss. The uneasy feeling, like wearing a second skin that didn't fit right it; persisted. Tony'd put it down to "premature evacuation" (pre-mission jitters).

Sarge was in great spirits, approving both my selections of canned entrée and dessert. Tacitly, as he wolfed down the food, he agreed to continue his guard duty of our somewhat more tractable charge. White picked distractedly at his plate while Sarge calculated his potential for leftovers. Just for a moment I may have actually pitied White, but it passed quickly; I hadn't lost sight of the damage he'd already caused, or deluded myself into thinking that he could be trusted.

The docking went smoothly at Doug's houseboat in spite of the wind, which had blown in quickly and was rising steadily. My skin prickled from the ozone-rich weight of the oncoming front. Behind me, I sensed rather than heard Tony jump, feeling the faint vibration as he landed lightly on the deck. Reaching to open the door, my thoughts were on the impending weather conditions. An invisible hand gripped my throat and twisted 'til I couldn't breathe. The fetid reek of Doug's dead body overwhelmed my senses. Rage and anger, like an injected drug, boiled hot in my veins. Gagging, choking back the tears, I slammed the door shut then returned to the cruiser to make sure Sarge stayed aboard.

Tony'd had the intestinal fortitude to weather the stench and cut the macabre wreckage of his friend from the chair, it now bobbed heavily in the water, visible through the open hatch. The quality of the air had only marginally improved. I had myself under control but the doorway was as close as I'd been able to go.

"Bring 'em in; let's get this done," Tony barked at me.

Breathing shallowly through my mouth, I tried not to look at the bloated thing floating in the water as I hauled two of the black tote bags inside. I wanted to say something but couldn't think of any words that would be appropriate. I stalled, unnecessarily checking to ensure that there were *indeed* two full sets of diving gear. Dreading the moment, I lay on the deck and leaned down over the edge. According to our plan, the equipment needed to be secured to the underside of the hatch coaming. Water reached up my arm and soaked the side of my head as I lowered the gear and fastened it in place on a row of eye-screws with nylon ties. I cannot begin to explain my revulsion at the greasy caress of dead flesh when Doug's hand brushed across my face. Mostly there was a profound sorrow for the loss of a comrade, and my shame at my inability to deal with the insanity that was our reality.

"Done yet?" Tony asked. Having finished the electric connections, he tested the soldered ends with a small meter.

"Just a minute," I said, biting down hard on my grief.

"I know," he said softly, understanding.

"Okay," I felt the zip of the nylon tie snug tight, "done." The last set was secure.

"Cast off the stern and make ready to leave." Tony directed, as he keyed the engines to life. "We need some way of keeping White on ice, any suggestions?

Tie him to the anchor and toss him overboard. I had a couple more, which I kept to myself; the last suggestion I'd been asked for had, more or less, ended up with my pulling a gun on Tony, I wasn't very proud of that.

"Hell, I don't know—why not just keep him on board? He's tied and gagged; where's he gonna go?"

"Maybe, but I'd kinda like him someplace *else*. There's no telling what kind of shit storm we might run into tonight."

The marine radio was tuned to the NOAA channel; according to the National Oceanic and Atmospheric Administration's broadcasts, that wasn't the only kind of storm on the way. A tropical depression formed in the turbid crucible where the Westerlies and the Trades spiral and hurricanes breed, was a little south of Key West, growing in strength, and heading right for us. If nothing else, it would keep the civilians off the streets and out of the way.

"Hah!" Tony'd apparently become the proud parent of a newborn idea. I knew I wouldn't have to wait long.

"No-no-no-no! No way." I fumed, when he'd laid it out.

"It's perfect. No one'd expect it."

"Because it's stupid. Think about it; two of their team go there then drop out of sight. Du-u-h! Doesn't that seem just the teensiest bit suspicious?"

"And, right after, who did you call? Rossi's got to figure you're not brainless enough to go back there. Reverse logic says—"

"Screw 'reverse logic. I don't like it."

Against my better judgement, Tony persuaded me into using the workshop one last time. Drugged and attached to the floor restraints, he convinced me White'd be safely on hold. The shop was heavily soundproofed and—I hated to admit it—it *was* the last place anyone would look for him. The only real argument I'd been able to offer was that bad, bad feeling, but I'd been having a steady stream of those ever since I'd come back from Georgia.

*   *   *

CHAPTER 94

Each carrying his own thoughts, the four of us made a strange party as we trooped up the dock, across the sliver of beach. Tony, in the lead with White in tow, carefully picked a trail through the tanglefoot and tripwires.

Tethered to the man who'd slain his brothers-in-arms, haunted his life, and made everything he'd fought for a lie; all in the name of greed and political expediency; I looked for any sign of what was going on inside of my friend. Tony was unreadable.

Bound at the wrists and on a tight leash, White appeared focused on keeping his balance; he limped a little, having sliced an ankle on a blade of roofing sheet. I enjoyed each twinge on Tony's behalf.

Sarge, the free-ranging flanker, intelligently went around through the neighboring grounds. Last in the troupe, I broke off for a dummy-check of the two G-men and to bring them some water. There were no signs of any escape attempts. Either we'd gotten very good at tying up people or these guys knew how to accept the inevitable.

I restated my promise to see them released, as soon as possible—they didn't deserve to suffer. I hadn't forgotten two others we'd left tied-up and defenseless, knowing that I would hear the flat, hollow sound of that explosion reverberating in my mind for years to come.

*　　　*　　　*

CHAPTER 95

Before peeling the tape from his mouth, Tony asked White if he was ready to cooperate. Feeling abused and abandoned by his master, Rossi, he nodded wearily in the affirmative.

White accepted a portion of the diamonds and a plausible cover story of his death in exchange for his recitation of the culpable parties, their roles and—should it become necessary—his testimony in a court of law. There was some reluctance with his agreeing to this item, until Tony convinced him that neither of us really wanted to pursue any course of legal action. Since we all knew that the removal of corrupt officials inevitably led to their replacement with soon-to-be-corrupt officials. If necessary, it wouldn't be the threat of public exposure but the will to execute it that would be a deterrent to further chicanery. White's agreeing to provide testimony, recorded on tape, would show that we had both the will and the wherewithal.

Wending our way through the wind-blasted streets, a world of corruption, conspiracy and collusion filled the van. Eavesdropping from the driver's seat, despair wrapped its fingers around my heart, as White sketched an outline of complicity and payoffs reaching the offices of the Joint Chiefs of Staff. Even in the White House, the prevailing opinion was that the preservation of the DEA outweighed the eradication of the problem it was created to solve. In a perverted way it made sense: power was a heady and addictive drug, and it wasn't an easy thing to give up. As White put it, "where was the need for a gatekeeper if the wolves are all dead?" As long as there were wolves, or the threat of them, there was power aplenty for the gatekeepers. In the political arena a grateful gatekeeper like the DEA, meant a strong right arm whose wolf-killing abilities could be used for anything from intimidation or to inflict retribution if the need arose.

Every moment I spent listening to how deftly woven into the warp and woof of the American Dream was the thread of deception, my resolve to go along with our plan weakened.

Twenty minutes later, Tony snapped the recorder off, put the tape in his pocket, buttoned the flap, and announced: "Ready."

Previously, when we'd hijacked the contraband shipment, I had believed we were in possession of a ticking bomb. Compared to the information recorded on the tiny cassette it was a soggy firecracker.

*   *   *

CHAPTER 96

Street lamps cast overlapping cones of illumination as far as I could see. Parked near the corner, a block and a half away on the opposite side of Angela Street, we had an unobstructed view in every direction. From our vantage point I could see two blocks beyond my house, down to where the asphalt ended and a black mound of road patch was piled up against the chain-linked perimeter.

Traffic, what little there was of it, was punctuated by a "heartbeat machine" rattling windows on houses as it pumped out rapper's rotes on full bass 'til the distortion fuzzed white-hot. Down the block on the left, a staccato rattle of Spanish flared quickly followed by a loud bellow and the crash of breaking dishes as Carmen and Shawndra entered the eternal round two of their turbulent marriage. Elsewhere, teen laughter or outrage—it was hard to tell the difference—shrilled. On the surface the neighborhood looked, and sounded, as it should.

Sarge and I approached the house on foot using, what can be best described as the-long-way-around-to-the-shortest-way-home method. We took it easy and were, to all outward appearances, like most folks on the Rock, in no hurry at all. Sarge gave an outstanding imitation of an average evening walk, sniffing and watering bushes in earnest.

My nerves, however, were in worse shape than I cared to admit. I'd almost taken cover and pulled my gun when a gaggle of rental-pink mopeds, each bearing a pair of sunburned college kids, noisily bleated their way down the street.

Within seconds of my flicking the porch light on and off, the van's lights came on in answer. Once inside the gate, before we let White out of the van, I took Tony to one side.

"It's too easy. We can't—I don't trust him." I had a problem with Tony's apparent acceptance of White's conversion, especially in light of the 'great Vietnam saga' he'd played out for me. Changing colors was something that came much too easily to White to suit me.

"And what would you have me do, kill him?"

That's exactly what I wanted, but I couldn't say the words.

Taking the lead, Tony insisted that since we were committed to a course of action that required our complete and utter concentration—a result of my own twisted machinations—it was a little late for second thoughts. He was right, so I kept my thoughts to myself and my mouth shut. This was Tony's play, and I wasn't going to rock the boat beyond what I'd already done. That didn't mean I was going to let my guard down. Sarge, like me, remained skeptical I noticed. After we let White out of the van and he was being directed to the shop, Sarge followed a little to the rear within easy striking distance.

White must have been none too comfortable either, seeing himself a prisoner returned to the place of his internment but he surprised me with his willingness to submit to one more night in bondage. Willing or not I took my duties seriously, securing him to the middle of the floor, eliciting a grunt as I tightened his restraints and added an extra cable tie for good measure. I hadn't forgotten the silent contemptuous promises of violence he'd sneered at me.

Sarge had an extra-large helping of food and water. I'd shaken out a padded mover's quilt and fashioned it into a comfortable bed for him. Still I was reluctant to leave. Kneeling, I put a hand on either side of his huge head and held him close to me for a moment.

"I'll be back for you, little buddy," I whispered into his furry ear, "that's a promise." I nodded towards White, saying, "Watch that guy. I don't trust him."

Sarge had the most soulful-looking eyes, and he used them to good effect.

As we set out into the night I was conscious of a big clock, ticking off the minutes and the seconds. That itchy second-skin feeling was back.

*　　　*　　　*

CHAPTER 97

The streets were virtually empty, most folks were snug inside, huddled around roaring television sets, warming themselves on promises of a new and improved life, or crowding the bars and clubs at the other end of Duval Street, down below Mile Zero.

I was parked in the shadows of a repair garage attached to a used car lot, the source of Tony's fleet of conch cruisers. Under row upon row of naked bulbs shimmering between plastic spinners and flapping pennants, highly polished sucker-bait stood prominently out front, a generous sprinkle of lemons garnished the display. My van was too conspicuous for the moves we were going to be making, and we would need to split up to accomplish our respective objectives. Browsing, separating creampuffs from the citrus, my choices had narrowed down to four.

Tony'd been gone for what seemed like an eternity. Five minutes earlier, moving between the cars like a broken-field runner avoiding tackles, he'd disappeared around the corner of the office, a mobile home up on blocks.

I was startled when the night was shattered by a loud crash—a door slamming or was it a gunshot? The human mind, wondrous thing that it is, not only can fill interludes when time hangs heavy on one's hands with our worst fears but has the inclination to do so. I tried not to think of someone waiting in the darkened office, killing Tony, someone signaling his accomplices who were coming for me. I saw a figure moving away from the building.

Stuffing one of two half-inch-thick blocks of money along with a set of keys into my hands, as we headed toward the front of the lot, Tony pretended not to notice my nervousness.

"That one's yours," he indicated a shiny black Jeep in the curbside row, one of the selections in my private survey. He got into the nondescript gray Honda beside it.

"See you at the motel, after." With that he was over the sidewalk and out of sight around the corner.

Automatically, when I got in, I looked to my right. Wishing Sarge was riding with me, missing his reassuring presence, I smiled at the thought of him invading the empty seat like a Panzer brigade, claiming it for his own.

*   *   *

CHAPTER 98

Rounding the curve onto South Roosevelt, paralleling the beach, a heavy blast peppered the side of my face with salty grit. Along the eastern periphery of the island, unimpeded by buildings, gusts of wind hustled shifting rows of sand across the road. In the distance I saw a pair of taillights. Small comfort to know that I wasn't the only one crazy enough to be out in this blow.

Listening to the unusual sound of heavy surf pounding Smathers Beach, I thought of how much had happened since that fateful day I'd brought Monk ashore, right there. How many would have been spared, if only—? What if Monk and L'Angousette were part of an inevitable reality from which there was no escape? I didn't want to—couldn't— let myself think of the futility of our efforts, if that was true.

Ahead, where the strip of manmade beach narrowed, waves broke over the seawall, rising up, flooding the sidewalk and drenching the road. The taillights ahead curved left then vanished. Moments later, like a fluorescent oasis in the night, a wing of low buildings on my left appeared through the mangroves. A moment later they disappeared, hidden behind the darkened brick bulk of the East Martello Towers, a Civil War Fort converted into a museum. *Civility in warfare?* An oxymoronic chuckle bubbled in my brain.

I entered the circular driveway, wondering why no one had come up with a better name? Perhaps "terminal" was intentional, a subtle reminder of the capriciousness and consequences of air-travel.

My watch beeped the hour—nine o'clock—as I crossed from the almost empty parking lot to the main building. Judging by the rising winds and the lone cabby hiding behind a newspaper, no flights were imminent.

The shabby concourse was virtually devoid of life; locked glass doors fronted a tired-looking gift shop. At the far end, muted rock music filtered through a pair of closed doors that led to the bar, popularly known as the "Augur Inn". Two coverall-ed workers, sonic earmuffs slung around their necks, walked past the empty luggage track, one poured coffee from a thermos into Styrofoam cups.

No one seemed to be paying me any attention as I consulted the arrivals/departures board opposite the bank of coin-fed lockers.

On the road again, my hand stole up to the soft denim of my shirt pocket every few seconds for a reassuring squeeze. It was an ordinary key with a round, red plate press-fit over the end. The number of the corresponding locker was stamped into the metal plate. There was a lot riding on this small piece of metal.

*   *   *

CHAPTER 99

"Sounds like *mes amis* are ready to go through with the trade." Tony said, ignoring my aversion to having a gun pointed at me when I opened the door. "Lobster-boy's downright antsy with that lump of loose cash around his people. Ya think maybe there might be a morale problem?"

L'Angousette had never been able to fool anyone for very long with his Uncle-Chuckles-the-beneficent-dictator role; he was a snake, pure and simple, and he attracted a like kind. Out of his element, with a quarter million in ready cash just sitting there for the taking, he had to be sweating. The more needles there were sticking him, the better I liked it.

A single high-pitched beep from Tony's watch signaled the half-hour. My own echoed the sentiment a beat later. I paused to cancel the feature from my well-worn Timex—congratulating myself for clear thinking. Tony noticed, nodding approval for not having to tell me the obvious. Considering what I needed to do, having it sound off at the wrong moment could cost dearly.

After several butchered French phrases, pausing for a protracted response, Tony disconnected then dialed a second number. Splitting his awareness between telephone and headset, he pointed at the door and said, "You're up."

The address Tony'd given the dispatcher was for a house halfway down the block on the street behind our motel. Armed with the sealed blank envelope holding the locker key, a sheaf of crisp twenties in my shirt pocket, and the balance of the block of money on my hip, I set off to meet our courier. Sweat beaded my forehead; the air was heavy, ripe with the promise of rain. I rounded the corner and a gust of wind staggered me backwards. The storm was gaining strength, fast; by feeling it was going to hit pretty hard. Maybe, I began to think, we should postpone. It was too late. I saw a dimly lit triangle floating above a pair of headlights when the cab entered the street. He slowed partway into the block then sped up, catching sight of me waving the white envelope.

I could see the hint of a sneer on the driver's stubbly face when I approached his window. A stormy Tuesday was probably not a hot night for fares. It must have appeared obvious to him I was going to cancel. The grimace warmed slightly when I handed him a twenty before giving him the envelope and the address where I wanted it delivered. He wasn't about to tell me I could have walked there in the time it had taken to call him. When I instructed him to ask for another envelope at the other end, I saw him frown. Not a virgin, obviously aware the Rock was still a place where you could get caught in the switches if you didn't think, he gave the envelope a quick fondle, hefting it to feel the weight and content.

"It's a key," I answered his silent question. "If anyone asks, you delivered it from Stock Island. There'll be another key in an envelope for me, a twenty for you, and another twenty waiting, as soon as you get back. Got it?"

"Right, boss." He smiled in anticipation of an easy sixty dollars. I should have known better but the smile, accentuating his weasel-thin face, bright rat eyes, and evidence of a chewing-tobacco habit, made me think about investing in burglar alarm futures. Like most people, I respond to exterior beauty in the belief that it's a reflection of the inner person. Probably, I thought, feeling sorry for the harsh joke life played on the driver, he was a decent person. I stepped back and watched him drive off.

Since there was nothing I could say about the gun pointing at me, I gritted my teeth, kept my tongue in check and flashed Tony a thumbs-up. His eyes dropped from mine focused somewhere into the middle distance as his attention was suddenly yanked into the headset.

"Here we go...the driver's at the door...the exchange is good, and...he's off! It's okay! They're not following him. Go-Go-Go!"

I was out the door at a run and just barely managed to beat the cab to the corner. On an impulse, I flagged him down and jumped in.

"Let's go."

There was no hesitation. He was on the gas pedal in a heartbeat. "Where to?"

Follow that car! I've always wanted to say that, but decided not to confuse the issue.

"Head to the Atlantic end of Duval."

He handed a pink envelope back to me over his shoulder. I put the promised twenty in his hand. The bill disappeared. By feel there was a key in this envelope, too, so far so good.

"Turn left up ahead. Let's take the tourist route," I suggested, turning to check for tails. "Head along the Atlantic Drive."

"Relax, Mister, there's no one back there. I've been watching."

Well, alright, I thought, the lights are on and someone is definitely home.

"Tell me, is Tuesday a slow night?" Nothing wrong with a little more improvisation, I thought, folding the envelope and tucking it into my shirt pocket.

"'Til the bars close, 'n that can be iffy. You want to hire me?"

This guy had a brain and he used it. It would be good to have a second pair of eyes along, someone to check my six.

"You know, with the sixty for this little turnaround, I was gonna duck the rest of my shift." He picked up the mike from the dashboard clip, mumbled something to his dispatcher then switched off without bothering to wait for an acknowledgment.

"Pull in to the next phone booth you see."

We were out near the public beaches on the southeast side of the island, just beyond the decayed brick ruins of the West Martello Towers, another ancient fort. A lit phone bubble was visible ahead. He slowed the cab, cruising easily through the empty parking lot towards the closed concession buildings fronting the deserted beach-walk.

Whirling in their suicidal dance of frustration, moths attacked the fluorescent ring inside the plastic privacy bubble. I fished the key out of the envelope and studied it under the blue-white glare. It was slim and brass colored not unlike the key I'd traded for it, on the head and part of the shank there a silvery abrasion showed where the numbers had been obliterated.

My favorite Night Manager answered then routed the call to the motel room. Tony picked up midway through the first ring. No voice, he merely lifted the receiver and waited. The thought of him pointing his gun at the mouthpiece, in case this was an unfriendly call, came to me unbidden, I stifled the giggle..

"It's me. What's up?"

"Feel like heading over to the market, for a case of Coors, maybe you could pick up a pizza; pepperoni okay by you?"

Not much of a code, but it gave me our next stop. Tony knew and shared my fears of being overheard. After reviewing our imprudent use of telephones, we'd resolved to be more careful. What we didn't need was Gollum involving himself again and extending a premature invitation to the police.

The place we'd chosen was a row of payphones outside the supermarket where we'd stopped earlier, Tony'd taken down the numbers. The reference to the beer and the pizza indicated that L'Angousette had sent his man to the airport and I should check in with Murph' then wait for a callback in thirty minutes.

"Okay. See you later." I hung up.

Murph' answered after the third ring.

"What's up?" He sounded wired, a combination of adrenaline and determination, all business. That, in and of itself, was a big comfort.

"Are you keeping tabs on Gallagher and Eaton?"

"Yeah, one of their main CI's leaked a rumor to them about some new druggies moving into town. They are primed and waiting to hear back from him."

Damn!

"Can you count on their "Confidential Informant" being around to do the right thing at the right time?" Understandably concerned, since a snitch, after lawyers and politicians, is arguably one of the lowest life forms on the planet, I began to get a sick feeling that I'd left too much to chance. I should've taken the time to sound Murphy out on the how and why.

"Not to worry, he's in the back of my patrol car as we speak. The bad news is I was only able to come up with one other assist. One of the two guys I wanted is out of town for a couple of days, but Rubeñas is in."

Now, he was doing good-news-bad-news jokes, was nothing sacred?

I had to ask, "What's a Rubeñas?"

I heard a dry chuckle through the earpiece. "How would you feel about a BMF?"

"'Depends on how big?"

"Six-six and two hundred eighty pounds of Cuban bad-ass."

"If he was on my side, pretty good."

"You got it, Toyota. Listen, any idea how much longer this *thing* is going to take?"

I appreciated his concern. One of Einstein's models supported the proposition that waiting for a phone to ring is the longest kind of time in the known universe.

"I'll touch base in an hour or so, no later than eleven. Everything should come down around midnight. Is this a good number to call?"

"No. I've been here too long already. Can I call you instead?"

Yeah, right, and the check's in the mail.

"Copy this down." I was about to give him the number of the booth at the beachside parking lot; I wouldn't be returning there and it was far enough from anywhere I planned on being. He interrupted and gave me a new number.

"It's a cellular," he explained, "I'll be down at the boat, waiting."

"Eleven at the latest," I promised. I was impressed; using a 'cell' phone had been a stroke of genius. Returning to the cab, I made a mental note to ask Tony if he could get a couple for us.

"Let's go get a coffee." I suggested to my driver that we use the twenty-four hour drive-thru adjacent to the location scheduled for our next contact, a food market that closed at ten. I wanted to see if anyone or anything out of the ordinary was going to happen along or happen.

"You're probably wondering what I'm doing—" I began.

"None of my business," the driver interrupted, "I don't get all emotionally involved with my fares, providing the money's right and nobody asks me to carry nothing illegal in my car."

Given the ground rules he'd set out, we struck deal for continued private taxi service and his discretion. I started at two hundred and allowed him to dicker me up to three-fifty; I was prepared to go a lot higher. If he did what was required and we survived the night, I'd give him a well-earned bonus.

The sweet aroma of hot coffee and donuts filled the cab. I'd been feeling a little guilty about my initial assessment of my new employee; he'd proven himself not only smart but resourceful as well, a pretty rare combination. Directing him to the phone pedestal in front of the market, I congratulated myself for hiring him.

One of the phones was already ringing as we neared the curb; I was out of the car almost before we'd come to a stop and reaching for it as the next ring began. I heard the disconnect an instant after I'd snatched it from the hook. A moment later the middle phone rang. I had it before the second ring started. It was seven past ten.

"Stay where you are! I'll call right back!" Tony sounded seriously rattled. What had happened? I replaced the phone but it rang again before I could release my grip.

"What?!"

The slurred voice desperately wanted to talk to Izzie. "Where is she?" the drunk blared into my ear. I slammed the phone back down. I'd clearly heard fear and alarm in Tony's voice, but something was preventing me from running panic-stricken in ever-tightening circles. The telephone rang; I paused, composing myself before answering.

"I got out with the equipment." Tony gasped, nearly out of breath.

"What's—?"

"Shut up for a second! I found a bug in the motel."

I blanked for a second—a cockroach? Then, I understood what he was saying.

"Wh—who?"

"How the-fuck should I know? Maybe your cop buddy, or the A-team. It don't matter. Shut it down. Shut it all down. There's no telling how badly we're compromised."

"Everything's in motion," I argued, feeling a sense of detachment, coolness in place of my previous proclivity for terror. "We've got to ride it out. Talk to me..."

Tony conceded that he *might* have overreacted. We discussed the content of any information that could have been overheard; it was surprisingly little, most of our final planning had been in transit. He agreed, finally, to place the call to L'Angousette while I waited for his confirmation.

The pay phone jangled again, I lifted the receiver.

"Iz-z-z-ie? Baby, it's Mark—"

I toggled the hook, disconnecting Mark. Almost immediately it rang again.

"There's several banks of night-access boxes at the Post Office on Whitehead."

Holding the key up close to the light I again looked for any trace of the identification number. A mass of gouges and scrapes obliterated

the numbers. With the number cover removed from our corresponding
locker key they were as much in the dark as we were. I closed my fist
around the key feeling the combined weight of nine deaths carried in
that slender bit of metal.

"I'm supposed to call them back at eleven. How're you doing?"

"Surviving. I've got a cab booked for the duration. Don't sweat it,"
I added before he could object, "the driver's cool."

"Just *you* remember to be cool. One of the frogs is on his way to
the airport."

"Call you from the post office," I said ringing off.

"Next stop Whitehead Post Office."

I sat back and tried—unsuccessfully—to relax. My stomach was
knotted up, the dice were in the air, the numbers were rolling, but there
was also a sensation of letting go-and-going with it. Tony, I'd known,
would do a better job dealing with L'Angousette and coordinating the
exchange. I'd wanted—needed—to be outside, in motion; it gave me
the illusion of being able to jump clear if things went out of control.
Like being trapped in a falling elevator, waiting for the last second as
it's about to hit bottom to jump up...it sounded good in theory.

Set well back from the corner, maybe fifty yards, the single-story
building squatted diagonally, a belt of grass and palm trees separating
the fan-shaped parking lot around the Post Office from the intersecting
sidewalks. A small green space, complete with a shiny white flag pole
fronted the brick facade. Nothing moved, except the wind gusting in
the branches.

After calling Tony with the numbers to the pay phones, I was
tempted to start trying the key at random until I got a look at the walls
of boxes; there were hundreds of them, far too many to check.

Almost directly overhead, a suddenly clear patch of sky appeared
in the brooding overcast. Briefly framed, my celestial guide, Orion
reminded me of the many times I'd relied upon the Hunter's glittering
belt and bow to find my headings in the night to reach a safe harbor.
Just this once more, I thought. Then the winds slammed shut the small
window of starlight. Not a very promising omen.

A strident jangle pulled my thoughts back to earth. Memories of
that gray, rainy New Orleans morning, so many years ago, oozed out
of the earpiece. L'Angousette!

I had to physically shake myself to concentrate on the here and now, as he gave me a post box number and told me to "go on, check it out."

I left the phone hanging from its cord. The number matched one of the large boxes on the lowest level. Inside, I found a briefcase, an old-fashioned leather style with an accordion base. Judging by the weight, it was full. My hands were shaking so badly I fumbled the locking strap several times before I got it opened.

Oh no! In the dim light, I could see the bag was full of freshly banded bricks of currency. This was a serious deviation: L'Angousette would never allow a stranger—someone who may have taken out one of his own people—access to his cash before he had the drugs already in his possession, unless he had a way to eliminate or control that 'someone'. My back muscles tensed, feeling an unseen gun sight zero in.

Skin prickling in anticipation of the bullet about to smash into my body, I walked back to the dangling phone. Scanning nearby cars, buildings and trees, my imagination saw gunmen everywhere, though nothing appeared out of place. I picked up the phone, forcing out the words around a mouthful of baked sand, I asked, "Okay, now what?"

L'Angousette's hearty peals of laughter constricted my heart with fear and loathing.

"It's simple, now you tell me where it is, this thing I have just bought from you, then you and your frien' you go away and spend my money."

It couldn't be. He had to have some angle but what was it? I gave him the room number and the name of the motel that matched the duplicate room key I'd left in the airport locker. Where was the anticipated reaction about the close proximity to his location? In that moment I had the identity of our "bug" installer.

"So, now we go our separate ways, no harm no foul?" I asked, playing my part.

"But of course, my frien'. It has been a great pleasure, this doing business with you. Goodbye and bon chance."

The click cut him off in mid-laugh. The volume of Langouste's humor was almost always in direct proportion to another's misfortune; he'd sounded awfully happy. I continued to hold the phone to my ear, reluctant to set it back on the hook. While speaking to him I'd heard the microscopic *crunch-squeak* of a bit of gravel or glass fragment underfoot. A noxious hint of chewing tobacco blew past my nose. Both had come from directly behind me. It was pucker time.

'Bring someone along to watch my six.' I heard my mind echo tauntingly. *'Brilliant! Absolutely brilliant!'* I'd played right into their hands. Wasn't he the lone cabby I'd seen at the airport earlier? I tried to remember. Who looks at cab drivers? Damn! *Think!* What would someone with a brain do? What would Tony do? Evaluate and assess. Pluses: I'd heard him and I had a gun. Minuses: the Beretta was snapped in its holster under my zipped up jacket, and he was probably standing on my shadow. My only weapon was salesmanship.

"Well you see Mr. L'Angousette—"

I was betting my life that hanging up would be the signal for my sudden departure from this world. I wasn't ready to leave, not just yet.

"Okay...well you see, *'Père,'*" I continued into the dead phone, forcing a tone of confidence into my voice that I didn't feel. "I'd be real happy to meet with you tonight."

I'd gained a little time, doing some fast-talking but had to continue selling the con, and I'd better be good. This guy had a kind of street-smart aura. I knew he'd catch on quick if my game was weak.

"Huh? Sure... "

As long as the driver continued to buy my act, I had a chance.

"Well, okay if you insist." I shrugged and laughed. "That was pretty smart of you...sure I'll tell the driver you said that." I chuckled again, as if to convey my having been impressed by his foresight and attention to detail.

The long, thin shaft of the ice pick slid with a slick ease through the soft tissues on the lower left side of my spinal column. Travelling on a slightly upward path, the needle-sharp point passed effortlessly through the layers of meat, puncturing the bottom of my left lung before seating itself into the right ventricle, paralyzing the muscle and arresting the flow of blood to the arteries. My heart gave a fluttering series of spasms and ceased beating....

'Stop it! Stop it! Stop it!' I screamed at the imp in my mind. I needed to focus on finding a way out, not indulging my worst fears.

"Right...I figure we should be there in, oh, say about fifteen to twenty minutes? Listen, would you like my partner to sit in, too...?"

I thought back to the conversation, Tony and I'd had only the day before. I had to assume the listening device was already in the room, otherwise none of this made any sense.

"...No, it's no problem at all. I'll give him a call—he can meet us there."

We'd essentially laid out the mechanics of our key exchange plan for the benefit of our unknown audience. How difficult would it be for them to lure a cabby someplace earlier in the evening and substitute their own driver? Not very, in fact, pretty easy. It would then only be a matter of waiting until we called for a taxi then canceling our call and sending their own man out instead.

"Good idea! Sure, we can pick him up on the way."

I wanted to turn around so badly that my body was twitching with the need. Instead, I concentrated on controlling the tremors in the hand feeding a quarter into the slot. Blood hammering in my ears almost drowned out the bonging coin signal. The receiver was slippery.

"You've reached the law offices of Montgomery Rothschild, if you—", began the answering machine.

"Hello...? Can you hear me? Hello...?" My voice was remarkably steady, despite the grotesquely sanguineous fantasies of my terror-stricken imagination. "Hello...?

I jiggled the hook several times, cursed, then fed more change into the phone. I was still breathing, so far.

I asked for my room, a moment later, Tony picked up.

"Yeah, that was me before, this line's much better, I can hear you now."

There was an intense, taut silence from his end.

"I just spoke to a Mr. L'Angousette.... Yeah, real friendly fella. 'Said he'd like to meet up with us before we leave the island. 'Says he's got another deal; something we might want in on.... From what I could tell, 'sounds like it might be interesting.... Yeah, I know; the phones are pretty bad tonight, must be the storm. Meet you at the motel room in about fifteen minutes.... Right. See you."

Please, think. I sent my silent plea to Tony.

The driver leaned casually against the front fender, examining his fingernails, looking suitably bored, as if he had never moved. Back lit by orange sodium lights, his shadowy silhouette gave nothing away. If I hadn't heard the telltale footstep I'd either be dead or unconscious. Or, had I imagined that too? No! The dome light in the car was now off and the front door was opened wide. My first evaluation was right: he was slick but not that slick; the light had worked earlier, which meant he made a mistake. If he made one he'd make others.

In a parody of a conscientious chauffeur, as I approached the taxi, he opened the rear door for me with a flourish then, dutifully waiting until I was seated, politely closed it behind me.

"What's up?" he asked, casual as could be, when he got in.

Opening the clasp on the briefcase balanced on my lap, I gave him L'Angousette's message. My right hand eased under my jacket while I ruffled through the packets of cash in the case with my left. I fluttered a cascade of hundred dollar bills down over his shoulder. Distracted, when he looked down at the money, I concealed unsnapping the safety strap on the pistol harness with the sharp click of the briefcase lock.

"Hey! You don't got to do this. Y'know, I get whatever I need from—"

"Listen, when I contract for a job I pay for the work. After all, you can never have too much. Right?"

"Yeah, I mean, *oh, yeah-h-h*! You got that right." He said, roping out a greedy laugh.

"Thanks to your Mr. L'Angousette—I mean *Père*—I might have just happened into a little extra money myself," I chimed in, laughing along, letting him share in my windfall, profiting from my feelings of goodwill and generosity. Life was one big happy joke. "So, consider yourself as having earned yourself that bonus."

"Well, alright!" Greed and a portion of green sugar were helping him swallow my lies. "Y'know," he said, warming up to me. "Y'er alright, too."

I basked in the warm glow of his approval, never forgetting for an instant what I had to do next; hating the very thought of it. There'd been too much killing and violence to suit me but I knew there would be more. By thinking those thoughts, I knew the driver was already a dead man. It was only a matter of where and when. Several blocks shy of our objective I directed him approach from the rear via the side street where he'd entered earlier.

"How come?" he asked, half-turning, seeking me out in the rear-view. I could see the twinge of suspicion stiffening his posture.

"Too many cars and people showing up at the same place at the same time could attract the wrong kind of attention. Maybe I'm wrong, but I got the impression your boss is a pretty smart fella, smart enough to appreciate discretion. Let's say we keep a low profile, huh?" It had sounded good to me, too, even as I said it.

"Yeah! Good idea."

At my direction he pulled in and parked on the verge near the spot where I'd first met him. This location had not been arbitrarily chosen; situated halfway between two street lamps, the scant light was further diminished under the prolific foliage of a huge Royal Poinciana.

*　　　*　　　*

**And the next instant
he was one of the deadest men that ever lived.**

- Roughing It, Mark Twain

CHAPTER 100

The silence was deafening; I could almost touch it; a physical presence inside the darkened taxi, the air so acrid and heavy with the stench of gunfire that it was almost impossible to draw breath. Tufts of upholstery stuffing and cartridge wadding floated like the tentative flakes of winter's first snowfall. The three-bullet burst had propelled the driver, sending him crashing into the door and steering wheel, after tearing up the car seat and his backbone on the way.

I regretted killing him in spite of the pistol I found clutched in his hand, cocked and ready to fire, right up to the moment when I opened the trunk and found, jumbled in beside a spare tire, gas can and jumper cables, another body. No mystery as to his identity; the real cab driver gazed into eternity aided by the empty eye socket in the center of his forehead. Had he been gulled under the pretense of a long trip and a big tip on a slow night? Did he have someone who loved him and would wonder where he was now that the daily ritual of his life had been stopped short? How long before he was missed? How long before he was forgotten? Tasting a salty wetness in the corners of my mouth, I swiped the blur from my eyes with my sleeve.

Common to most on-duty cabs, the key was sticking out of the trunk lock. It went onto the ring along with the taxi's ignition and the post box key. The second driver would be safe enough in the trunk and he wouldn't be lonely. If need be, we had a sufficiently anonymous late night transportation. Also, it was, if circumstances warranted, the vehicle L'Angousette would expect to see; that *could* be useful.

I melted into the foliage behind the motel parking lot, well hidden behind the straggling trunks of the massive Banyan tree until I was opposite the main entrance. An involuntary quiver ran down my spine and an irritating itch began on the exposed area of the back of my neck; bugs or nerves, I wasn't sure which, so I pulled my collar up, speculating on the futility of detailed plans, timetables and schedules.

'One step forward, two steps back,' played over and over again in my mind, like the maniacal refrain of a sometime-remembered nursery rhyme.

L'Angousette had tried for an end run and failed; we now had his cash and had deleted another of his crew. Though I would have given much to be the proverbial fly on the wall, to see his frustration, to savor his irritation firsthand, I preferred standing quietly in the bushes feeling the wind build; gusting, shaking branches overhead. Rumbles of thunder were getting closer. Mountains of bruised cloud were lit from inside. The rain wouldn't be far behind.

Someone or something was directly behind me, close, very close. I reacted fast and hard when a hand grabbed my shoulder. Driving an elbow back towards the attacker's solar plexus, spinning to deliver the second, decisive strike, I found myself on the ground.

"The red wolf howls in the full moon saloon," the dark figure above me whispered then laughed softly. "What's the countersign?"

I squeaked a vulgar response down deep in my throat, which was held tight in a hard hand. The grip loosened.

"Unh, would you get offa me!"

"That was good, real good," Tony smirked, as he helped me up. "Next time, pick on the bad guys and use more hip and less shoulder."

"I, uh, guess I wasn't really paying attention."

"Really? He smirked then, shifting gears, asked: "Tell me, what happened?"

I broke it down then laid it out for him. In turn, Tony agreed that L'Angousette figured for the bugging. How? We didn't know. Tony's finding the bug when he had, had probably saved him from being taken or taken out. By insinuating their own man as our driver and using the cash to bait the hook, he supposed I was probably meant to be followed, taken, and used one way or another to get the 'goods' for them. By a freak series of circumstances, starting with my unwittingly hiring their driver, we were provided with the opportunity for hunted to become hunter, and in so doing, we could, if we wished, delete

L'Angousette and his outfit from the equation. I suggested we proceed directly to phase-two without them. Tony seconded. We still might be able to patch things together from the Gallagher, Eaton, Murphy end, so we dared not lose our momentum.

Tony gripped my hand, our eyes met, silently communicating the things men are usually too embarrassed or self-conscious to speak of, especially to each other, or will seldom acknowledge—it felt good just the same—then he was gone. One moment he was there, the next, he had simply vanished into the Bamboo and Hibiscus-rich swath of jungle landscaping.

*   *   *

CHAPTER 101

Juicy, half-dollar-sized drops spattered the ground with flat, afflictive slaps, stinging the roof of the taxi. By the time I had reached the end of the block the rain was falling with such intensity that I was forced to a crawl in order to find my turn at the first cross street. Crossing the four-lane boulevard was simple—no one else was stupid enough to be driving in this downpour. A thundering boom split the air. House lights on either side flickered briefly then winked out. The local utility company (better known as "The Powers of Darkness") had again succumbed to a greater force. With only headlights to define the shape of the road, visibility was down to only a few feet.

CRAAACKKKOOM-M-M!

Thunder followed close on the heels of the heart-stopping crash and sizzle of a lightning bolt striking close by. The memory of a gray Honda, on the other side of the entrance to the project, had been seared into my brain by the blast of energy. I stopped beside the driveway of the large split-level condo-complex adjacent to the work site, and waited for my night vision to return. Zipping my jacket up to my neck, preparing to throw the door open, I held my breath—similar to diving into water—before stepping into the downpour.

A sheltered corridor bored through the heart of the concrete condo structure, leading to the private beach next to the debris-laden grounds of the job site next door. From the top of the steps leading down to the water, I could see the whole world had been plunged into darkness. Across the bay a scatter of generator-powered buildings and a few fixed headlights showed the shape of the road. Stretching out into the inky waters red and green channel lights stood like glowing sentinels in the dark. Below, at the end of the dock, a faint glimmer of light shone through the curtain of rain. Another flash split the sky; the booming rumble even closer behind as the heart of the storm drew near.

Sprinting across the narrow sandy strip, I was soaked to the skin before I'd reached the first plank.

"It's a fitting night," Tony said unnecessarily, lending a steadying hand as I tripped over the raised doorsill into the wheelhouse. Standing in the middle of the small lake I'd brought aboard, I gave him the briefcase full of money then peeled down and toweled off. Pulling on dry sweat pants, as Tony gloated over the stacks of money, I voiced my concerns.

"This blackout, the phone lines might be down, too"

"Yeah," Tony cut in, "Whyn't you just try making the calls first, okay? We'll figure out something if you can't get through."

"Do you have cellular—"

"A cell-phone?" he interrupted, reading my thoughts and shaking his head, no. "Good idea, wish I'd thought of that. We'll have to do the best we can with what we have. 'Better be gettin' on and going."

*   *   *

CHAPTER 102

Aromas of ancient sweat billowed up and around me, as my body heat warmed the inside of the rain suit. I clumped along the dock in my borrowed white shrimper boots, two sizes too big. Bright orange foul-weather gear would not have been my first choice for the kind of work that lay ahead, but it had been all there was onboard and it was dry. Hopefully, I would be perceived as nothing more than a concerned boat owner, if, in the rain and almost pitch darkness, I could be seen at all.

The phone was answered immediately. "I'd almost given up on you." Murph' did not sound pleased. That made two of us.

"Something came up—is everything ready?"

"Everything's *been* ready for three hours."

I heard the frustration in his voice over a background of voices and idling motors.

"This storm, how much of a problem is it going to be using a boat?"

"For me, plenty—"

I saw the plan coming apart.

"—I get seasick."

I waited; whatever was really bothering him I knew wouldn't take long to appear.

"Eaton's had the police cutter standing by with a crew all night; they're waiting for the signal to go. I don't know where Gallagher is; they usually team up on something major, so they may be linking up later, I think he'll chance it alone since no one's seen Gallagher since morning and, and this is *un*-usual, I don't know if I'm going to—"

"Call you right back. Sorry." I'd already disconnected, so only the empty room heard my apology. Murphy was half-a-step away from calling it off. I'd heard him working up to an ultimatum; a deadline, something I couldn't commit to was imminent. My fingers sped across the keypad, tagging in numbers.

"That room doesn't answer," the night clerk said, "you can leave a message—"

I've got your money; I've killed your people; where are you?

I hung up. A sense of everything coming to a screeching halt was destroying my resolve. Any chance of pulling this together would be gone once I told Murphy we couldn't cover our end. Rain pounded the roof filling the empty concrete shell with noise, filling my mind frustration, welling up into an insane bubble of rage.

"Arrrrgggh!" Throat rasping, eyes tearing, I roared my frustration. It would be impossible to put this thing back together after tonight. I had to call Murphy, tell him it wasn't happening, if only to give him enough time to try and avoid getting in trouble for staging a hoax. I couldn't seem to make my fingers enter the numbers.

"Where?" I asked the phone in my hand, "where are they?" I rapped the unresponsive plastic receiver against my head, vainly trying to drum an idea into my brain. "Think, dammit, think!"

"What the—" I stopped in mid-curse. Something I thought I had seen in the last sizzle and crack of lightning, something impossible, had frozen me in place. Highlighted against the construction fence, picking their way across the trash-strewn compound, heading toward the docks was what, by size, could only have been Gordo, followed by L'Angousette and two others.

Nerves, and the shock of seeing a different, unanticipated ending to our night stalking, caused me to punch in the wrong numbers, twice. It *could* still happen, but only if I could get through.

"Yeah!?"

"End of Hilton Haven Drive," I shouted into the receiver, "on the bay side, a white cabin cruiser: *NEVER AGAIN III*, it'll be at the dock or tied to the last houseboat at the southeast end of the bay. Move!"

I didn't wait for a reply; I was already half way across the great room before the phone hit the floor.

Wind and water knifed through the gaping holes in the wall and tore at the shredded plastic sheeting. I looked out into the horizontally driven rain. Between howling gusts I heard fragments of the throaty diesels idling at the end of the dock. I stripped off the bright reflective-orange rain gear. Groping for hand and footholds, I scrambled down the exposed ends of rebar and ragged cinder blocks. Somehow, I had to warn Tony or prevent L'Angousette from reaching him.

"Distract then attack." I recalled one of Tony's axioms. If I could keep them busy or make enough noise, it might give Tony a chance to get away and finish what we'd started. I saw a handle sticking out of a box of nails beside a flat of cedar shakes, something to throw? Even better, a shingler's hammer with its flat axe-blade would serve as a fearsome weapon providing I could get close enough. I scattered a box of roofing nails over the path they would take once they passed through the courtyard. Gathering a handful to throw when I attacked, I measured the distance and waited. It would be a desperation play but—

S-S-Z-Z-Z-A-K-K-K!

Every inch of skin, each hair on my body tingled from the close proximity to the charged track of pure blue-white energy. A bolt of lightning had struck the site power pole. An explosion; sparks spewed out in a yellow-orange rain. Frozen, the four Cajuns stared up in shock at the sputtering pyrotechnics coming from the annihilated transformer overhead before hitting the deck. The moment they dropped, in the booming aftermath of thunder, I put on a burst of speed toward the jetty. During the headlong dash through the jagged obstacle course, slicing, sliding and twisting treacherously underfoot, I lost my right boot and almost slammed face first into a discarded air conditioner. Stumbling, tripping, overrunning balance, reaching the dock, I slipped on the rain-slick planks then fell. Rolling, scrambling to get up, half-running, half-crawling. Insanely, I still held onto the hammer. Out of breath, gasping for air, I reached the boat, threw the bowline from the dock cleat then heaved against the hull. Pushing against the wind, the bow moved away from the dock with an agonizing slowness. I was whimpering hysterically in frustration and terror. Cycling, the wind softened; the lull and direction shift allowed the bow to pick up momentum, swinging away from the dock. Sensing movement, Tony looked out. I shouted to him but he couldn't hear me over another boom of thunder. Looking astern, at the changing perspective, he turned, saw me, what I was doing, and came forward.

"Are you nuts!" The smirking grin vanished the instant he saw my face; the terror must have been stamped clear.

"Get us outta here!" I yelled, running past him, leaping into the aft deck. He immediately jammed the throttle to the stops and cranked the wheel hard over. The engines scaled up to a roar, the deck tilted, I lost my balance and went down. The stern line stretched and narrowed, tightening itself impossibly into the cleat. Grabbing the shingle hammer from the deck, I pulled myself off my knees and raised it up. Teak and fiberglass exploded from the transom in front of me. Something slapped the hammer out of my hand. A sharp *rap-a-pop* of pistol shots was followed by the *paloop* of the hammer hitting the water. Winking fireflies of gunfire sparkled at the end of the dock. L'Angousette and his men were attacking.

Tony had the power cranked. The bow was out of the water. The rear deck slanted down as the stern threatened to bury itself.

Br-r-rap! The braided rope shredded under the three-round burst. With a sickening lurch that almost threw me overboard, the yacht leapt forward. I slumped to the deck, leaning against the kill-box, gulping in huge draughts of air, sobbing at the razor-thin closeness of our escape. My hand shook so badly I couldn't re-holster the Beretta.

"Where are we?" Tony asked calmly about our operation, when I stumbled across the heaving deck into the wheelhouse. Leaning back against the flapping door, shutting it, I told him.

"How?" I asked, "How did they know? We never mentioned the boat or the dock."

"Take the wheel! Stay in the channel," he ordered. Pulling me to the helm, Tony yanked up the bench lid, pulled out the briefcase, and dumped the money. Sifting the stacks of cash, he pawed and riffled through each of the money bundles.

I kept to the channel, heading for the houseboat. We were running slightly abeam of the wind, taking the blow on our starboard side. The boat shuddered, shunting to port as each wind-driven wave thudded against the hull. The deck yawed wildly. I had to hold onto the wheel as much to steady myself as to maintain our course.

"You saved our collective butt. This"—he held up what looked like the guts of a transistor radio, about the size of a credit card—"was tucked into the lining of the briefcase."

There seemed to be a few more wrinkles in Tony's face. He wore the same look I'd seen on some of the vets returning from the wars, it was called the Thousand-Yard-Stare.

"Are we screwed?"

"What's your intuition tell you?"

"Nothing." I slap-searched imaginary pockets. Must'a left it in my other suit." For all the good it did, the wisecrack might have been best left unsaid.

"What would you have done if something like this had happened in 'Nam?"

He thought for several seconds, "You're right," he said, puzzling me.

It felt good to be right. *What*, I wondered, was I right about?

"This'll work just as well."

Whoever he was talking to—it wasn't me—must've made a good suggestion. The next question was, evidently, meant for me.

"How's our clock?"

"In this weather it might take an hour, at top speed, for the cops to get to the houseboat. L'Angousette and his bunch are probably right behind us." I shivered with the thought. Of course, it might've been due to my being wet and underdressed. Noticing, Tony took the wheel, allowing me to dig a pair of Farmer John's out of the diving stores and start pulling them on.

"Don't count on it."

He sounded so sure; I thought he was wrong.

"What's to stop them hot-wiring one of the boats at the dock?"

"Not much—"

A welcome sight, seeing his spit-in-the-Devil's-eye grin, though I knew stress and danger must've been taking a heavy toll on his reserves; they were close to driving me to my knees.

"—if I hadn't done a little preventive maintenance this afternoon. Kinda hard to start an engine without sparkplug wires, it'll take them a bit before they get any of those boats working so's they can steal one, and we're going to need every minute."

The boat took a sudden and violent slam of wind and water. The deck tilted sharply. Loose gear came crashing down on and around us, as the vessel heeled over almost sideways. Another hit held us from recovering. For a very long moment, I wasn't sure we would. Tony hung one-handed from a rail overhead, one foot braced against the bulkhead, his other hand clasped the wheel in a grip of iron. I clung tightly to a stanchion, my wetsuit pants at half-mast, feeling our center of gravity slowly shift back.

"Maybe longer...?" I offered.

*   *   *

CHAPTER 103

We were bow straight on; alternating from six to twelve feet away from the houseboat. Tony feathered and boosted the throttle, working the helm to compensate for the buck and roll of the waves. He brought us in as close as he dared. Even in the lee of the houseboat, the cruiser pitched underfoot like a mechanical bull in a rodeo bar. I was a little surprised, when I reached the bow pulpit, to see a partially submerged kayak still tied to one of the cleats where we'd left it.

I sensed the rhythm in the set of waves, felt the momentum rise then jumped. The upsurge catapulted me over the guardrail. I slammed into the wall, hard, then fell backwards onto a rising deck that punched the wind out of me. Dazed, gasping for breath, not quite believing I'd managed to hang on to the mooring line, I lurched to my knees. Tony gave me a thumbs-up; his mouth moved silently, wind stole the words as they were uttered. I caught his meaning along with the first carryall, as he began passing them down from the boat.

Inside, the door closed against the ravings of the storm, we could speak again. The soft red light played on the rush and gurgle in the open and empty hatchway.

"Doug's gone!" I noticed.

Tony nodded grimly as he set to work.

*   *   *

I tell you not for your comfort,
Yea, not for your desire,
Save that the sky grows darker yet
And the sea rises higher.

- Gilbert Keith Chesterton

CHAPTER 104

Ominous creaks, strained anchor cables groaning, filled the stygian blackness. It wasn't so much that it was dark, rather, it was as if light had altogether ceased to exist. Tony was right next to me; I could touch and hear him, yet he and everything else was invisible. Sight deprivation supposedly engenders a compensatory increase in the remaining senses, for me it was tactility. My mad scramble down the jagged building face and headlong dash through the construction debris had left me feeling pretty ragged. Salt water pointed out, with ruthless efficiency, just how ragged. Razor-edged barnacles shredded any undamaged flesh remaining on my hands. I clung desperately, resisting the clutch and pull that threatened to tear me from my hand-hold, trying to keep from crashing through the floorboards overhead as the houseboat peaked and squatted in the raging swells. Plunging down each wave trough, like a runaway freight train, the heavy barge felt like it would bore straight through to the bottom, taking us with it, crushing our fragile bodies.

Claustrophobia had never been a concern or something I'd ever considered before; in that hellish nightmare it became an inescapable reality. I clamped my teeth down hard on the rubber mouthpiece to keep from screaming. Only an inch of wood separated us from the muffled voices and footsteps clumping directly overhead.

WWHAMPPP!

I felt rather than heard the flat, percussive detonation in the room above us.

Tony had placed the homing device and empty briefcase beside the booby-trapped canister. Instead of triggering C-4 plastic explosive, any attempt to remove its contents or lift the canister would activate a spring-loaded switch causing a pair of gas cylinders to simultaneously flood the small room with their contents. "CS and DM gasses," Tony had explained earlier, in his classroom mode, while we prepped the houseboat for visitors, "are only mixed together for violent crowd control situations. CS, your garden-variety tear gas, is colorless and odorless, which of course, causes tears. DM, is a whole 'nother thing: kinda smells sweet, like licorice, this shit will do a real number on you," he read from a sheet, enumerating; "severe chest pains, like a massive coronary; uncontrolled vomiting, and defecation."

'Better living through chemistry,' I recalled thinking at the time but wisely kept it to myself.

I gagged at the stench when we levered the deck hatch open. After taking a couple deep breaths from my regulator, I tied a wet bandana over my face, slipped out of my harness and went up. A scene from an Hieronymous Bosch Halloween card greeted me. I hauled on the pulley rope, lifting the deck-hatch, then tied it open for Tony.

"We've—"

He was gone.

"Tony...?"

There were only ten minutes left on the bottom end of our time-table for the early arrival by the cops, but there was something wrong. Terribly wrong.

*   *   *

Now of that long pursuit
Comes on at hand the bruit;
That Voice is round me like a bursting sea:
'And is thy earth so marred,
Shattered in shard on shard?
Lo, all things fly thee, for thou flyest Me!'

- Francis Thompson

CHAPTER 105

"Maybe you should sit down a little while, my frien', don' you think...?"

I spun around.

L'Angousette!

He stood just outside the open doorway. The red interior light painted his wet face like a bloated Lucifer from a watery Hell. I was rooted to the deck, paralyzed by the twin bores of the sawed-off 12-gauge that stared at me from his fist.

"Take off the mask," he ordered, gesturing with his gun. "I want to see your face before I kill you."

He handled the shotgun with its foot-long barrels and cocked scroll hammers with ease. In his huge paws it looked like a dueling pistol.

"I know you...!? Merde!" He leered above the howl of the storm. "It is, *You!*" he roared, laughing with great gusto. "How come you don' greet your old frien'? Hien?"

I was speechless.

"You and your ami, did you think you could catch me so easy? Have you forgotten who it is you deal with?" he roared, chortling with obvious glee.

My mind raced frantically, I couldn't go through the open hatch before he could pull the triggers. My pistol was wrapped in plastic against immersion in the salt water and snapped tight in its holster.

"Your partner, you'd better call him out. Now, I think, or I will have to shoot you a little," he crooned sweetly.

I was frozen.

"Call him!" The softness left his voice, replaced by savage rage as the velvet facade split open to reveal the crazed beast within.

"Right here, asshole...."

L'Angousette's hands flew up, the wind left his body in a gust, his eyes rolled back, the shotgun cartwheeled from his senseless hands. Like a felled oak, he crashed face first onto the deck revealing Tony, framed in the doorway, holding an air tank like a battering ram.

BBLABBLAM-M-M!

Two wells of flame exploded up from the deck. I felt myself lifted off my feet and hurled back against the bulkhead.

Numbly, I became aware of Tony looming over me, his eyes wide with alarm, furiously jamming something under my wetsuit jacket.

"I'm okay," I wanted to tell him. "It doesn't hurt." I couldn't seem to make the words come out.

That's strange, I remember thinking vaguely, lifting my hand into the red light; fingers looking like I'd dipped them in blackberry syrup.

*   *   *

O Woman! in our hours of ease,
Uncertain, coy, and hard to please,
And variable as the shade
By the light quivering aspen made;
When pain and anguish ring the brow,
A ministering Angel thou!

- Sir Walter Scott

CHAPTER 106

"Can't you see how bad he's been hurt?"

I cracked my eyes open; they watered immediately; I quickly closed them. *Ouch!* That light was bright.

"Are you going to get him to a doctor, or am I?"

"Stop!" I yelled. What I heard come out was scarcely a tiny little murmur. "Hey...! Can you hear me?"

I tried opening my eyes again. Tony's face hovered above me. He was wearing a huge smile. Tears were coursing down his face.

"What's wrong, somebody die or something?" I shouted in a reedy whisper.

Tony laughed aloud; strain washed clean by his obvious relief at my return to the land of the living; or, at least, the semi-living.

"Jerk! You had me scared shi—"

"What's that?" I croaked, interrupting. Across the room from me a wood frame dominated the whole of the wall. The top third looked like a piano with its long row of vertical strings exposed. The rest, as much as I could see of it, was filled with wildly colored abstract imagery.

"Huh? A, a weaving, one of my sister's tapestries. You're in her house. How're you doing? How do you feel?"

I had been taking a mental inventory of the moving parts: other than a pounding headache and a numb sort of stiffness in my chest and shoulder, I felt pretty fair.

"Not too bad. Why? Feel like a workout?"

"Knucklehead!" The insult was uttered with kindness.

He leaned forward and gently put his hands on either side of my lower ribcage and lent me some of his strength, so I could sit up. The little guy with the big hammer went after the soft spot inside my head. I think I must have faded out because the next thing I knew Tony was entering the bedroom a leather shaving bag in his hands.

"Where'd you go?" my voice mewled.

"You passed out. Here, put these under your tongue."

I took the pills he gave me and immediately regretted it. They filled my mouth with a sour searing taste. Soon, I began to feel a little surge of energy. My awareness sharpened and became a little clearer. I lay back against a stack of pillows and tried to focus my thoughts. The last sequence that came to mind was the flare of sparks when a bolt of lightning took out the T-pole; being on the boat and ducking bullets; shooting the rope then speeding away from the dock; then leaping onto the houseboat and hitting the wall. Everything else was a black hole yawning wider and wider in front of me. I was about half way down the hole...suddenly I was sitting on a hornets nest.

"You with us again?"

I opened my eyes again. After what seemed like an hour, I gave up trying to move my left hand to see my watch.

"It's two o'clock," Tony's voice answered my query. "You've had quite a time tonight, partner. I hate to push it, but I need—"

I began twitching. What was going on? I was close to bursting at the seams; every part of me felt pumped tight. Power surged through every muscle and cell. I was invincible.

"What! What did you give me?"

"Amphetamine Bisulfate and a healthy shot of Dianabol."

I looked at him, uncomprehending, as he dismantled a syringe and stowed it in the leather bag. Indomitable or not, I wasn't tracking.

"Speed and 'roids. What every growing boy needs. Feel better?"

Like tearing a few phone books in half, is what I felt. The power-rush was unimaginable. Tony's voice had a hard time getting through the torrent of blood booming in my ears. There must have been some sign from me indicative of my improved condition, because he flashed me a quick grin then picked up a pencil and note pad.

"What's the number?"

I looked at him blankly. My head spun, he made a move to catch me. I motioned him off.

"Stay cool and concentrate, we've got to call your cop and find out what went down. Believe it or not, but this might be all over."

"S'really something." I mumbled. It was difficult to understand the importance of anything other than reveling in the magnificent wonder of the super-human power flowing through me, the awesome marvel of my newfound strength.

"The phone," I demanded, cresting the surge of power, "I'll do it."

"No!"

My sudden movement precipitated a cascading wave of dizziness. I reached out to steady myself. A yellow and red sheet of agony tore up and across my body. Everything went from red to black.

"Wake Up!"

" For God's sake, let him alone. He should be in the hospital."

The voices sounded disembodied and very far away. I felt myself being lifted like a child and placed on something soft, a bed, maybe. I opened my eyes and saw concern in Sola's eyes.

"The number, man, the number. Think." Tony's face leaned over me.

"Unnhh...."

"I think he's trying to say something." He looked into my eyes, questioningly, as he held a glass of water in front of my face. I nodded slightly, he helped me to the glass and I gulped at it urgently.

I must have replied, because the next time I touched down to earth, he was stabbing the buttons on the telephone with his finger as he left the room. Left standing at the doorway his sister looked at me with such sympathy and tenderness that my heart went out to her. Just for a second I thought I might've seen something else. A sudden flush of emotion caused my blood to pump at an accelerated rate. Within seconds, my invulnerability had returned. For some reason—I'm not sure why—I needed to get up and take command of the situation. As surely as action follows thought I flung the covers back to stand like Hercules unchained. The carpet rushed up and surrounded me as I fell endlessly into a soft dark cavern.

*　　　*　　　*

CHAPTER 107

"...moved."
What moved? I wondered.
"...coming around."

I opened my eyes and saw A S h o l e scrawled across one wall and knew I was in my own bedroom.

It's dark out, I don't have to get up yet, I thought. Then, sensing I wasn't alone; that there was someone else in the room, I kept perfectly still and listened. Questions, pieces of dreams, images bombarded my mind. I knew I was home in my own bed, but how? The last thing I remembered was the storm, being on the boat—no—Tony and I were at Sola's. How did I get there? How did I get *here*? I tried to think but nothing came. Had it all been a bad dream? Since I hadn't heard any sounds in the room with me for almost an hour, I figured it was safe to sneak another peek.

"I told you. He opened his eyes."

I tried to turn my head. Filled with lead and bolted to the pillow, it wouldn't move. Everything faded fast.

*   *   *

In truth, he was a strange and wayward wight,
Fond of each gentle and each dreadful scene.
In darkness and in storm he found delight.

- James Beattie

CHAPTER 108

Hot! I was hog-tied in a sauna and suffocating. It wasn't so much a gradual, gentle process of waking up, as having been parboiled into consciousness. Light, despite the closed drapes, flooded my bedroom with the luminescence specific to the Tropics. The stifling accumulation of heat in my room said I'd been out for some time. For how long, I wasn't sure? I wasn't certain of anything except the steady throbbing pulse that emanated from my left side; from hip to head my body was a massive toothache.

Feebly, I kicked free of the blanket's sweaty embrace. Sometimes the very old and infirm will move with a similarly frail desperation. The effort threatened to send the blackness washing over me again. Resting, letting soft breezes played across my skin, drying the film of sweat, I resisted the urge to fade until it receded. The evaporation process was a delight, I luxuriated in the simple pleasure of just being alive.

I had been hurt, that much was obvious. Exactly how? I wasn't sure. Suspicious of the momentary calm, of being in a place I never thought I should see again, wondering what would be the direction and form of the next sudden intrusion of violence, I listened. Other than the faraway sounds of the outside world rolling along fat, happy, and ignorant, I was alone. There were no guns pointing at me, no sounds of gravel crunching beneath stealthy feet. For the moment the world was wearing its benign mask. There was something I needed to do. What was it? I couldn't think.

My left arm was wrapped tight across my chest. I swiveled my head in search of the time.

02:18AM: The red display flashed, on-off-on-off, pulsing in time to the red flares in my brain. I rolled back and closed my eyes, waiting for the pounding to recede.

02:19AM: In the wake of the tempest and the power outage, the display on the clock radio may have been less than accurate. From the angle of sunlight on the walls, it was late morning, a little before noon; but what morning, what day?

"You're awake?" More a statement of fact than a question, I tried to speak but my mouth was glue. Tony guided a bent straw between my lips.

My first tentative sip spurred a desperate need to gulp, to drink down as much beautiful cool as I could.

"Hey, slow down."

Too late I realized, he was right. The coughing spasm threatened to rip me apart. Once the painful constriction in my chest eased and I was able to breathe again, I looked up at him in bewilderment. I hurt all over and the pounding inside my head, having gained volume and momentum, was crashing away with blinding effect.

He dropped a couple of tablets in my mouth. This time I took it easy on the water.

Slowly, too slowly, the hammering eased back to a steady, dull thud.

"What happened?"

"Hungry? Feel like some food?" Tony wasn't looking at me and I got the feeling he was avoiding eye contact for some reason.

"What is it? What's wrong? Talk to me, please..."

"First food, then talk."

Whatever had happened could obviously wait. Tony'd shown he, too, could be stubborn; the mere mention of food had precipitated salivating and the audible rumblings of my stomach clamoring for attention.

Once the debris of the meal, from my inhalation of everything but the plate, the first one I'd eaten in a week had been cleared away, I set out to satisfy my curiosity.

"What's wrong, what's happened?"

"What's the last thing you remember?"

I understood the logic; clearly there were chunks missing between approaching the houseboat and waking up in my own bed encased in a swath of bandaging that covered half my body. There was no need to tell me what I already knew, true, but Tony's responses to my queries seemed evasive.

Following my discovery of the Cajuns at the job site, the pieces fell into an unsettling pattern as he took me through our escape from the dock, arrival at the houseboat, and subsequent confrontation with L'Angousette. My stomach did a slow cold churn as he described the double blast I'd taken in the chest and shoulder when his shotgun had discharged as it struck the deck.

(That answered that question).

There were, according to Tony, two elements contributing to my survival: the severely shortened barrels had dissipated much of the blast force over the distance; and my holstered pistol, which shielded my left side, deflected any potentially lethal shot away from my heart.

"You are," he promised, "going to have the granddaddy of all scars." He went on to say that, since the Egg Harbor had been cut loose—probably, thanks to L'Angousette—and was nowhere in sight, he'd pulled the kayak on deck, drained it, lowered me into the front half, and zippered the hatch cover closed. He went back inside and set the strings of blasting caps, squib-cartridges, and flash-bangs he had prepared earlier. With the detonators connected to radio-receivers, he strategically positioned L'Angousette and his three soldiers with their weapons cocked and loaded then barred the front door from the inside. After arming the charges, he lowered the hatch back in place over-head, swam out from under the houseboat, launched us into the night, then moored us to the channel marker anchored several hundred yards away.

Tony told it all so matter-of-factly, as if he'd only gone for a walk to the corner store. I guessed at the things he wasn't saying; knowing what I'd helped plan for L'Angousette's group, his initial rejection of the idea, and from his having to set the stage for their role in that plan by himself. I didn't know how to apologize for that. Maybe, it could never be said.

"It was maybe another twenty minutes or so," he said, "before the police cutter arrived and tied up outboard of L'angousette's stolen vessel. Two other boats arrived shortly after, separately, neither of them showed running lights; they lay further out. I figured who they probably were but couldn't tell which was which. It was like a regular convention out there."

I tried to focus on what he was saying, envisioning the layout in my mind's eye. Thinking about it made the room tilt and spin a little.

"The cops seemed to be doing it by the book; they made it look so pretty when they moved in. If I hadn't been worried about you, I think I would have enjoyed being out there. It was real thrilling stuff," he drawled sarcastically.

"Sorry I ruined your fun," I quipped.

He had carried the weight of the scenario I'd engineered; it was a heavy weight, I sensed. Perhaps, in time he might forgive me. Would I, I wondered, be able to forgive myself? Could I again face the guy in the mirror, look into his eyes, without seeing the multiple masks of his deceit? I didn't know.

"Apology accepted."

The fleeting trace of his smile acknowledged my weak attempt at humor. I sensed there was a deeper understanding; of what, I couldn't yet say. He knew; I thought. That made it a little easier, though it was something that we'd have to find the right moment to try and work out or it might always be between us.

"Those guys weren't novices. You should have seen 'em when I touched off the pyrotechnics. One second they were calling through the bullhorn, you know: 'Throw down your guns; come out with your hands up,' all that good cop stuff; and the next; they were ducking, dodging and diving overboard.

Maybe, this was the right moment and the right way? Get it out, detail by detail, not personal; treat the moment for the deadly farce it had been.

"Kinda like Khe Sanh and the Fourth of July all rolled into one, it was trés magnifico! You should have seen it."

"I was the unconscious, shot-up guy in bottom of the kayak, remember...?"

"Yeah, sorry 'bout that...."

He'd once told me the standard response in 'Nam, to everything bad that happened: "...your wife's left you for a folk singer, sorry 'bout that...you stepped on a land mine and you're gonna spend the rest of your sexless, miserable life in a wheelchair, sorry 'bout that...you're shot in the guts, dying, and we can't Med-Evac you outta here, sorry 'bout that.... He was right; I had to get over it and stop feeling sorry for myself. *We* were the good guys, I was still pretty sure of that.

"Anyway, this one guy shot-gunned the door off the hinges and his partner pops off some tear gas."

I winced knowing what was coming.

"I gave them a five-count before I lit off the second string. They were just starting to put their heads up. Suddenly, it was like they were in the middle of a war; machine gun sequences; shotgun blasts; M-80's...man, you'da thought it was the real thing. *They* did. Two of them started chucking in flash-bangs... *Pow! Pow! Pow! Pow!* And the rest charge in, like commandos, firing from the hip. Kinda wished I'd had a camera. Think I might've missed my calling; maybe I should've been a movie director."

I quailed, thinking of bullets pumping into unconscious bodies.

"After a few minutes of coming and going, they carried two stiffs off in body bags and escorted L'Angousette out in cuffs."

"And...."

"What do you mean 'and...'?"

"There were four of them; you only mentioned three."

Tony looked deeply embarrassed at having been caught in such a serious oversight.

"Think. Was it Gordo—the big guy—or—?"

"It was kind of hard to tell from that distance...." He took a deep breath, remembering, then let it out saying: "Nope; I'm sure that was L'Angousette. So..."

I'd sensed uncertainty behind an attempt to reassure me.

"...after the police cutter moves off," he continued, "someone onboard flashes a light and the closer of the two boats sitting out in the dark started in. Guess who? Gallagher. I have to give him credit. He can handle a boat and it was rough out there."

"That much I do remember."

Tony gave me an indulgent smile.

"He didn't try to dock it. Did a touch-'n-go, close enough for his partner to toss a duffel or something on board then he booted out of there in one quick hurry. A minute or so goes by and the other boat out in the dark—prob'ly your pal—moves out after him. And that, my friend," Tony got up, saying, "is what happened."

He went over to the window and stood there, back to me, staring out at nothing. I could only guess what was going on inside him.

Tony's narrative filled in some of the blanks but that only made way for twice as many new ones. Mainly, I was concerned over the missing fourth man, but I—*we* were in no position to do anything about it. Something else didn't feel right. A rat, called doubt, began to gnaw at my insides.

"What have you heard from Murphy?" I asked impatiently.

He let the curtain fall shut and turned to face me. "'You remember being at Sola's place?"

"Your sister's? Sort of. How'd we get there from the kayak? And, what's that got to do with Murph'?"

"Just cool your jets and listen. Okay...?"

I kept my mouth shut. He paused for a moment before continuing.

"It was blowing so heavy that we were way past the mall before I could get us close to shore. The rest is simple. I hiked back and called from the pay phone outside the theater. Sola drove over and picked us up."

"She must have been thrilled, especially after that last time we woke her up."

"No, it wasn't that bad. Once I explained you were injured I couldn't have stopped her if I'd tried. Personally," he seemed amused at the thought, "I think she might have a thing for you, partner."

I was dumbfounded. A fireworks of ideas exploded in my brain, but my mouth said: "Then what?"

"I won the argument, so we took you to her place instead of the hospital. We picked the shot out of you, got the bleeding stopped again then got you cleaned and bandaged. She wanted to call the ambulance, but I wouldn't let her. Anybody saw you woulda known right off you'd been blown up by a shotgun. That, Bubba, is something that has to be reported."

I waited for him to continue. I was finding it easier to ignore the filler and let him tell it at his own maddeningly drawn-out pace.

"I got you to give me Murphy's cell number, but I couldn't get through until somewhere around five in the morning." He stopped and looked at me. It was a look that carried some hidden meaning that I couldn't quite define. Maybe it was because I seemed to be on the verge of nodding off, which I must have done, because the next thing I recalled was opening my eyes in a dark room.

I was alone. I could hear voices in the next room, but I was too weak to call out, so I contented myself with just lying there.

Over! It was over, I thought, really over. Now I could get on with my life again: The construction job...? Considering what had gone down, I could pretty much shine-on any chance of finishing that project. Monk wouldn't be up to honoring any contract. In typically sleazy lawyer-fashion, he'd neglected to sign our agreement. Not that he'd be signing anything ever again.

A number of thoughts regarding Monk and his condition came to mind. I wasn't proud of them. Perhaps, with time, I thought, I might be able to forgive him and release that demon but I didn't think so. Also, I wasn't going to have as much of a nest egg as I had begun to count on for my move to the mountains, but I had gotten by on a lot less in the past. I shut my eyes and smiled in anticipation, the mountains! Yeah!

*　　*　　*

He is gone on the mountain,
He is gone to the forest,
Like a summer-dried fountain,
When our need was the sorest.

- Sir Walter Scott

CHAPTER 109

Free and happy to be alive, I was soaring high above a network of mountain ranges. Low-lying mists filled the valleys giving the appearance of a primordial river of cloud in a prehistoric past. The sun was shining, but the light it gave off was thin and brittle. At this altitude, cool bordered on cold; I regretted wearing only a T-shirt and jeans. The high-pitched rush of wind was loud in my ears. By using the tone and volume of sound as a guide I knew my speed was still within the do-not-exceed parameters for safe operation, but something was wrong. Guilty of having rushed my recovery period, my left side was still tender from the recent wounds. Keeping the glider on track was starting to give me some trouble. I was letting my left wing dip a little, a little too much. I could feel the glider start to side-slip out of the sky. I began losing altitude fast—too fast. The wind shrilled loudly through the rigging wires. I was getting close to exceeding the design limitations. Shifting my weight as far back and to the right as my harness would allow, to compensate for my injury, I could not raise the lowered wing. Desperately, I pushed out hard, full-arm extension, trying to slow my descent by initiating a stall condition. Faster and faster, I augured in toward the ground in a dizzying counter-clockwise spin. I could see the raw crags of the mountaintop reaching for me, coming closer as I plummeted out of control. The wind screamed deafeningly through the flying wires, louder and louder. Imminent disaster filled my senses. I was about to hit at full speed. There was nothing I could do. I tensed, anticipating the impact....

"Ready for some breakfast?"

My heart was rattling like a jackhammer. Barely able to catch a breath, I opened my eyes. In the kitchen the kettle whistled fiercely. It was morning, and from the coolness of the room, a lot earlier than yesterday. When *was* yesterday?

"Yeah." I groaned, still shaken by the vivid and terrifying nature of my dream. "What day is it?"

"Saturday. What do you feel like having? I've got to warn you, I make a pretty mean omelet."

Tuesday to Saturday? No wonder I felt out of it, I'd been gone for three days.

"What's it going to be?" he asked.

"Huh? Uh, whatever you're having's fine with me."

The distracted tone caught Tony's attention. a metallic whirring outside started then stopped; started and stopped again. I wondered what it could be? He sat down on the side of the bed and pulled the sheet down and checked the mound of bandages on my torso.

"You okay?" he asked. There was serious concern.

"No. I've been shot." I twitched the corner of my mouth, to let him know I was joking. "You're not my regular nurse, are you?"

He looked up at me and started to cackle with laughter.

"I was wondering if you'd get that rotten sense of humor back, I haven't had a decent groan in days. How 'bout I fix up some food?"

"Sounds good. I'm kind of curious about a few things."

The noise started up again. I turned my head in the direction, trying to identify the cause.

"Where's Sarge?"

The noise repeated a few cycles, then stopped. I looked around in time to see Tony's back moving down the hallway.

Hey...!"

*   *   *

CHAPTER 110

"...so I came back into the bedroom and there you were, passed out and bleeding all over the floor. Sis' freaked right out. She doesn't handle the sight of blood very well." Tony paused to take a slug of coffee. "I suppose you don't remember Joe and I carrying you, or the drive over here?"

"'Last thing I recall is jumping from the boat, hitting the house-boat wall and falling on my ass. After that everything—getting shot, being in the kayak—*everything* is a blur. Speaking of Murphy, where is he? You've been edging around something, I want to know what it is."

"Alright-alright, let me get a refill and I'll see if I can bring you up to speed."

I got the feeling he was holding back, that something terrible had happened and he didn't want to talk about it. But I wasn't sure. Waking up just about to crash into a mountainside can seriously affect one's perceptions in real-time.

The whirring sound outside my window cycled a few more times, but a little further away than before. What *was* that?' It was almost familiar. The sound cycled again then stopped, shortly after I heard a door close. Whatever it was, the sound didn't return. A few moments later Tony came into the room carrying his mug.

Something was on his mind. I waited for him to speak.

"I take back all the static I gave you about getting your cop friend involved. Truth is—"

He sipped his coffee; focused internally, as though remembering something. Lowering the mug he took a deep breath.

"You and I could not have gotten along without him," he then quickly added, "once you decided to run the whole damn' show."

Tony gave me a hard look, telling me that I'd crossed a line and I'd better not do it again. I got the message: Few had dared, fewer had lived to tell the tale. He then softened and smiled as if to say that he'd taken the body blow to his ego and survived it; we were still friends, but on a different, perhaps a higher level.

"Thanks, that means a lot to me." As if a huge weight had been lifted, it felt very good to be alive. Maybe, I wondered, he might tell me what it was that had been between him and Charlie. That, I thought, could wait for another time. I smiled.

"Now, would you mind, telling me what happened to Gallagher and where's Murph'?"

"'Mind if I answer that one?"

Turning, I saw dark green tropical foliage with hot pink flowers growing up one side of the doorway. Murph', resplendent in a lurid Aloha shirt, tried to hide a broad grin behind his coffee mug. I couldn't begin to imagine the buzz he must've created in the police department. The Deputy Chief had not struck me as someone willingly tolerant of departmental embarrassment. What he must have gone—be going through, I could only guess. Though, most definitely out of uniform, Murphy did seem in positive spirits. In Charlie's parlance: He'd been there, seen the elephant, and had come back in one piece.

"Trying to get anything out of this character is nearly impossible." I pleaded to Murphy, "maybe now, I can get a few straight answers."

"Consider yourself about to be told, but first I think someone else would like to say hi."

I didn't know what to expect when they both left the room as if on cue. A minute later they came back carrying Sarge who was wearing almost as much bandaging as me.

"Sarge! Is this a joke? Is he hurt?"

"Relax, he's okay," Tony said as they brought him next to me. His head was a swell of white bandaging. His left shoulder and stretched out front leg were set in a plaster cast that was hooked into a full-body walking-frame with wheels that extended below his front paws. There were several shaved and sutured patches on his back and sides. In the middle of it all was a huge, beautiful Rottweiler grin; a furiously wagging stub accentuating the other end. I could only pet him gently between the bandages with my one good hand. Tears spilled freely down my face. We must have looked quite the pair of bandaged book-ends.

"White?!" I asked.

Tony slowly nodded his head in the affirmative, as Murph' shook his negatively, answering both of my questions at once.

"When we got you here," Tony explained, "both house and garage were wide open, Sarge was lying in the doorway in a pool of blood. Give him—" Tony gestured with his mug. "—some serious credit."

I turned but Murphy was already in the other room, ostensibly gone to retrieve his coffee mug.

"He carried Sarge to his car and blasted off down the road; sirens, lights, chickens flying, the whole nine yards. Got the vet outta bed and stood over the poor guy until he knew Sarge was gonna pull through."

Murphy ambled back to the doorway and leaned against what was fast becoming his favorite place.

"I owe you," I said, my eyes brimming. "Thanks, for Sarge...for everything." I could see he was uncomfortable with the attention and my heartfelt appreciation.

"You promised to tell me the background for..." He made an all-encompassing gesture. "Do that and we'll call it even."

"Done," I agreed. Tony and I, with the aid of another pot of coffee, launched into a no-holds-barred narrative on everything prior to my calling from the job site and giving Murph' the green light.

"That's unbelievable." He shook his head in amazement. "If I hadn't been part of it I would have said you guys were ready for the psycho ward."

"The way it felt, while it was all happening, you're not too far from being right.

"So, how about returning the favor? Every time I ask about that night, Tony changes the topic, makes an omelet or something else." I was feeling beat up and pretty near exhausted, but determined to be more curious than tired.

"Okay," Murph' began, pulling a chair close to my bed. "When I got your call, it was a few minutes after midnight. I hauled Gallagher's CI to a payphone and coached him what to say. Once he was done, we handcuffed him and locked him in the back of my car. I'd been following the radio-chatter all night. Eaton was all over the air taking care of business. 'Sounded like he was preparing for D-day. The idea of all those drugs just waiting for him must have been quite the incentive. A friend of mine runs a boat rental at Land's End marina; he had a twenty-one-foot Mako ready and waiting. Ral' and I left the dock about ten after." He saw the unasked question and answered: "Ral, short for Raoul, ...Rubeñas?...remember?"

"The BMF?" I confirmed, hearing Tony's snort of laughter.

"The same. I don't mind saying I would've preferred being home instead of out in the shit in that little boat."

From what I'd remembered, it hadn't been my first choice of places to be, either.

Murphy grew introspective.

"We only had a little Tee-top on the boat for shelter. 'Didn't matter we had foul weather gear, both of us were soaked minutes after leaving the dock. That was some scary water, that night. I lost a perfectly good lunch out there."

He grimaced at the memory then grinned at his play on words.

"Ral's a local boy. He knows the waters around here blindfolded. Lucky, 'cause we were running without lights and the pounding we were taking kept winking the radar out."

He looked at the mug in his hand as if he'd forgotten it existed, took a sip, made a face and put it down.

"At one point" he continued, "about half way there, the police cutter must've passed within a hundred yards of us. I knew Gallagher was out there somewhere nearby, too."

"All that traffic, I'm surprised no one ran into anyone else," Tony said, echoing my own thoughts.

"Ditto, that." Murph' agreed. "We saw the houseboat, soon as we rounded the head. It was lit up by the cutter's lights, so Ral' and I shut down to wait and see what was going to happen. A few minutes later —while were waiting out there in the dark—another boat arrives and stood to maybe an eighth of a mile, or so, closer in than us. We figured it was Gallagher, seeing how he wasn't showing running lights either. When we heard shooting I started wondering what was going on but we stayed put."

Murphy hadn't guessed and I was glad Tony saw no need to be overly forthcoming about how we'd set that up.

"It wasn't long before everything settled back down, and about ten-fifteen minutes later the cutter left. The other boat powered up. I could see it was Gallagher when he got close to the houseboat and he and Eaton did their now-you-see-it, now-you-don't' act. When he left," Murph' explained, "we followed."

Most of this I'd gleaned from Tony, but it was enlightening seeing it through someone else's eyes.

"Gallagher headed northwest, about forty minutes or so. Thanks to Ral' we were able to lay back a bit and use the radar to track him. There was a loose connector, and he got the problem licked while we were bouncing around out there waiting for something to happen.

"The wind had shifted quite a bit and we were now running with the storm, making pretty good time until he started turning back east once he passed Boca Chica. It was close after three when Ral' figured he was making for the Big Coppitt bridge, so he pushed us along full out. We must have been doing well over forty knots. I didn't think so while we were getting slammed around in that little boat, but it was a good thing he did, otherwise we might have lost him in the clutter."

I knew the area: It was jammed with every kind of boat dock and slip imaginable. Big Coppitt Key was a little further up the road from the Rock; many people traded off the drive against lower "berth rates." I chuckled, remembering one of Charlie's favorite groan lines then regretted the attendant memories. Feeling the stab of his absence, he should have been here with us, considering how much a part of what had happened was due to our love and respect for him.

"'Time he started slowing down," Murphy continued, "we were just about close enough to see him without his running lights. Right about then he vanished off the screen. He'd gone somewhere into the jumble of private docks and boathouses, but he hadn't been that far ahead. So, we killed the engine and drifted. I began to think we'd lost him until I saw a light go on in one of the boathouses."

Murph' paused for a moment. Probably, remembering the smell and feel of that night. Sarge creaked open a mammoth yawn then looked me in the eye until I resumed ruffling the fur under his chin, which he endorsed with a thoroughly contented grunt.

"We paddled over to the next dock to wait." Murphy continued. "I figured Eaton wouldn't be able to stay away, and I'd be damned if I was going to jump early. We musta' donated a couple pints of blood that night; every mosquito in the world was out there with us, but I wasn't going to settle for the tail...I wanted the whole dog."

I thought of several smart remarks, and to everyone's unknowing gratitude, kept them to myself.

"Maybe an hour or so later, 'little after four, Eaton finally showed. He came straight down from the main house to the boat shed, like it was just another day at the office. I guess they'd been doing this kind of thing for so long that he didn't expect anything unusual.

"Ral' stayed with the boat; I went through the neighbors' yard crossing over until I reached the head of the ramp. I gave a couple quick breaks on the radio. Ral' started the engine, goosed it right into their boat, and gave a hillbilly "yee-haw.' They came tumbling and falling over themselves out of the shed, pistols drawn, ready to scare off what they must've thought was some loudmouth drunk, but they never thought to look behind them...it was almost too easy.

"They threatened, they joked, they whined, then, as soon as the cuffs were on, they offered to cut us in and keep us well-greased with some pretty outrageous numbers. Lucky for them I take my job seriously, 'cause bribery's a dangerous insult to both Ral' and myself. 'Soon as the sheriff's people showed up and took them into custody, they dummied-up and refused to say a word. That's when I switched on the phone and got Tony's calls. The rest you..." he gestured first to me then to Tony, "...*you* both know."

There was something I wasn't being told. Whatever it was, had been and was still between them. It was in the way he'd repeated "you" then locked eyes with Tony. I thought I saw something pass between them. Tony turned his head away from Murphy and locked his eyes on me.

I looked at the man who'd helped me wage a war and win it. He'd always had my best interests at heart. Never-failing, he'd fought by my side, doing what needed to be done, risking all and asking for nothing but honor and decency in return. Tony had guided me through the battlefields of our collective past where we'd lost friends, avenged them, and killed wrongly. We would each carry the weight of those things forever. *"Enough,"* his eyes seemed to say.

I'd doubted him once; never again, I silently promised, nodding slowly. Tony understood.

Murph' appeared about to pursue the point, regardless of our tacit accord, when Sarge grunted loudly, as if in agreement with us, which turned into a strange gurgling growl. It sounded as if he was laughing at the silly humans, worrying about the "before" when the "now" is the only thing that mattered. Probably, he was wondering what new delicacy awaited him in the imminent *now* of his food dish?

Our little drama wasn't on a par with "Miami Vice" adventures but, like Sarge, I'd take steak over sizzle any old day of the week. Sarge knew the how and when of putting things into perspective.

Laughter, whether canine or human, is infectious. Sarge was the undisputed catalyst of our being able to lighten up an awkward moment. I had also noticed that Murph' had deleted any mention of the life-saving run he'd performed on Sarge's behalf from his retelling of the events. Chuckling, he caught my look; knew what I was thinking then smiled in acknowledgement of my unspoken thanks.

"Ral' and I are both on indefinite leave, with pay, I might add, until the trial is set. Some vacation...." He consulted his watch then sighed, "Thanks to those ass—to those apple-heads we get to spend it in Tallahassee, Fun 'n Sun capital of the South...*Not!*"

I remember thinking how it might've been more appropriate to debrief them in Orlando, given the Mickey-Mouse way things had gone up to now, besides it would've made a perfect cover. The price of a G-job was beyond what I would've willingly paid; getting yanked from a comfortable, familiar day-to-day reality only to be plunked down in the middle of a town full of strangers at a moment's notice, with no control over your life. No thanks!

"We're supposed to leave in about four hours," he continued, "I heard how, when Gallagher and Eaton didn't get cut loose right away, they got plenty scared about being "at risk" if they spent any time in the jail system, so they started singing."

"They're right," Tony snickered. "No shortage 'inside' of people who'd like to skin 'em slow...people they put there."

Murphy understood, agreeing with a nod at Tony's insight. "The State's Attorney wants to keep them," he added, "and us, out of harm's way until he can get us-all in front of a special grand jury. According to some of the rumors I've heard they're only the tip of the ice cube." Murphy grinned at his play on words, which I didn't understand. But, considering what he'd done for Sarge, he could make all the lame jokes he wanted and I'd keep on smiling. Tony sat quietly, his mood reflective, a gentle look on his face. I could guess some of the things he was going to try to put back together in his life, now that Gallagher and Eaton were off his back for good.

It was finally over. We could all relax. I felt myself starting to drift again. This time, I didn't fight it.

*　　*　　*

**Each lonely scene shall thee restore,
For thee the tear be duly shed;
Beloved to life can charm no more,
And mourn'd, till Pity's self be dead.**

- William Collins

CHAPTER 111

A sharp pain jabbed under my chin. A sharper whisper was in my ear. "Wake up, dead man. Rise and shine!"

I froze; my heart, gripped in ice, was wedged in the back of my throat. White!

I felt the bite of nylon as he grabbed the cable-ties binding my ankles. Stitches in my chest tore loose and my eyes flooded with tears; a band of duct tape kept the scratchy block of wadded sweat sock in my mouth, muffling my scream of agony as he yanked me off the bed and let me fall to the floor. I saw it coming, tried to move my head, but I was helpless to avoid the pistol butt in White's hand or the skyrocket blaze and the blackness that followed.

"Tony...?!"

He was looking right at me, his face only three or four inches from mine. We lay on the floor of the workshop. My head pounded in sync with the burning pulse that encased my chest and shoulder. There was something wrong with his eyes; there was no focus.

"Ohhhh..." I moaned, devastated, as the realization sunk in.

"Where is it?"

That deadly whispery voice. It *was* White. I'd thought I'd been having a nightmare. What was he doing here? Obviously, getting even, but there had to be more. I had to concentrate, but I couldn't seem to focus.

"Where is it?"

I didn't know for a moment what he was talking about; it was hard to think straight. There was a strange spitting sound, I felt a tiny sting, like a pair of insects had bitten me. Suddenly, I couldn't breathe. A huge claw picked me up and was shaking me like a terrier worrying a rat. My teeth were vibrating. The cheap metal-spoon taste of blood filled my mouth. I think I may have tried to cry out. Oblivion rose up, covering me in a merciful, black blanket.

*   *   *

**For secrets are edged tools,
And must be kept from children
and from fools.**

- John Dryden

CHAPTER 112

Alone, in my workshop, by feel—rather than the lack of feeling in my feet and my restricted movement—I was cinched tight by the ankles to one of the staples set into the floor and by my right wrist to another. I was thankful the sock had been removed from my mouth though the flavor remained. A terrible memory of having seen Tony dead persisted. Had I imagined that, too? His body wasn't where I'd thought I'd seen it. Nothing made any sense...well, almost nothing. I had, with Tony's assistance, pretty well fouled White's prospects and probably his life expectancy. He had nothing left to lose. Ironically, the one thing he wanted I couldn't give him. Tony'd never divulged the final hiding place for the smuggled load of drugs and diamonds. Until this instant, it hadn't seemed important to know where, only that they were safely hidden. I pictured him, that night, standing in the doorway, dripping on the floor, empty-handed when he'd returned to Charlie's warehouse. If White really had killed Tony then he'd burned his only bridge. I almost giggled at the insanity of it all.

The belief he held in my knowledge, I was sure, was the only thing standing between me and him adding one more winding-turn to his karmic cycle. At the very least, Tony's wishes would be honored. Those drugs would never be put on the street to hurt another person. When I was gone that would be an end to it.

'When I was gone...?!'

That kind of thinking wasn't going to help. Resolving to deprive White of any kind of victory, after all of Tony's and my efforts, I had to find a way to fight back, so not knowing what else to do I started with the things that I could.

What would Tony do? Inventory, assess then adapt and improvise. First, I was hurting all over, no surprise there; judging by the dried blood on my bandages, my wounds were apparently closed for the moment. Second, my mind seemed to be functioning, a little wooly, but rational. Third, while my right hand and feet were immobilized, my left, swathed in bandages, was not. If I could get my hand free and there was a tool or weapon within reach. Fourth, from my position on the floor I could see no tool or weapon within reach.

* * *

It hath been often said, that it is not death, but dying, which is terrible.

- Henry Fielding

CHAPTER 113

"Shall we talk?"

I refused to give White the satisfaction of reacting when he ripped the duct tape from my face. It felt like I might never have to shave again. Shock after shock jolted through me, contorting my body into backbreaking arches and spasms, lifting me again and again in that phantom grip then, repeatedly bashing me against the concrete floor. Unable to draw breath, I was severely weakened and getting weaker. Each time I came back to consciousness it seemed to take longer to get over the effects of the punishment. I knew I couldn't take many more of those sessions. I'd given up any pretense of bravery after the first round and told the truth, but he didn't, wouldn't, or couldn't believe it. I lied. He checked what I told him. Then, having discovered my deceit, in his rage he'd beaten me senseless when he returned empty-handed.

I could see the insanity growing in his eyes, hear it in his voice. Knowing I'd helped push him over the edge with no way back made it all the worse. My howls of pain from the kicks he aimed at my injuries and my genitals resulted in his gagging me with another piece of tape. All I could do was hang on and endure. For how long or to what end I didn't know.

*   *   *

> **If, of all sound words of tongue and pen,**
> **The saddest are, "It might have been,"**
> **More sad are these we daily see:**
> **"It is, but hadn't ought to be!"**
>
> **- Francis Brett Hart**

CHAPTER 114

At one point, I remember wondering, quite objectively, whether I would bleed to death or die more slowly from the steady diet of electric shocks and beatings. I'd long since abandoned hope of anyone riding to my rescue. Murphy and his friend were sequestered somewhere safely testifying against Gallagher and Eaton. There was no "anyone" out there. If something was going to be done it was solely up to me. The nylon ties anchoring me to the floor were so tight they'd cut off all feeling. Other than a steady, thick thud-dub sensation in my right hand and feet, they were dead meat at the end of my limbs. My thrashing about from the Taser shocks had caused the nylon to cut deeply, and a thick crust of dried blood surrounded each tie. Recalling Monk's wounds and the outcome, I wondered if death might not be preferable. With effort, I pushed my mind away from going down that path; it led to surrender and something far worse: acceptance.

When I rolled to my right and pushed up into a sitting position, my field of vision narrowed then pulled back, like looking through the wrong end of a telescope. I waited a minute or an hour, I wasn't sure how long, for the disorientation to pass.

My heart leapt. The Ramset! It was still on the workbench where I'd left it. There was a red charge-strip sticking out of the gun. A weapon! Somehow, if only I could get loose.

White must have thought my left arm broken. Strapped across my chest by wraps and layers of bandage, immobilized, to keep me from tearing my stitches loose, a reasonable assumption.

Gritting my teeth against the pain I tried to wiggle my hand down and out from the lower edge of the elastic bandage, felt something rip and pull high up, near my shoulder. Tears flooded my eyes, the pain triggered a wave of nausea, causing the little telescope in my mind to reverse itself. I took deep slow breaths as I waited for it to pass, for the world to come back into focus. After two more trips to the edge of blackout, each one requiring slightly more recovery time, my arm was fully extended. The bandaging hung loosely around me. Fresh blood dripped off the ends of my fingers. Something *had* opened up. Loss of blood, in my weakened state, could be critical. I had to hurry or risk passing out. If that were to happen, as slim as this chance was, I'd have none at all.

The Ace-bandage was about fifteen feet long; fully stretched it might reach maybe twenty or more. That would be ample for what I had in mind, but I needed something to weight one end. Other than bandages and nylon restraints, I was buck-naked, there was nothing within reach. The wreckage of wood framing from the table saw extension White had ripped loose, stood against the near wall, a little less than eight feet away. I layered the bandage carefully. Holding onto the two ends I leaned as far over to my right as I could. Then, rolling back to the left, I threw my arm out as far as I could reach and let go the sling.

I wasn't sure how long I'd been out, but I had been gone. The first thing I saw when I opened my eyes was a loop of bandage lying atop the pieces of broken wood. One, that had two bent-over nails sticking out, had been my intended target. I'd reached it! The long, stretching-out throw had done damage. My chest and shoulder felt as if they'd been torn apart and shredded. I could see blood puddling, spreading out from under my arm.

Using my fingers, I gathered the ends of the stretchy fabric to me. The loop curled as it dragged over the piece of plywood. About two inches shy of the nail-hooks the fabric hung up on a narrow splinter along the broken edge. The bandage stretched tighter and tighter...the plywood started to shift...I held my breath, gathering in a little more... the elastic cloth narrowed under the strain...the panel moved again. Suddenly, the splinter broke and the bandage sprang back from the wood to fall in a loose pile by my outstretched arm.

The frustration was devastating. I wanted to cry.

Gee whiz! That'll help. Denying the sarcastic critic in my mind—perhaps, because of it—from somewhere down deep in the place where I keep strength, resolve, and tenacity, I gathered up enough for another try.

Concentrating, measuring the distance, I took my time then let fly another desperate toss. The back of my head cracked onto the concrete floor with a flat pinging ring, like smacking a brick with a hammer. Vision vibrated. The room shifted a half step to each side, doubling, yawing queasily before centering again. I shut my eyes tight, clamped down hard, withstanding the roar of agony that tore across my body.

Stay conscious! I screamed in my mind.

Not daring to look until I'd managed to slow down my runaway breathing to a series of controlled gasps, I opened my eyes. One end of the bandage had come loose from my hand and lay about a foot and a half beyond my fingertips. I traced the other end to where it extended across the floor and lay just on top of the bent nails. I stretched over, teased the loose end back with the tips of my fingers then gathered the slack in until the bandage started to curl and wrap itself around one of the steel points. The fabric strained. My fingers twitched. Nerves, muscles convulsed. The tremors started almost imperceptibly, quickly growing in intensity and speed until the bandage was twanging in the air like a guitar string. Fearful I might be destroying my one chance, I forced my cramping hands to slowly unclench. The fabric slithered through my fingers. The spasms, if anything, worsened. Impulsively, I slapped my free hand against the concrete hard enough to bring tears to my eyes. Again and again, I beat it against the floor until the convulsions stopped, replaced by a burning pain. I was breathing in great ragged gulps, sick with frustration and hurt, but the tremors had subsided.

Again, I gathered in the slack, saw the nails bite into the elastic, the fabric curled, folding around the sharp points. I took in just a little more until the plywood moved ever so slightly then I felt the shakes starting again, saw the bandage beginning to vibrate. In one final, all-or-nothing risk, I gave everything I had in one last, hard, teeth-gritting yank.

"Got it!" I cheered into my gag.

Feeling that piece of scrap wood gouge a chunk from the side of my leg was one of the most wonderful sensations imaginable. My breath rattled harshly in my throat with the effort and success, I felt like a winning marathon runner breaking the tape; the rush of blood thundering in my ears sounded like the roar of a cheering crowd. Getting fuzzy around the edges, the room receded, and threatened to disappear.

Slowly, too slowly, it came back into focus.

The chunk of plywood I'd hooked, once a triangular gusset, was about fourteen inches long with an arch cut out of the hypotenuse. Single-handed, I fashioned a noosed bowline around its center.

So far I'd been very lucky, I couldn't afford to rest, there was no way of telling how long that luck would last. I had to keep at it even knowing I might have already used up whatever had been allotted me. At any moment, White could decide to have another go at me. The closed door vibrated, it swelled, seemingly about to open in the next instant.

Get busy! Do something! My mind demanded.

The workbench stood waist-high and ran the length of the wall; near the door, close to the edge, the Ramset lay across its open metal carrying case. At most, it was six feet beyond the stretched-out tips of my fingers. I worked the loose end of the bandage into and around the numb fingers of my right hand. For all the feeling, it may as well have not been there. Other than a dull, thudding pulse-beat from my wrist, I'd lost virtually all sense of feeling. I knew if I didn't find a way of getting loose....

Wonderful things they're doing with prosthetics these days.

I tried to push away the images of Monk's devastation. The warm and husky little purr of a woman's voice on a telephone, sounding so much like Nicole, as it kept repeating in my ear, "... post surgical recovery... satisfactory condition..."

Concentrate!

I leaned my weight on my right elbow and hefted the small plate of wood in my left hand, finding the balance of it. Curling my arm across my body, twisting from the waist, I saw the target in my mind, imagined where I wanted my line to fall then skated the plywood out in a backhand throw.

Whang!

The edge of the plywood hit the toolbox squarely, driving it back an inch or so. The Ramset teetered on the edge of the box for what seemed an eternity, threatening to fall back out of sight and beyond reach. I groaned into the taped gag. Slowly, my perspective on the room and the tool stopped wobbling, and both settled back in place. I let my breath out.

The wrap on the plywood was still in place, the knot had held. I reeled it in for a second try. Fresh blood glistened, trickling down my chest; cold sweat beaded my forehead, my stomach churned and my mind started to reel. Resting, concentrating on breathing until the nausea receded, I steeled myself for another go, tensed...aimed... twisted back...then rolled out and lofted the panel up and over the box.

"Ohhh..."

I watched in horror as the plywood gusset flew off the end of my heaving line, bounced off the wall and crash-landed behind a saw-horse on the other side of the shop.

"...Nooo!" I moaned softly.

"'Nothing wrong with talking to yourself, nothing at all. 'Perfectly natural thing to do." Charlie'd once explained to me. "Interrupting the conversation's what you got to watch out for."

Hearing the distant sound of his rolling chuckle, I started to laugh along. Gagged as I was, I heard the sharp edge of hysteria.

My lifeline, what I could see of it, was mostly draped across the bench and toolbox. If only....

"If," I remembered Charlie saying, "is the middle word in Life."

Not knowing if the knot was still intact, if it would catch, if anything, I reeled in. Slowly, steadily over the smooth red-painted surface of the Ramset, the fabric flowed. Gravity conspired with momentum. I quailed, watching it slicker down faster and faster, falling, rippling into loops on the floor.

Then it stopped.

The knot or loop had caught on something; I couldn't see what. I gathered in the loose folds. Slowly, the fabric stretched tighter and tighter. It started to slip from my cramped fingers. Sweat stung my eyes. I blinked it away, held on tight and pulled hard.

Grit grated under the sheet metal box. Only a fraction of an inch, but it had moved! I tightened my grip, straining. It shifted again, another fraction then it stopped. Muscles twanging, nerves vibrating, I went through the pain and pulled as hard as I could. Things started to go fuzzy and dim.

All at once, there was a screeching scrape as box and tool skidded forward, to the edge, balanced, wavered then came tumbling, crashing, down, falling on top of me. I scrabbled for the gun, gathered it to me, and held on to it for dear life.

The room started fading.

"NO!" I bellowed in a muffled roar. The rush of anger pushed back the dark enveloping edge of unconsciousness.

What if White had heard the crash and was about to burst through the door? I tried to think. What to do? I racked the barrel, opened the firing piston; only two crimped brass tips remained at the end of the red plastic charge strip. The rest of the .25 caliber loads were safely stored in a locked cabinet on the other side of the shop. Whatever I was going to do, I had two chances. I fed the strip back in then pulled the barrel back cocking it. Shaking fingers inserted a three-inch long plate-fastener into the end of the barrel. The nylon bushing on the shank would keep the nail from falling out. Armed, as I was, I held my weapon at the ready.

Until several long anxious minutes had passed by uneventfully, I began to believe what little luck I had might still be with me. I had been so intent on getting the Ramset that I hadn't thought much about what I was going to do when I got it. I thought about shooting through the nylon ties; both shots would have to be perfect, if they weren't...at the very least, White might take a dim view of my resourcefulness, and call me bad names.

I giggled insanely, felt like crying, understanding the desperation and futility a snared rabbit must feel, as it waited for the trapper's club.

Think!

If I didn't want to be the rabbit then I had to be a fox, but everything would have to look normal if it was going to work.

The shop was spinning in earnest by the time I got the toolbox shoved under the bench and the area around me clear of telltale debris. The concrete floor started pitching like the deck of a small boat. My mind wobbled and yawed, tumbling forward, as I struggled to gather in the loose folds of bandage around the bright red of the Ramset and cover it with my body. I saw Monk's Hobie-cat come cartwheeling across the sky before slamming into the water sending up cascading sprays of rainbow shards, then I passed out.

*   *   *

> **Suspicion all our lives shall be stuck full of eyes;**
> **For treason is but trusted like the fox,**
> **Who, ne'er so tame, so cherish'd, and locked up,**
> **Will have a wild trick of his ancestors.**
>
> **- King Henry IV - William Shakespeare**

CHAPTER 115

"Mmmpph!" I wailed into the tape gag over my mouth, awakened by a sudden blaze of agony that flared from my kidneys. Forcing myself to resist the instinctive urge to arch away from the attack, I pulled in hard against the nylon cables cutting me to the bone, squeezing myself into fetal curl around the pile of bandaging covering the Ramset, as White methodically moved around me raining kick after kick into my helpless form with an excruciating accuracy.

A hard shoe slammed into my face; the vision in my left eye flashed hot bright white, then red dimming to black.

"Enough! Please! I'll tell." I sobbed into the gag, furiously nodding my surrender and compliance.

White stood above me, breathing heavily. I could still see a little out of my right eye; the left was swollen completely shut. That side of my face was numb. Blood dripped off the end of my nose onto the floor. He leaned over and slowly pulled the tape from my mouth; I felt my lips peel and split.

"No more, please! It's in the, the...." My voice trailed off into an unintelligible whimper and mumble.

He bent down on one knee, resting his weight on one hand, as he prodded my cheek with his gun. The safety was off. I saw the white dot bright against the matte black of the pistol.

Sobs wracked my body, obscuring the words when I tried to tell him where the drugs and diamonds were hidden.

He leaned closer to hear.

With every last grain of strength remaining in my body, I jammed the point of the shot-nail into his forehead as hard as I could and pulled the trigger.

Two explosions simultaneously echoed cries of pain and surprise. I felt a stunning blow to my head. Merciful blackness washed over me, and I knew nothing.

*   *   *

Three blind mice, see how they run!
They all ran after the farmer's wife.
Who cut off their tails with a carving-knife,
Did you ever see such a thing in your life
As three blind mice?

- Deuteromelia, Thomas Ravenscroft

CHAPTER 116

I was having a nightmare from which I couldn't seem to awaken. In my dream a heavy weight had me pinned against a sheet of ice. Strangely, a colony of fire ants were burrowing into my chest, my head was clamped into a vice being tightened by a huge, evil-smelling ogre with very mean red and yellow eyes. He held something over my mouth, laughing as I suffocated.

I tried to open my eyes. I could see nothing.

Oh God! I thought, *I'm blind!*

Then I understood where I was and what had happened. In dying, White had befouled us both. A rank stench assaulted my senses when I struggled to move his corpse off me. Bad air or not, I was alive and I could breathe, a little more freely. My left eye throbbed and was swollen shut; the vision in my right was vibrating a little, but I could see.

A nail trimmer, a pocketknife, anything!

I searched his pockets then searched them again. I almost wept. White carried nothing, save a set of keys and a spare pistol magazine.

The tip of the unbelievably heavy handgun wandered back and forth. It took several attempts before I had the muzzle pressed against the nylon tie around my wrist. I squeezed the trigger. Within the confines of the small workshop the report was deafening. My head imploded.

It seemed to take a very long time before I was able to steady my vision again. I suspected, from the way everything was fading in and out, that I had probably sustained a concussion.

I missed the next shot, then missed again on the next two tries, as I attempted to free myself. The fourth seared a burning hot groove across the palm of my right hand and cost me the tip of my little finger.

*   *   *

But what am I?
An infant crying the night:
An infant crying for the light:
And with no language but a cry.

- Alfred, Lord Tennyson

CHAPTER 117

Several days had passed since Sola came to the workshop and found me, curled up next to White's maggot-infested corpse, an empty pistol near my hand. Several distorted flashes; impressions of a panicked race to the hospital then nothing; nothing until I woke up in a private hospital room, manacled to the bed frame with an armed military guard on duty.

Fragile but free of White and his tortures, I quickly discovered that I was trapped in another kind of nightmare: Deemed physically stable enough to have visitors, I was subjected to a continuous barrage of city, state and federal officials of all shapes, sizes and prominence, many of whom remained anonymous. Hour upon hour, day after day, they pounded at me for information. Some were nice; most were not. I remained numb and dumb to all.

With everything gone, nothing mattered anymore. I should have been dead several times over, yet I was still here. That had to have some purpose. The damage had to stop, I decided it would stop with me. Once I'd made up my mind, for the record, to forget everything that happened—that was my story or lack of one—I stuck to it. Without knowing how much Murph' had told the authorities, or what they had deduced on their own I wasn't about to volunteer anything that might sink him.

Whatever was going to happen to me next, was beyond my control, so I sank down into the womb/tomb of my mind, listening to all but hearing nothing save the sound of my heartbeat, as I waited for that *it* to happen.

A month inched by then another.

The medical authorities conferred, after having administered their latest battery of tests, asserting that the combined effects of Traumatic, Retrograde, and Hysterical Amnesia were plausible, attributable to the extent of the extreme mental and physical abuse I had suffered. Due to the untreated multiple concussions, permanent and debilitating brain damage, they determined, was feasible.

My act was so convincing—or there really *was* damage—that there were moments when I began to doubt whether anything actually had happened. The marks on my wrist and ankles gradually faded; only the broad expanse of puckered and discolored flesh, below the lethargic face in the mirror, said otherwise. Tony was—had been right, it was a "granddaddy" of scars. I didn't have to see it to feel it, even after the physical body stopped hurting. Unseen, some nights, it was a terrible thing in the dark cutting deeply into me, ripping my heart to pieces.

There were too many of those nights when I awakened, trembling, as icy-cold fingertips clutched at me; images lashed my brain: going berserk at Nicole's funeral...Gordo crushing my arm... Monk's mother, the General, screeching at me...Doug in his chair laughing at me from a second bloody grin...a dead cabdriver, beside the spare tire, beckoning to me...a bloody-faced diver rising from the water...Tony's vacant eyes staring at me....

Food was brought, I ate it; sunlight tracked across the sky, I stared at the changing patterns on the walls; the lights went out and, sick at heart I shivered alone in the dark until the meds' kicked in and put me out of my misery.

Soon, the texture of my interrogators' attempts to communicate with me slid from suspected criminal mastermind, through collateral witness, down to toddler/retard. Some of my visitors suspected I was faking it, even after the physicians, psychologists and psychiatric minds deemed my condition precluded the possibility of their learning anything of substance. Eventually, they lost interest in, as one jokester, an assistant to the State's Attorney opined, "...talking to the broc'." To them I was a vegetable. Soon the only interrogations were those I precipitated with myself.

"Why be anything," I asked myself, "if you're nothing?"

"If I am nothing then why do anything?"

There were debates aplenty but I won none of them.

Whatever case the government planned on making would have to be accomplished solely by Murph and Rubeñas' testimony, supported by forensics and circumstantial evidence.

No longer a part of their strategy, I may have been left alone but I was not forgotten.

*   *   *

...waking I often observe the absurdity of Dreames, but never dream of the absurdities of my waking thoughts; I am well satisfied, that being awake, I know I dreame not; though when I dreame, I think my selfe awake.

- Leviathan, Thomas Hobbes

CHAPTER 118

Late one morning, I awoke to find I had been whisked away from my hospital room during the night. Apparently, I was now in a double occupancy officer's quarters, stripped for one, on a military base somewhere in Florida. Which one or how I had gotten there was a mystery; the last thing I' remembered was nuzzling deep down into my pillow and floating away on a cloud heavily laced with some delicious morphine derivative.

During my 'recuperative' stay, I was afforded all the comforts of home...almost. I had a television, tuned exclusively to movie and cartoon channels. If I found the continuing adventures of Porky, Bugs, Tweety and Sylvester too challenging, I was allowed to request books and games brought to me from the library; newsmagazines, radios or newspapers were forbidden.

Neither Larry my afternoon guard, nor his two partners, carried any unit insignia or identification on their uniforms. Stationed outside my door, they wore the same daily change of unlabeled, unremarkable khakis provided for me. Three times each day, a tray was delivered from the mess hall, which I quickly discovered was not a misnomer.

Days became weeks each blending seamlessly, one into the next, without a ripple. The only variables were the natural rhythms of rain and sun, night and day. When I perceived that there might be no end to having my life put on hold, and began wondering if that might not be for the best, something in me snapped.

The unanticipated response to my smashing television, furniture; everything I could lay my hands on before covering the walls with mashed potatoes, gravy and lima beans, was my having to live in the mess I'd created until I promised to be nice and requested cleaning supplies and replacements.

On the one occasion when I tested my guardians, Curly's speed in the application of retaliatory force permanently dissuaded me from any such course in the future. After regaining the full range of motion in my arm joints, I resigned myself to waiting until either they decided what they were going to do with me or they made a mistake. It was to that end, focusing all my energy into planning my escape, that may have saved what little sanity I had left. To succeed, my plan must employ subterfuge or guile. Unfortunately, I was fresh out of both and complicity was hard to come by. My guards never spoke, other than was necessary for day-to-day functioning, nor did they relax their vigilance for an instant.

While working on my latest stratagem, calculating shift changes garbage schedules, factoring in the lunar cycle, my door swung open. Standing there, instead of Moe, my mid-morning keeper, was Officer Joseph Murphy, resplendent in the uniform of a Sergeant of the Key West Police Department.

I was a deer in the headlights; my mouth hung agape as Murphy walked in, a little stiffly, and took a seat opposite me at my collapsible everything-table without saying a word. Stunned, I couldn't think, the thousand-and-one questions that boiled and bubbled in my mind refused to come out. His eyes silently flicked from mine to the still open door, and he was "Murph'" again, warning me against saying anything. I shut my mouth.

A moment passed then another before the assistant to the State's Attorney, the comedic pencil-neck from my hospital stay, strutted into my room followed by a stenographer-aide in close order formation. Since I hadn't incriminated myself, thanks to his warning, by saying something that couldn't be unsaid, whatever dog-and-pony show had been set up was about to begin. Clearly Murph's presence was not optional.

Our exemption, we were then told, from prosecution on a host of charges was conditional on our continued good behavior [i.e. silence] and subsequent relocation to any non-adjacent states as soon as we could "put our local affairs in order, in a timely manner."

Moreover, Murphy and I were "strictly proscribed from having any contact with each other, under pain of revocation and repeal of said exemptions followed by the swift imposition of appropriate and commensurate disciplinary action."

Apparently, someone did not want us putting our heads together, or else.

We signed the forms stuck in front of us and that was that. The whole production lasted maybe a total of five minutes. Throughout, Murph' sat silent as a post. I followed suit. When the deed was done he was the first to leave.

Alone again, my thoughts were even more confused than before. This latest episode was so off-the-wall I began considering that I may have been hallucinating. Had Murphy, the suits, the session, only taken place in my mind? I had nothing to prove they'd ever been there, except the dimly remembered impression of having held a pen and signed my name in triplicate.

Two days later, I woke up back in the same private hospital room I'd occupied however many months earlier; at least, it looked like the same room.

My hold on sanity, tenuous at best, slipped several notches lower. What must have been a massive dosage of drugs in my previous evening's meal hadn't helped. Perception of reality shifted to a place well off center and it wasn't switching back. I wondered if maybe I hadn't dreamt it all up. Was I dreaming about dreaming about being in a hospital?

I threw back the blankets and went to the door. Finding it locked I attacked it, pounding at it until the guard, the same guard as before, entered. My mind began to crumble. Where were the Three Stooges? Had they really existed outside of my imagination?

The last impression I recall was being pinned to the floor by two large men in white, and feeling a pinprick as someone jabbed a needle into my arm.

*   *   *

I seem forsaken and alone,
I hear the lions roar;
And every door shut but one,
And that is mercy's door.

- William Cowper

CHAPTER 119

Sola Amundsen insisted I spend a week following my discharge from the hospital in her studio cum guest cottage. A marked improvement, it was awkward being there without Tony. His ashes, she'd told me, had been scattered over the coral reefs; just a small, simple ceremony off the stern of a hired boat.

There was a tap on the door and she bustled in with fresh linen for the bed.

"I really appreciate being here," I began, "but—"

When she looked at me, her eyes were at once the saddest and fiercest I've ever seen; tears brimmed, threatening to spill over.

"All I meant was—"

Tears sliding down her cheeks, she shook her head *no,* slowly, repeatedly negating my comprehension of what was the matter.

"I haven't—" her voice, a hoarse whisper, faltered. Choked with emotion, she tried again. "I've been trying to work up the guts—the courage to tell you—" Again words failed her. She buried her face in the yellow flowered sheets and turned her back to me, to compose her self. Meanwhile, my heart pounded and my imagination conjured up demons galore.

"While you were *away...*" she began, in a stronger voice, before turning to look at me, "Your house, on Angela Street...everything you had is gone."

Numbed, before I could speak she put down the bundle of bed-clothes and went outside leaving the door standing open. A couple of minutes passed before I heard her footsteps returning, during which I began to understand how the logic of damage control would demand such action take place.

She entered, holding out a newspaper folded open to a page with two paragraphs circled. The fire, according to the exceptionally brief article, was ascribed to "accidental causes".

"Your clothing, tools and some of your personal effects are in a storage locker," Sola began, handing me an envelope. In it, I found a receipt for a year's rental and a brochure with a map showing the location of the storage facility in Homestead, a small town adjacent to a large military base on the Florida mainland. Stapled to the back was an index card with a phone number. I held up the card, the unspoken question apparent.

"That's for the office at the City Hall where you pick up the key, on your way *off island*, for good."

The Iron Works was pretty much the same except for a great, empty black hole where Tony used to be. One of the provisions of his will, Sola told me, was that she inherited the gym. A codicil dated only days prior to his death, requested I help her out in the daily operation until she found a buyer or decided I was superfluous.

Why not, I reasoned? There were worse things I could be doing. Though it may have come awfully close to invalidating the provisions of my agreement with Big Brother, until she asked me to leave my "local affairs" were not "in order". In essence, I neither would nor could conscience refusing to honor Tony's last request.

Mostly, I sat behind the counter watching Sola take care of the customers. My job was companion for Sarge; I'd thought he was going to go crazy the day we walked into the gym together. Other than a patch of black-fur-turned-white that covered a large area between his ears, he was in perfect shape. Those mementos, his and mine, were a symbol, a bond between us. They were all that was left to show that anything had ever happened.

The gym regulars had no idea what had transpired; I perpetuated the boating accident myth the Authorities had deemed appropriate for general consumption. With time, even the lie became easier, but an all-consuming depression had settled in to fill the void left in the absence of the pharmaceutically induced oblivion to which I'd been subjected.

It lasted until late one night when Sola stopped into the guesthouse for a visit. We talked a little about the shop and the day's business. She became very quiet then got up from the futon couch, where she'd been sitting. I thought she was leaving. I stood to see her out and she walked into my arms. I didn't know or care who was comforting whom; I only knew that that for the first time in a very long time I was feeling and acting like a human being again.

After we made love, I cried myself to sleep in her arms, awakening the next morning to find that it hadn't been a dream. At her urging, I quit the cottage and moved into the main house. Her gentle love, compassion, and understanding became the foundation for days that built into weeks.

Gradually, the nightmares receded into a dim haze.

*   *   *

In nature there are neither rewards nor punishments — there are consequences.

- Robert Green Ingersoll

CHAPTER 120

One evening, just after we'd closed up for the night, Murph' showed up unannounced. Newly returned from an extensive audience with some wondrous personage who dwelt in some hallowed corridor of power or other, for all I knew it might have been the man behind the curtain, pulling the levers and switches in the Land of Oz.

"I'm not here, and never was," was the first thing he said.

Immediately, *'a red wolf howling in the full moon saloon'* came to mind, I kept those thoughts unspoken.

The three of us, with Sarge curled at my feet, stayed up most of the night in the guest cottage, with Murph' doing most of the talking.

Gallagher and Eaton, I learned, much to our disappointment, had been channeled into the witness protection program.

"First to squeal gets the deal," was how Murph' had aptly put it.

They'd been part of an organized ring of corrupt cops stretching from Miami to Key West. Fearful of the fate awaiting them *inside* they hadn't balked at trading-up, implicating their superiors. Apparently, quite a number of prominent careers had come to a screeching halt behind their joint testimony. Evidently, there'd been enough talk about contracts and hit men to warrant putting them on some far out-of-the-way shelf; a comfortable country-club shelf, no doubt.

However, with reference to the machinations of the DEA, nothing was ever done; there was no evidence of wrongdoing and other than poor, certifiably brain-damaged little me, there were no witnesses.

Monk, I then learned, had died months earlier, amazingly, from a broken neck when the ambulance transporting him to an inquest on the mainland drove—or, was driven—off the road into the ocean. When found, Murph' said he'd heard, Monk was smiling.

I thought I understood why.

"Odd," he went on, "only one of the two attendants' bodies was recovered from the wreck. The other, a recent employee, was never seen again. Odder still, his records, when sought for, had been inexplicably misplaced. It was as if he'd never existed."

"Another visitor from the Twilight Zone," Sola suggested.

I said, "Gosh! You think...?" which earned me a gentle jab in the ribs. I kissed her in apology, promised to keep my mouth shut, and signaled for Murph' to continue.

Gordo Valtierre and his co-conspirators, Murphy said, had been returned to Louisiana; two for burial with Gordo catching a 25-to-life stretch in Angola, Louisiana State penitentiary. And, Pierre Auguste L'Angousette, New Orleans businessman, friend and sometime-client of the late Montgomery Rothschild Esq.; he was vouched for by the bereaved mother of the unfortunate Key West attorney, Martha (the General) Rothschild, as having been in West Palm Beach dining with her on the night in question.

A melancholy settled over the room, as we silently grappled with those revelations, each according to our own needs. Sola kissed me softly, made her excuses and went into the main house.

Murphy confided he was less than enchanted with the morals of his—for lack of a better term—superiors. He told me he was making plans to do something different with his life but refused to elaborate. We briefly discussed flying in the mountains together; good intentions aside, too many things had passed between us; it would never happen.

After he'd gone I recalled the scene from the movie *Deliverance,* near the end, when the fat guy—I forget his name—the one who was raped, tells the others he thinks it's a good idea if they don't see each other for a while, it was apparent the friendship was gone for good. In my heart I knew Murph' and I had made our own farewells.

That night, for the first time in months, the dreams came back, and with a bloody vengeance, so I retreated to the guest cottage. When they persisted, again and again, over the next succession of nights, I moved my things. Sola was hurt and confused, thinking I was rejecting her, but I couldn't explain the substance of my dark mood without opening the door and letting the storm clouds I felt gathering inside of me loose to darken her horizon.

She gave me the space I needed and in it a chasm opened between us that I was powerless to close.

My thoughts were on the General and the betrayal of her son. Mostly, I focused on L'Angousette. I knew that he was out there somewhere, waiting.

*   *   *

**Go, litel book,
go litel myn tragedie.**

- Geoffrey Chaucer

CHAPTER 121

On that, and the following nights when I couldn't sleep, I passed the dead hours completing the journal I'd started such a very long time ago. It was a painful reminder of everything I had been trying to understand but hadn't known how. When I found it still under the passenger seat in the van, in the bag of road maps, a little mildewed around the edges but intact, I had no desire to open it or those wounds again. Neither, had I been able to throw it away. Until the night Murphy showed up I hadn't given it much thought. Afterwards, I felt there was a need.

Rereading the events of those first few days, I was soon caught up in a morbid fascination with the progression of events. The treadmill, once started, proved impossible to stop or get off. I soon came to believe that by completing it, getting it all down as it happened, somehow might serve to drain off some of the poisons and put to rest the monsters that stalked my nights. Gradually, I noticed a profound difference in me. The lassitude that had plagued my mind had been replaced with something akin to the old vigor. I began looking forward to each new day and started to take an active interest in the operation of the gym, until....

It was about three in the morning and I had just finished writing down the details concerning my discharge from the hospital, after what turned out to be almost a year in custody, when I found the following note written on the last page:

Well partner, I couldn't resist reading this. You make me sound like some kind of hero. It ain't so. I'm just as scared as you, and if I didn't have you to back me up, I don't think we'd have gotten this far. I wasn't going to do this, but I've been having a bad feeling for the past few days. So, if you're reading this it means I didn't make it, and I need you to take care of something for me. Go see Sis', she has a map. On it seven locations are marked, six black and one in red. I'd like you to see that one of those containers goes to each of my family, Marisha, my kids, June and Amy-Rose, and Sola. There's one each for you and Joe. You stuck by me like a brother when I needed you, so this is my way of saying thanks. The last one you know about. Do yourself and the world a favor and leave it rot where it is. The only thing in there is bad luck, and there's enough of that in the world already.

Tony

EPILOGUE

Mountains surround the little township in northern Georgia, close to where I've been living. The land is rich, nourished by fresh clean water from an abundance of rivers and streams. Each breath of air cleanses the soul and brings a quiet smile to the heart. The people here look you in the eye when they talk to you—and they talk *to*, not *at* you.

Funny how life sometimes conspires to give what is needed: After the gym was sold, Sola came up here to be with me but shortly after she arrived, her artwork was discovered by an important New York gallery. After struggling most of her life to have her work recognized she became an overnight success. I still get an occasional card from her, from different parts of the world where she's creating her great art pieces on commission, though not as many as when she first left. The offers to join her are fewer too. Still, I am happy for her success.

And, Sarge...? He spends most of his time on the next farm over, where he's fathered eleven of the nicest looking pups I've ever seen. To my eyes every one of them is the pick of the litter. The neighbors are a nice couple with a large family, who love and look after him better than most folks treat their own children, so I won't have to worry about him when I go.

I try not to think that much about Florida anymore, except for those nights when I can't sleep and I find myself awake, wondering about how things might have been if.... I think you know what I mean.

Now this record's complete, there remains only one piece of unfinished business. Tony'd once remarked about Cajuns and their blood feuds, he'd been only half-right because I am finally ready to deal with things left undone for too long.

Unexpectedly, I'm actually looking forward to my next Mardi Gras.

THE END

LaVergne, TN USA
13 December 2010
208587LV00001B/98/P